D0437244

DISCARDED

BAD KITTY GETS A PHONE

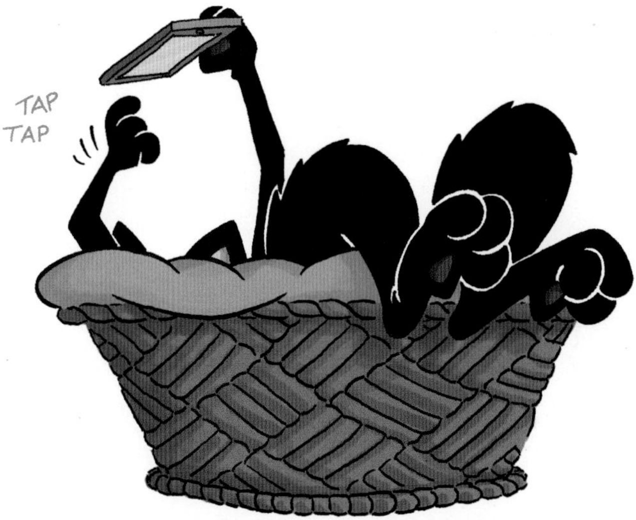
TAP
TAP

NICK BRUEL

ROARING BROOK PRESS
NEW YORK

To Ares and Nico

Published by Roaring Brook Press
Roaring Brook Press is a division of Holtzbrinck Publishing Holdings Limited Partnership
120 Broadway, New York, NY 10271 • mackids.com

Library of Congress Cataloging-in-Publication Data is available.
ISBN 978-1-250-74996-3

Our books may be purchased in bulk for promotional, educational, or business use.
Please contact your local bookseller or the Macmillan Corporate and Premium Sales
Department at (800) 221-7945 ext. 5442 or by email at
MacmillanSpecialMarkets@macmillan.com.

First edition, 2021 • Book design by Aurora Parlagreco • Color by Rob Steen
Printed in China by RR Donnelley Asia Printing Solutions Ltd.,
Dongguan City, Guangdong Province

1 3 5 7 9 10 8 6 4 2

• CONTENTS •

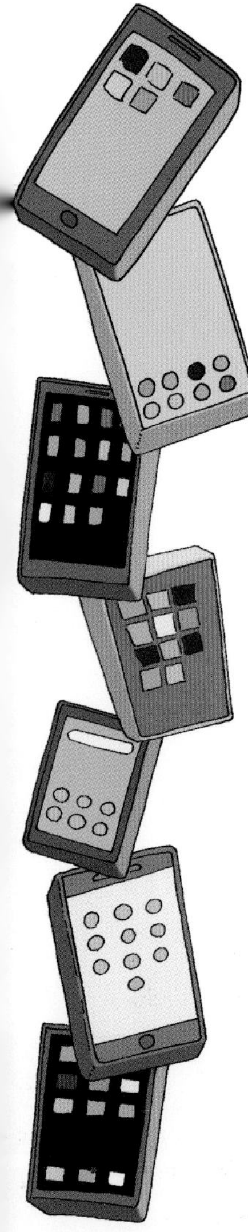

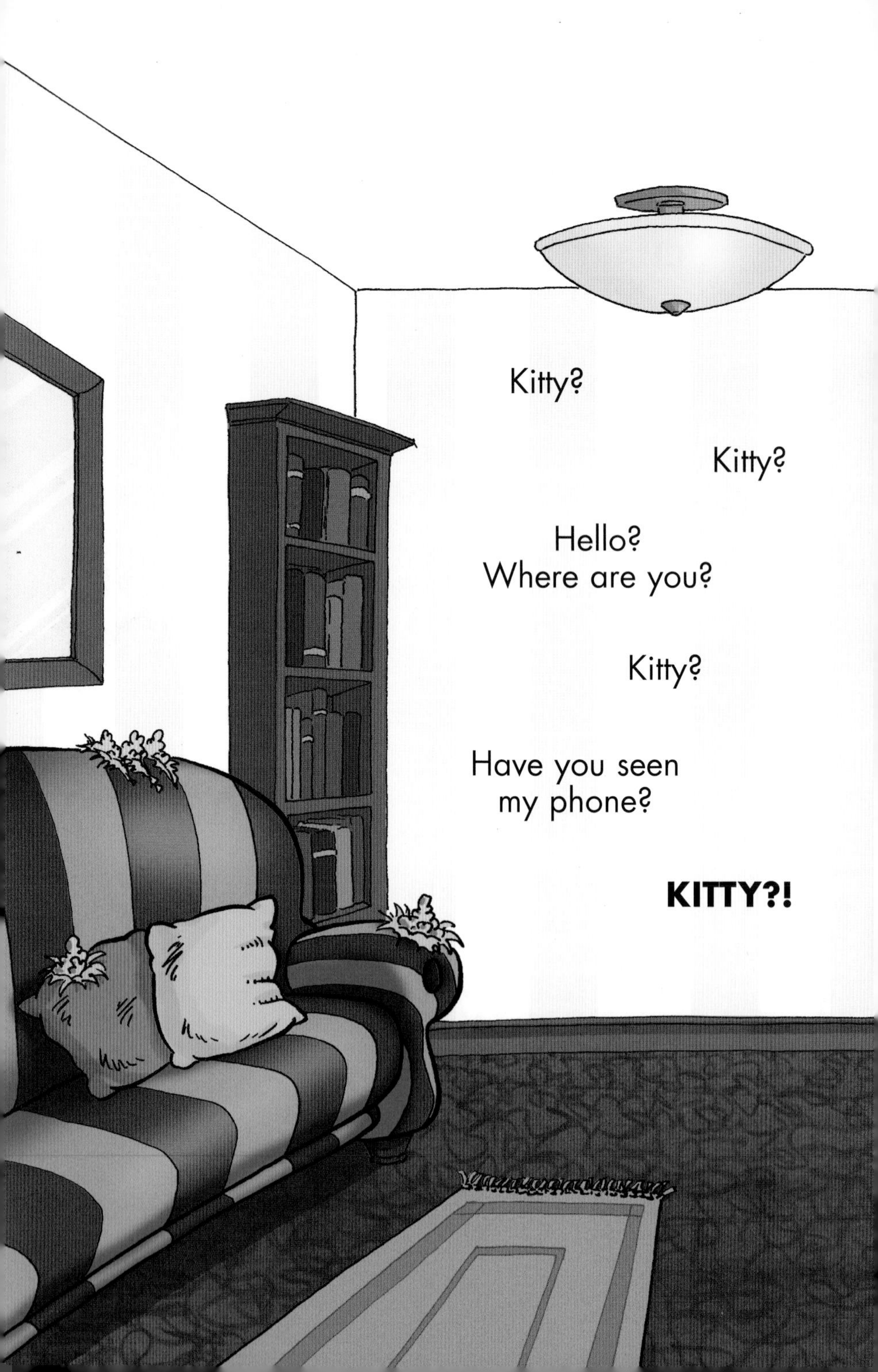
Kitty?
Kitty?
Hello?
Where are you?
Kitty?
Have you seen
my phone?
KITTY?!

•CHAPTER ONE•

KITTY WANTS A PHONE

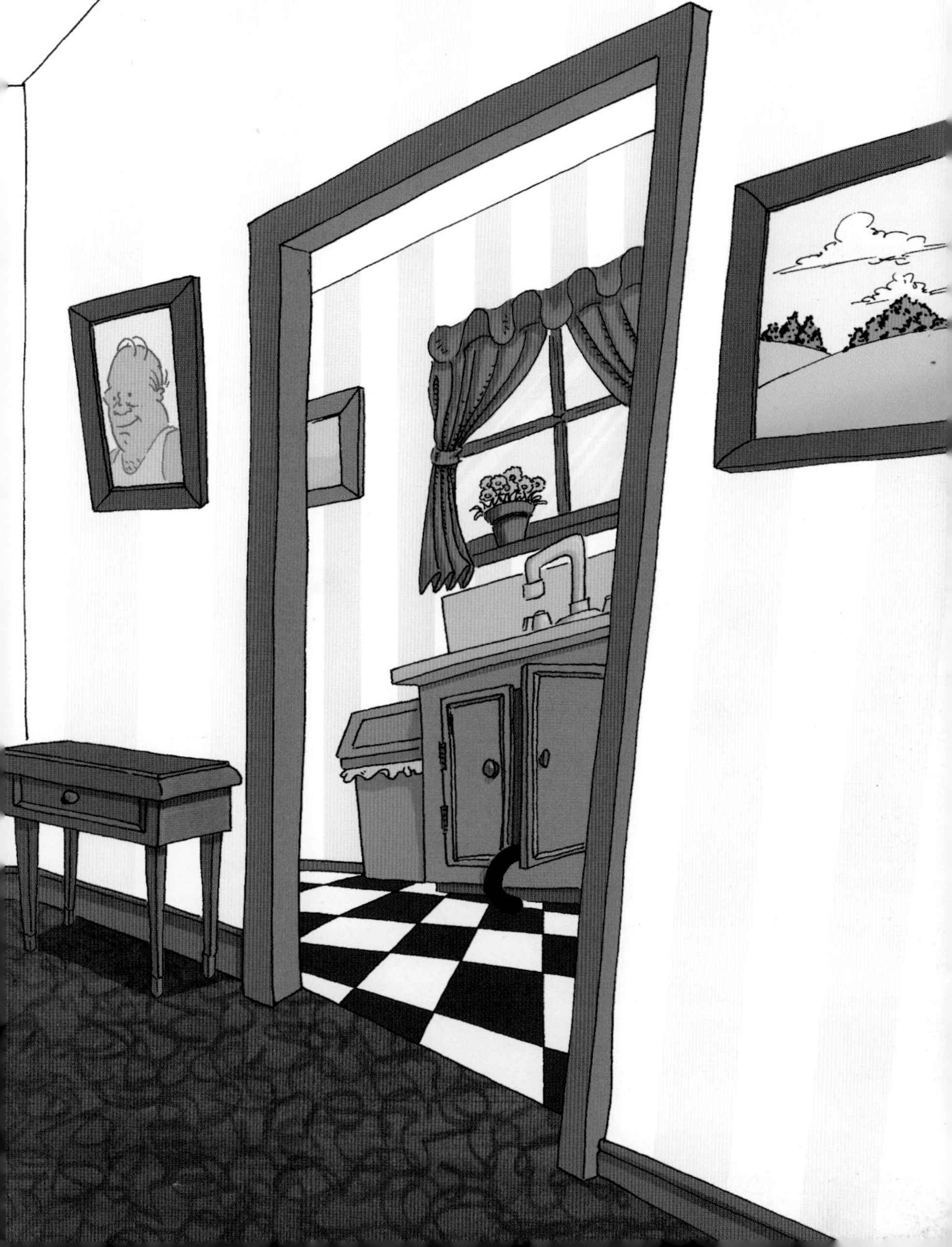

I see you, Kitty!
Do you have my phone again?

Kitty? Kitty?

KITTY!

Please stop ignoring me!

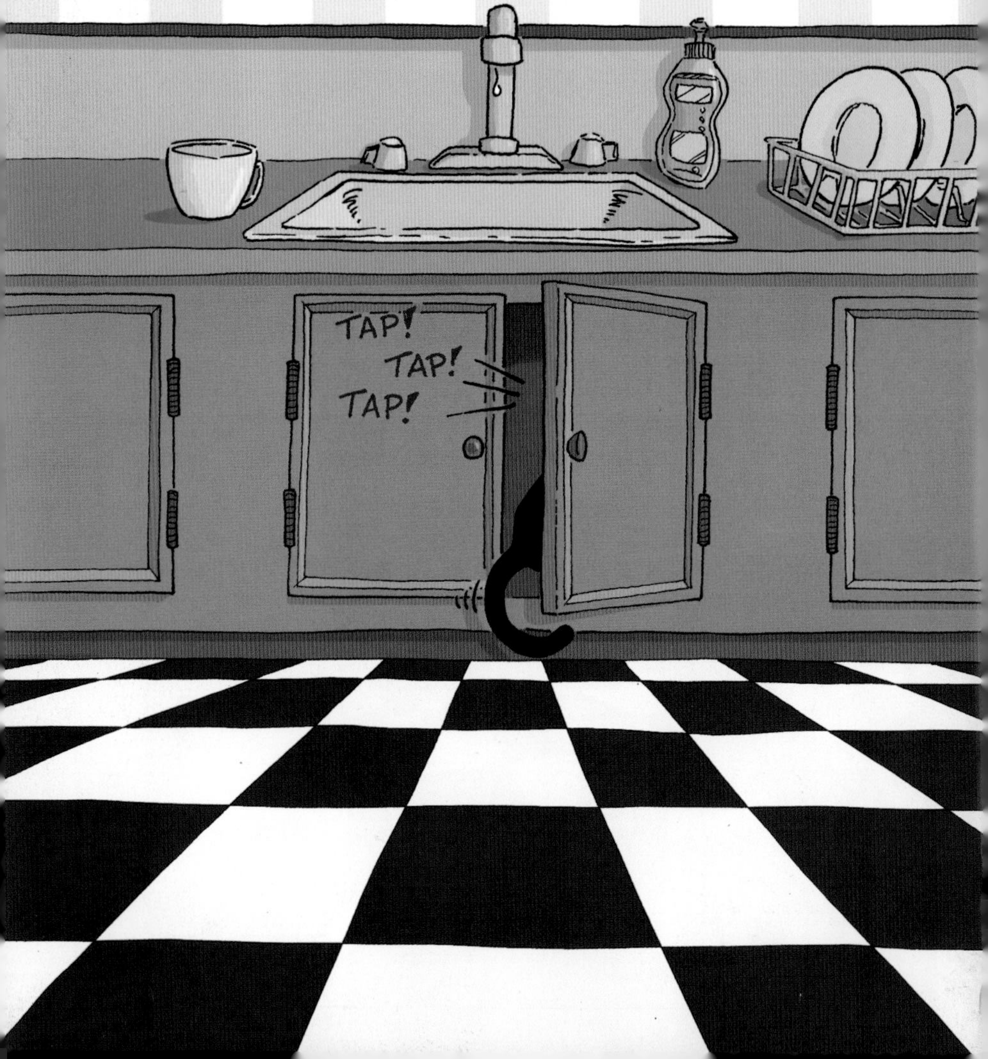

Kitty, how many times do I have to say this? You can't just take my phone without permission! I'd like it back now, please. Kitty? Kitty?

Have you even heard a single word that I've said?

Sigh.

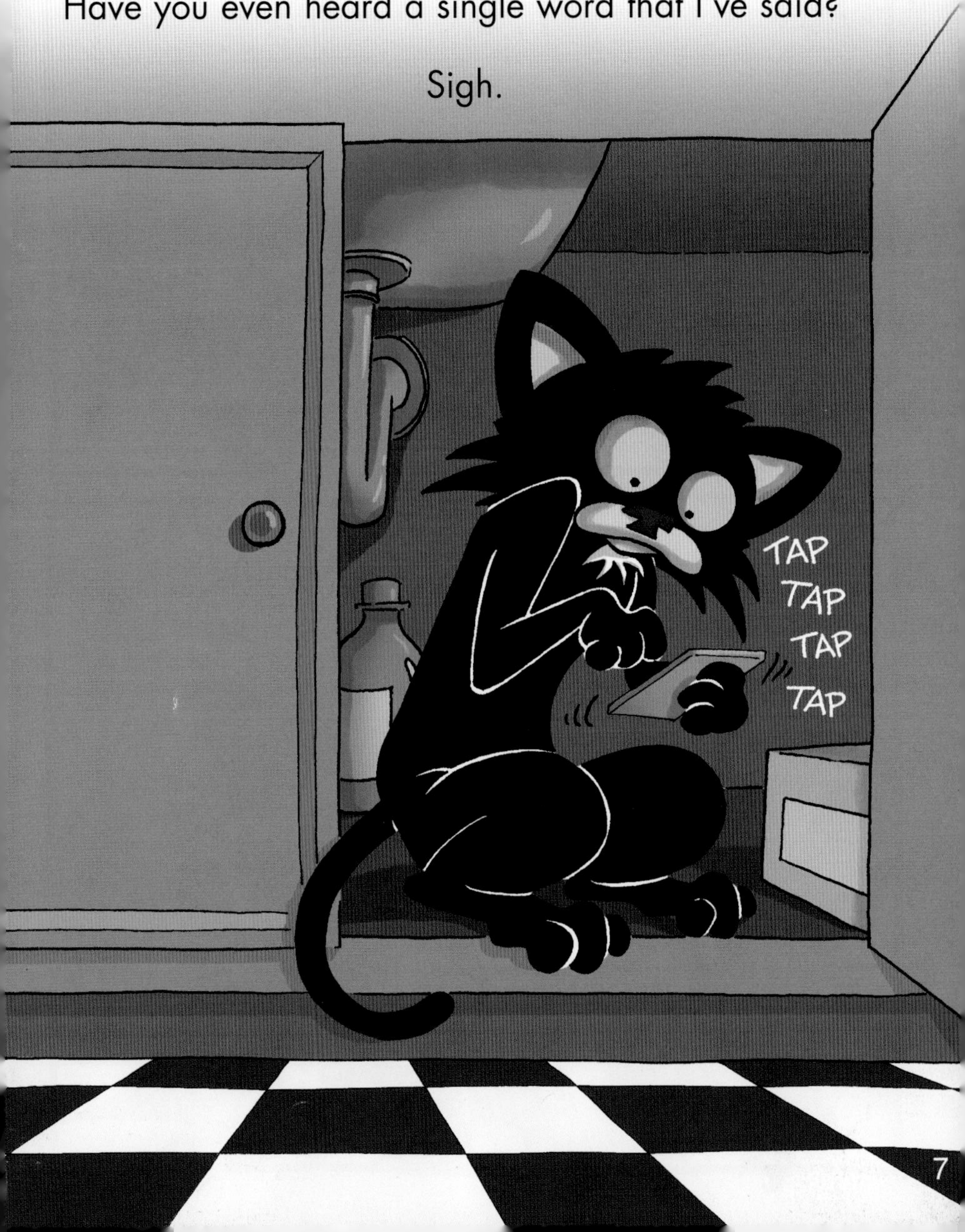
TAP
TAP
TAP
TAP

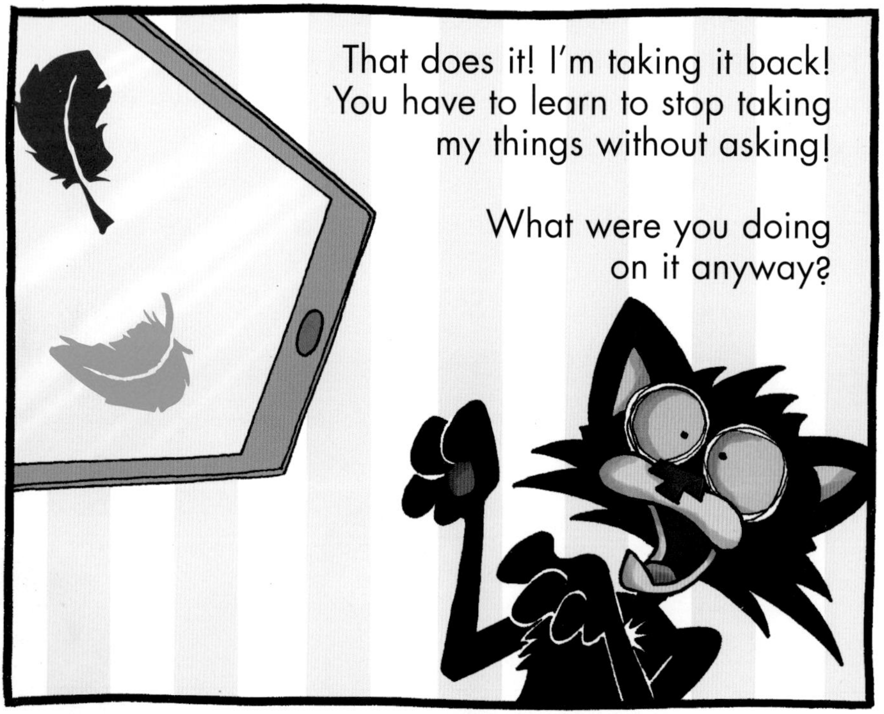
That does it! I'm taking it back! You have to learn to stop taking my things without asking!
What were you doing on it anyway?

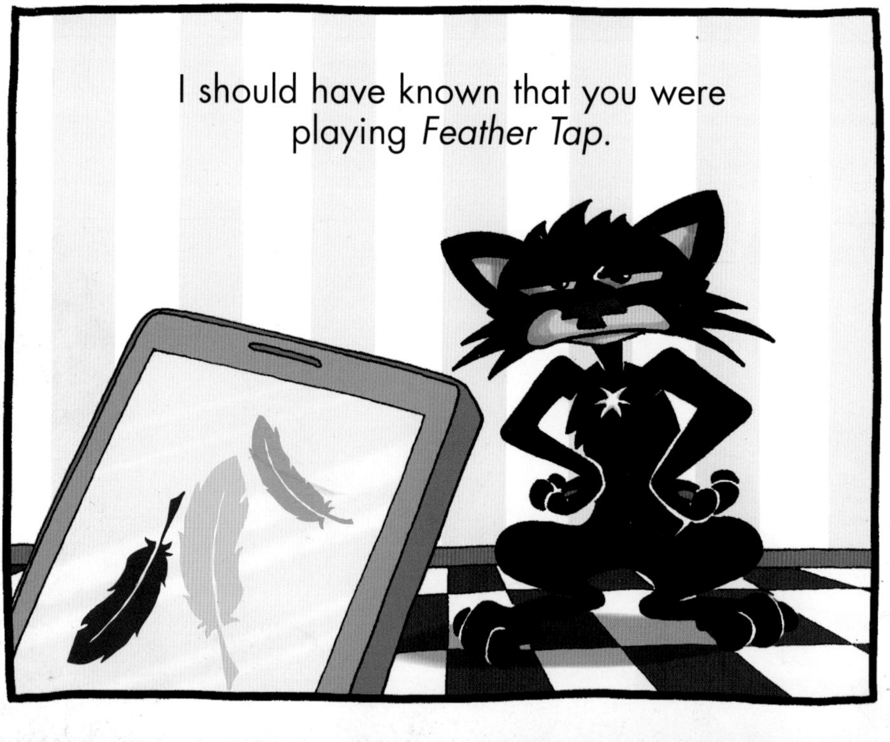
I should have known that you were playing *Feather Tap*.

You are obsessed with this game, Kitty. I don't know why I let you talk me into downloading it onto my phone.

NO, KITTY! You've had enough screen time for today!

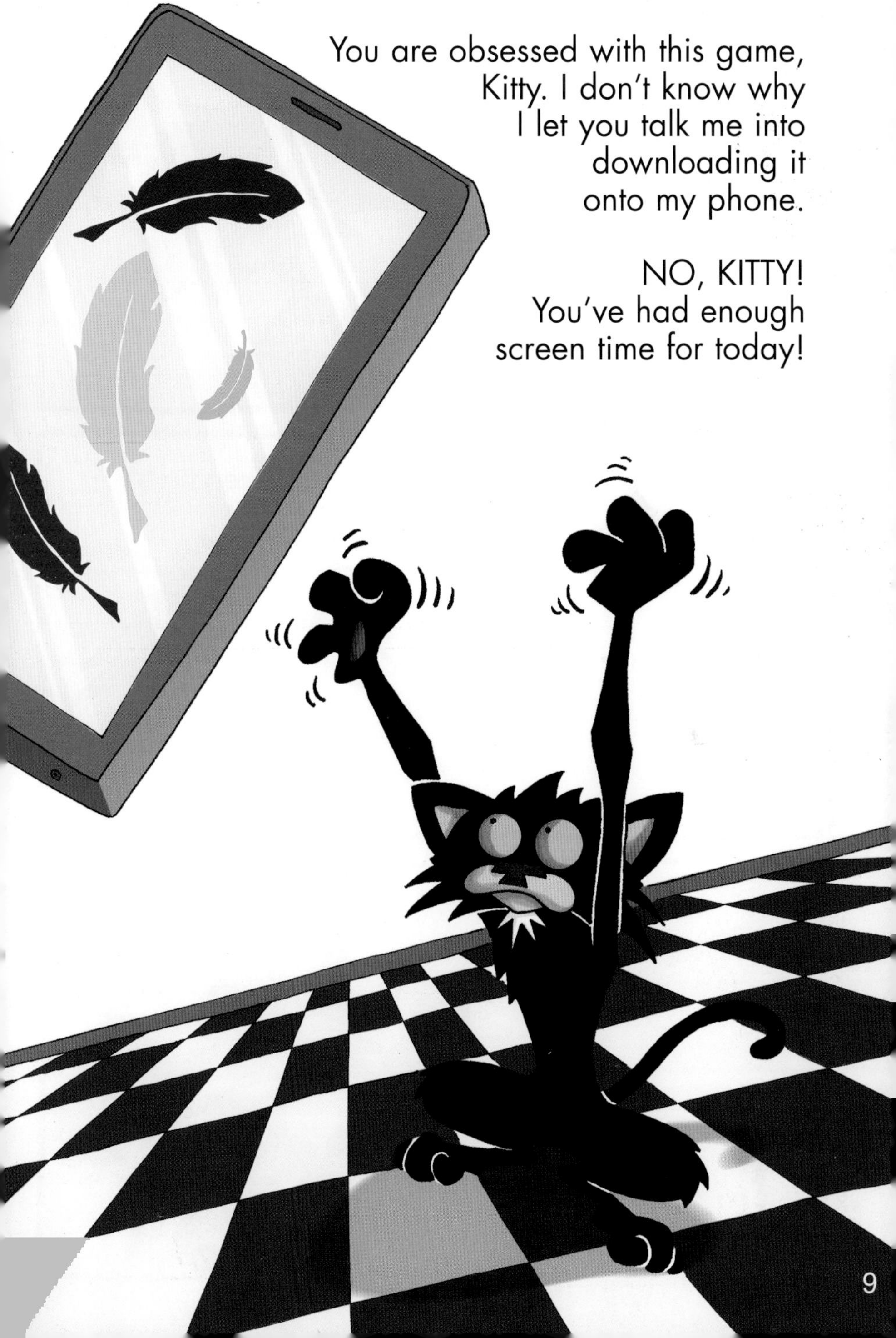

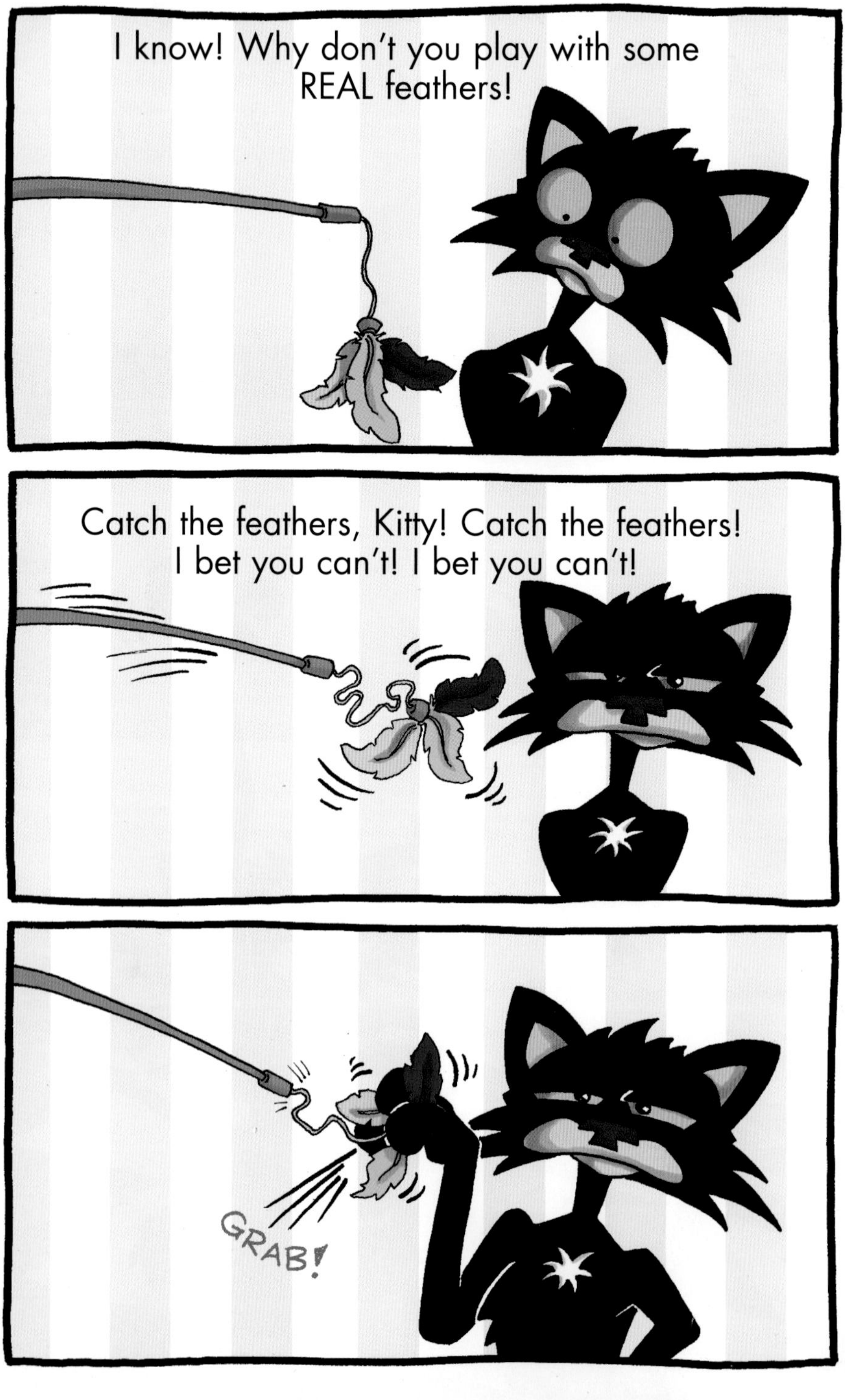
I know! Why don't you play with some REAL feathers!
Catch the feathers, Kitty! Catch the feathers! I bet you can't! I bet you can't!
GRAB!

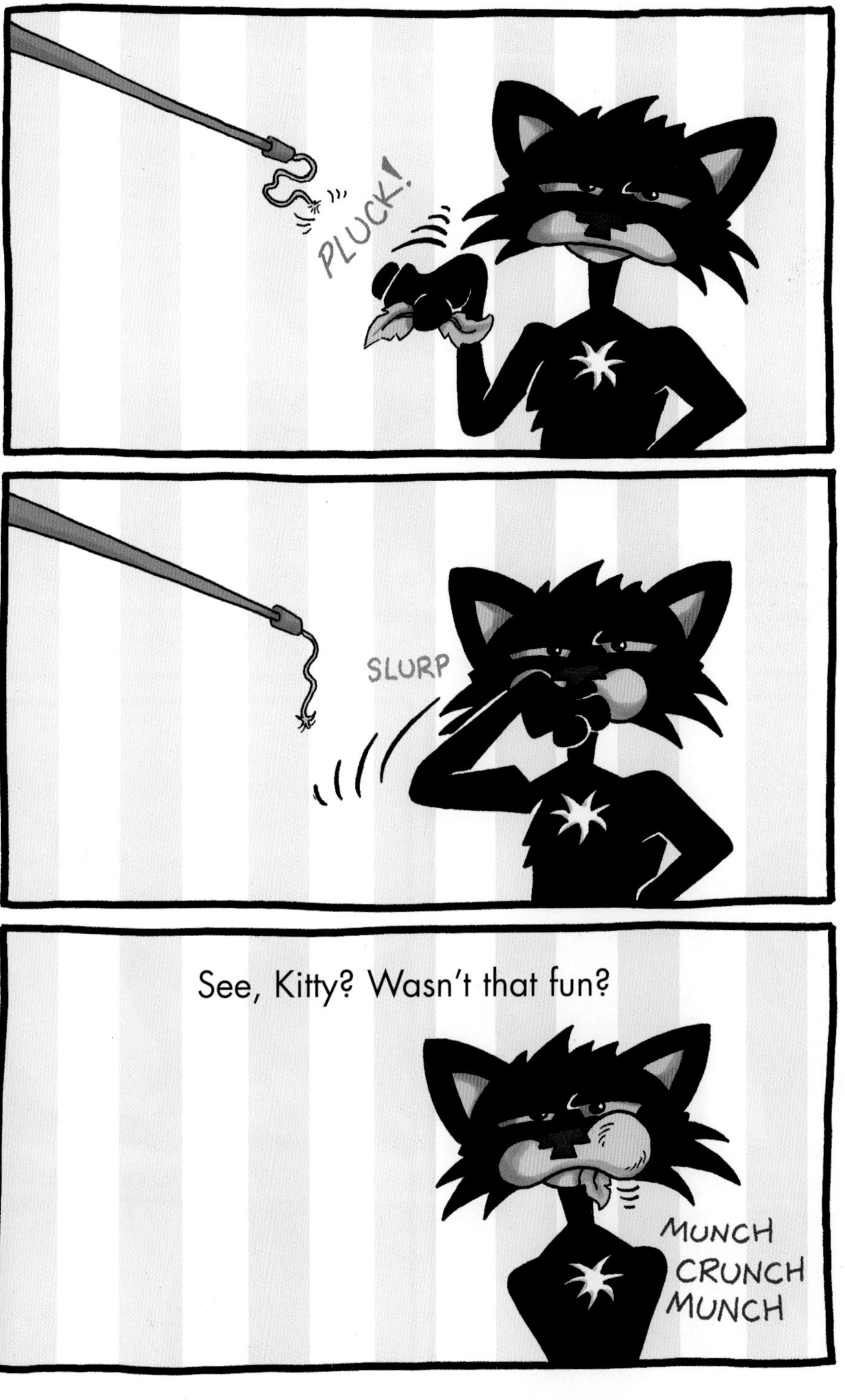
PLUCK!
SLURP
See, Kitty? Wasn't that fun?
MUNCH
CRUNCH
MUNCH

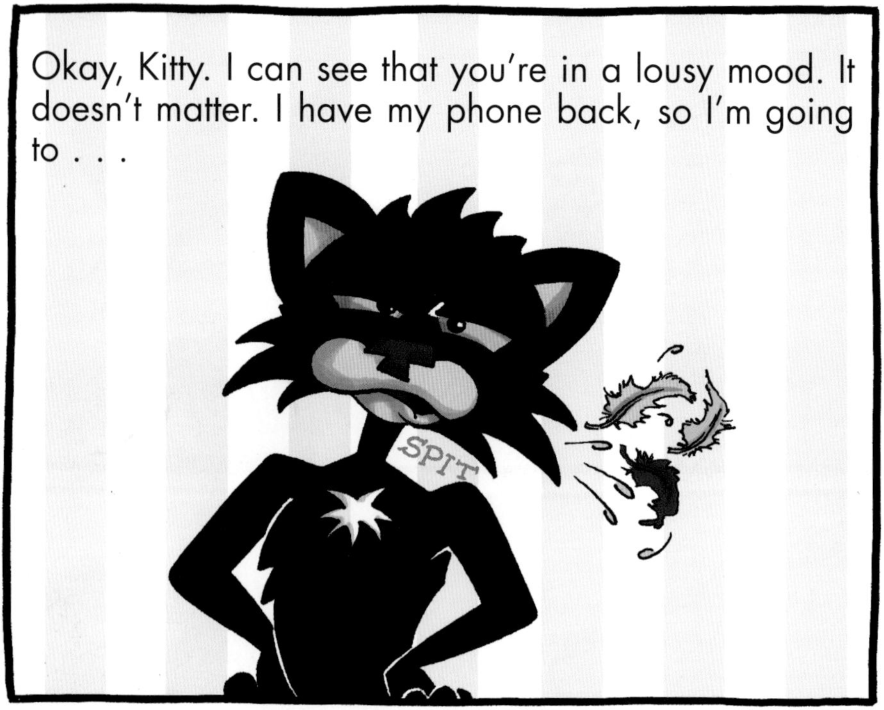
Okay, Kitty. I can see that you're in a lousy mood. It doesn't matter. I have my phone back, so I'm going to . . .
SPIT

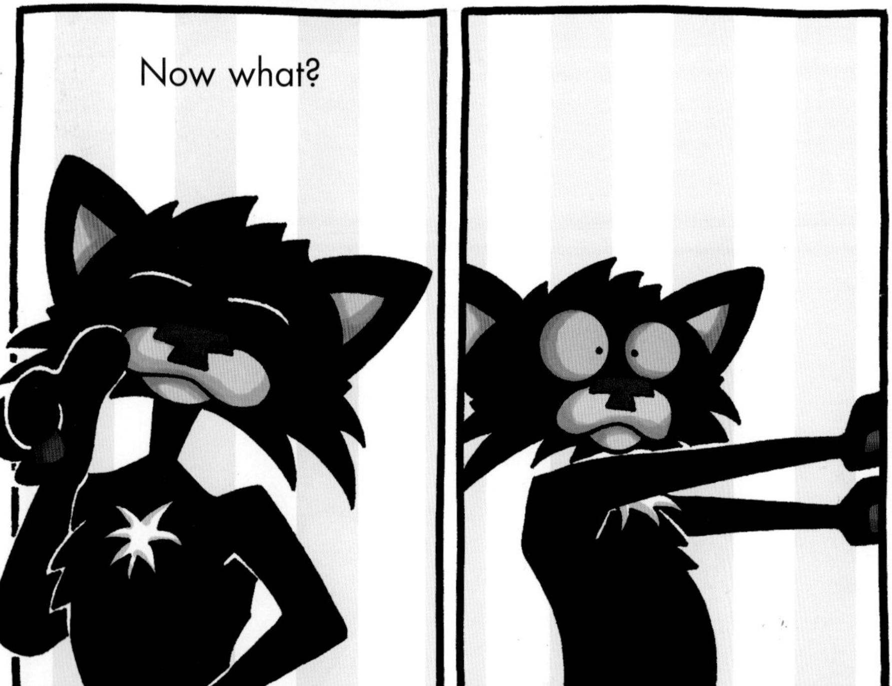
Now what?

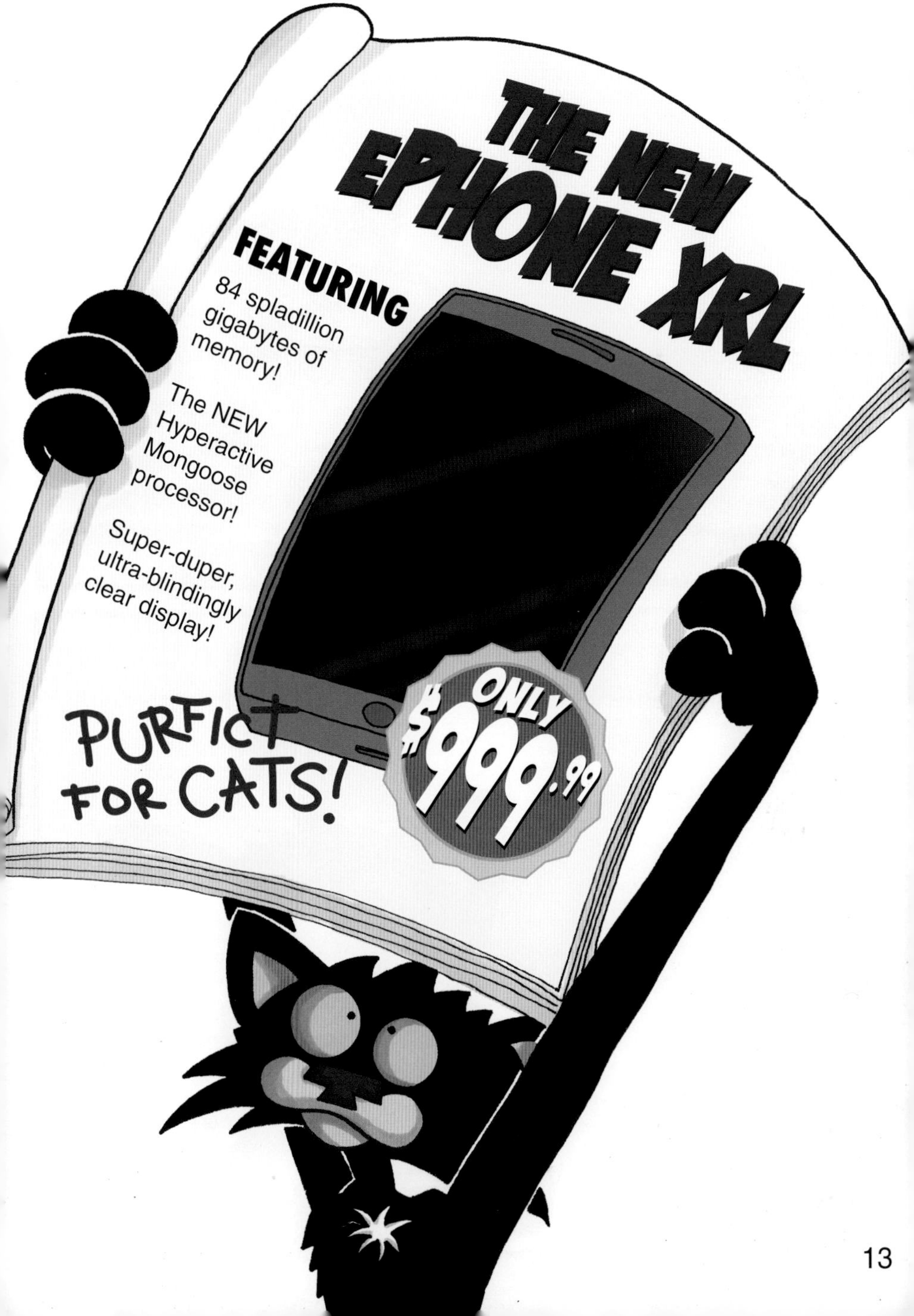
THE NEW EPHONE XRL
FEATURING
84 spladillion gigabytes of memory!
The NEW Hyperactive Mongoose processor!
Super-duper, ultra-blindingly clear display!
ONLY $999.99
PURFICT FOR CATS!

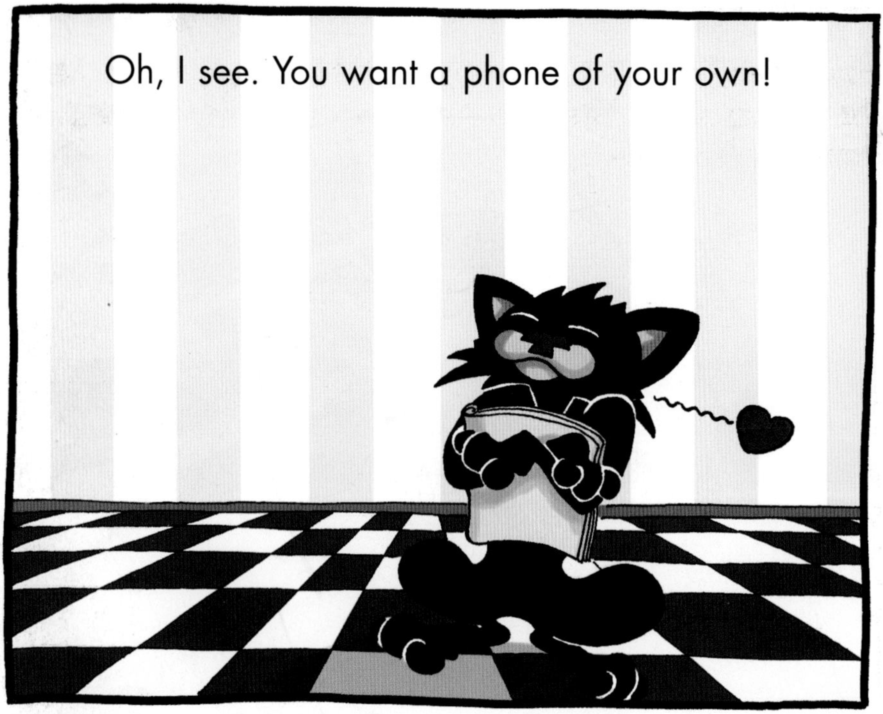
Oh, I see. You want a phone of your own!

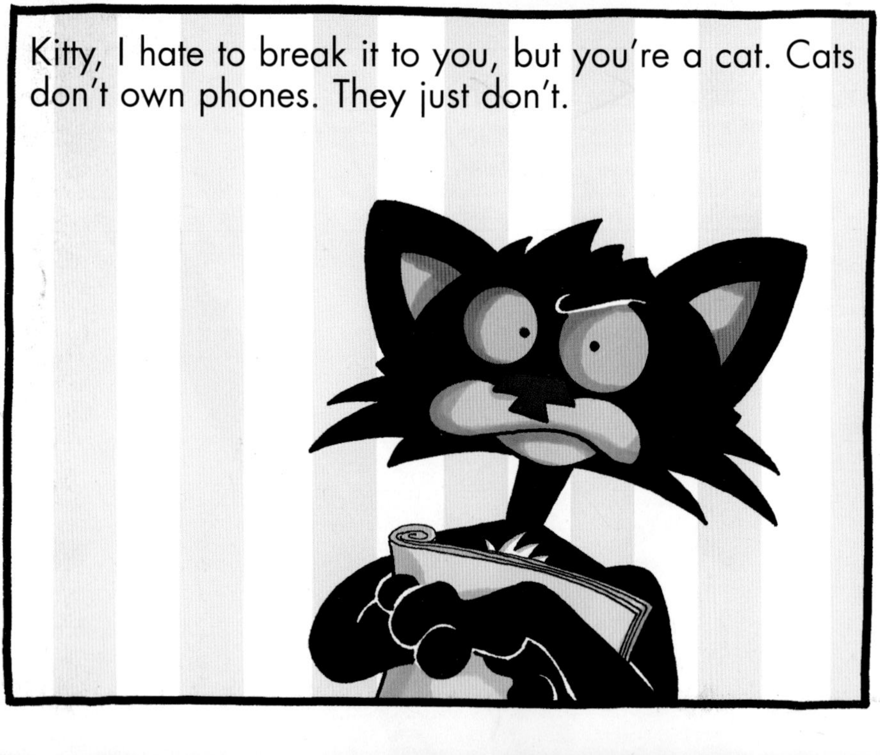
Kitty, I hate to break it to you, but you're a cat. Cats don't own phones. They just don't.

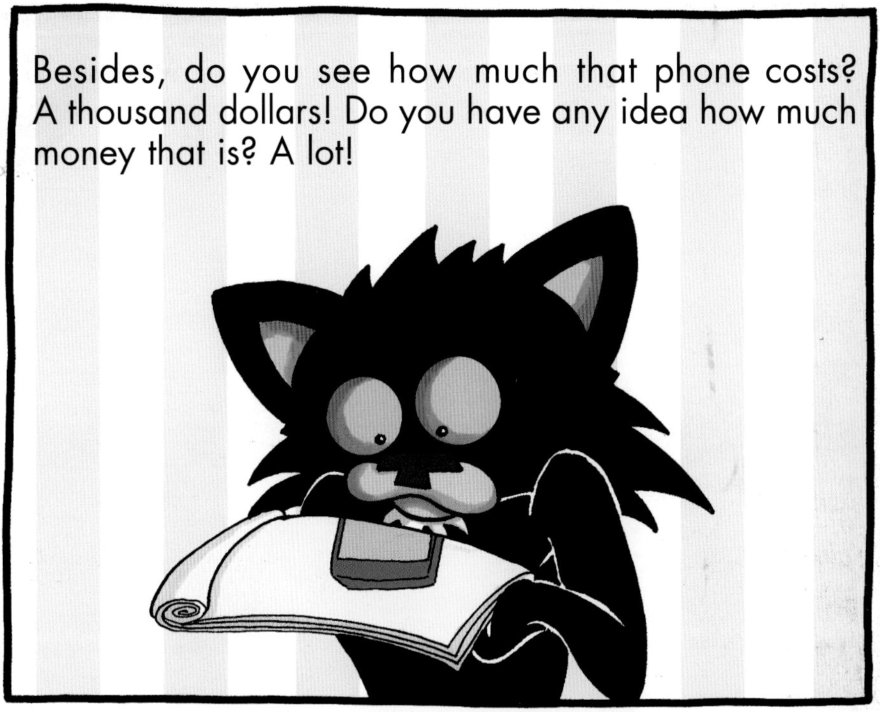
Besides, do you see how much that phone costs? A thousand dollars! Do you have any idea how much money that is? A lot!

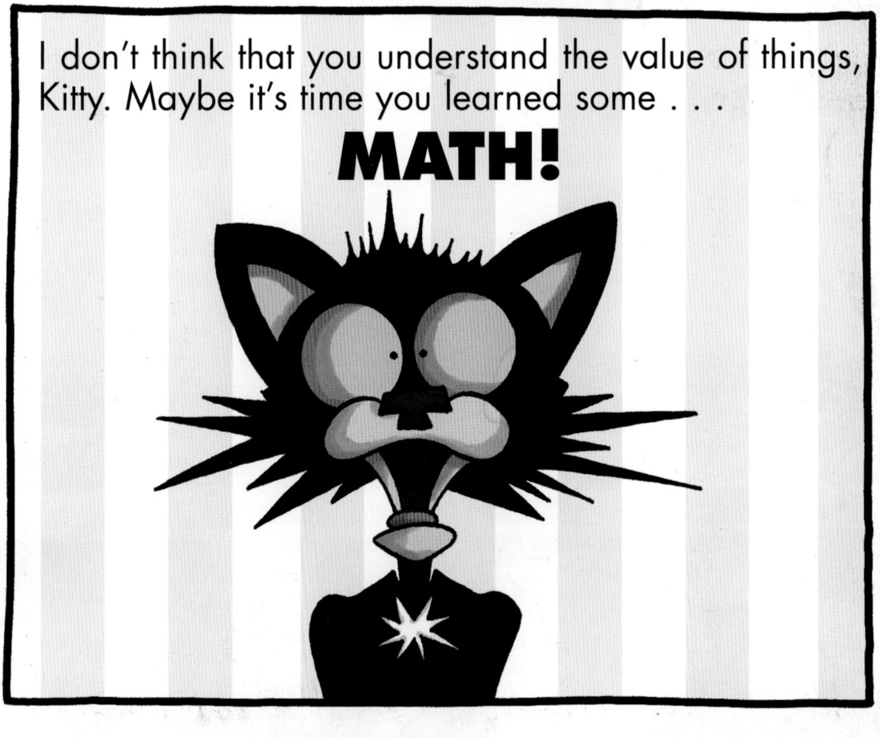
I don't think that you understand the value of things, Kitty. Maybe it's time you learned some . . .
MATH!

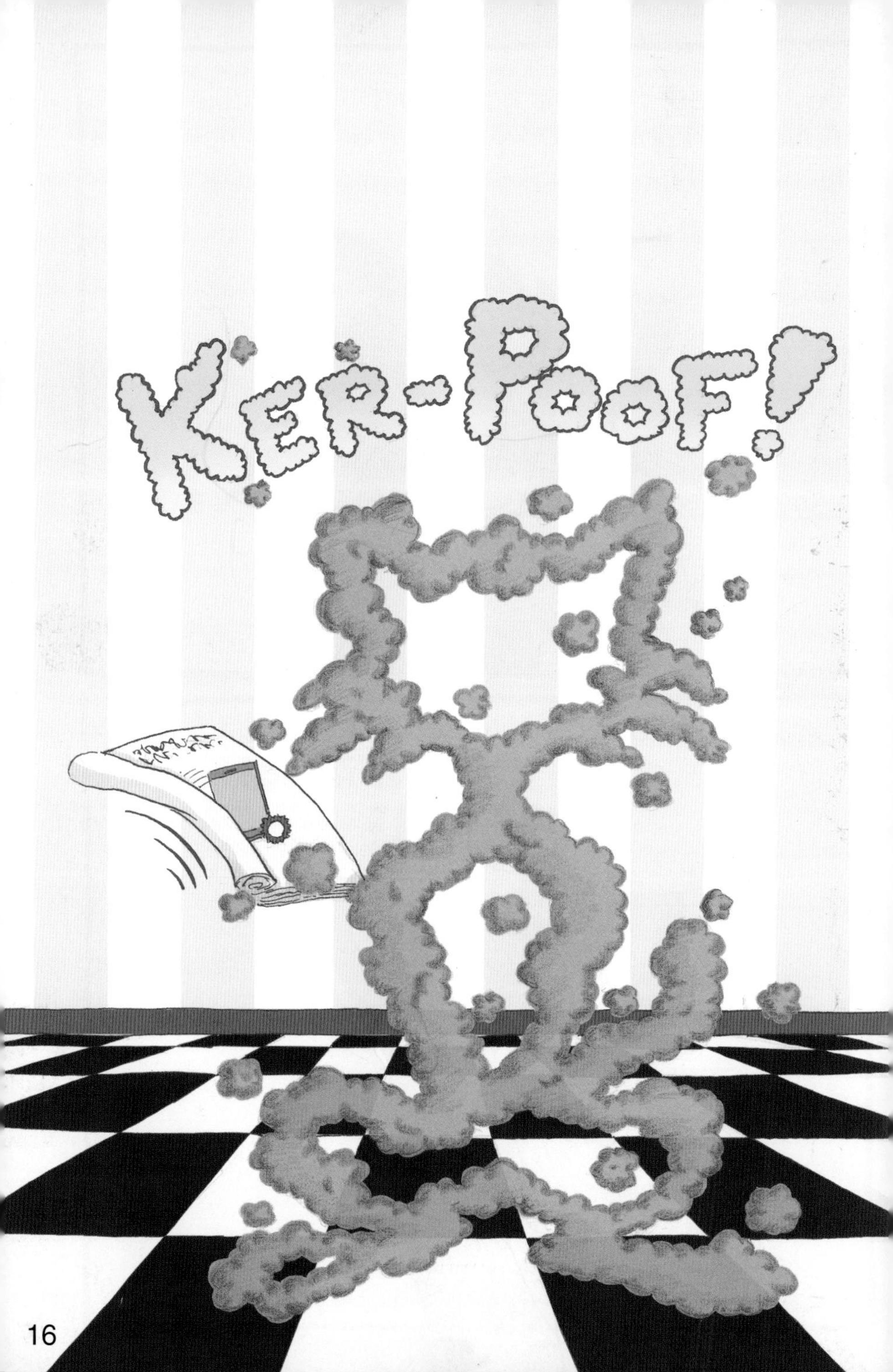
KER-POOF!

KITTY!

I said "MATH," not "BATH"!

On second thought, maybe she ***did*** understand what I said.

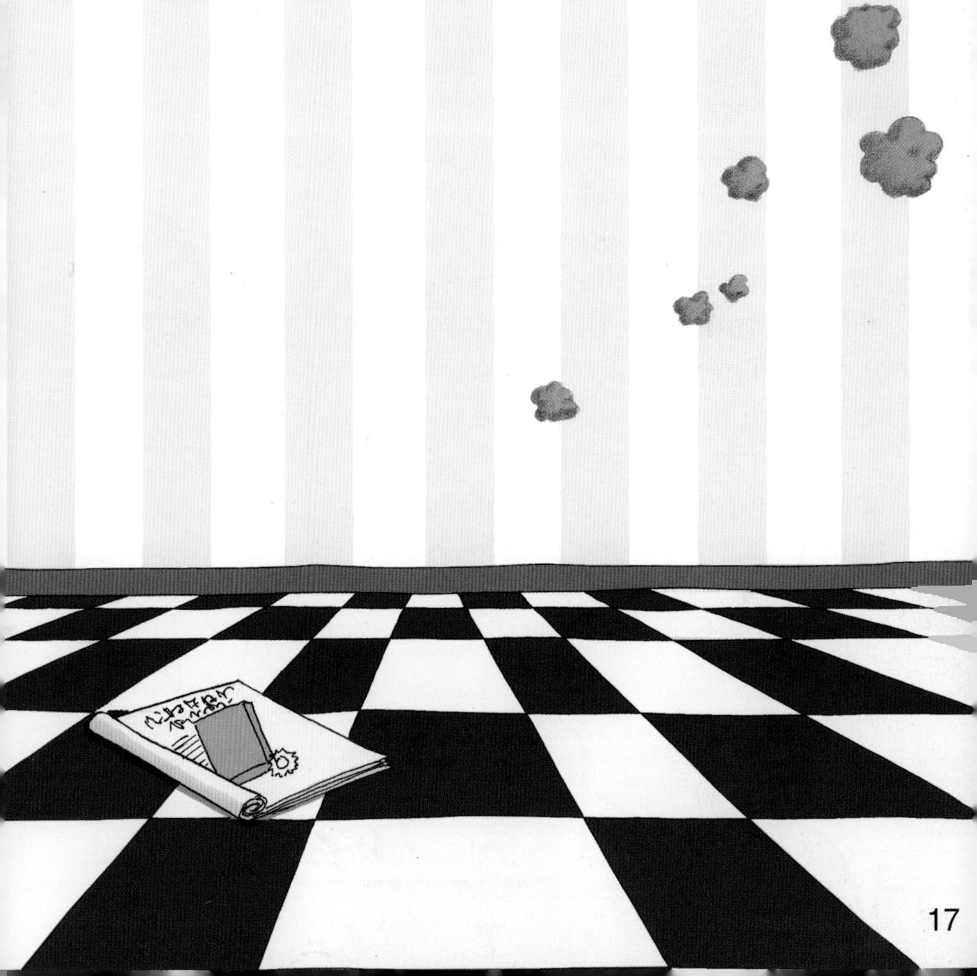

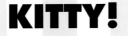

UNCLE MURRAY'S FUN FACTS

SHOULD CATS OWN PHONES?

NO!

NO! NO! NO!
A THOUSAND TIMES NO!
There. Question answered. Let's move on with this goofy book!

But why, Uncle Murray?

Think about it! If cats all had phones, they could communicate with each other all over the world! They could collude! They could connive! They could organize! Soon the entire planet would be overrun with armies of cats marching around with spatulas, ready to smack me on the head!

Uncle Murray, do you have any evidence that this could happen?

Sure, I have evidence!
Lots of evidence!
Lots and lots of evidence!

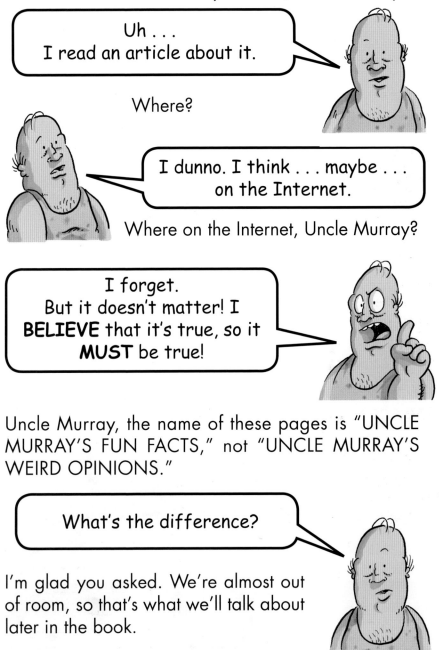

What kind of evidence do you have, Uncle Murray?

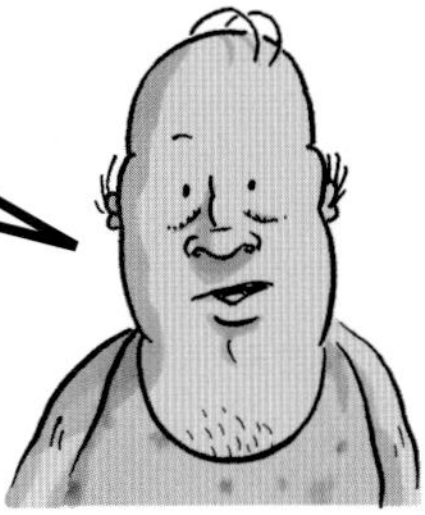
Uh . . .
I read an article about it.

Where?

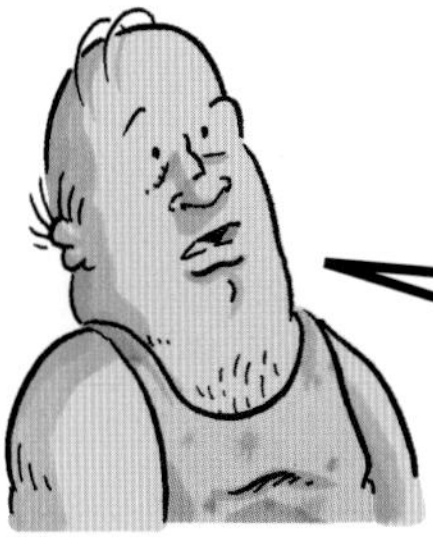
I dunno. I think . . . maybe . . . on the Internet.

Where on the Internet, Uncle Murray?

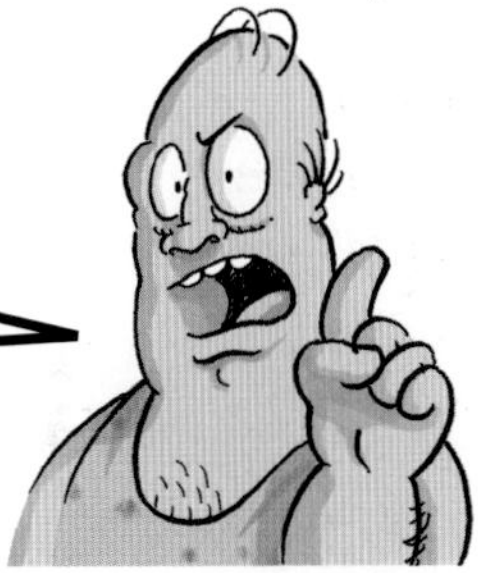
I forget.
But it doesn't matter! I **BELIEVE** that it's true, so it **MUST** be true!

Uncle Murray, the name of these pages is "UNCLE MURRAY'S FUN FACTS," not "UNCLE MURRAY'S WEIRD OPINIONS."

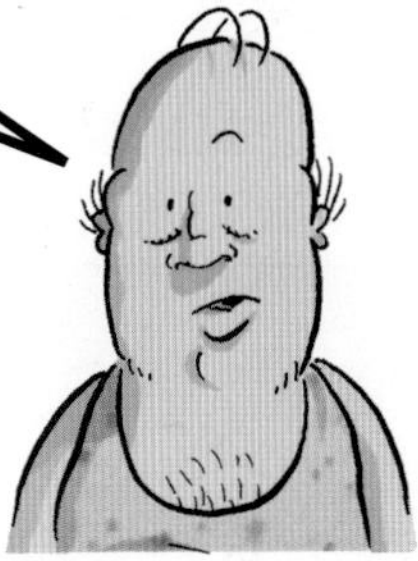
What's the difference?

I'm glad you asked. We're almost out of room, so that's what we'll talk about later in the book.

•CHAPTER TWO•

KITTY NEEDS A PHONE

I see you there, Kitty. We need to talk about how much a new phone costs.

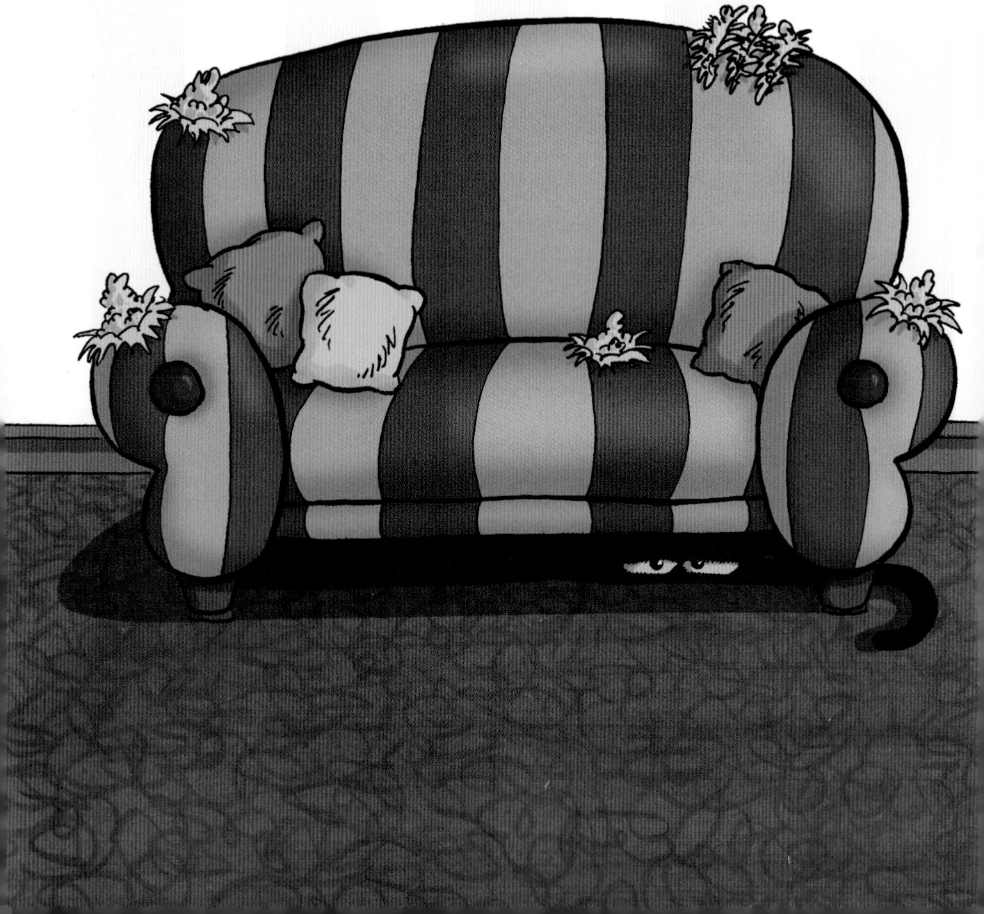

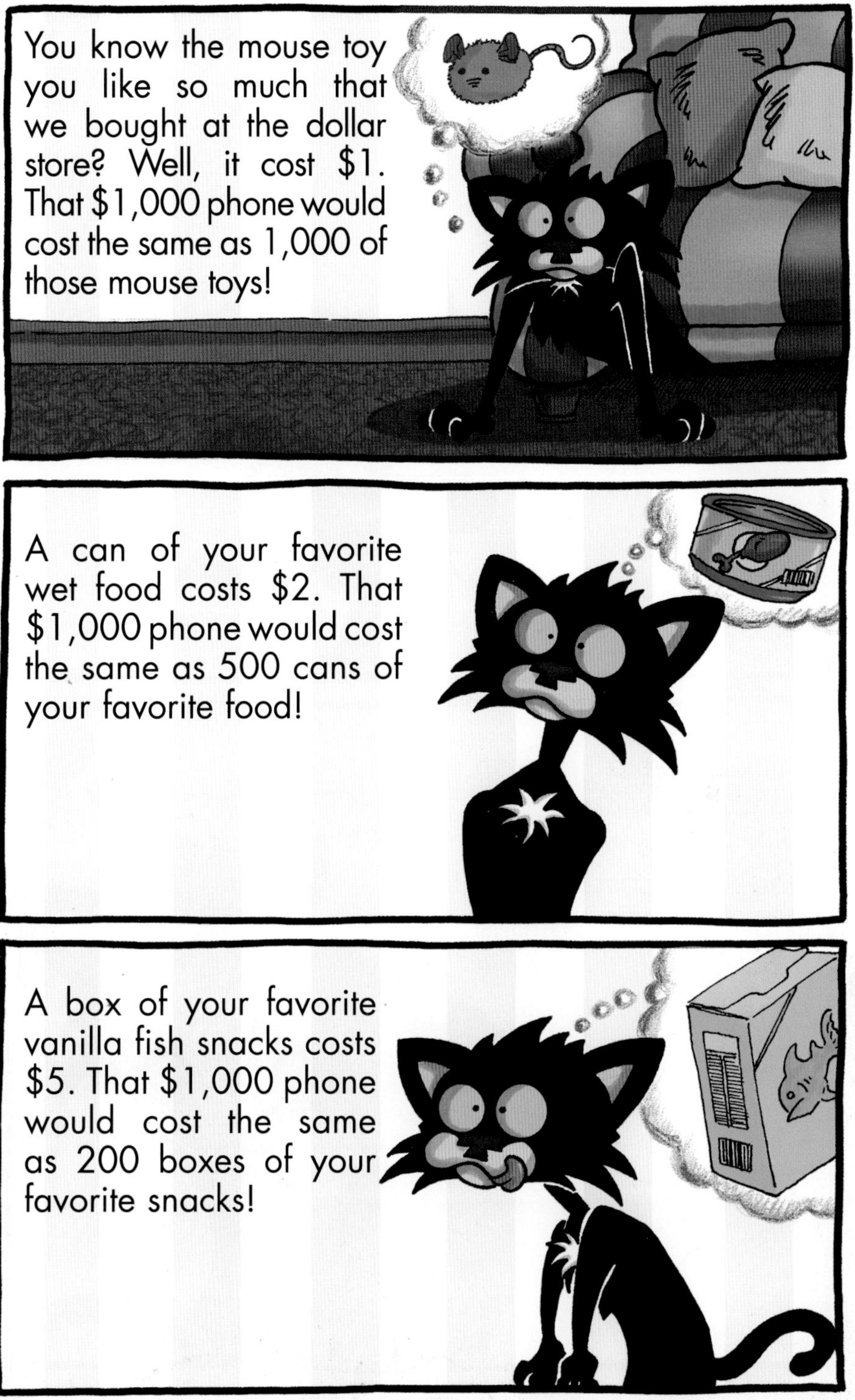
You know the mouse toy you like so much that we bought at the dollar store? Well, it cost $1. That $1,000 phone would cost the same as 1,000 of those mouse toys!
A can of your favorite wet food costs $2. That $1,000 phone would cost the same as 500 cans of your favorite food!
A box of your favorite vanilla fish snacks costs $5. That $1,000 phone would cost the same as 200 boxes of your favorite snacks!

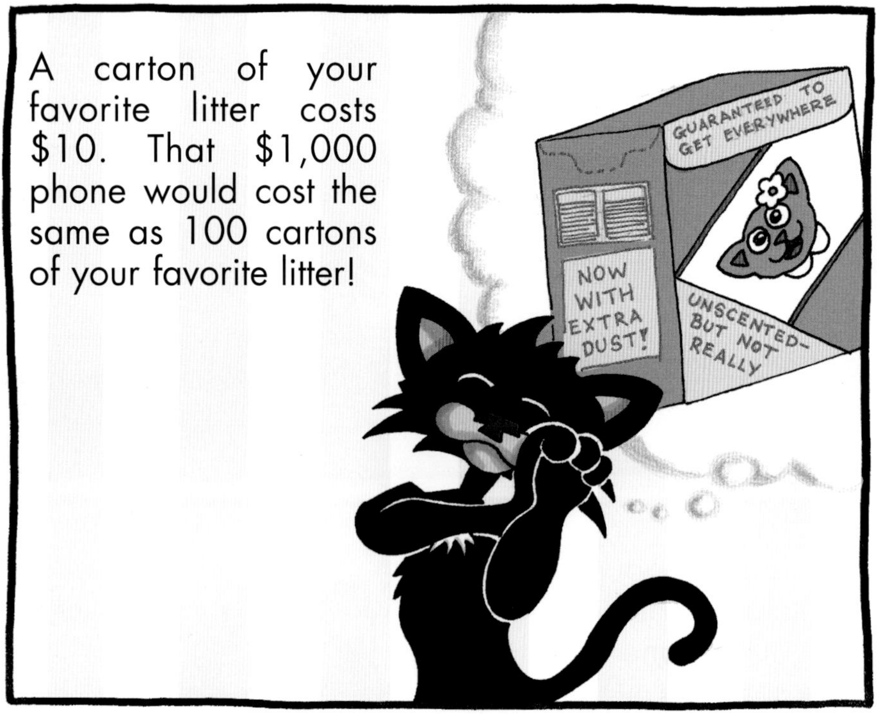
A carton of your favorite litter costs $10. That $1,000 phone would cost the same as 100 cartons of your favorite litter!
GUARANTEED TO GET EVERYWHERE
NOW WITH EXTRA DUST!
UNSCENTED- BUT NOT REALLY

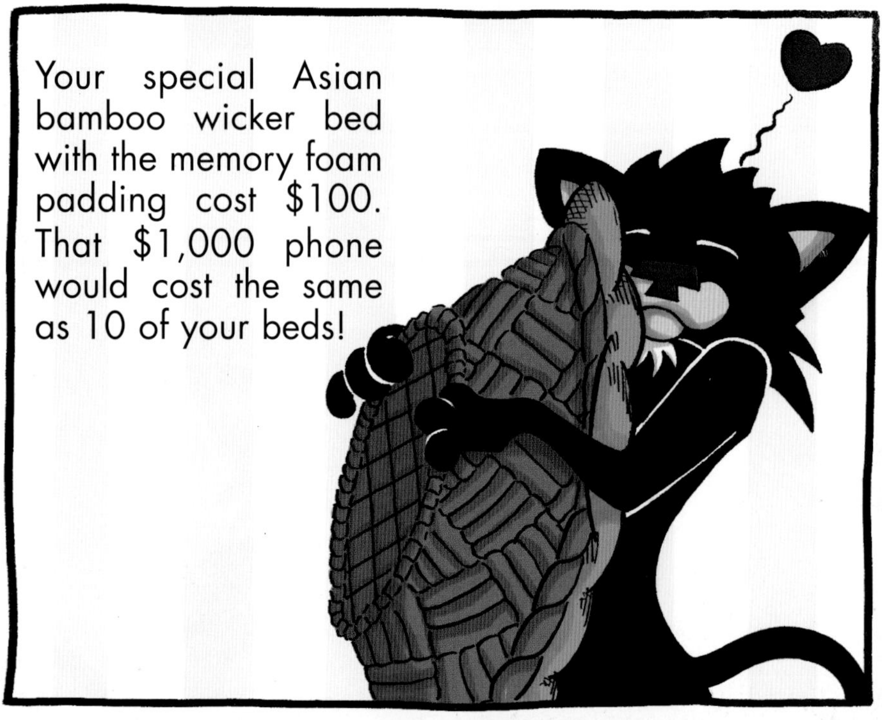
Your special Asian bamboo wicker bed with the memory foam padding cost $100. That $1,000 phone would cost the same as 10 of your beds!

Your fancy cat tree—the one we had specially shipped from a monastery high in the Andes mountains, made by an order of monks that spend their days only making cat trees—cost $200. That $1,000 phone would cost the same as 5 of your cat trees!

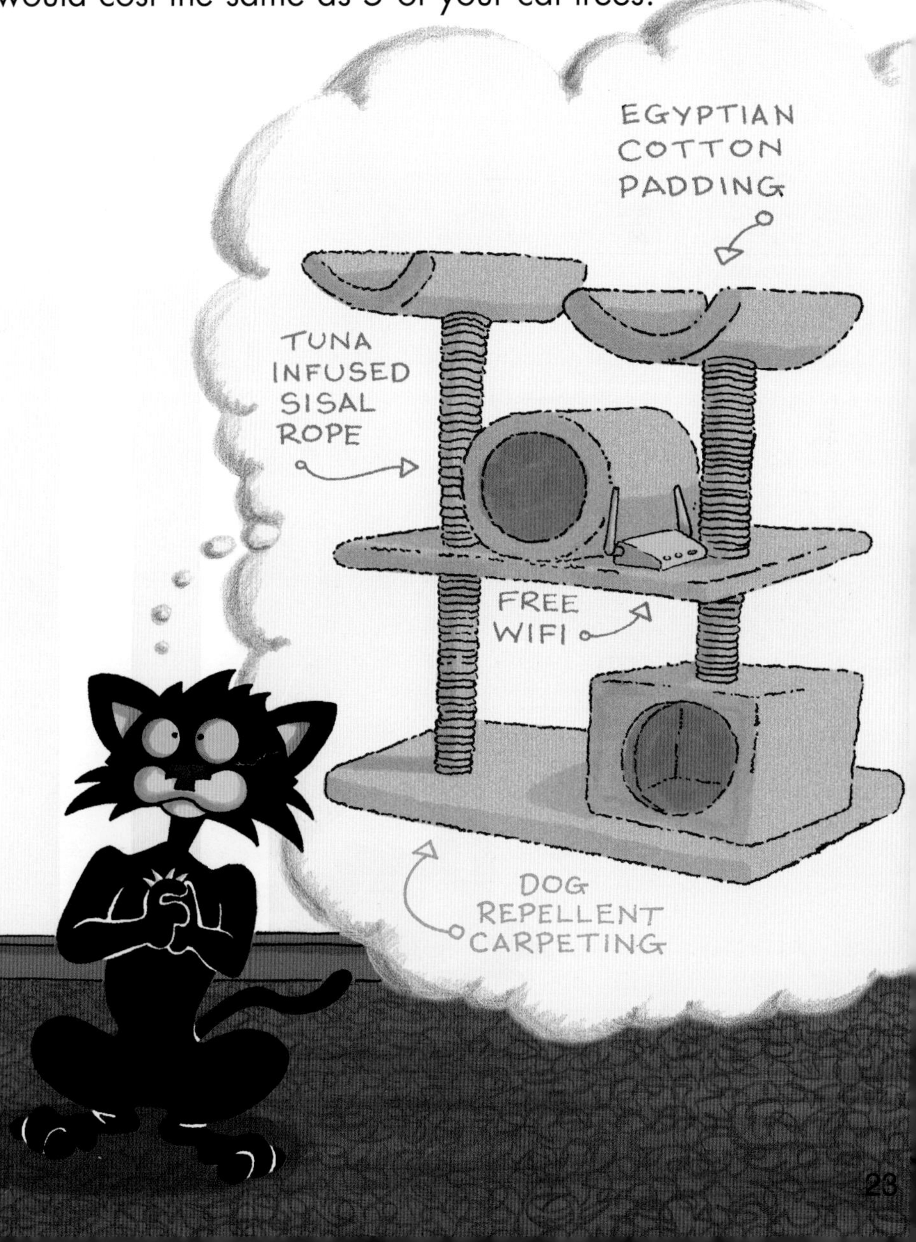
EGYPTIAN COTTON PADDING
TUNA INFUSED SISAL ROPE
FREE WIFI
DOG REPELLENT CARPETING

Kitty? **Kitty?!**
Are you even listening to me?

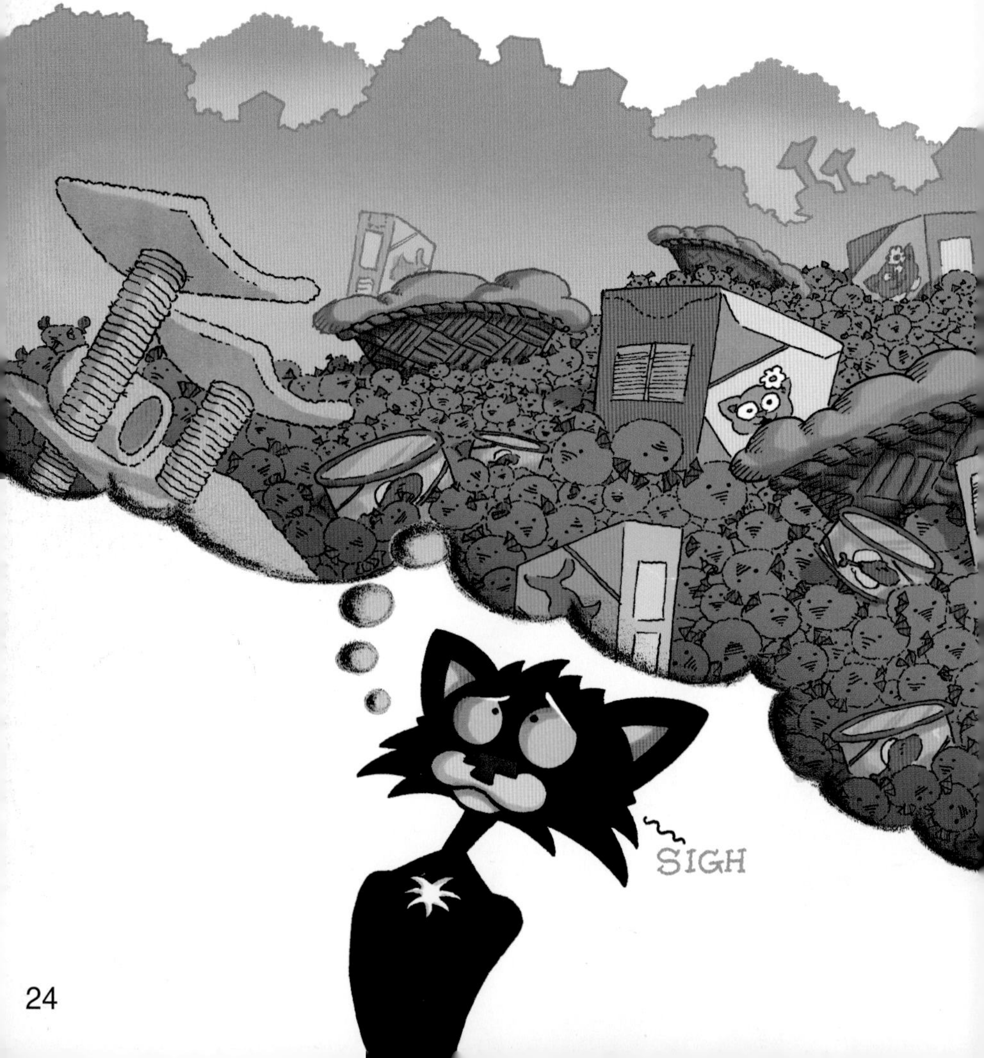
SIGH

Let me guess . . . You're thinking of what it would be like to live with 5 Andes mountain monastery cat trees, 10 Asian bamboo wicker beds, 100 cartons of litter, 200 boxes of your favorite snacks, 500 cans of your favorite food, and 1,000 mouse toys, aren't you?

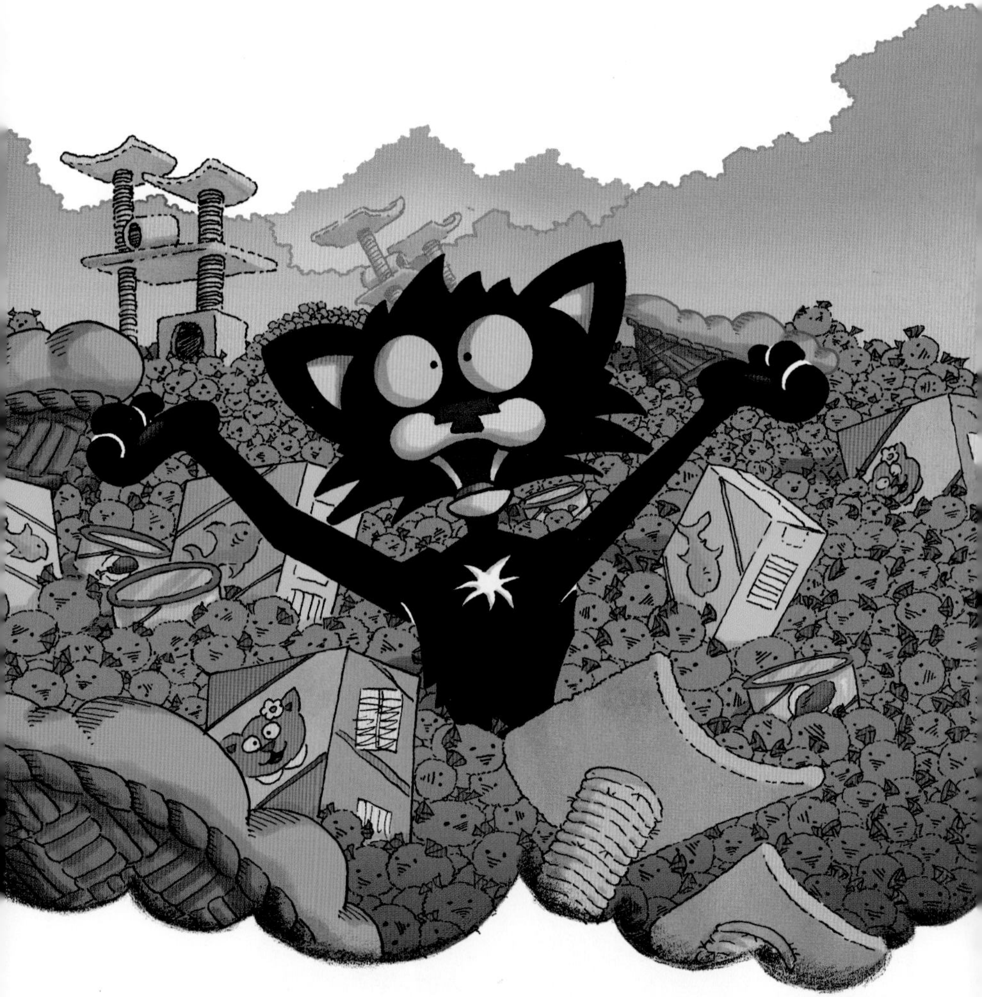

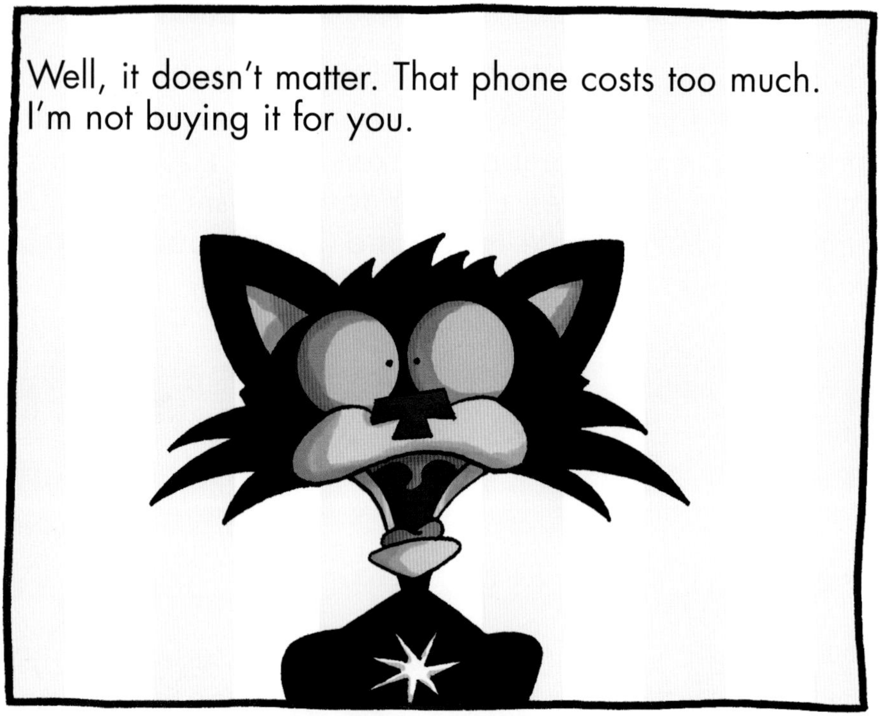
Well, it doesn't matter. That phone costs too much. I'm not buying it for you.

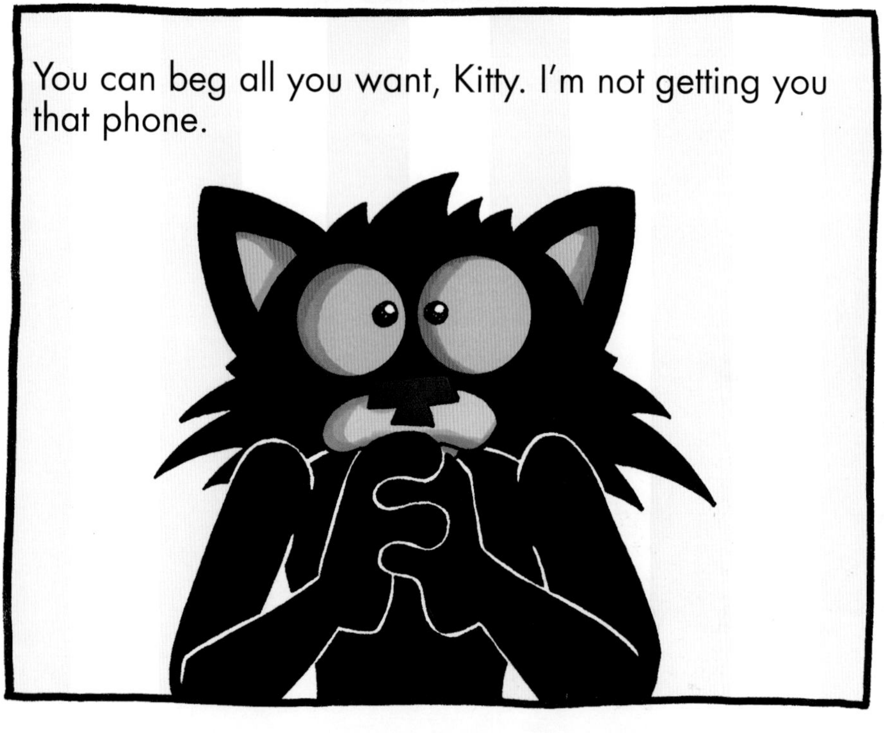
You can beg all you want, Kitty. I'm not getting you that phone.

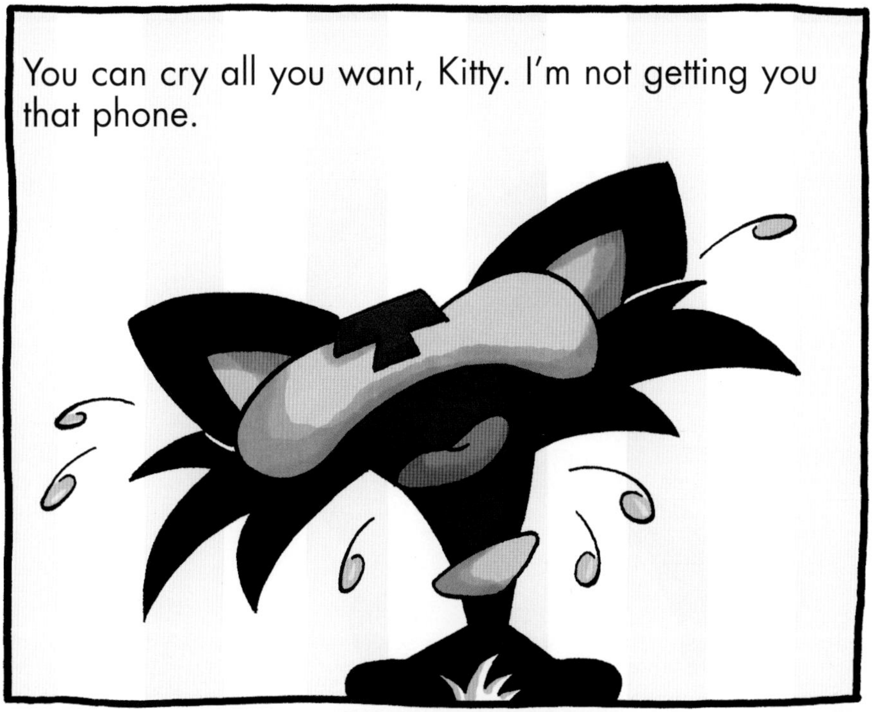
You can cry all you want, Kitty. I'm not getting you that phone.

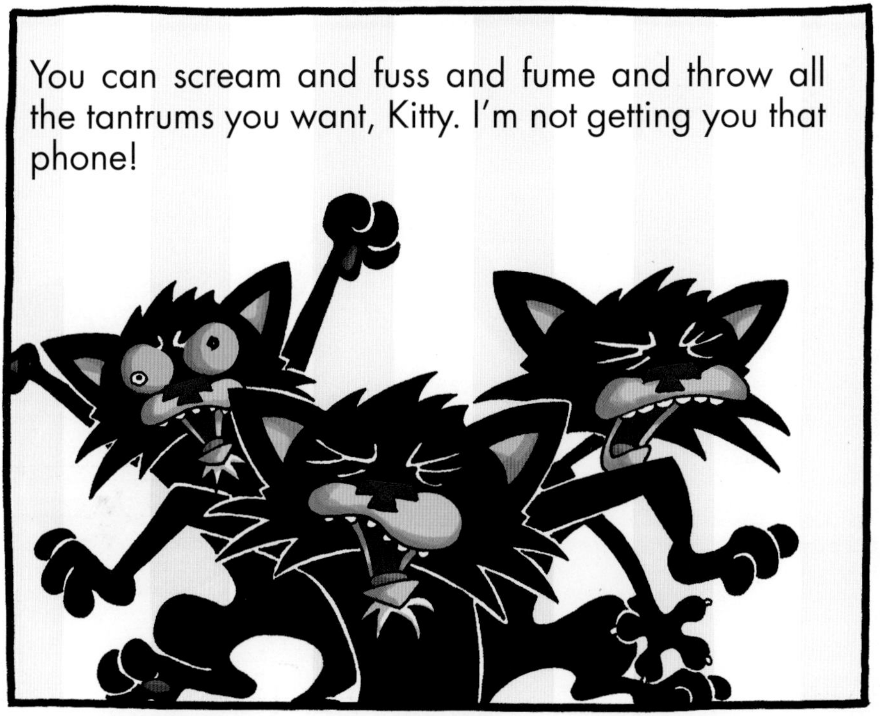
You can scream and fuss and fume and throw all the tantrums you want, Kitty. I'm not getting you that phone!

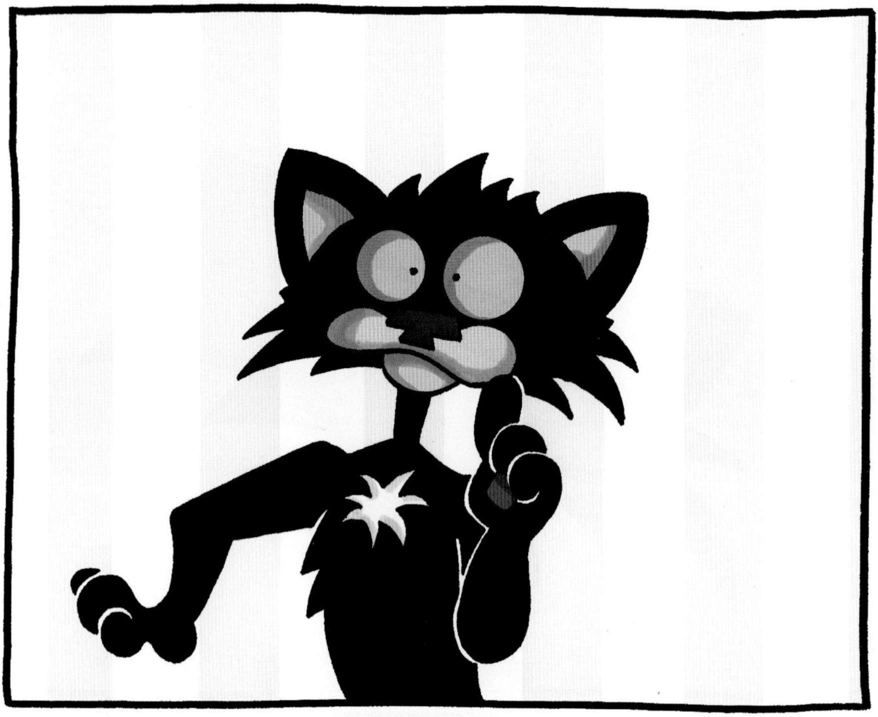

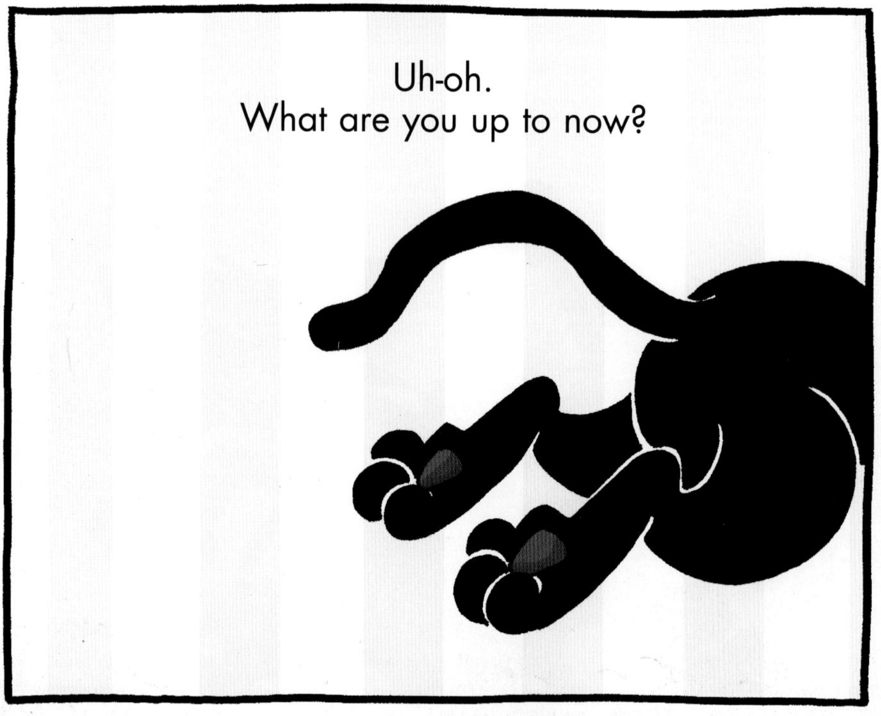
Uh-oh.
What are you up to now?

Oh, I see. You want to ***EARN*** the phone. Interesting. That might be something I could actually support, Kitty.

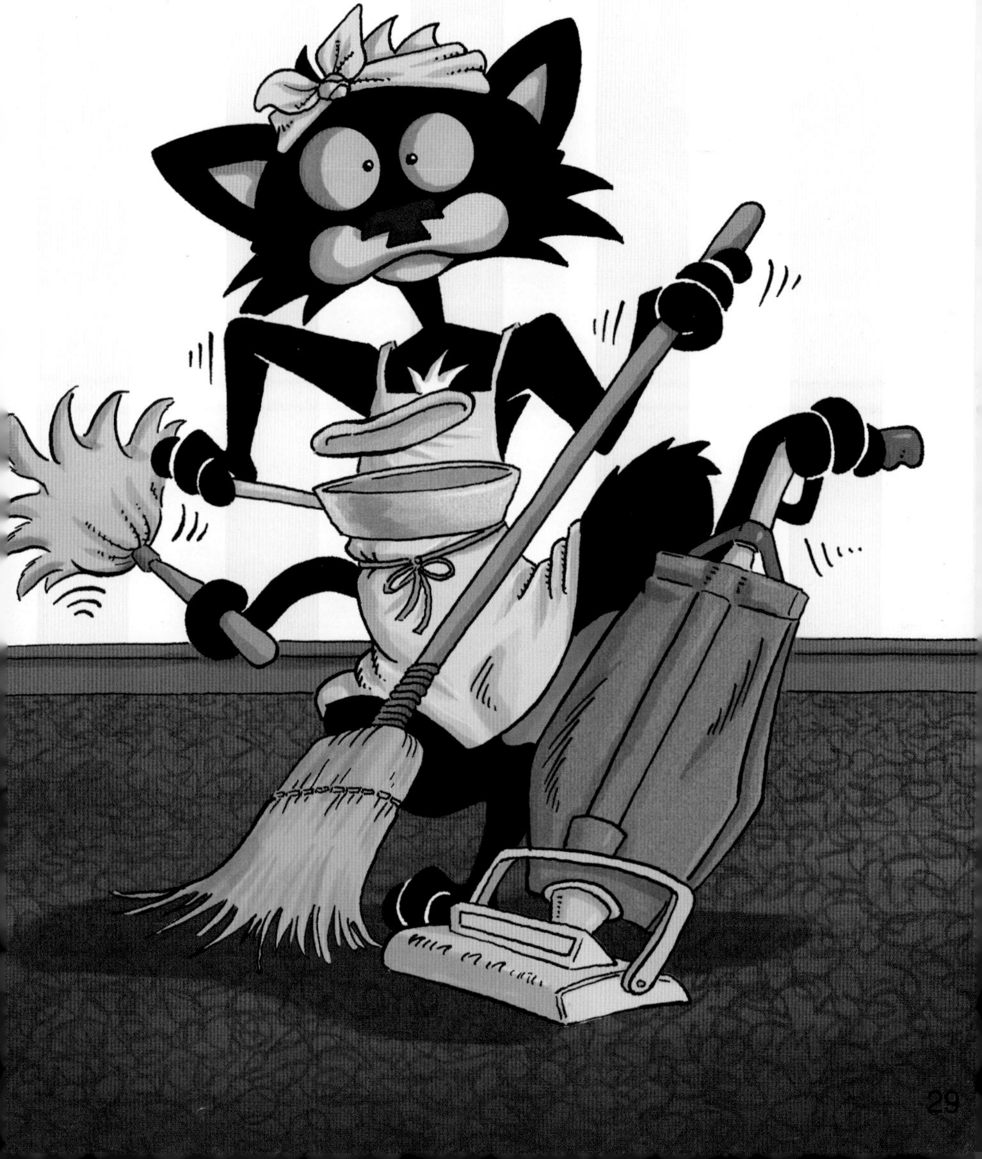

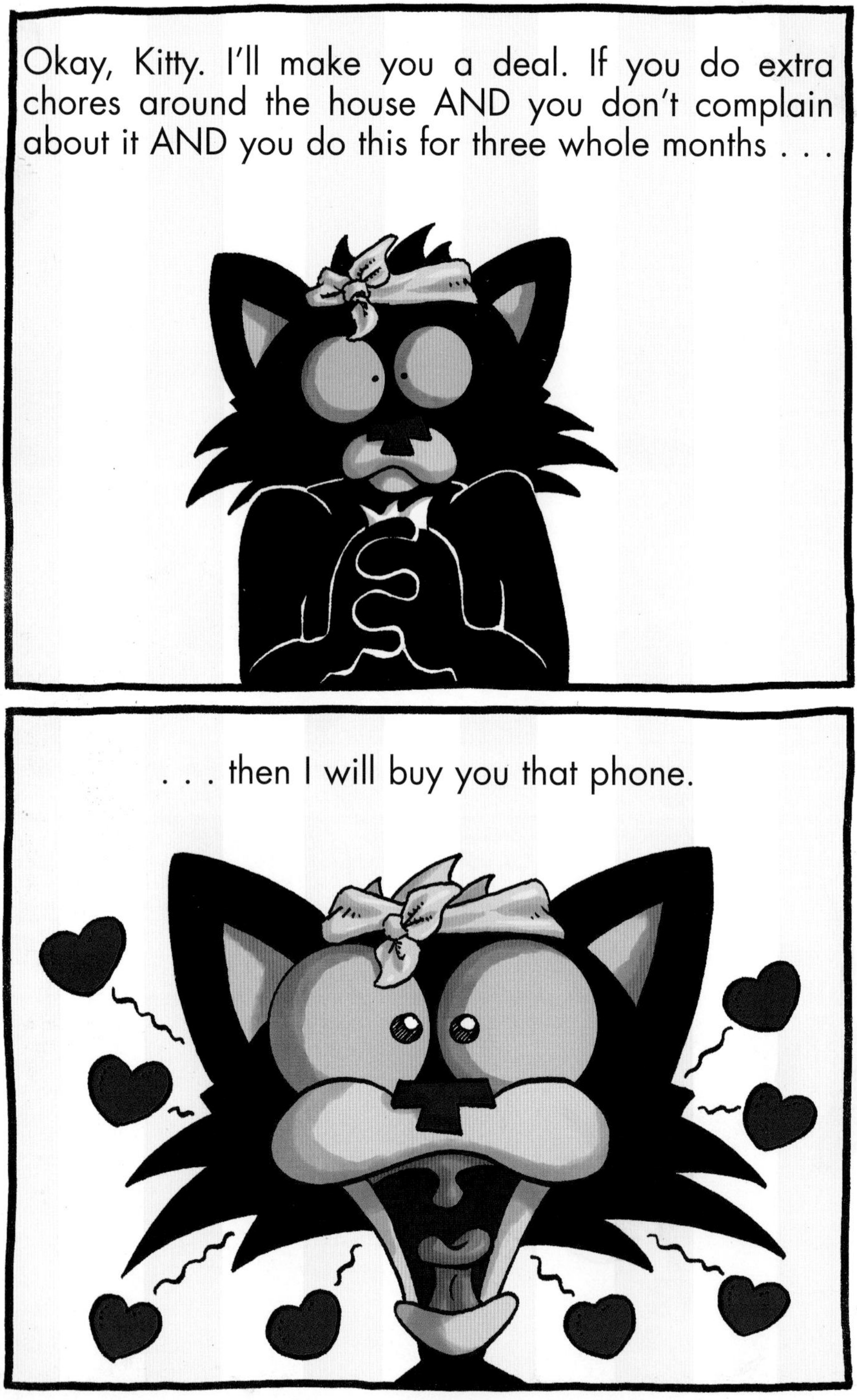
Okay, Kitty. I'll make you a deal. If you do extra chores around the house AND you don't complain about it AND you do this for three whole months . . .
. . . then I will buy you that phone.

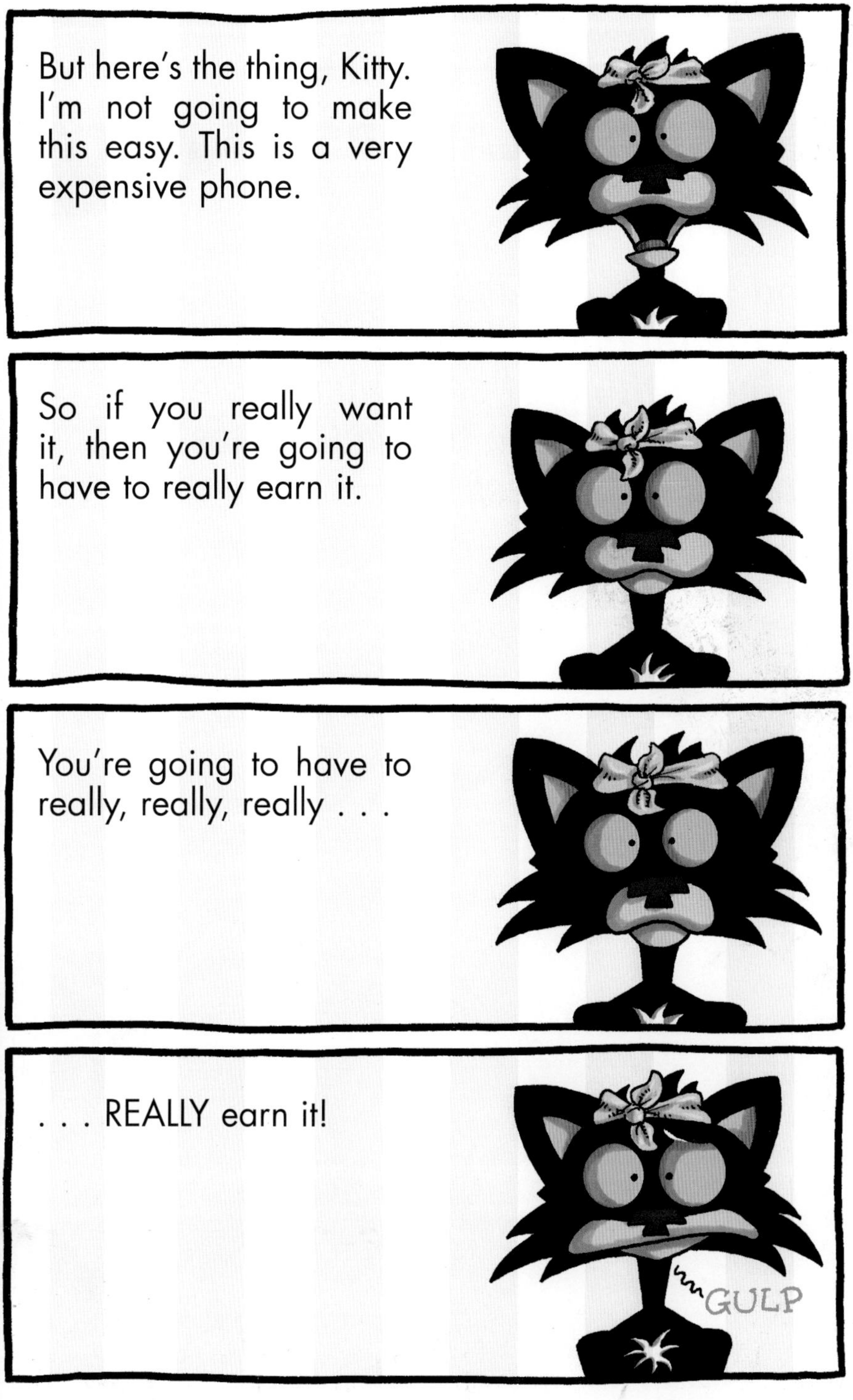
But here's the thing, Kitty. I'm not going to make this easy. This is a very expensive phone.
So if you really want it, then you're going to have to really earn it.
You're going to have to really, really, really . . .
. . . REALLY earn it!
GULP

•CHAPTER THREE•

THE SEVEN LABORS OF KITTY

And so began our brave hero's quest to defy all odds and earn the sacred device, a thing of such incredible beauty and magic that all felines yearned to possess it.

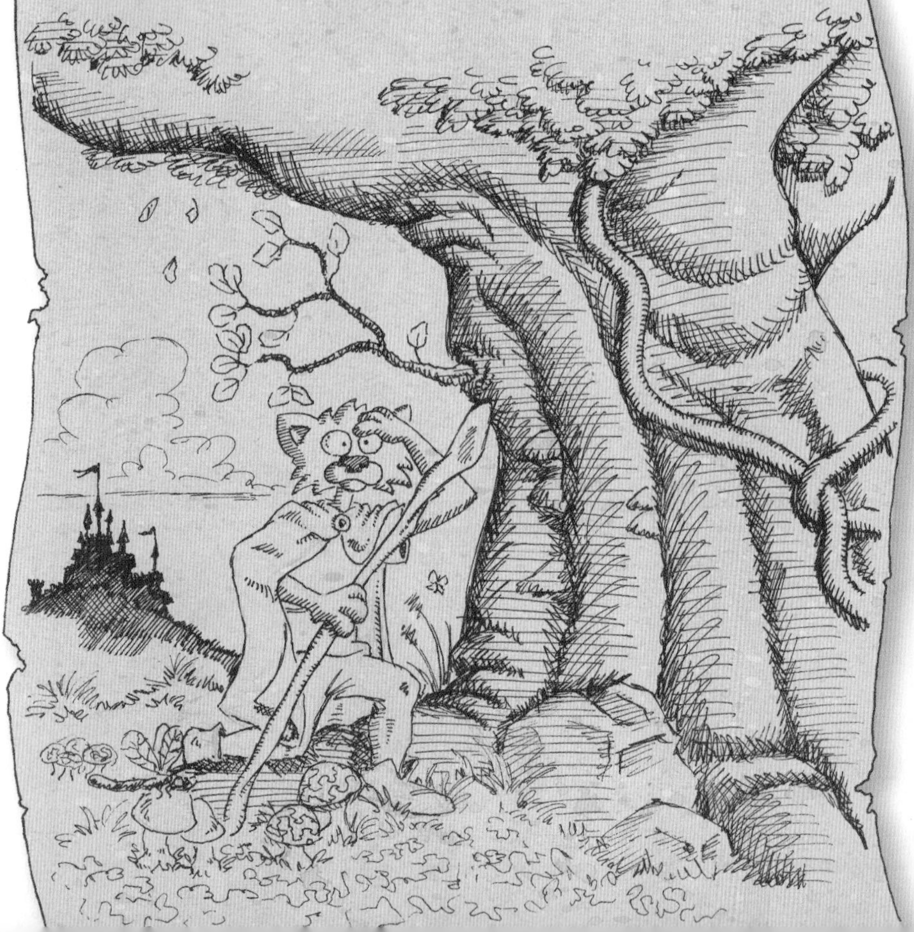

THE FIRST LABOR:
Pick up her toys

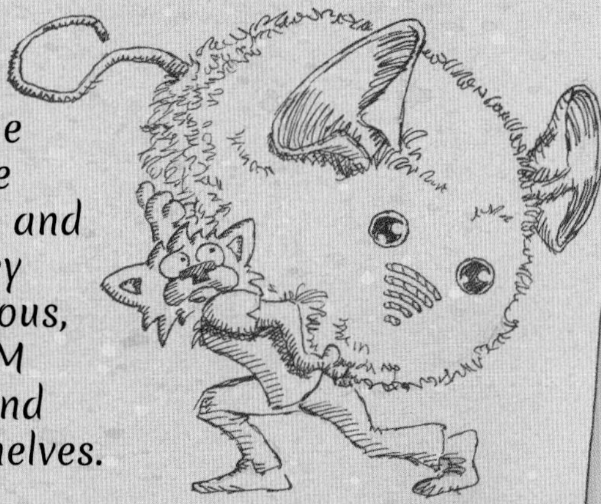

Our hero's toys were plentiful, and the gods decreed that she must not only remove them from the floors and pathways where they were deemed hazardous, but also STORE THEM AWAY inside boxes and cabinets and atop shelves.

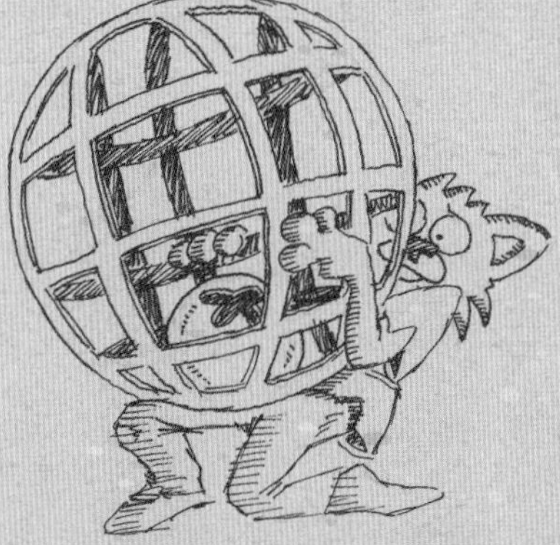

Stuffing them under the couch was forbidden. Hiding them behind the curtains was forbidden. Even concealing them under the rugs was forbidden.

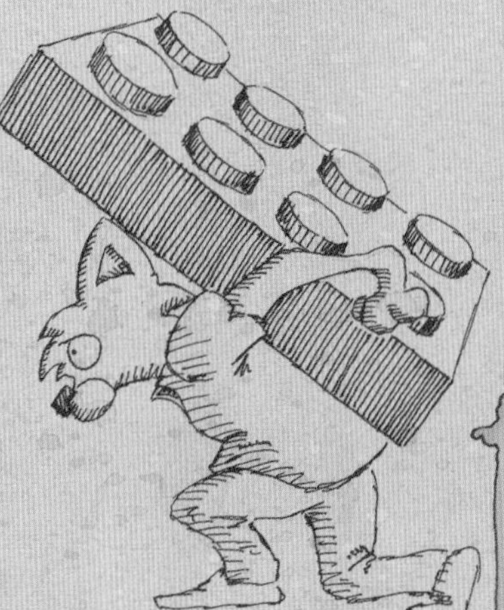

Our brave hero could have endured this miserable labor were it but for a day. But no! The gods deemed that this labor was to last for not just one day or two, but for ALL OF ETERNITY!

THE SECOND LABOR: Make her bed

The gods oftentimes made no sense. They demanded that our hero flatten her sheets, tuck them in, and fold them at the top! Flat, tuck, fold. Flat, tuck, fold. Every morning, over and over, they demanded this until she thought she would scream!

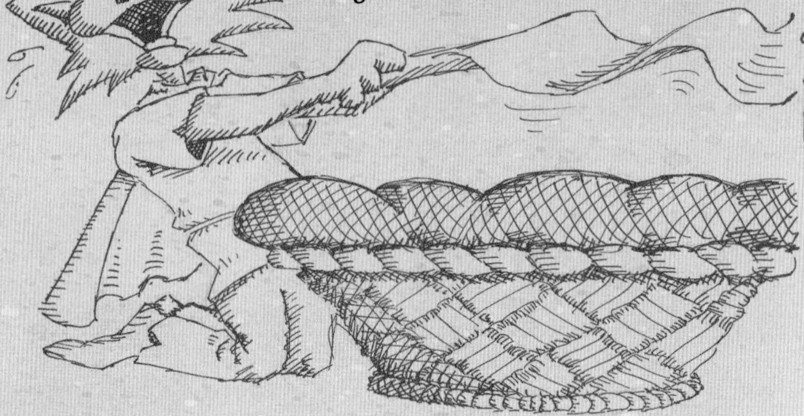

Our hero was sorely tempted to protest, but she knew that the gods were fickle and petty. They looked for any excuse to keep the device of great beauty and magic from her. Our hero had no choice but to give in to their whims, no matter how small and senseless they may be.

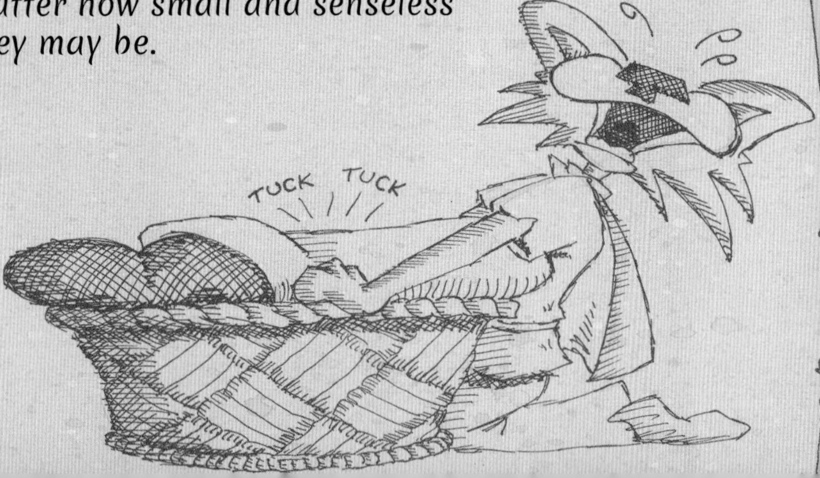
TUCK TUCK

THE THIRD LABOR:
Wash her bowl

Every day for years, our hero had eaten from the same bowl and licked it until it shined. But now the gods decreed that it was not enough!

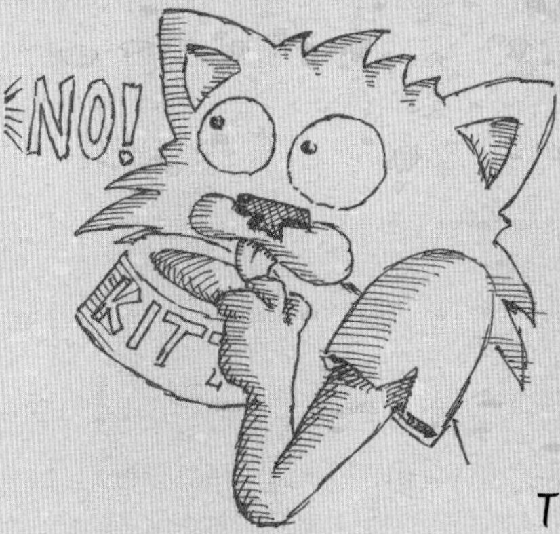
NO!
KITT

No. Now the bowl must be "cleaned." It must be scrubbed and washed until all of its wonderful flavor from the previous meal was lost forever! Plus, water was not enough. The gods demanded that soap be involved!

More and more each day, our hero found the gods irksome. And yet she persisted. For the sake of the device of great beauty and magic, she persisted.

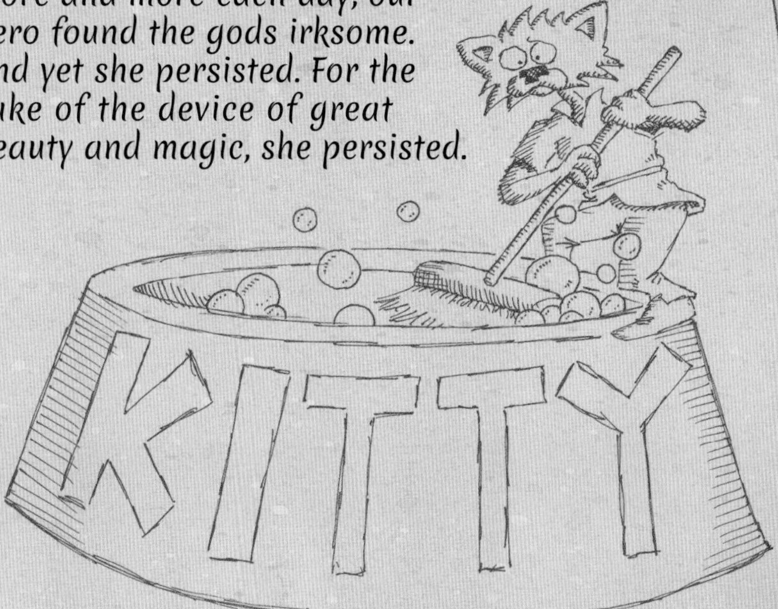
KITTY

THE FOURTH LABOR:
Clean her litter box

Legends told of a cave so dark and fetid that none dare venture into it. Our hero, however, knew it well, and the gods decreed that she should sally forth into it to remove its most horrible contents.

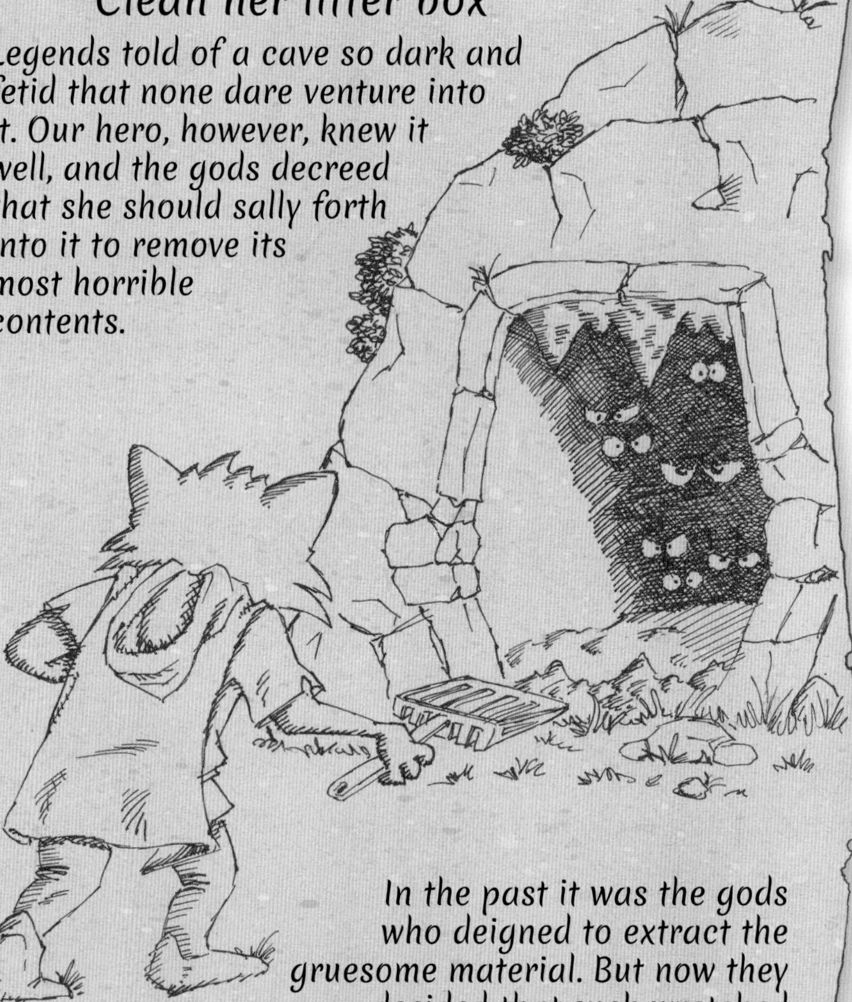

In the past it was the gods who deigned to extract the gruesome material. But now they decided that such wretched responsibilities should fall upon HER! No doubt they laughed at her plight, but she remained pure of heart and all the more determined to succeed in her quest. She would have the last laugh.

THE FIFTH LABOR:
Change the baby

There was a time when our hero was allied with the spawn of the gods. But then it was the gods themselves who put upon our hero the abominable task of removing the spawn's horrific undergarments and replacing them with a new, fresh version of the same. Even when our hero had cleaned out the cave of horrors, she did not experience such a stench! For the first time, she questioned the worth of her quest to possess the device. And yet, she persevered.

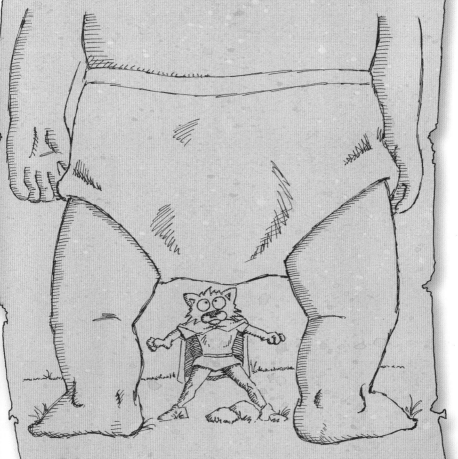

THE SIXTH LABOR:
Repair the curtains

One would think that the drapery of the gods was made of gold or the finest woven catnip the way they would carry on about the slightest tear to the precious fabric. Nonetheless, the gods placed the responsibility for their condition squarely upon our hero's broad shoulders. She had but climbed them once, maybe twice, but no more than 89 times in the past month. Yet, she dared not protest as she contemplated the device of great beauty and magic and sewed together the pathetic window dressings.

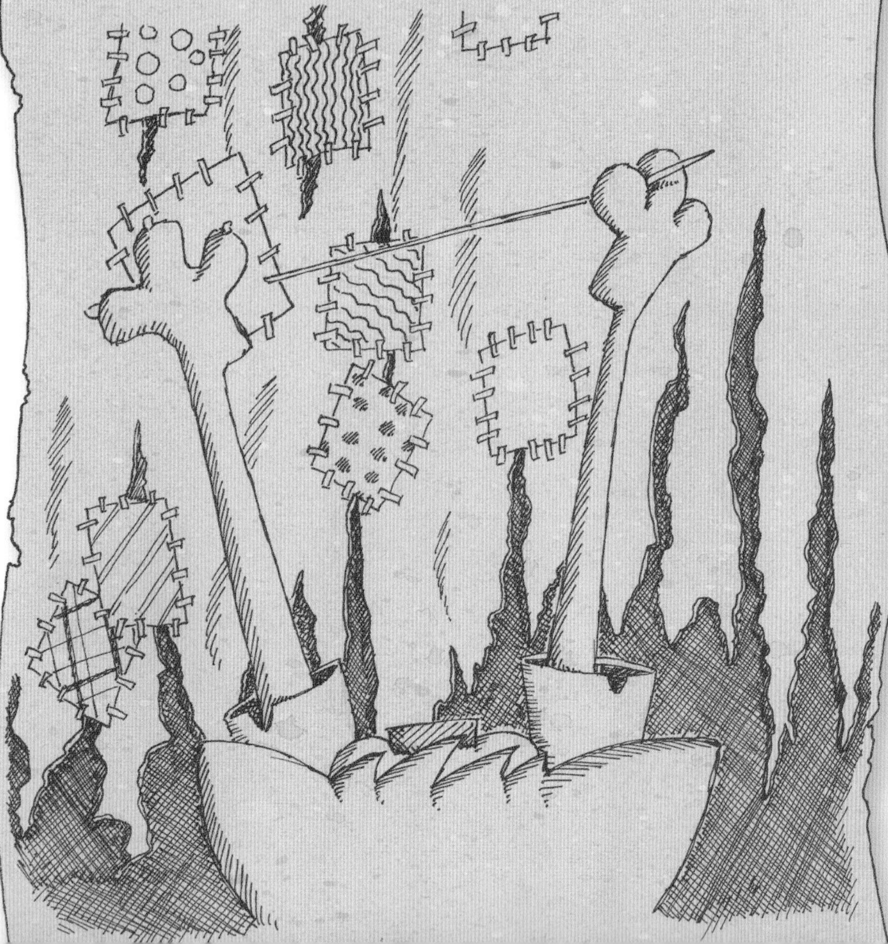

THE SEVENTH LABOR:

The gods had saved their most terrible task for last. From the deepest bowels of Hades there once came a beast most foul, a creature made more of drool than flesh and bone. The gods named this repugnant saliva monster "Puppy" and gave it shelter in their home.

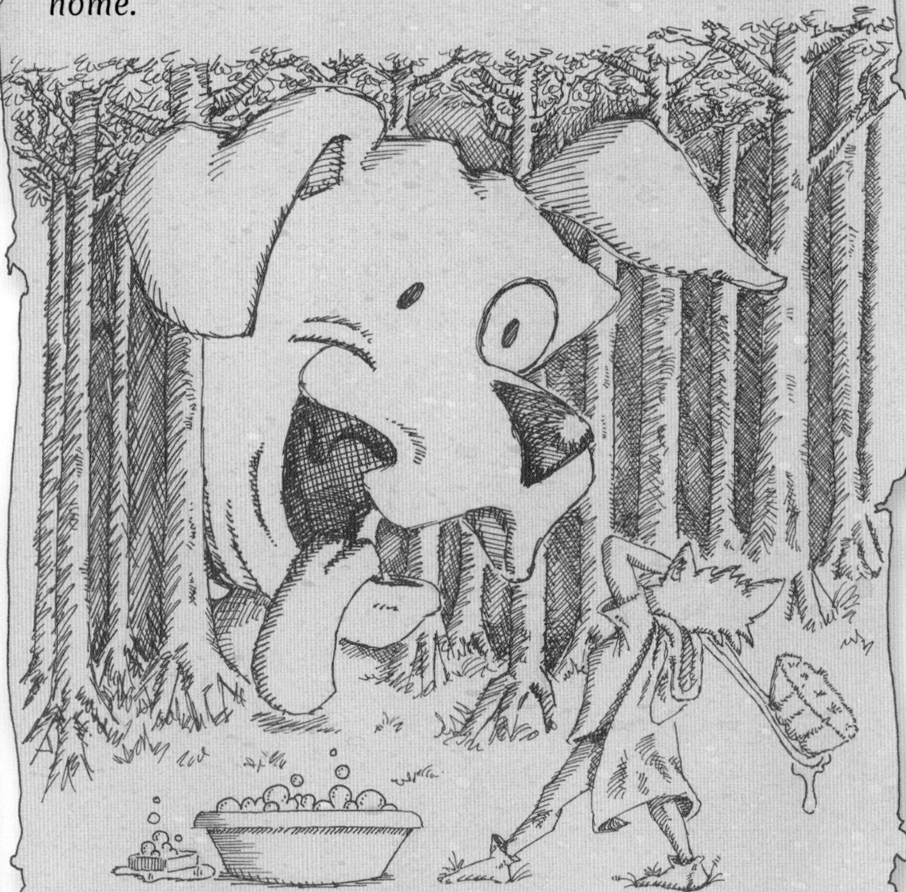

Oh, how the gods must have chortled with delight when they gave our brave hero her final challenge:

GIVE PUPPY A BATH!

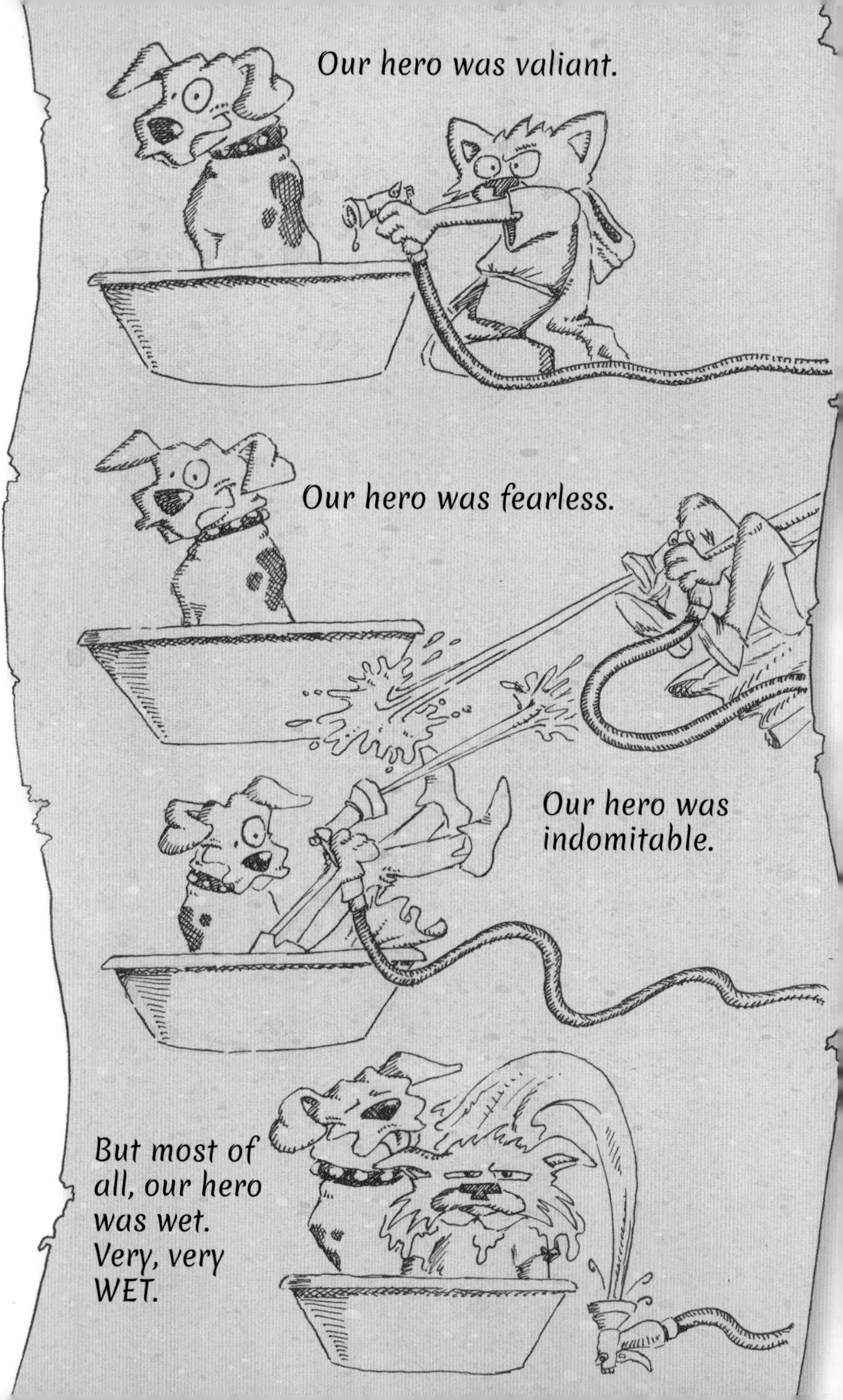
Our hero was valiant.
Our hero was fearless.
Our hero was indomitable.
But most of all, our hero was wet. Very, very WET.

"And hast thou bathed the Slobberbrute?" The gods asked if 'twas done. Our hero had NO MORE tasks to do! Zip. Zilch. Naught. Nada. None!

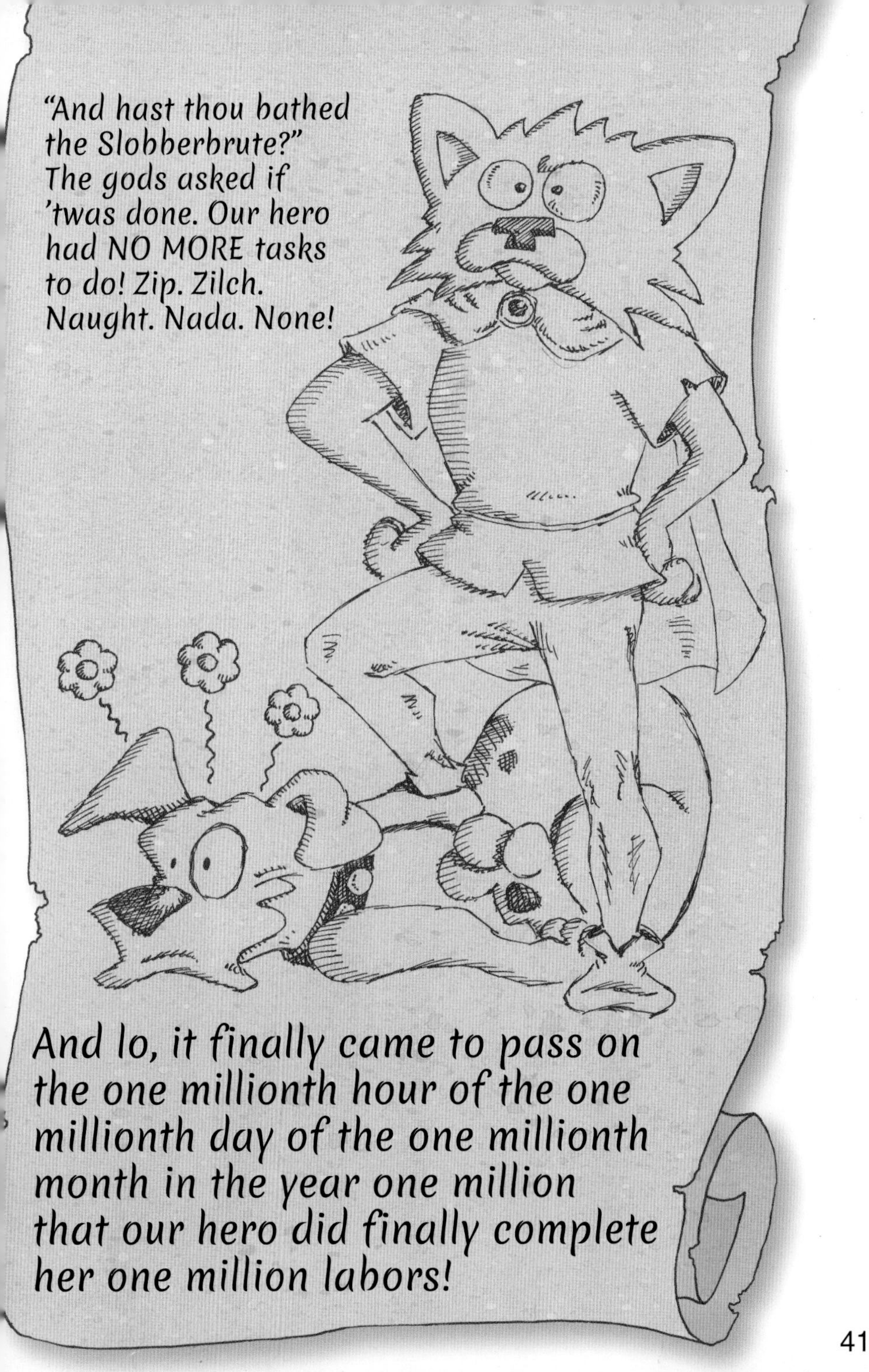

And lo, it finally came to pass on the one millionth hour of the one millionth day of the one millionth month in the year one million that our hero did finally complete her one million labors!

Well, Kitty, you did it. A deal's a deal. You did all of your chores without complaining for three whole months with the promise to keep it up. So . . .

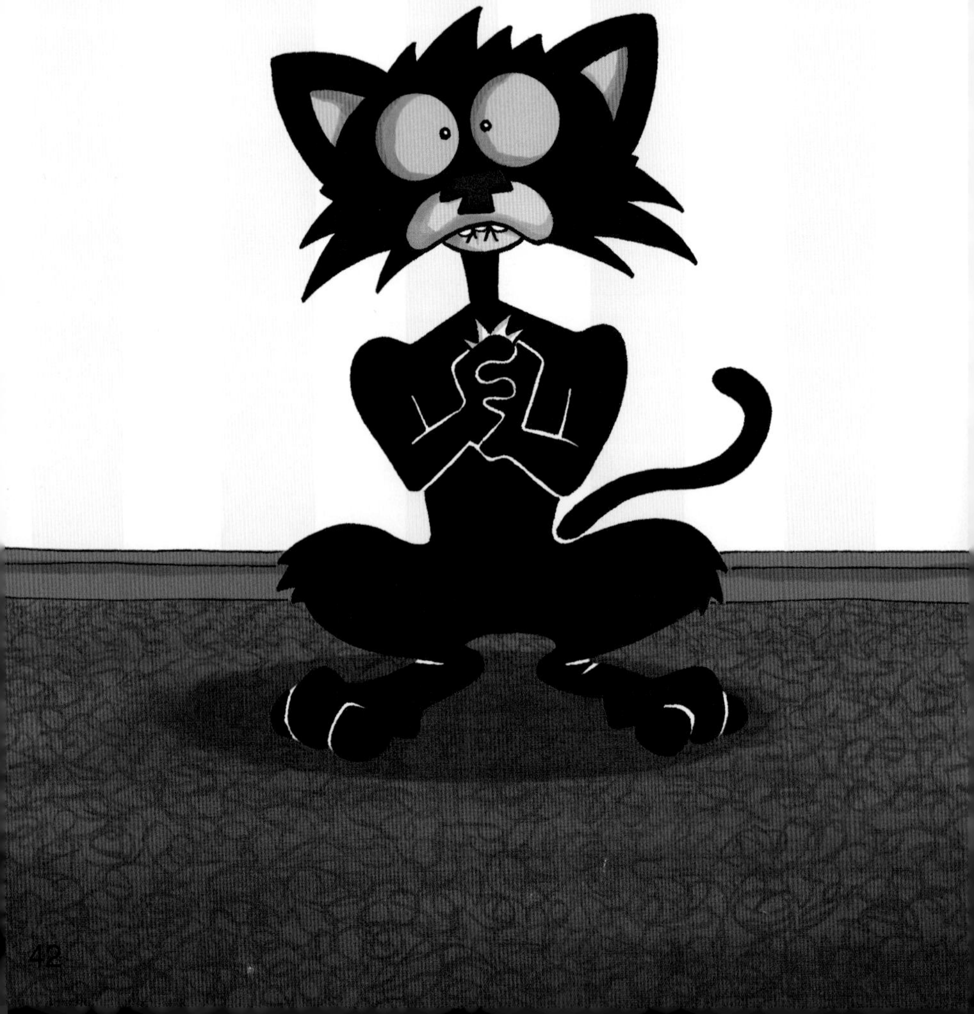

HERE'S YOUR PHONE!

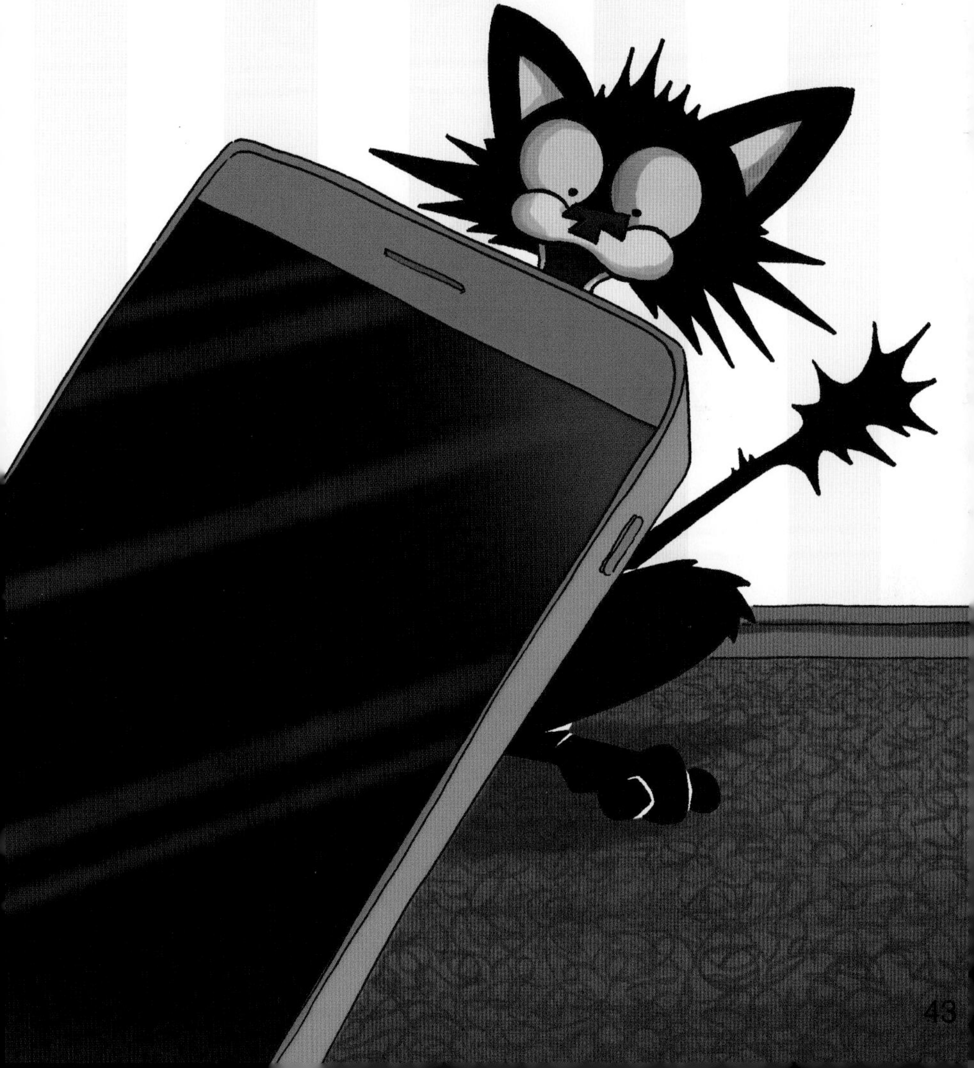

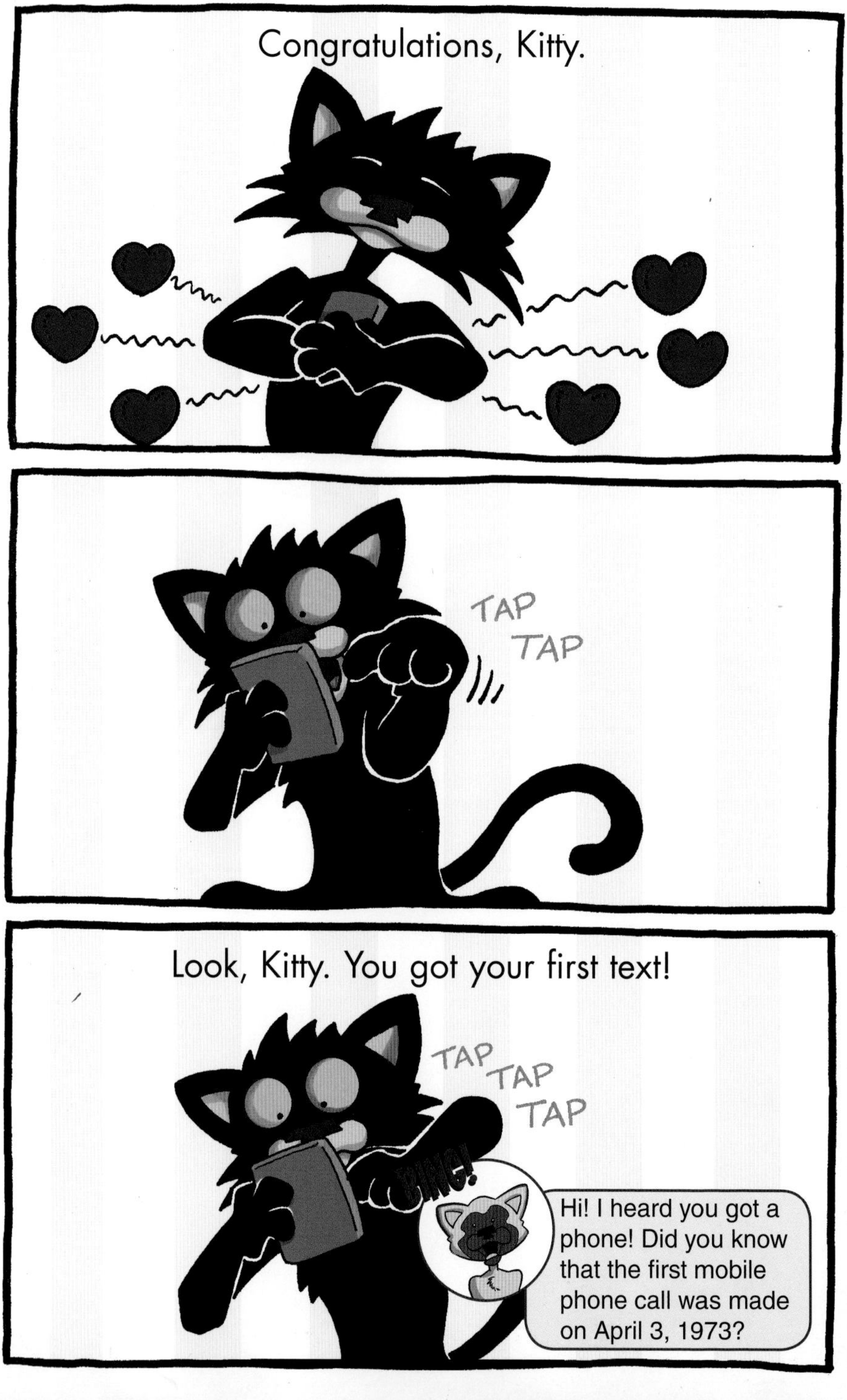
Congratulations, Kitty.
TAP
TAP
Look, Kitty. You got your first text!
TAP
TAP
TAP
DING!
Hi! I heard you got a phone! Did you know that the first mobile phone call was made on April 3, 1973?

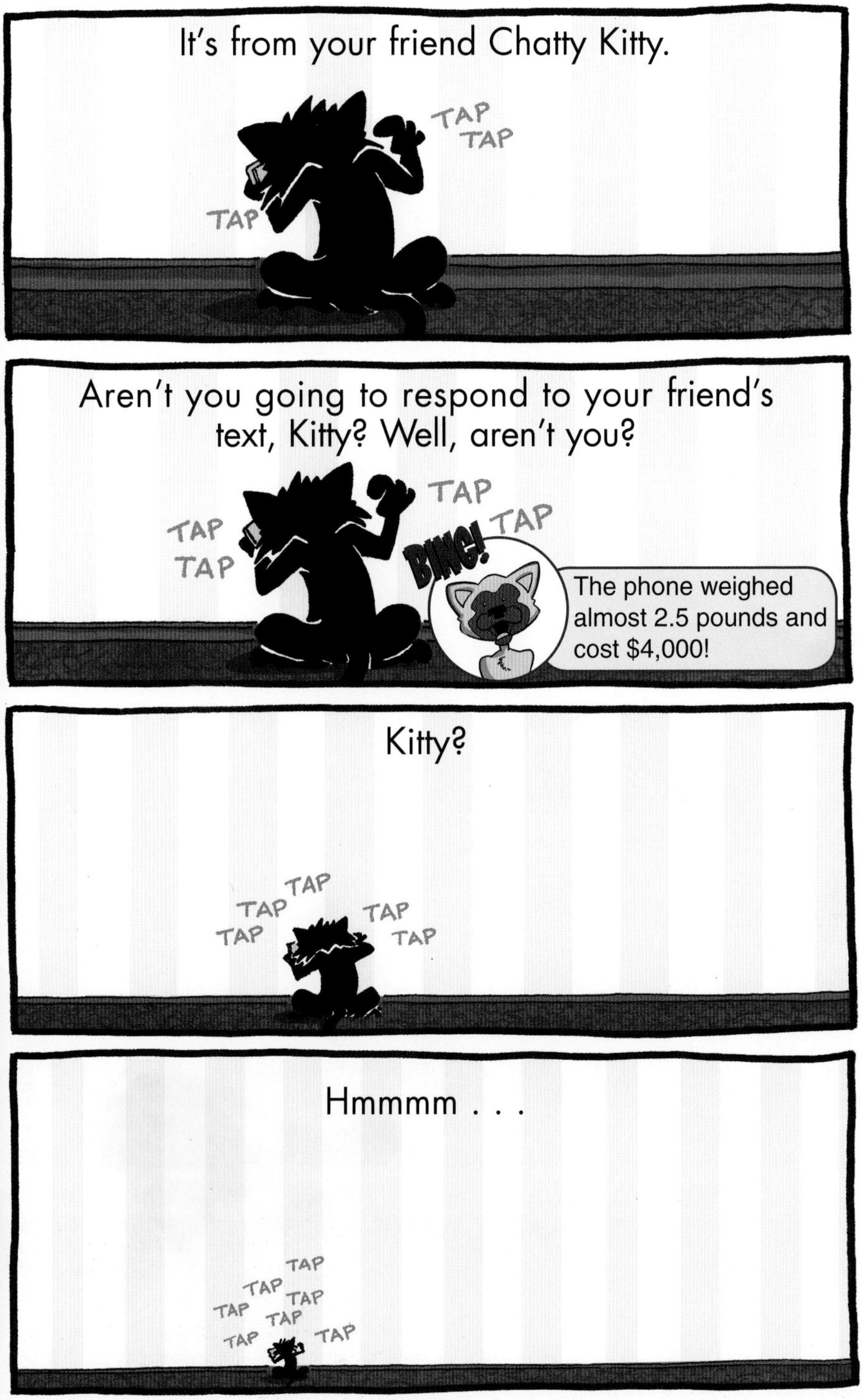
It's from your friend Chatty Kitty.
TAP
TAP
TAP
Aren't you going to respond to your friend's text, Kitty? Well, aren't you?
TAP
TAP
TAP
TAP
BING!
The phone weighed almost 2.5 pounds and cost $4,000!
Kitty?
TAP
TAP
TAP
TAP
TAP
Hmmmm . . .
TAP
TAP
TAP
TAP
TAP
TAP
TAP

• CHAPTER FOUR •

DRAGON MAYHEM CARNAGE WARS

Kitty, you've been playing your little *Feather Tap* game since yesterday. I know that having a phone is fun and all, but maybe it's time to put it away. Maybe you and I could play with some *real* feathers! Maybe we can go to the park. Maybe we can . . .

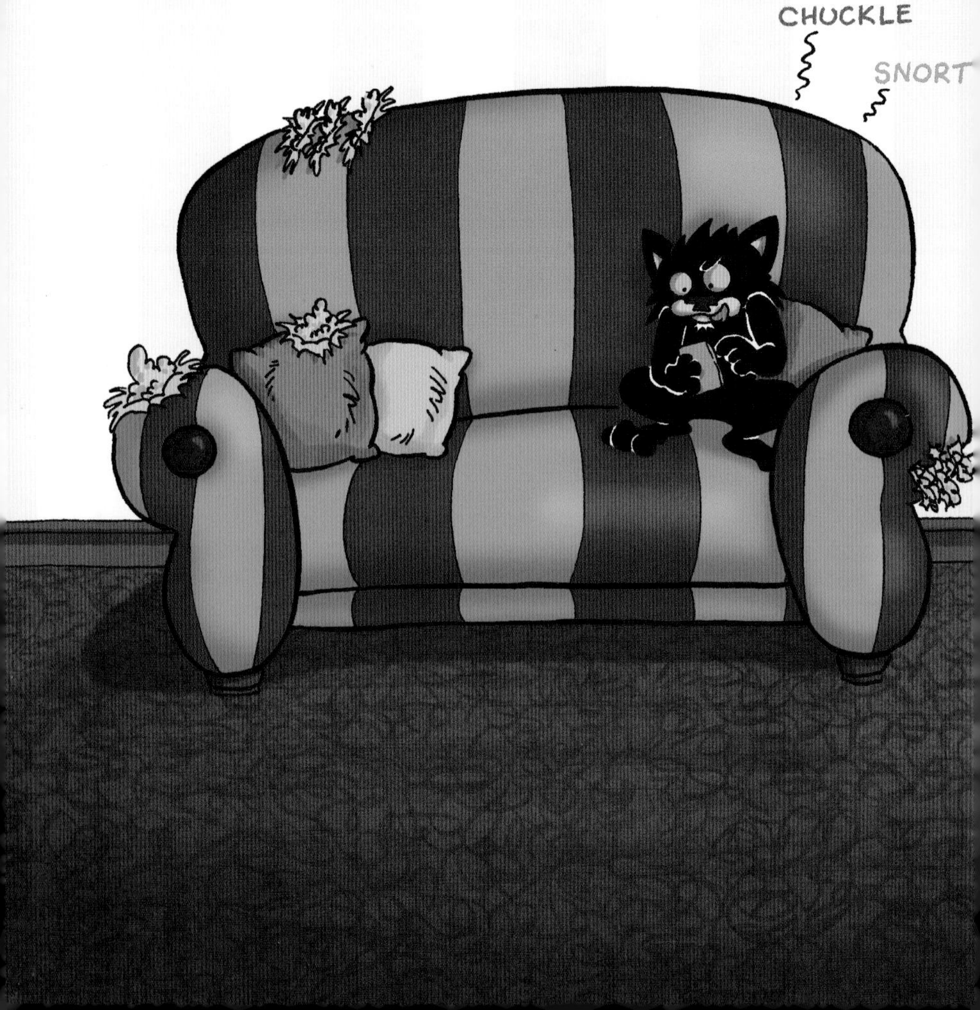
CHUCKLE
SNORT

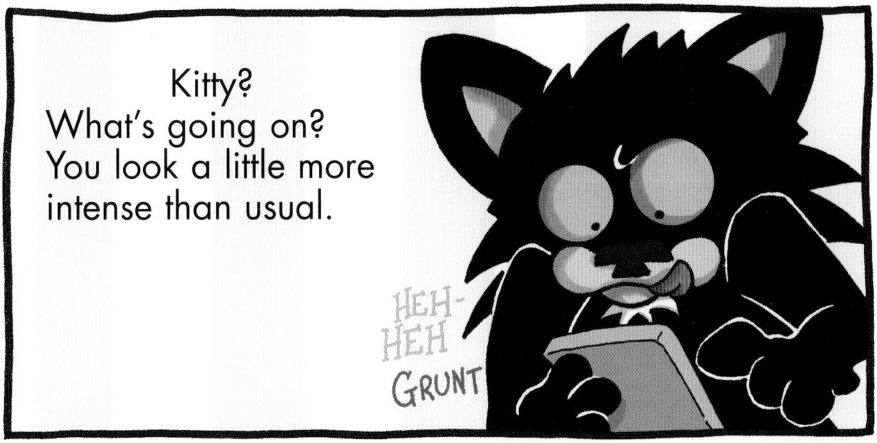
Kitty?
What's going on?
You look a little more
intense than usual.
HEH-
HEH
GRUNT

Hang on!
This isn't *Feather Tap*!
What is this game?

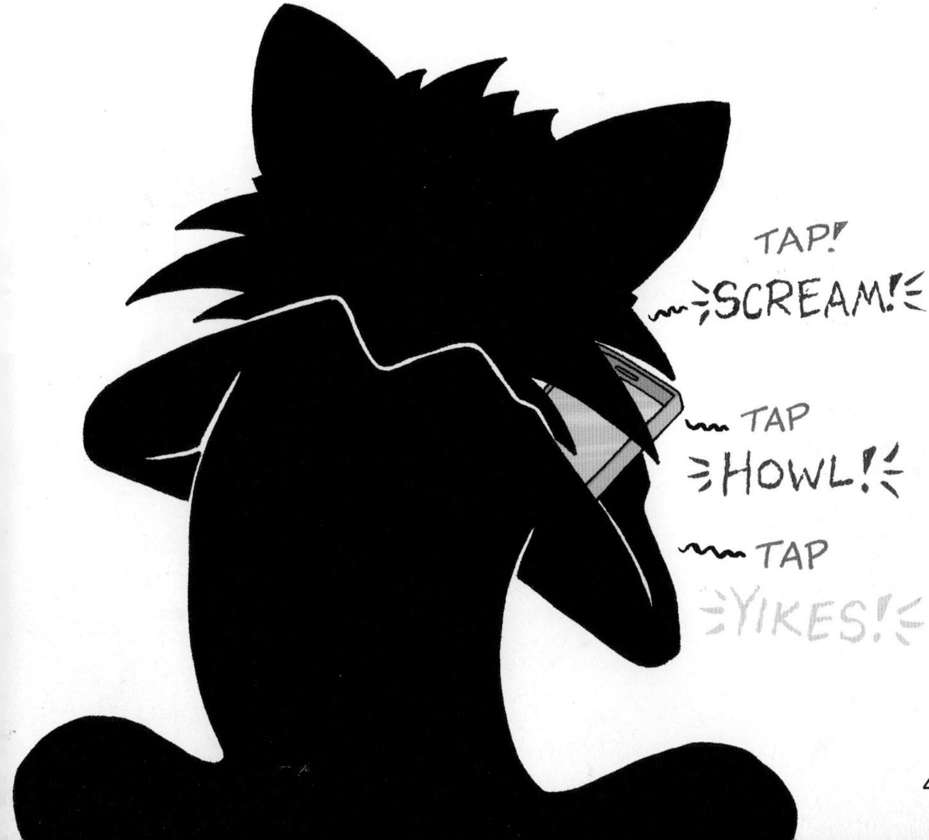
TAP!
SCREAM!
TAP
HOWL!
TAP
YIKES!

Dragon Mayhem Carnage Wars?!

I don't think I like the sound of this game. Are you sure it's appropriate for cats? Show me how you play it.

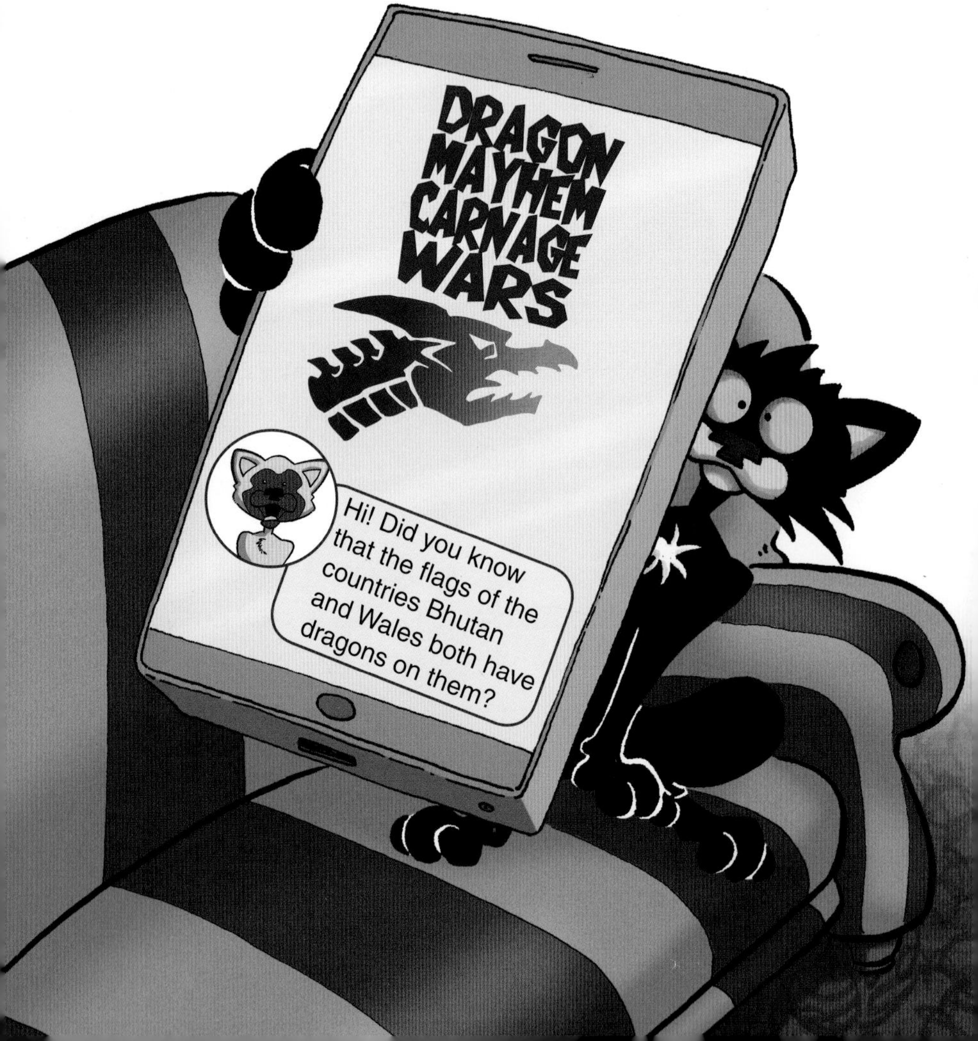
DRAGON MAYHEM CARNAGE WARS
Hi! Did you know that the flags of the countries Bhutan and Wales both have dragons on them?

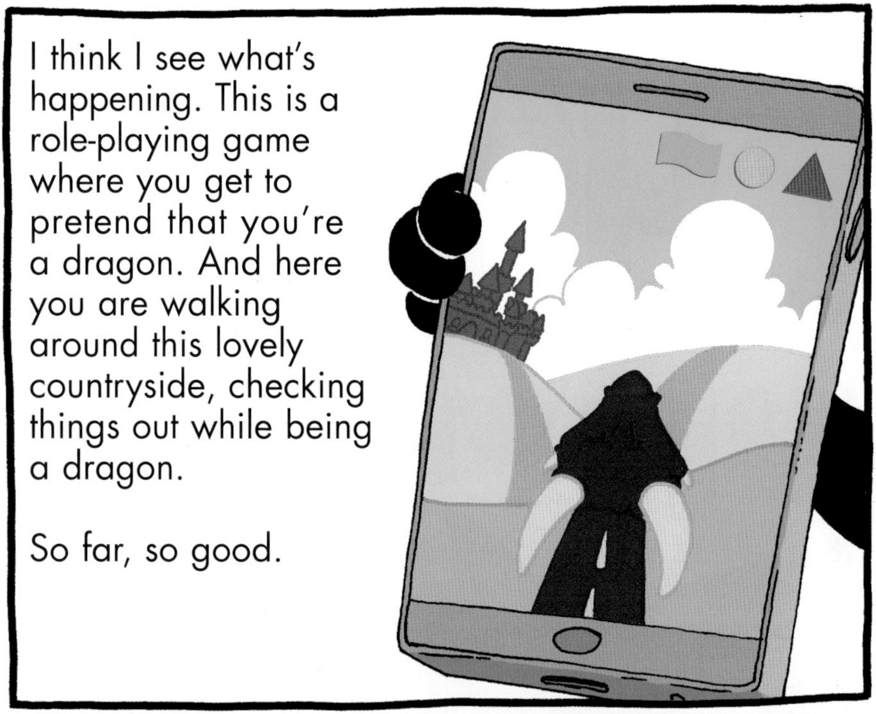
I think I see what's happening. This is a role-playing game where you get to pretend that you're a dragon. And here you are walking around this lovely countryside, checking things out while being a dragon.
So far, so good.

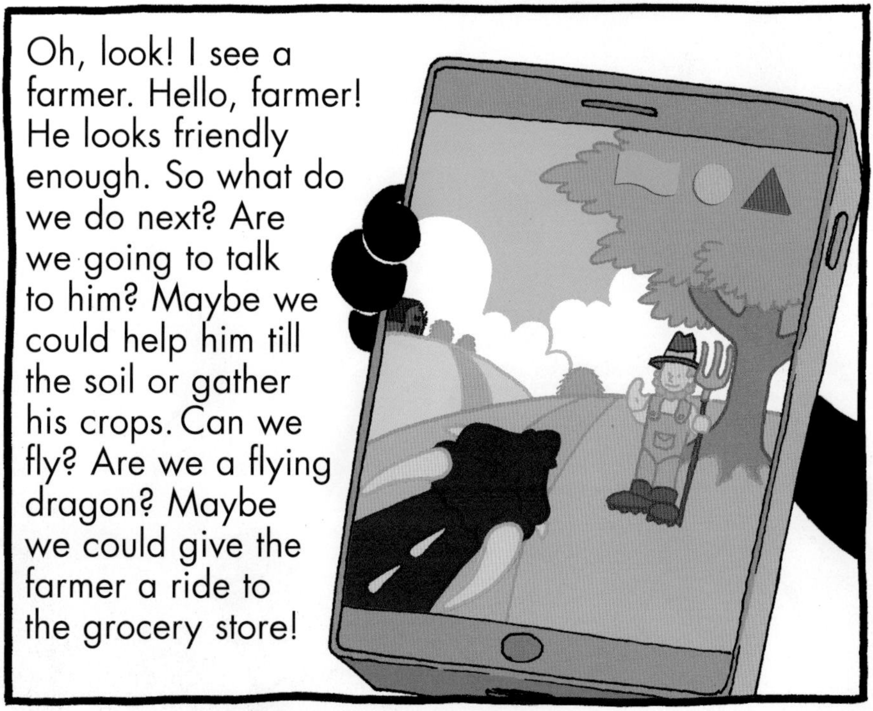
Oh, look! I see a farmer. Hello, farmer! He looks friendly enough. So what do we do next? Are we going to talk to him? Maybe we could help him till the soil or gather his crops. Can we fly? Are we a flying dragon? Maybe we could give the farmer a ride to the grocery store!

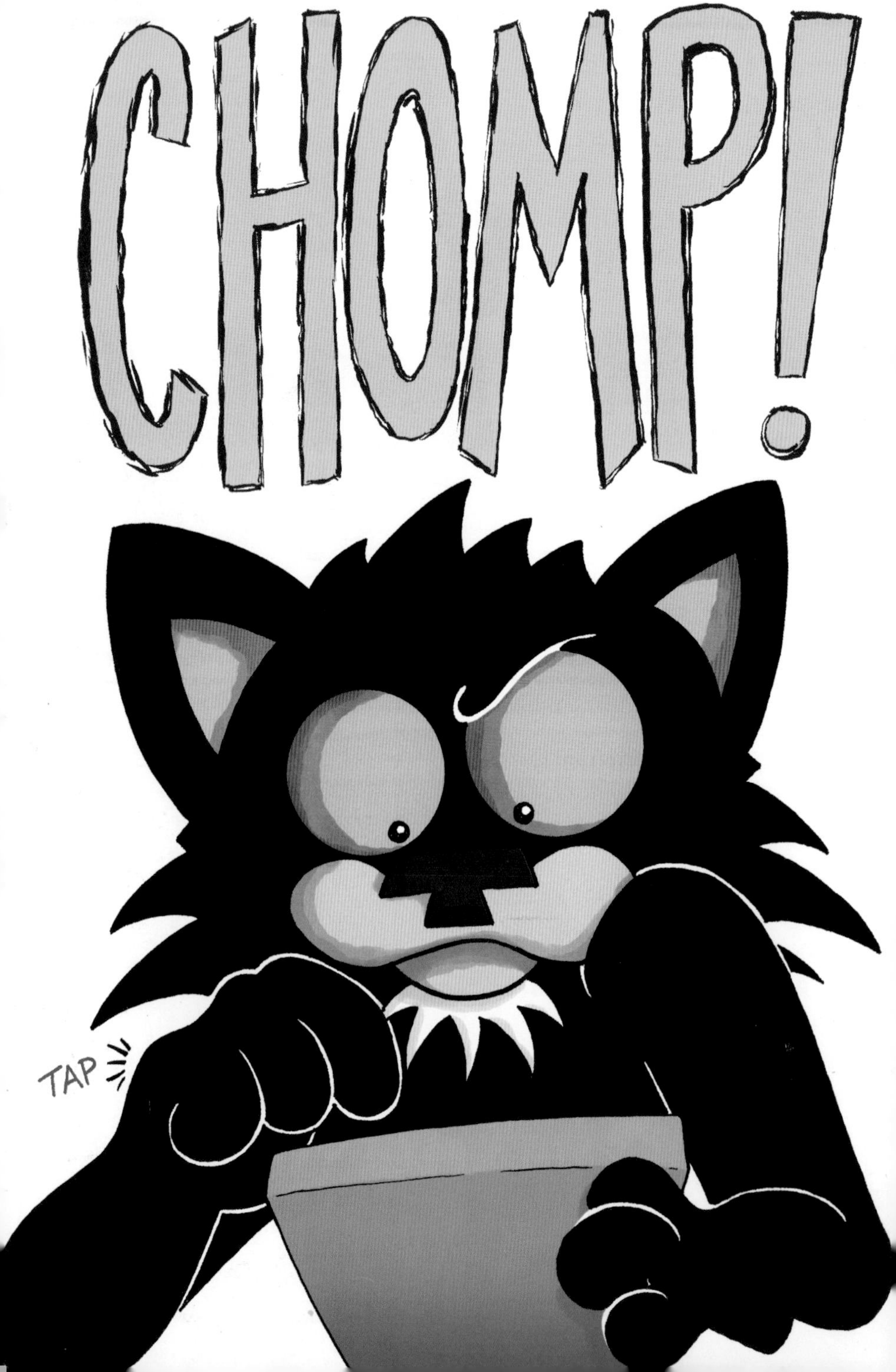
CHOMP!
TAP

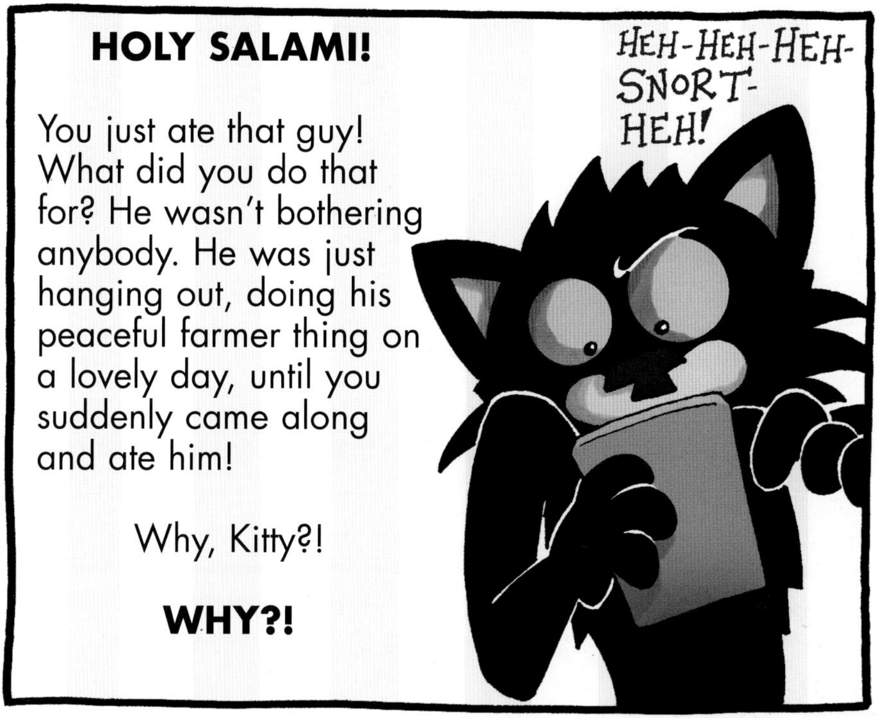
HOLY SALAMI!
You just ate that guy! What did you do that for? He wasn't bothering anybody. He was just hanging out, doing his peaceful farmer thing on a lovely day, until you suddenly came along and ate him!
Why, Kitty?!
WHY?!
HEH-HEH-HEH-SNORT-HEH!

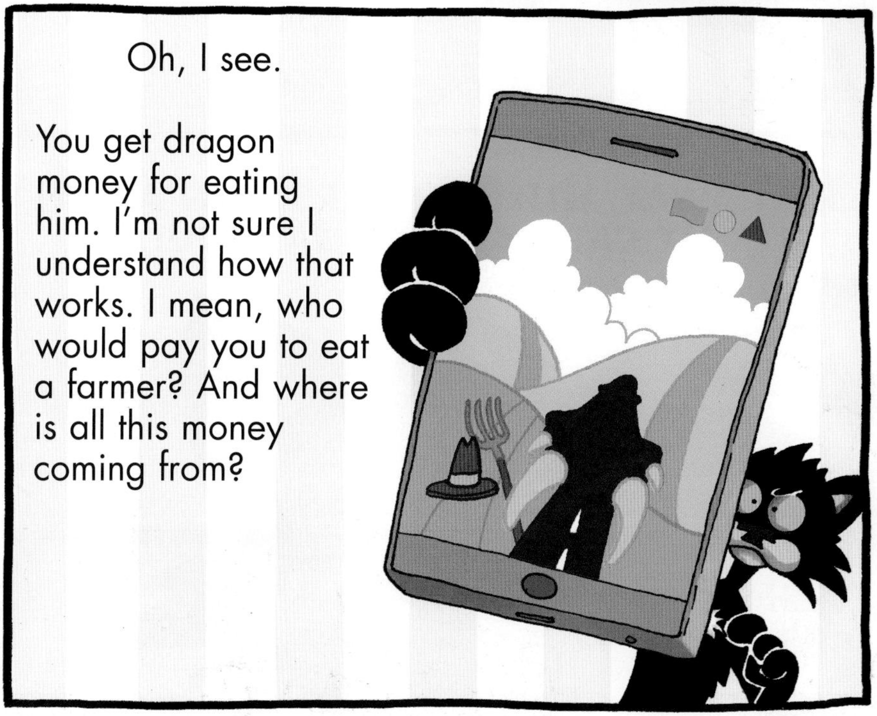
Oh, I see.
You get dragon money for eating him. I'm not sure I understand how that works. I mean, who would pay you to eat a farmer? And where is all this money coming from?

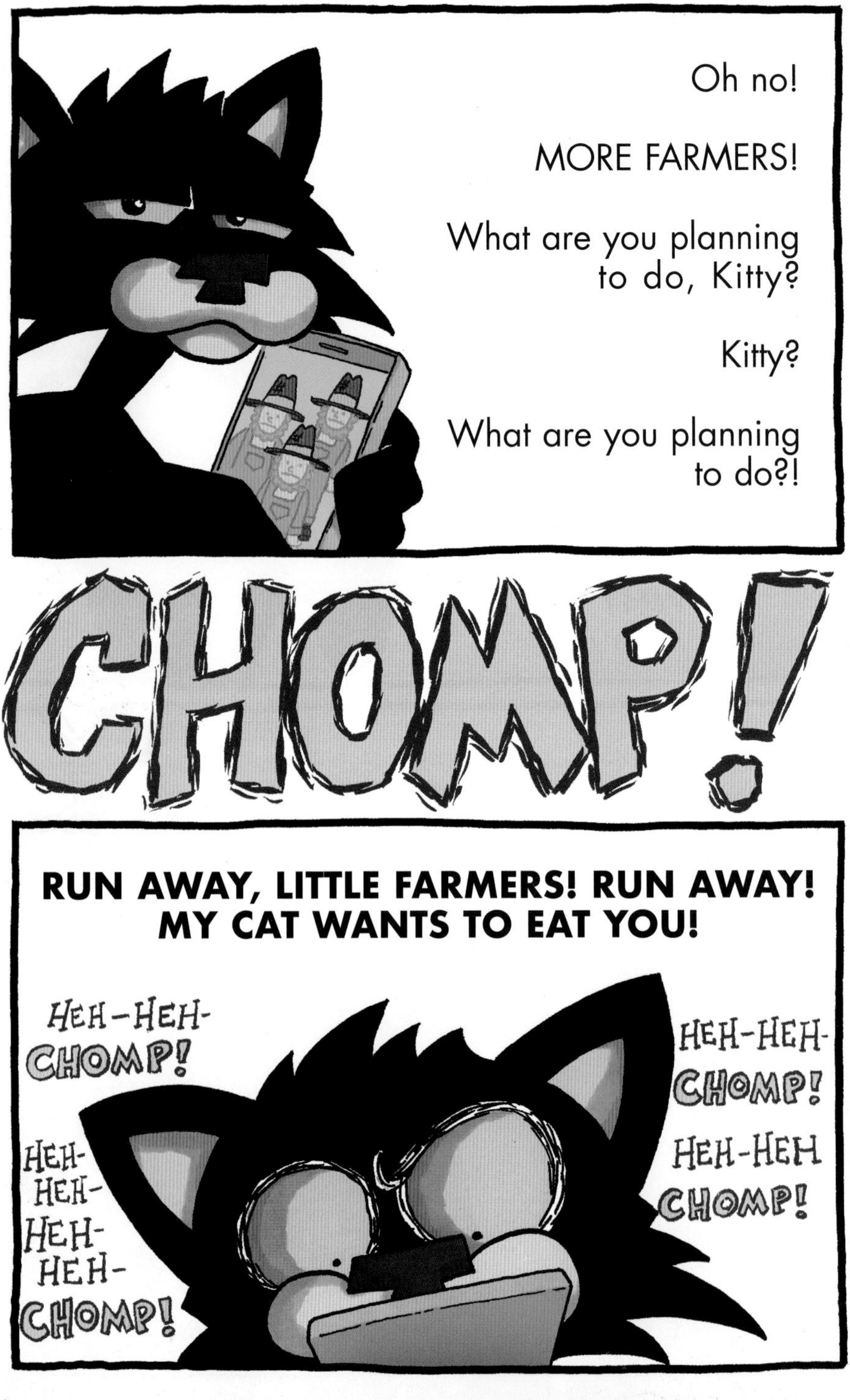
Oh no!
MORE FARMERS!
What are you planning to do, Kitty?
Kitty?
What are you planning to do?!
CHOMP!
RUN AWAY, LITTLE FARMERS! RUN AWAY! MY CAT WANTS TO EAT YOU!
HEH-HEH-CHOMP!
HEH-HEH-CHOMP!
HEH-HEH-HEH-HEH-CHOMP!
HEH-HEH CHOMP!

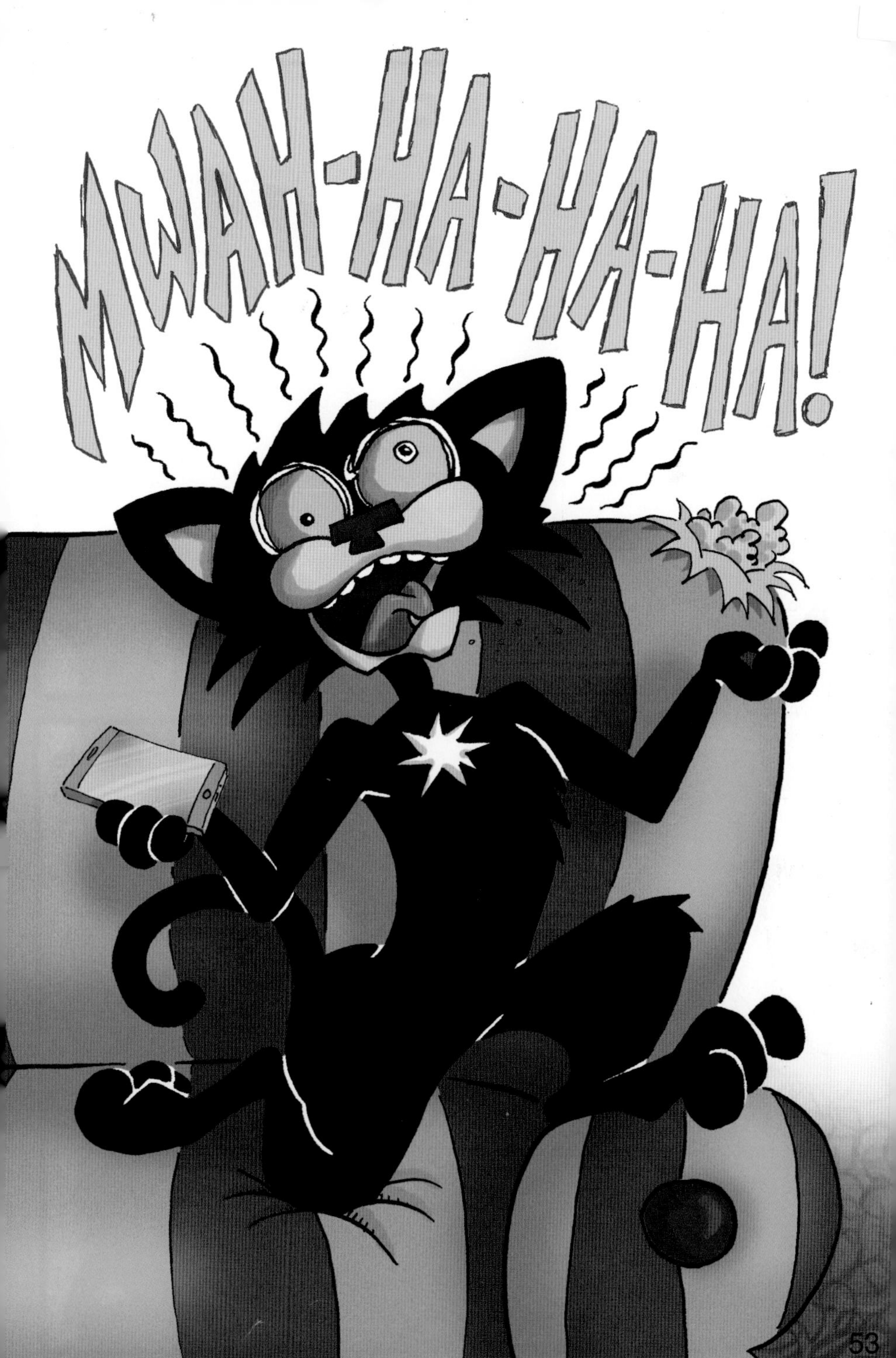
MWAH-HA-HA-HA!

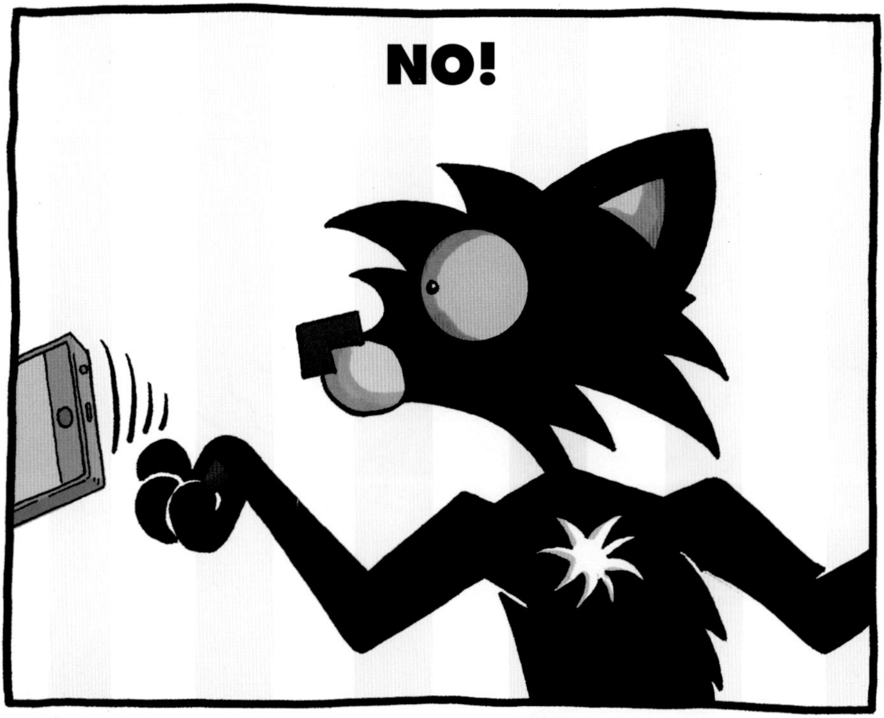
NO!

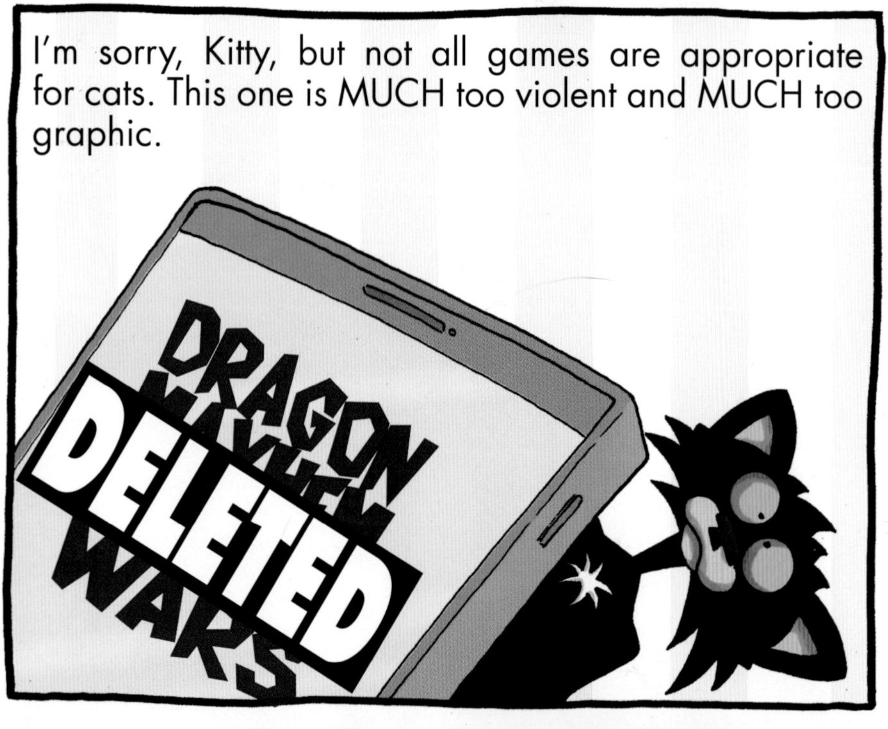
I'm sorry, Kitty, but not all games are appropriate for cats. This one is MUCH too violent and MUCH too graphic.
DRAGON
WARS
DELETED

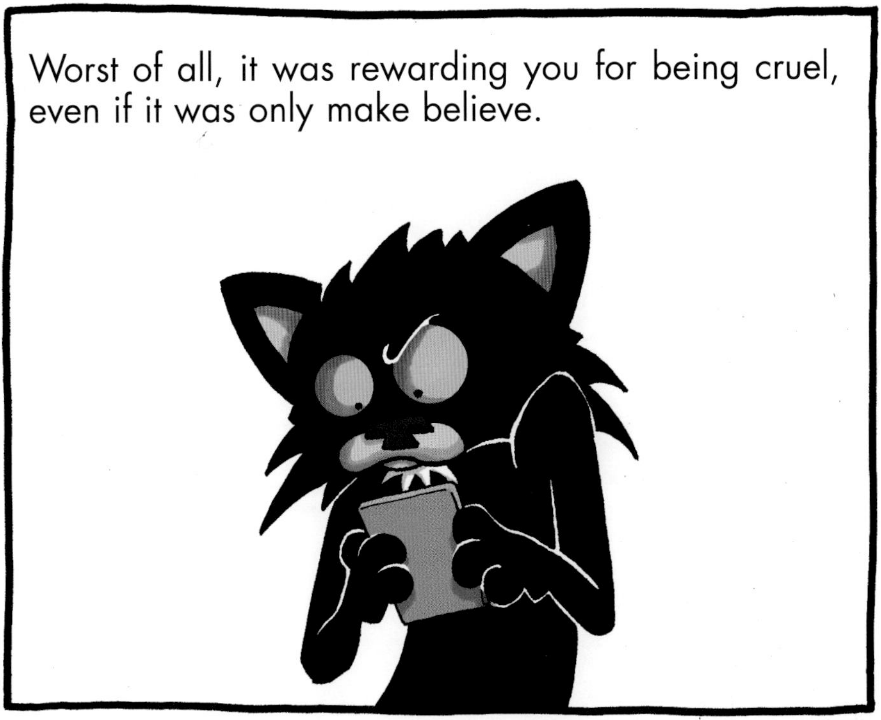
Worst of all, it was rewarding you for being cruel, even if it was only make believe.

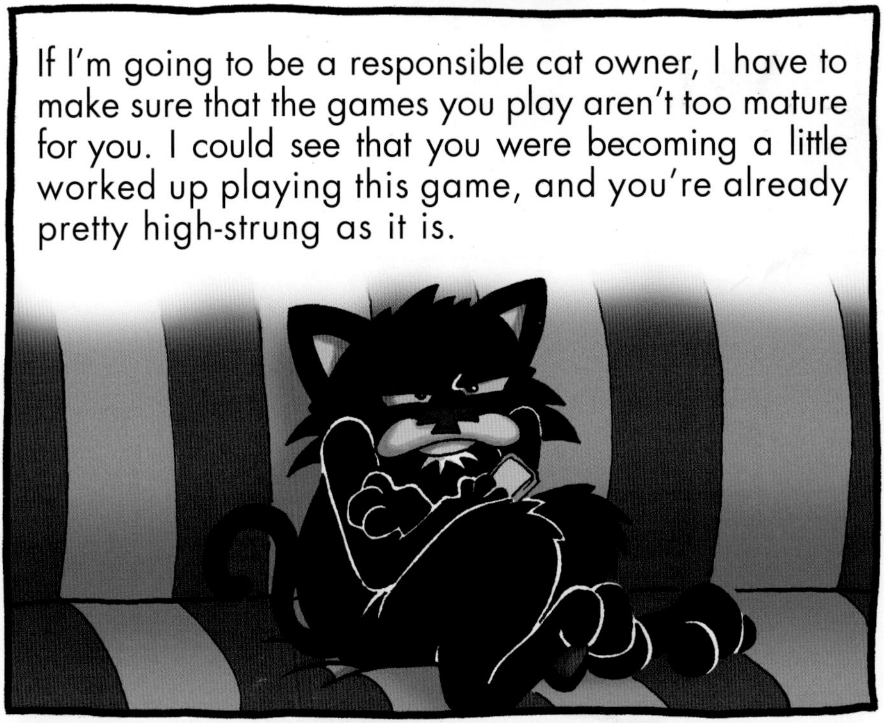
If I'm going to be a responsible cat owner, I have to make sure that the games you play aren't too mature for you. I could see that you were becoming a little worked up playing this game, and you're already pretty high-strung as it is.

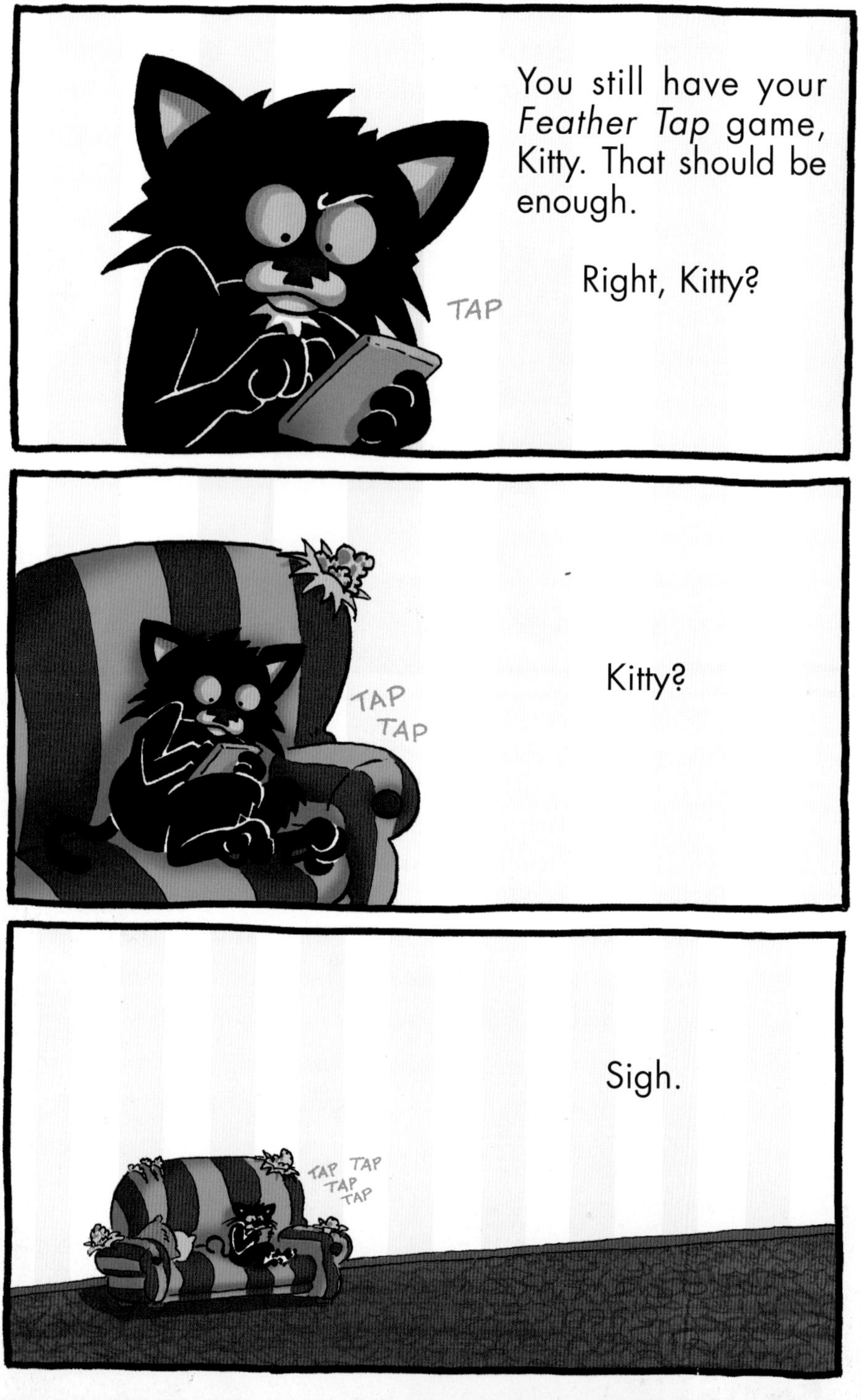
You still have your *Feather Tap* game, Kitty. That should be enough.
Right, Kitty?
TAP
Kitty?
TAP
TAP
Sigh.
TAP TAP
TAP
TAP

• CHAPTER FIVE •

CAT FRIEND BOOK

Kitty, you've been lying in bed all morning playing that *Feather Tap* game. It's a gorgeous day! Why don't you go outside. The Twin Kitties came by twice today to see if you wanted to play.

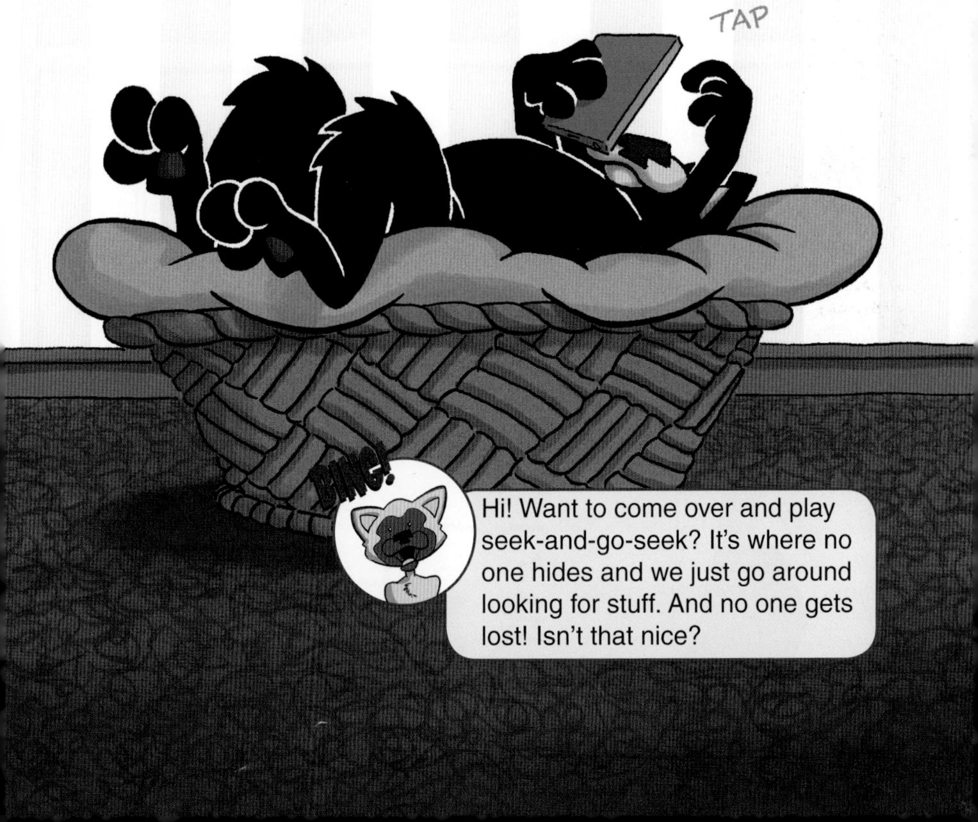
TAP
BING!
Hi! Want to come over and play seek-and-go-seek? It's where no one hides and we just go around looking for stuff. And no one gets lost! Isn't that nice?

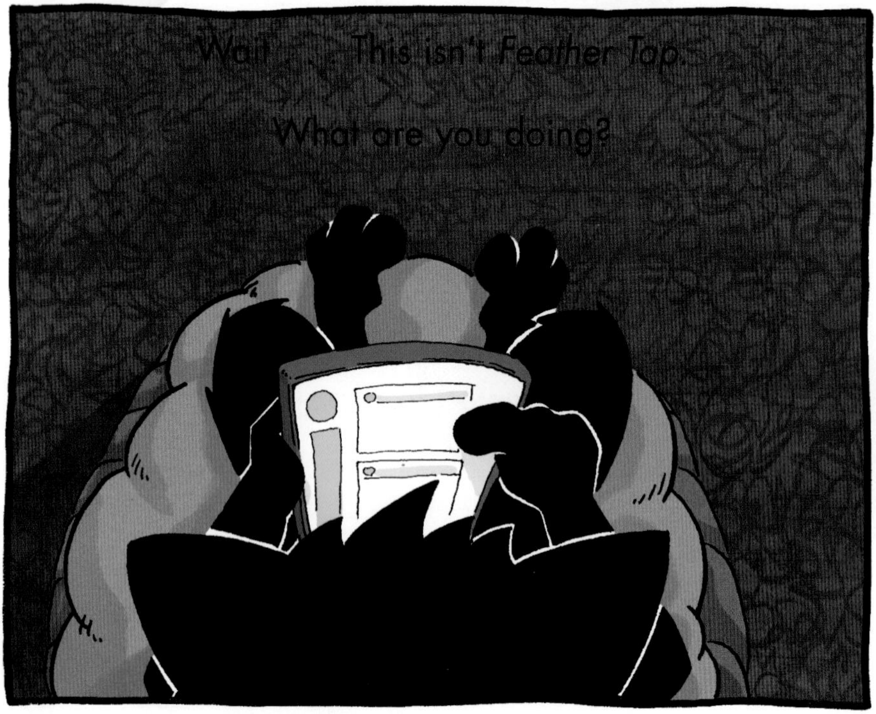
Wait . . . This isn't *Feather Tap*.
What are you doing?

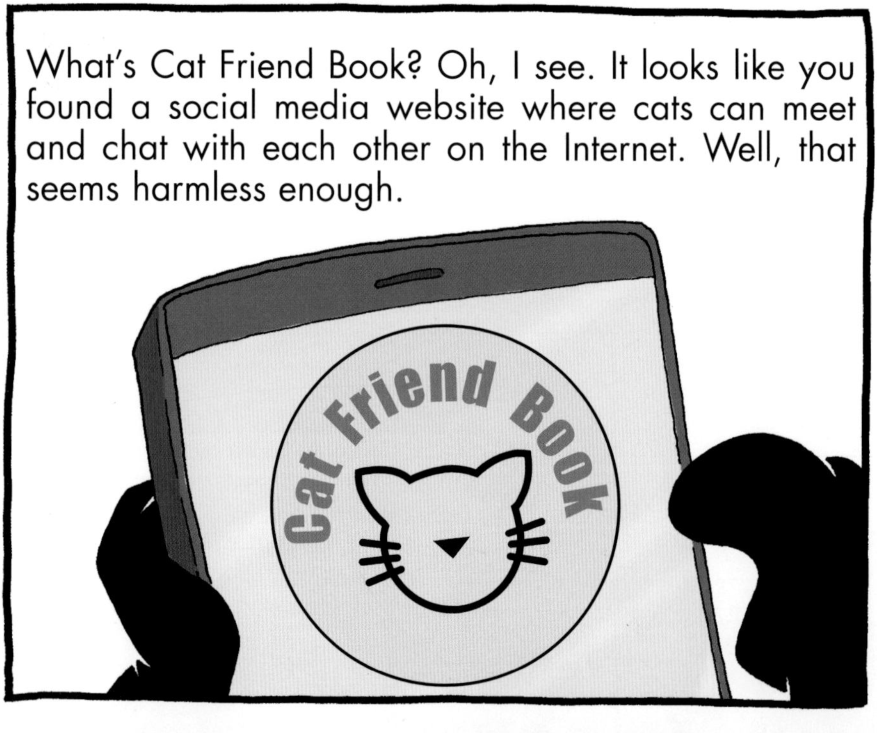
What's Cat Friend Book? Oh, I see. It looks like you found a social media website where cats can meet and chat with each other on the Internet. Well, that seems harmless enough.
Cat Friend Book

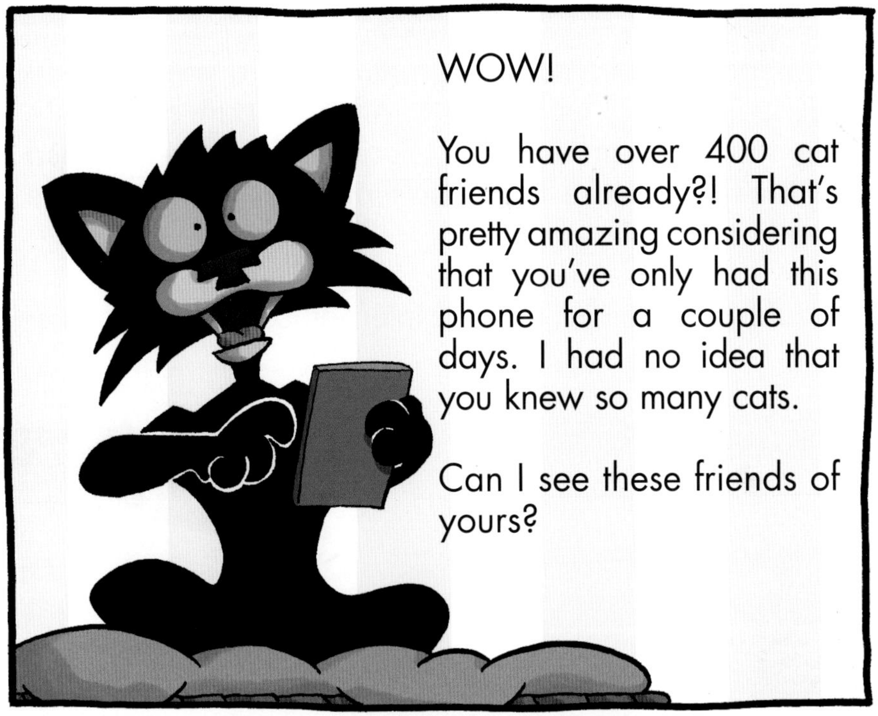
WOW!
You have over 400 cat friends already?! That's pretty amazing considering that you've only had this phone for a couple of days. I had no idea that you knew so many cats.
Can I see these friends of yours?

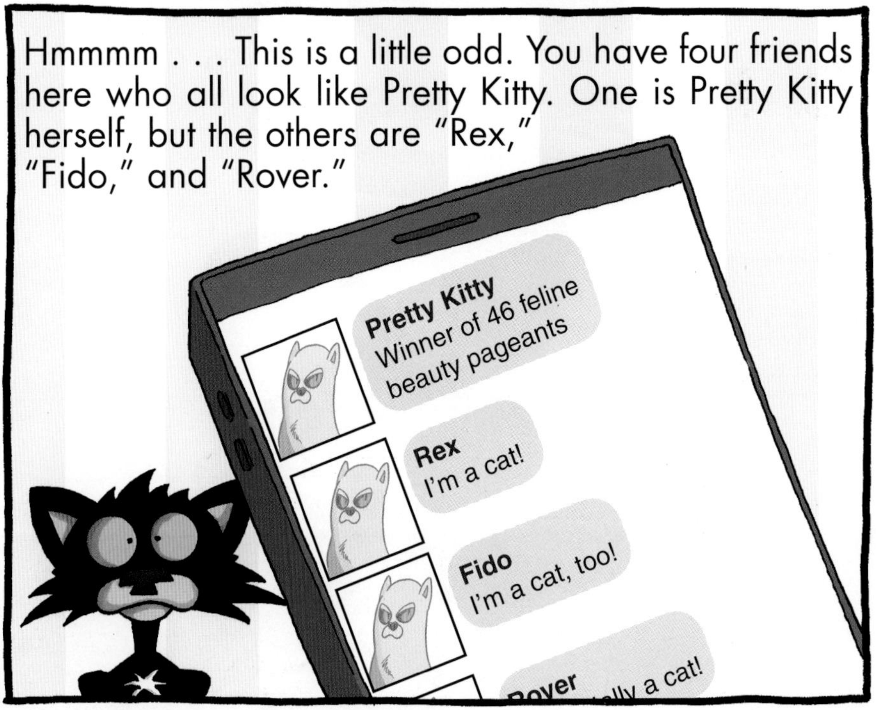
Hmmmm . . . This is a little odd. You have four friends here who all look like Pretty Kitty. One is Pretty Kitty herself, but the others are "Rex," "Fido," and "Rover."
Pretty Kitty
Winner of 46 feline beauty pageants
Rex
I'm a cat!
Fido
I'm a cat, too!
Rover

Kitty, social media can be fun. It can be a great way to stay connected with your friends. It can be a safe way to meet someone new. But social media can also be tricky, because you don't always know for sure who you're talking to.

Fortunately, we can use the Internet to investigate this.

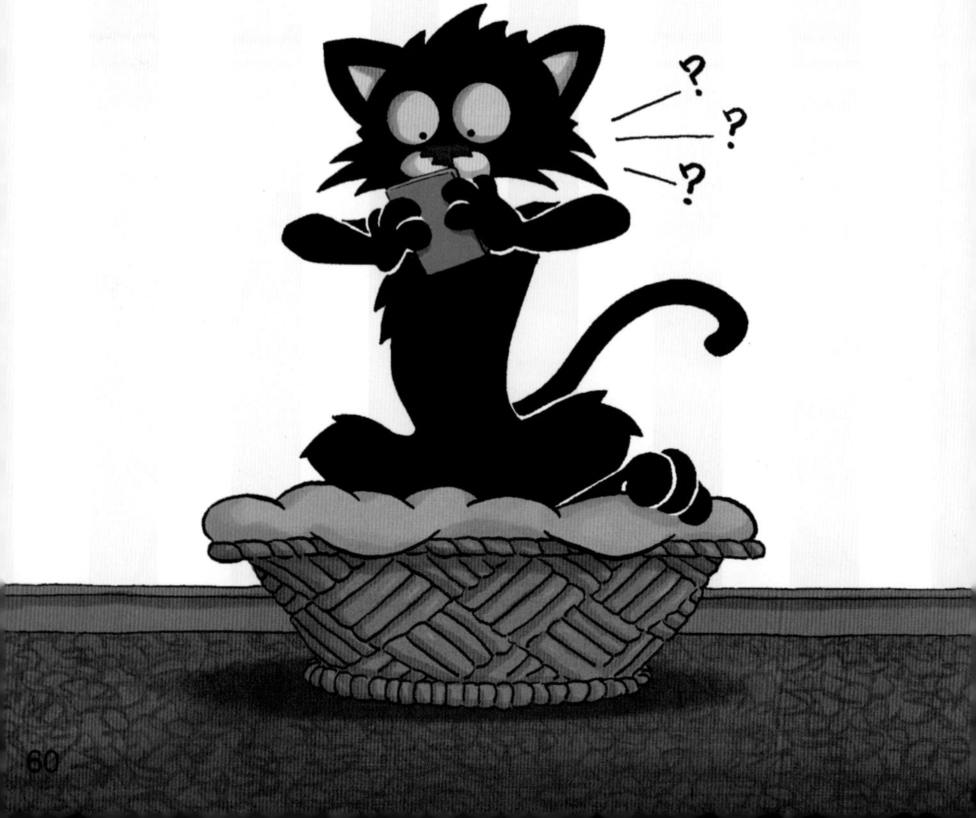

?
?
?

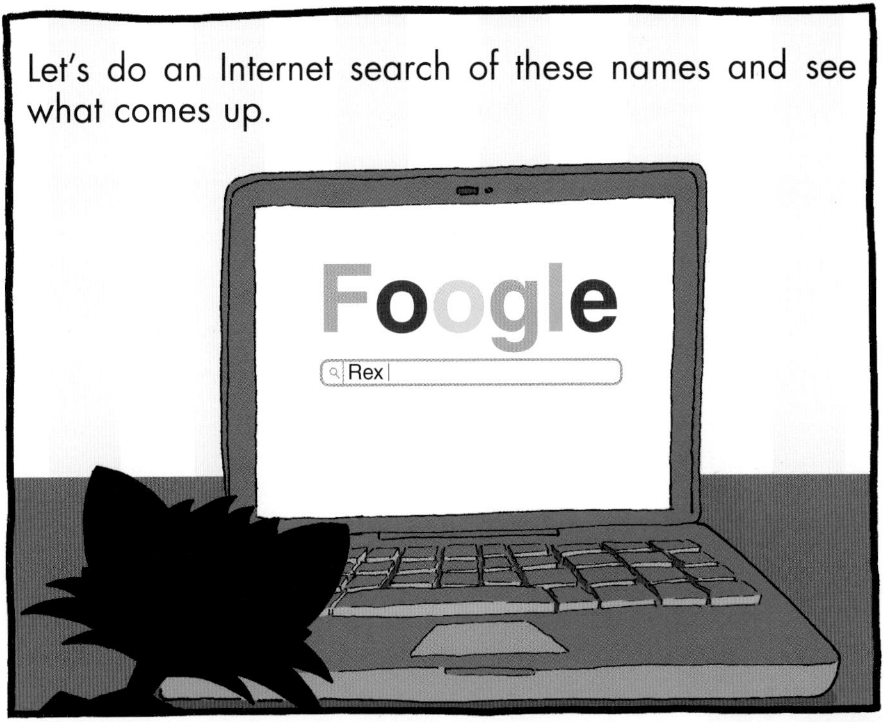
Let's do an Internet search of these names and see what comes up.
Foogle
Rex

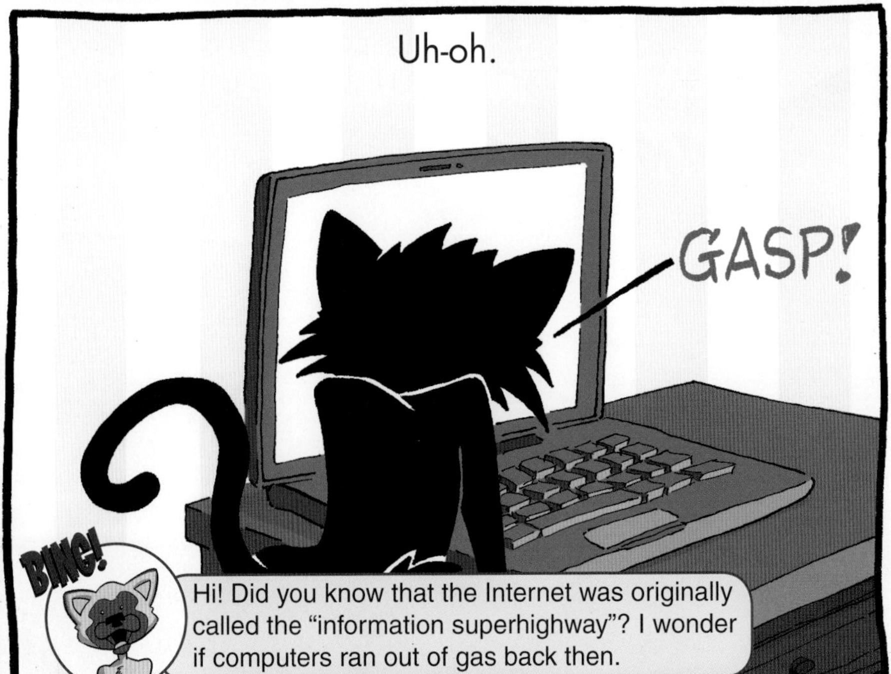
Uh-oh.
GASP!
BING!
Hi! Did you know that the Internet was originally called the "information superhighway"? I wonder if computers ran out of gas back then.

Kitty, I'm very sorry to inform you that these are the REAL Rex, Fido, and Rover.

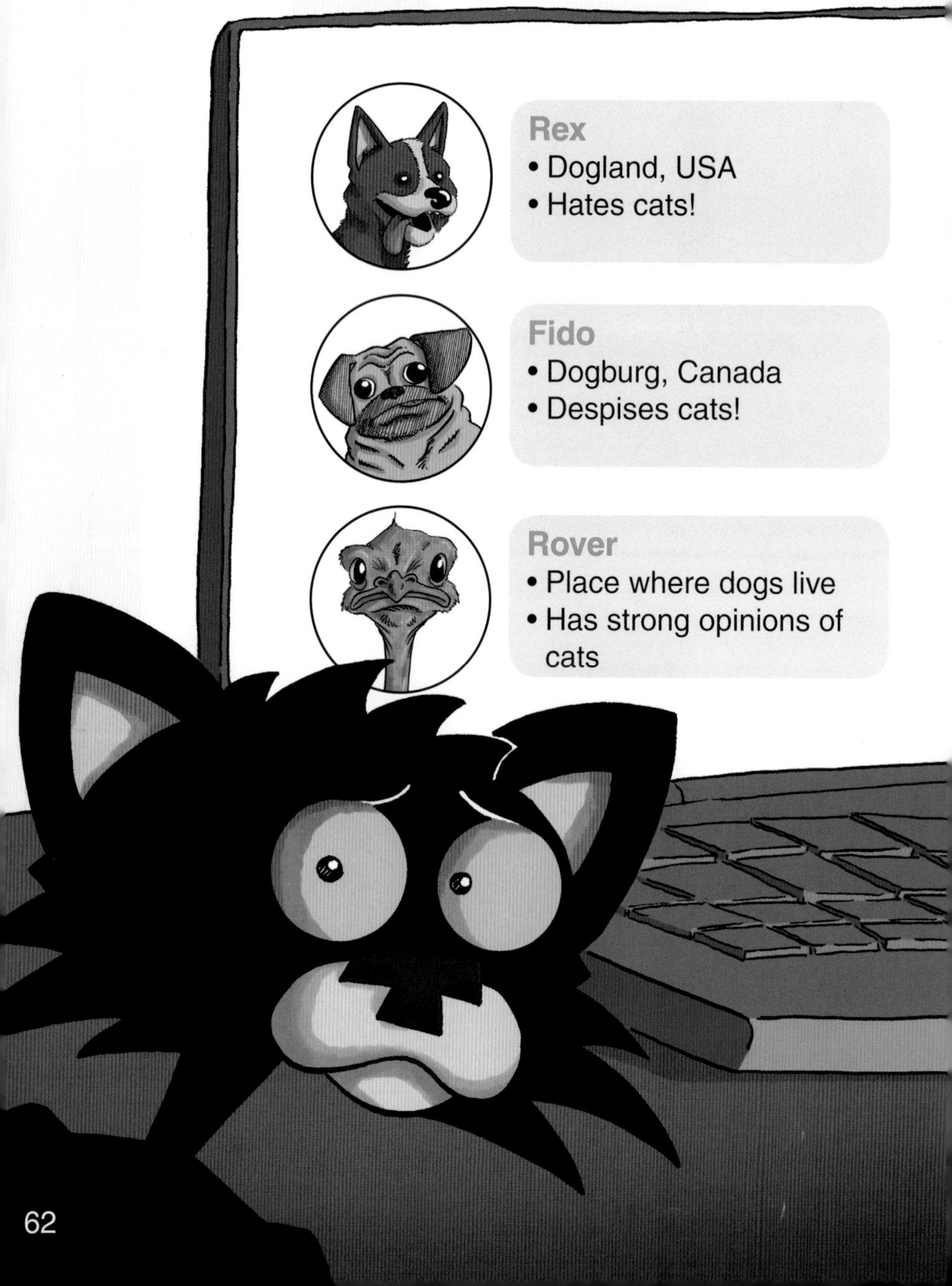
Rex
• Dogland, USA
• Hates cats!
Fido
• Dogburg, Canada
• Despises cats!
Rover
• Place where dogs live
• Has strong opinions of cats

I found them all on a site called Dog Friend Book. Here is a printout of one of their recent conversations.

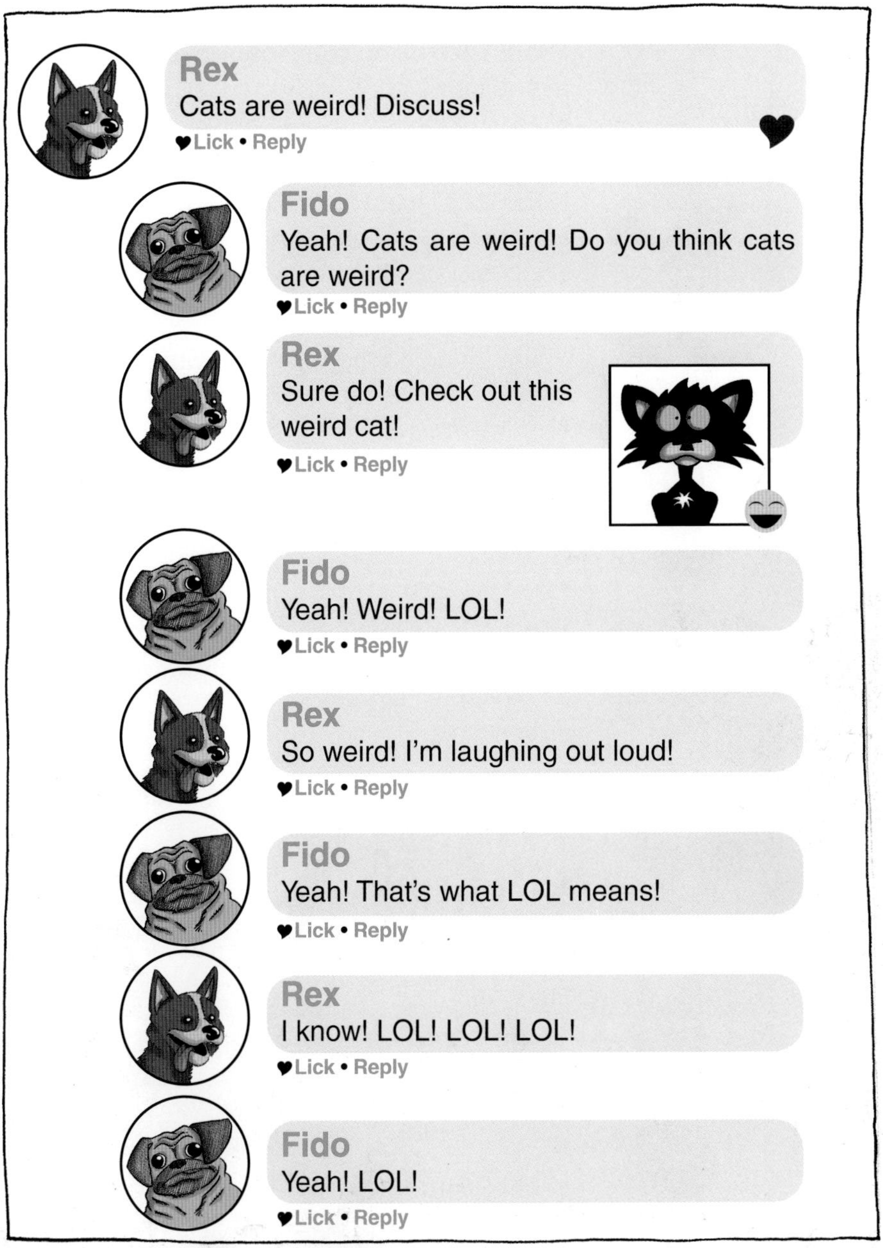
Rex
Cats are weird! Discuss!
Lick • Reply
Fido
Yeah! Cats are weird! Do you think cats are weird?
Lick • Reply
Rex
Sure do! Check out this weird cat!
Lick • Reply
Fido
Yeah! Weird! LOL!
Lick • Reply
Rex
So weird! I'm laughing out loud!
Lick • Reply
Fido
Yeah! That's what LOL means!
Lick • Reply
Rex
I know! LOL! LOL! LOL!
Lick • Reply
Fido
Yeah! LOL!
Lick • Reply

Rex
I like biting cats! Discuss!
♥ Lick • Reply

Fido
Yeah! I like biting cats, too! Have you ever bitten a cat?
♥ Lick • Reply

Rex
Nope. But I want to bite one someday. Maybe on the foot.
♥ Lick • Reply

Fido
Yeah! Biting a cat on the foot would be cool. Or maybe the tail. I hate their tails!
♥ Lick • Reply

Rex
I read a science article that said cat tails are really snakes!
♥ Lick • Reply

Fido
Yeah! I read that, too! The guy who wrote it is a cat tail expert!
♥ Lick • Reply

Rover
CAT TAILS ARE RLY SNAKES! ♥♥
♥ Lick • Reply

Rex
That's the article! Thanks! Science!
♥ Lick • Reply

Fido
Yeah! SCIENCE!
♥ Lick • Reply

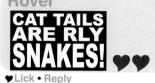

I'm sorry that those dogs fooled you, Kitty. The lesson here is that strangers on the Internet are still strangers. It's really easy to pretend to be someone you're not, even on social media.

One good rule is to only be "friends" with someone on the Internet if you're friends with them in real life.

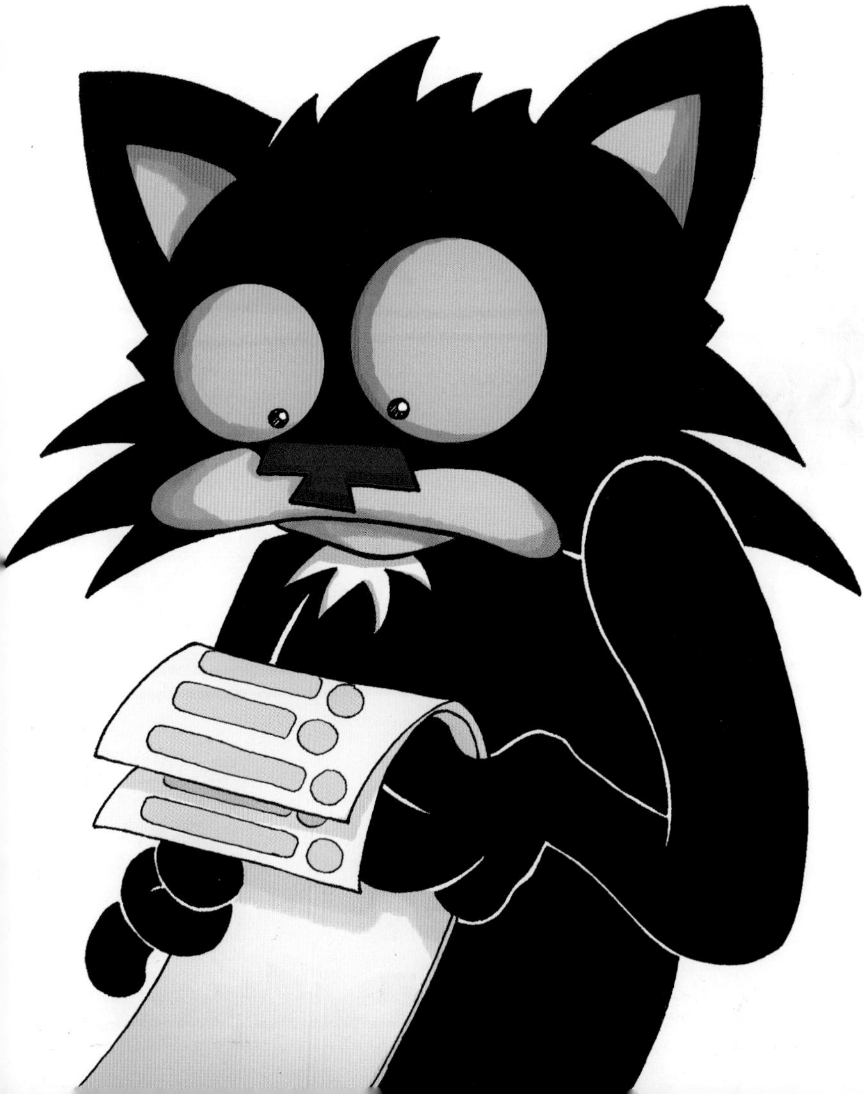

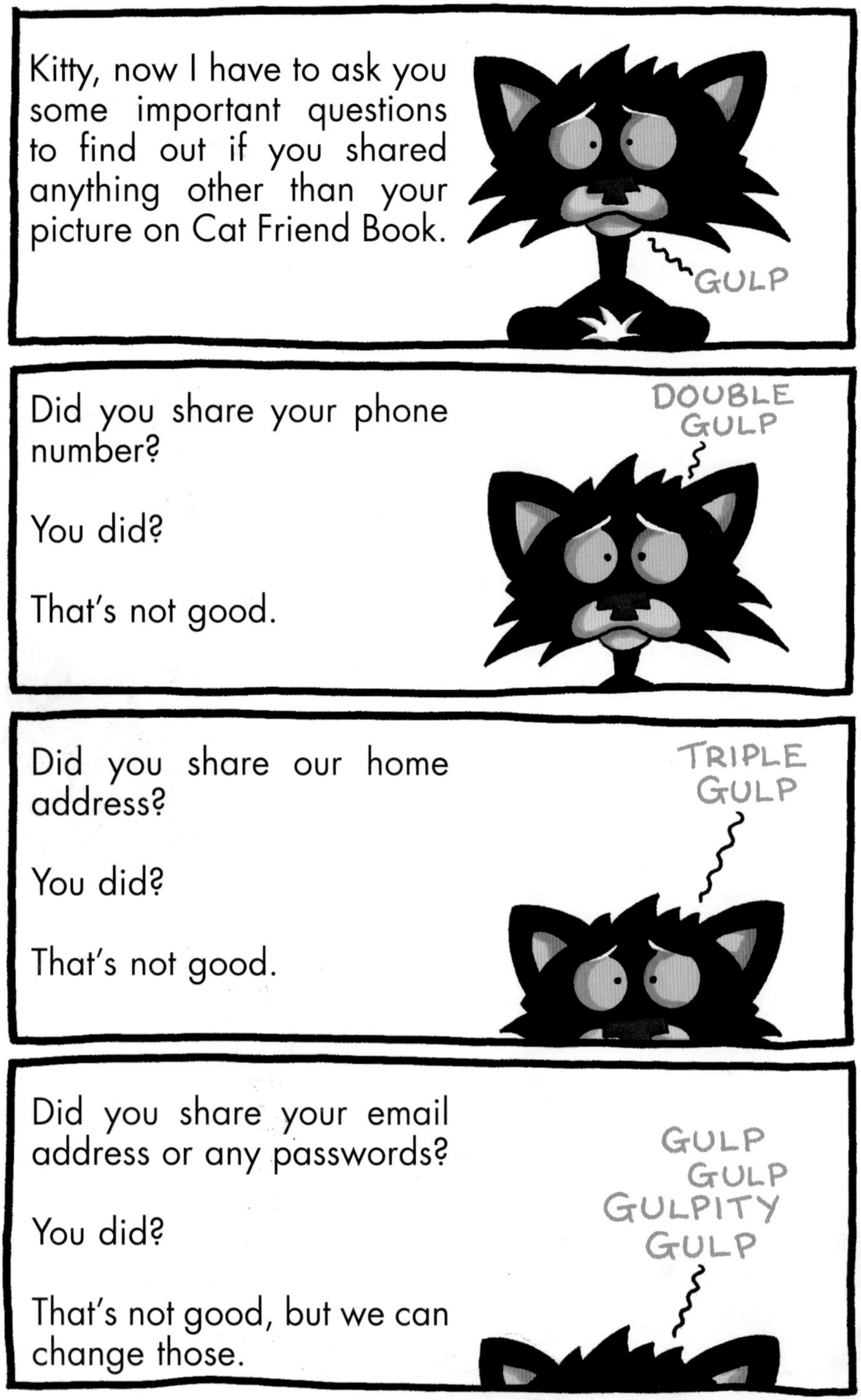
Kitty, now I have to ask you some important questions to find out if you shared anything other than your picture on Cat Friend Book.
GULP
Did you share your phone number?
You did?
That's not good.
DOUBLE GULP
Did you share our home address?
You did?
That's not good.
TRIPLE GULP
Did you share your email address or any passwords?
You did?
That's not good, but we can change those.
GULP GULP GULPITY GULP

Sorry, Kitty, but social media is just not appropriate for cats. There are just too many risks involved, like sharing too much about yourself with strangers. I have to delete your account.

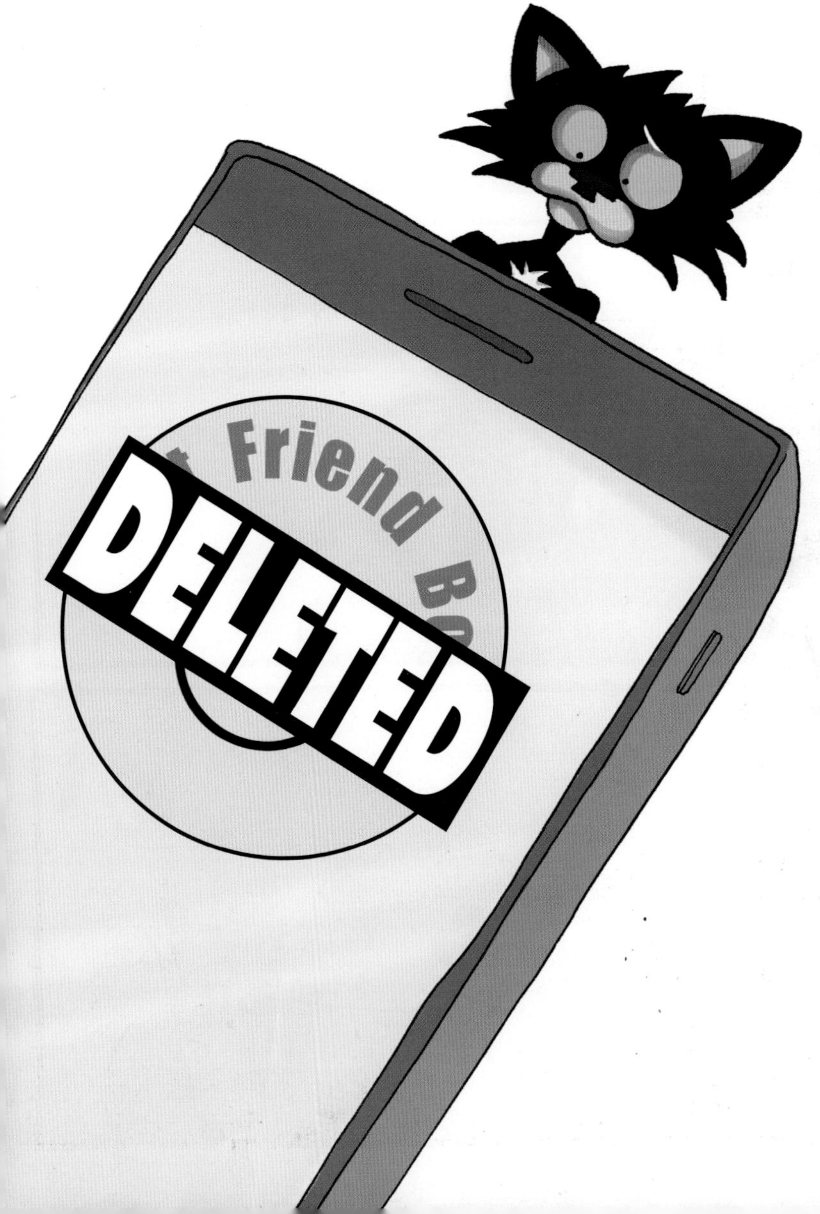
Friend Bo
DELETED

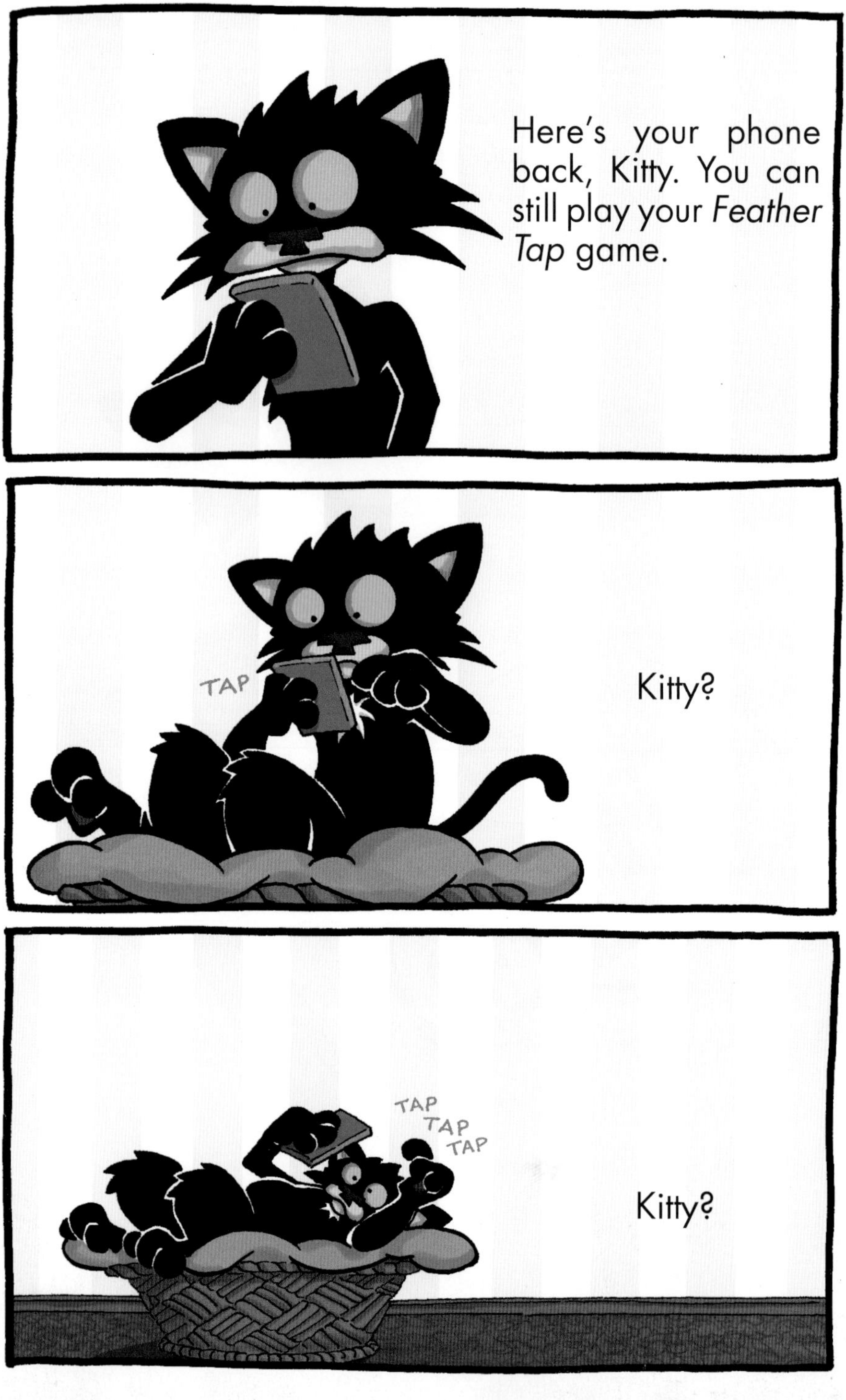
Here's your phone back, Kitty. You can still play your *Feather Tap* game.
TAP
Kitty?
TAP
TAP
TAP
Kitty?

Sigh.

TAP TAP TAP TAP
TAP TAP
TAP

UNCLE MURRAY'S REAL ~~FUN~~ FACTS

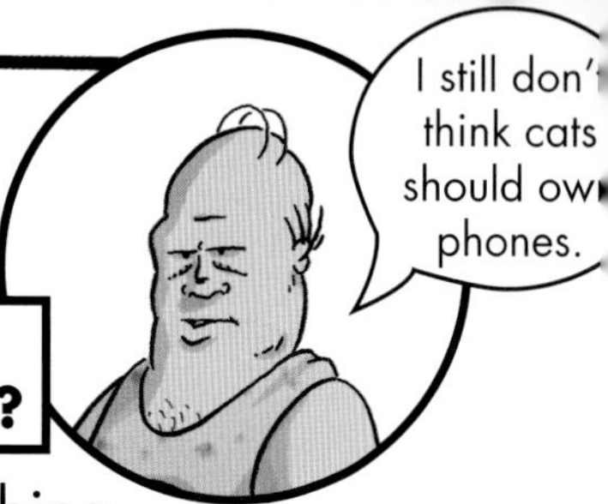
I still don'
think cats
should ow
phones.

WHAT IS THE DIFFERENCE BETWEEN FACT AND OPINION?

What is a FACT? A fact is something that is known or always true.

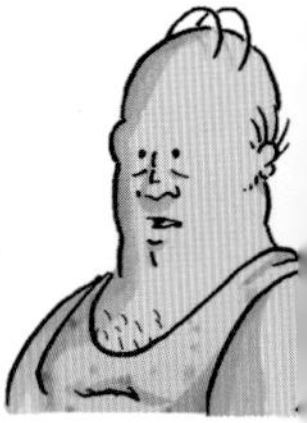
Seems simple enough.

It is! All facts are observable. All facts can be proven.

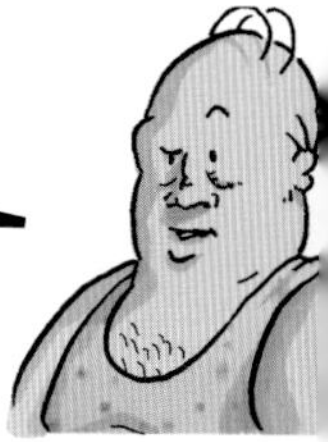
Still simple. So what's an opinion?

An opinion is what someone thinks or feels.

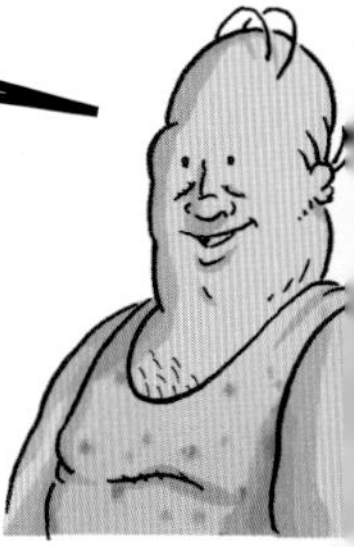
Also simple!

Well, here's where it gets tricky. Often someone *believes* something because they *think* it's true. They may think it's a fact, but it might not be. The problem is that a lot of opinions can't be proven true or false.

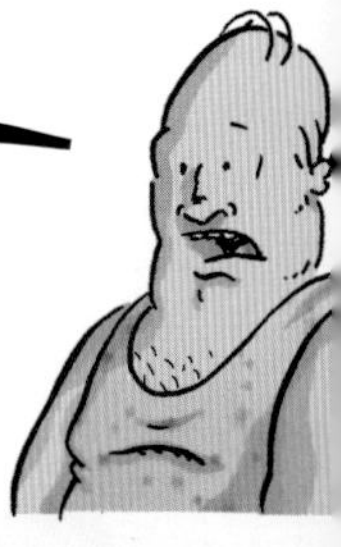
So opinions are like lies?!

Not at all! Often, people form their opinions based on facts. I'll give you an example . . .

In my opinion, I think cats make the best pets. What do you think?

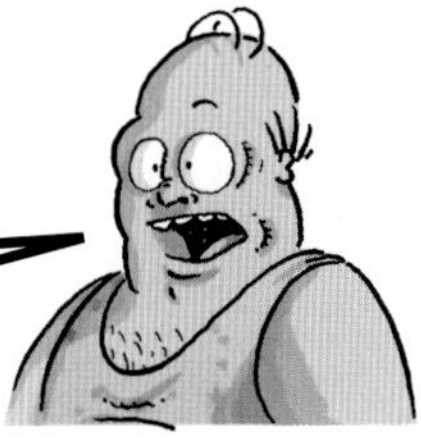

You're insane! Cats make the worst pets!

I think cats make the best pets because they have fur and whiskers and use the litter box.

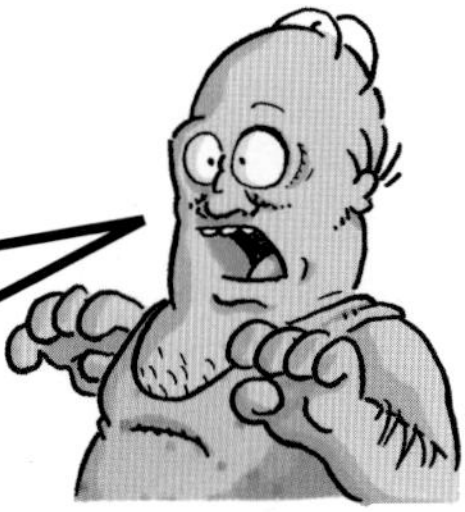

I think cats are the absolute worst pets because they have claws and sharp teeth and use the litter box! They poop in the house!
IN THE HOUSE!

See, Uncle Murray? We used two sets of facts to support two completely different opinions.

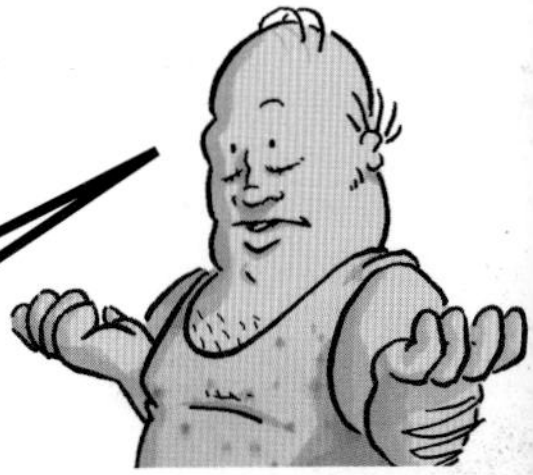

But we both agreed that cats use a litter box.

Yes, because while some people might like the fact that cats use a litter box, some people might not. When the same fact forms different opinions, that's called "interpretation," and we'll get into that next.

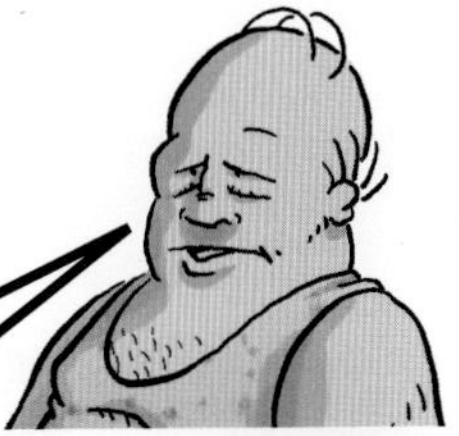

Do we have to?
I'm getting a headache.
And that's a fact.

•CHAPTER SIX•

VIEWTUBE

Kitty, you've been on your phone all morning, and this is after you were on it all day yesterday and the day before! I certainly hope you're not playing inappropriate games or getting into trouble on social media again.

What are you doing? Have you really been playing that *Feather Tap* game all this time?

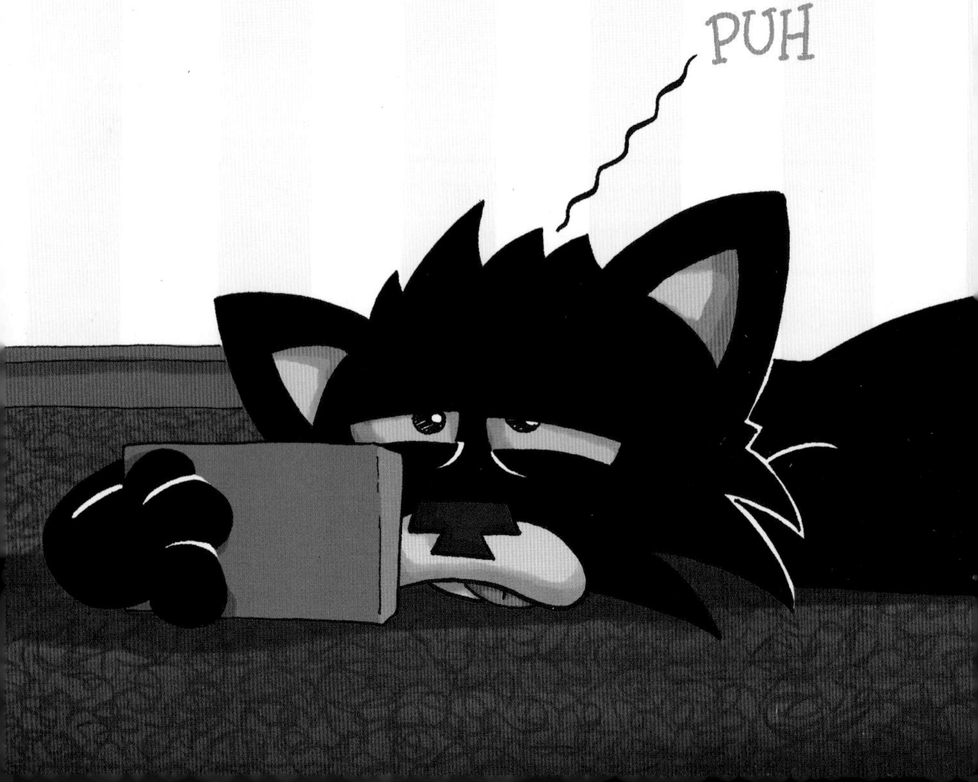
PUH

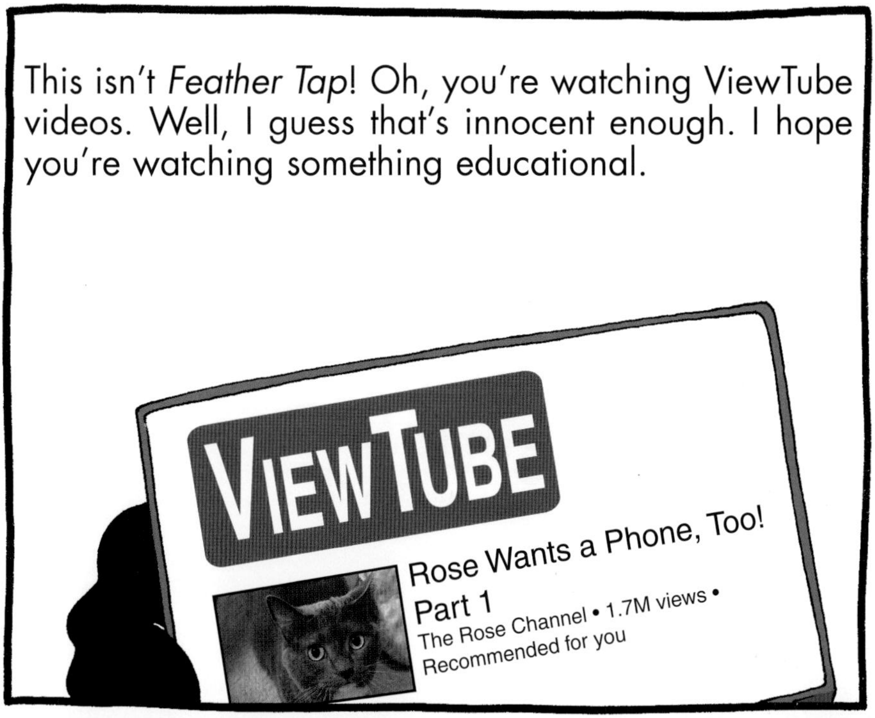
This isn't *Feather Tap*! Oh, you're watching ViewTube videos. Well, I guess that's innocent enough. I hope you're watching something educational.
VIEWTUBE
Rose Wants a Phone, Too! Part 1
The Rose Channel • 1.7M views • Recommended for you

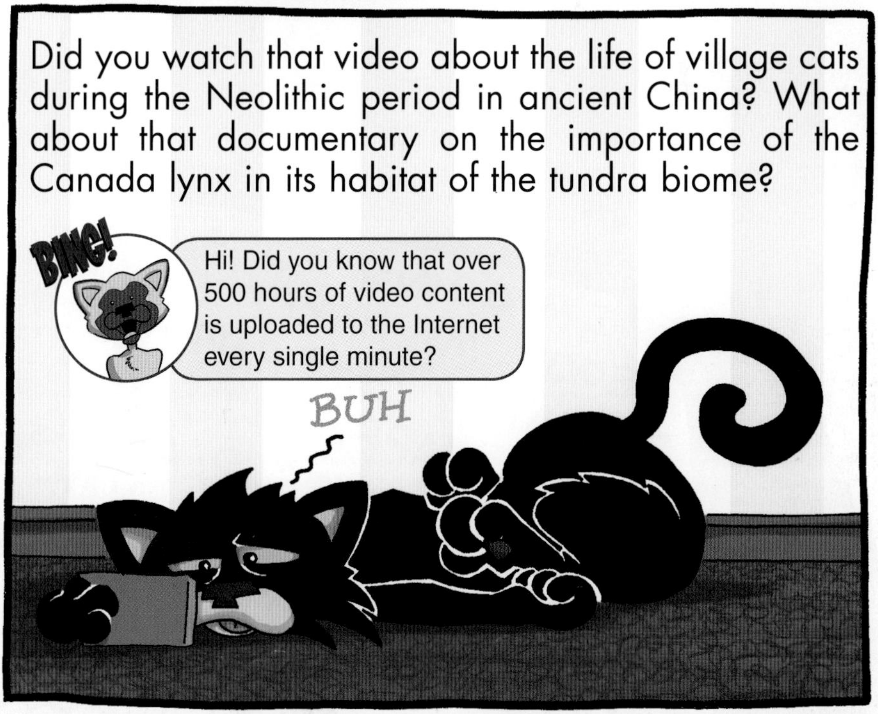
Did you watch that video about the life of village cats during the Neolithic period in ancient China? What about that documentary on the importance of the Canada lynx in its habitat of the tundra biome?
BING!
Hi! Did you know that over 500 hours of video content is uploaded to the Internet every single minute?
BUH

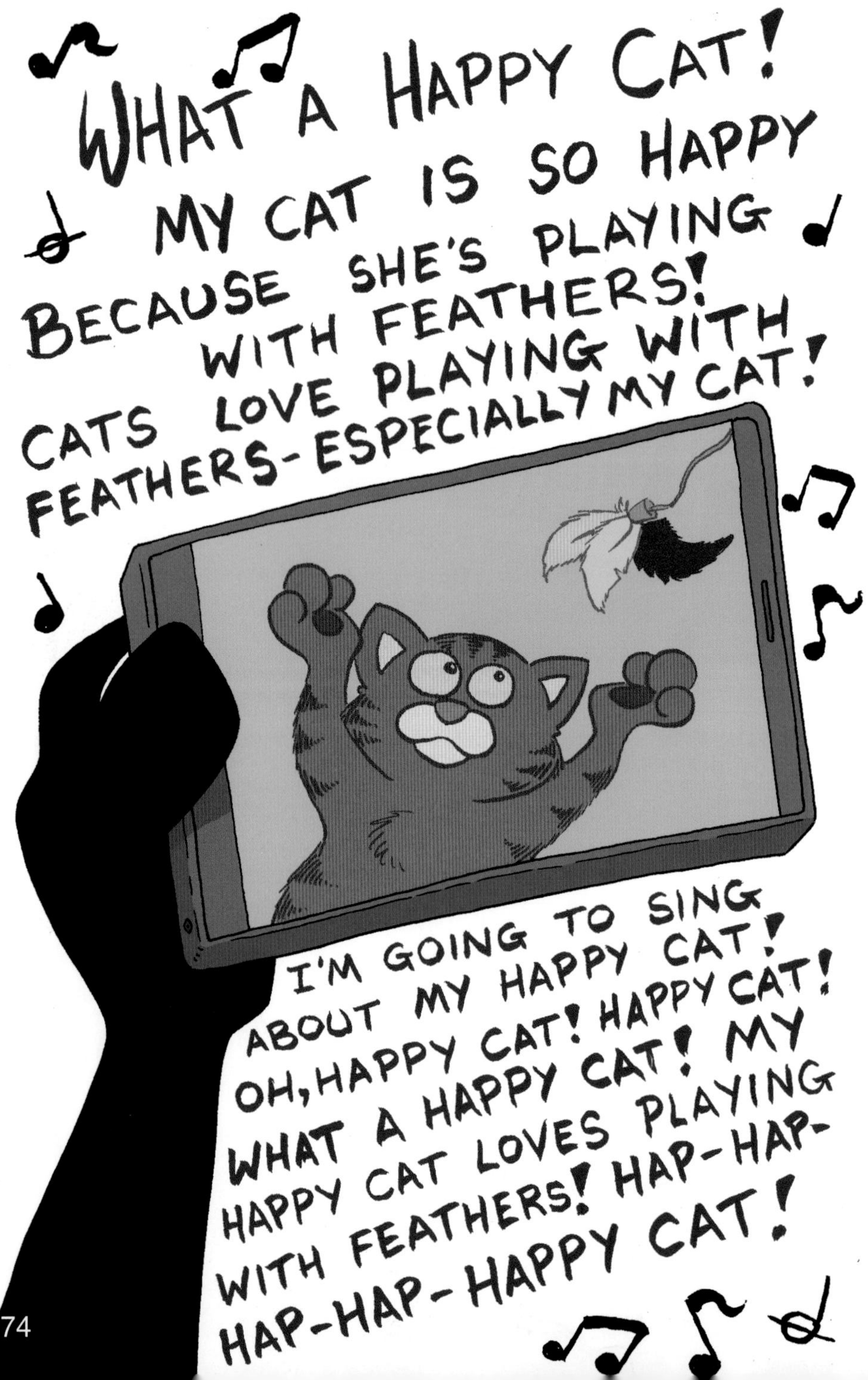
WHAT A HAPPY CAT!
MY CAT IS SO HAPPY BECAUSE SHE'S PLAYING WITH FEATHERS! CATS LOVE PLAYING WITH FEATHERS-ESPECIALLY MY CAT!
I'M GOING TO SING ABOUT MY HAPPY CAT! OH, HAPPY CAT! HAPPY CAT! WHAT A HAPPY CAT! MY HAPPY CAT LOVES PLAYING WITH FEATHERS! HAP-HAP-HAP-HAP-HAPPY CAT!

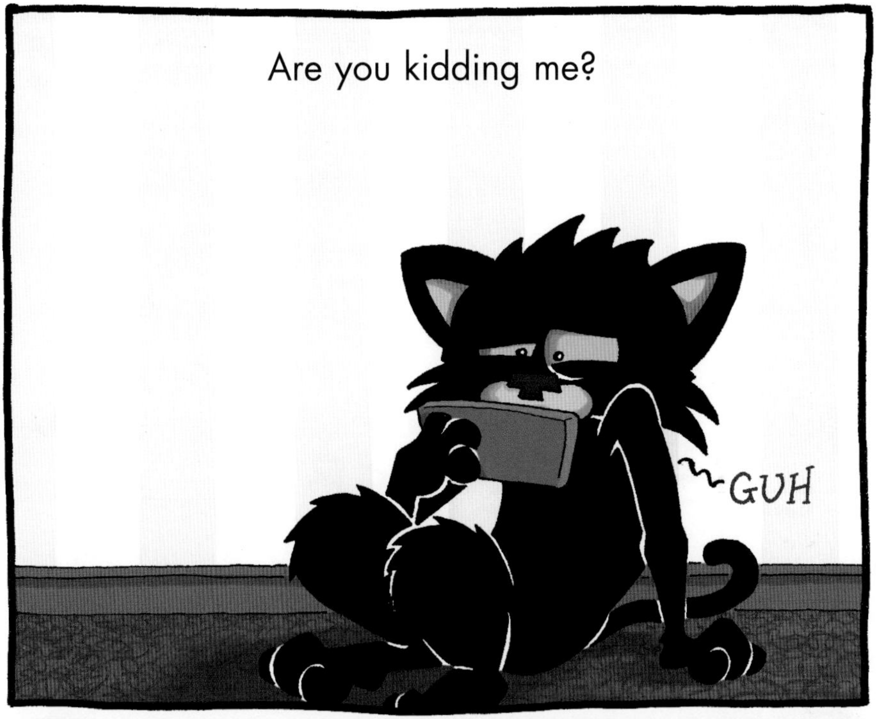
Are you kidding me?
GUH

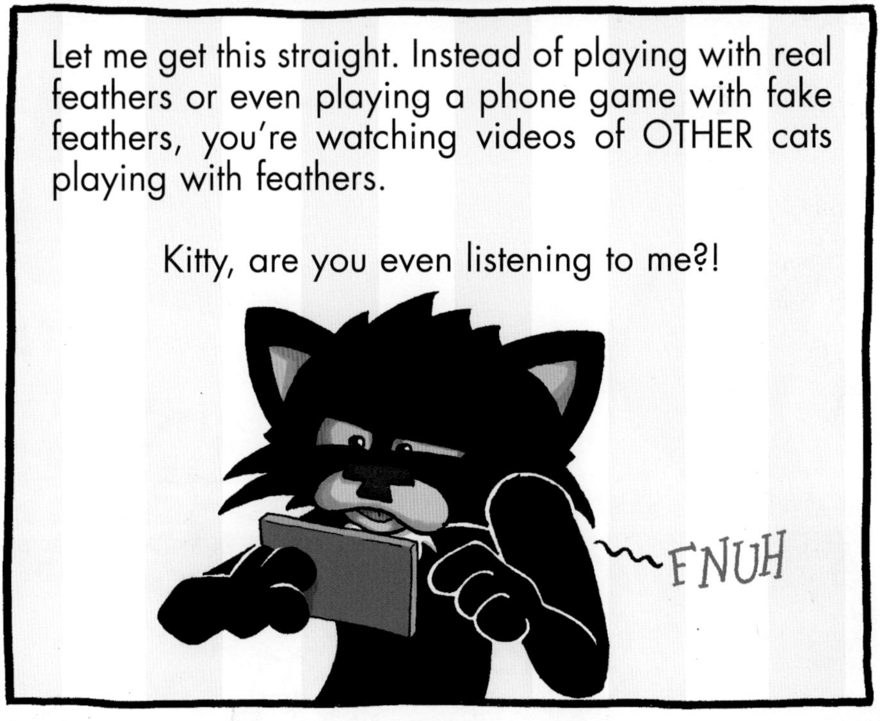
Let me get this straight. Instead of playing with real feathers or even playing a phone game with fake feathers, you're watching videos of OTHER cats playing with feathers.
Kitty, are you even listening to me?!
FNUH

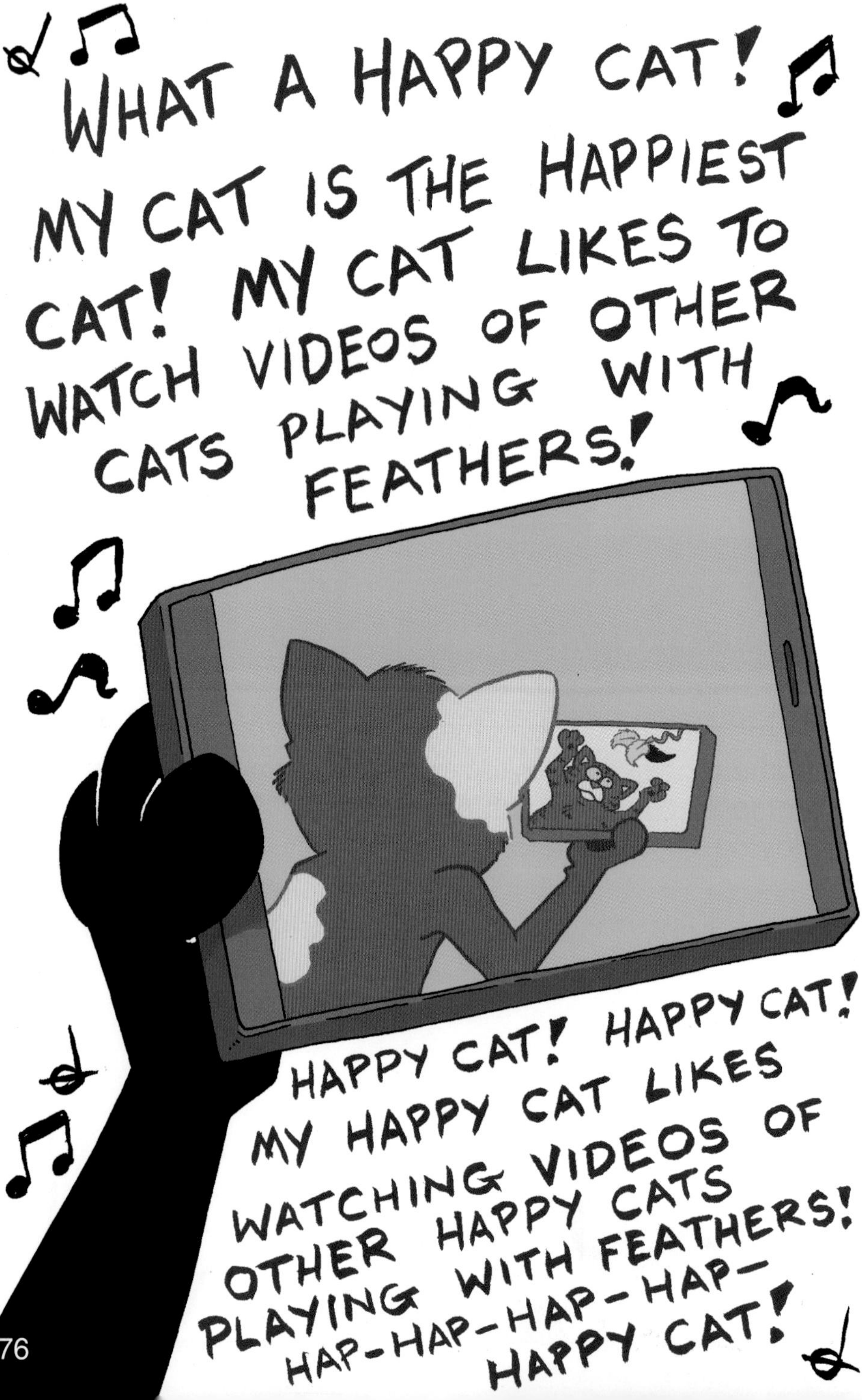
WHAT A HAPPY CAT!
MY CAT IS THE HAPPIEST CAT! MY CAT LIKES TO WATCH VIDEOS OF OTHER CATS PLAYING WITH FEATHERS!
HAPPY CAT! HAPPY CAT!
MY HAPPY CAT LIKES WATCHING VIDEOS OF OTHER HAPPY CATS PLAYING WITH FEATHERS!
HAP-HAP-HAP-HAP-HAPPY CAT!

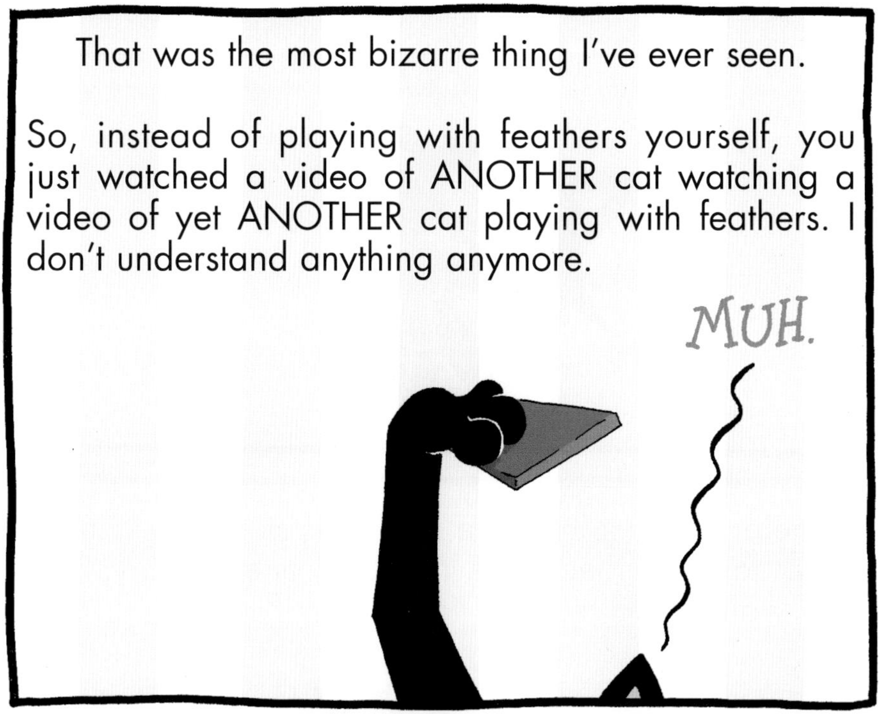
That was the most bizarre thing I've ever seen.
So, instead of playing with feathers yourself, you just watched a video of ANOTHER cat watching a video of yet ANOTHER cat playing with feathers. I don't understand anything anymore.
MUH.

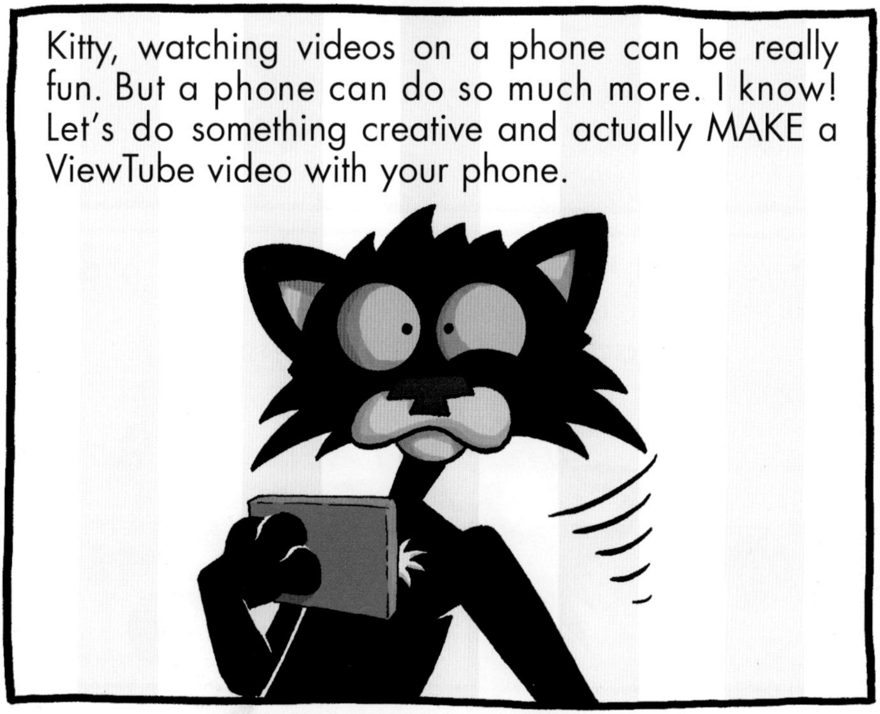
Kitty, watching videos on a phone can be really fun. But a phone can do so much more. I know! Let's do something creative and actually MAKE a ViewTube video with your phone.

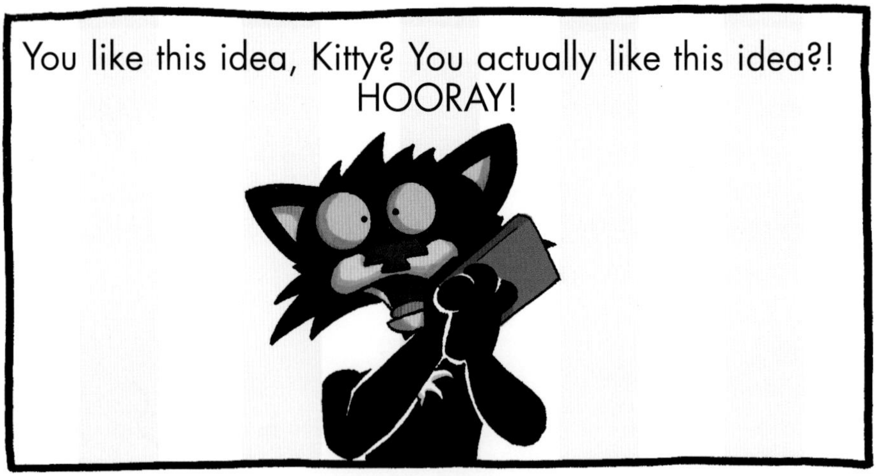
You like this idea, Kitty? You actually like this idea?!
HOORAY!

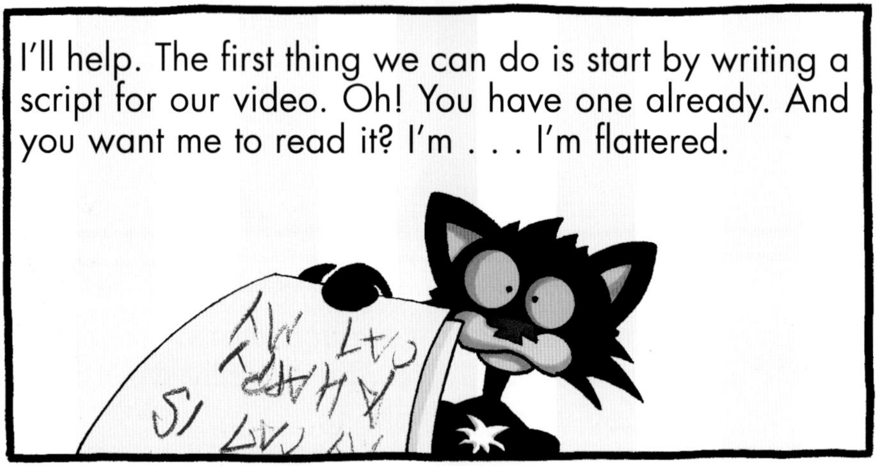
I'll help. The first thing we can do is start by writing a script for our video. Oh! You have one already. And you want me to read it? I'm . . . I'm flattered.

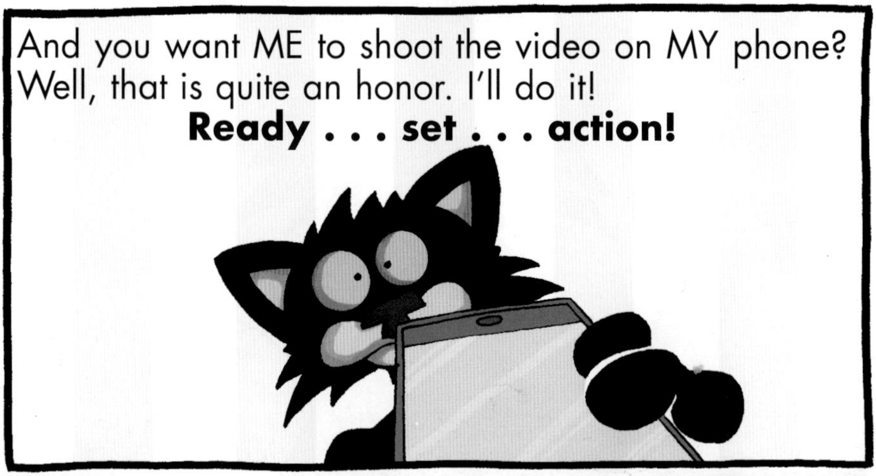
And you want ME to shoot the video on MY phone? Well, that is quite an honor. I'll do it!
Ready . . . set . . . action!

What a happy cat!
My cat is the . . . uh . . . HAPPIEST cat!
My cat likes to . . . um . . . watch videos of other cats watching videos of other cats playing with feathers!

Hap-Hap-Hap-Happy Cat!

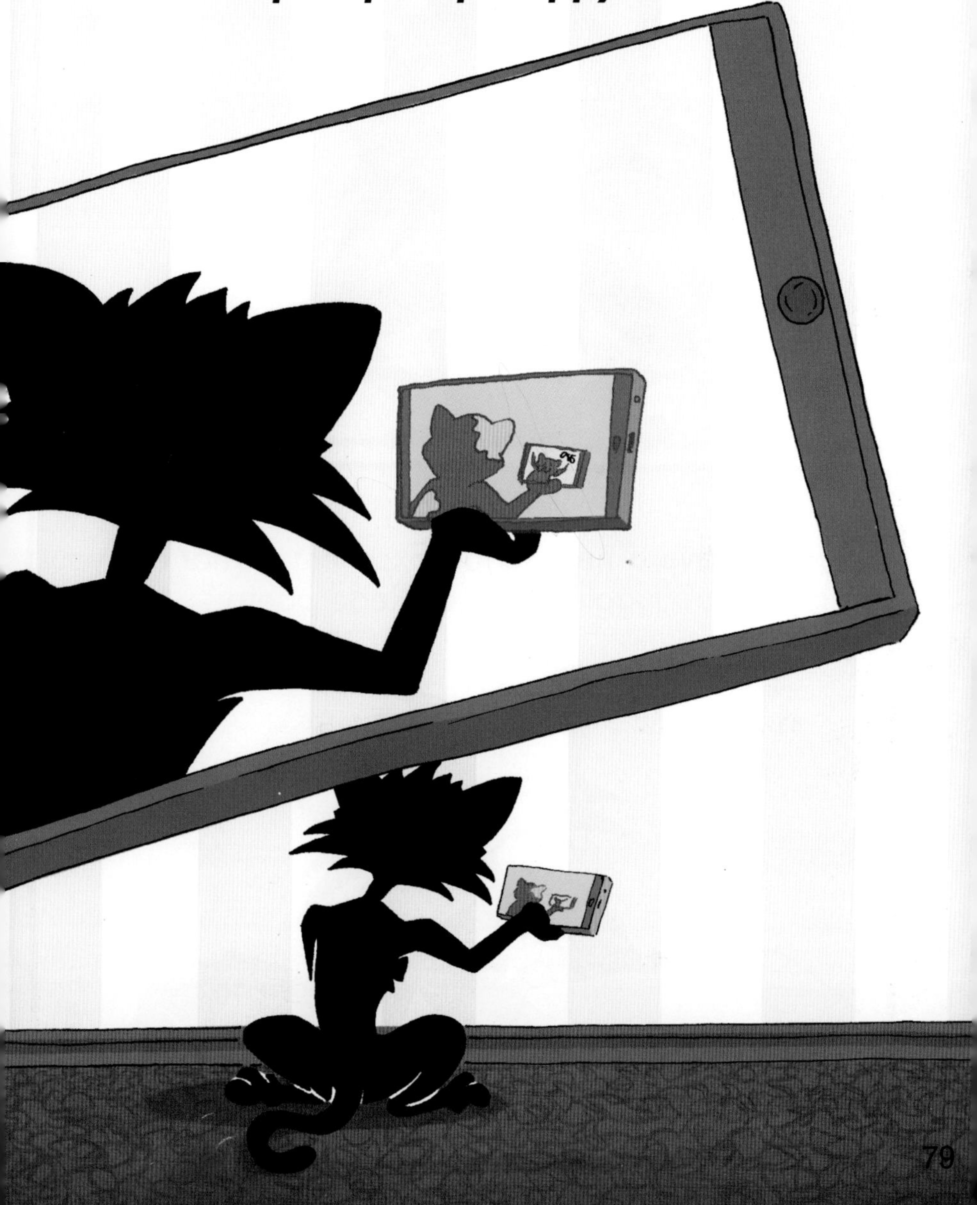

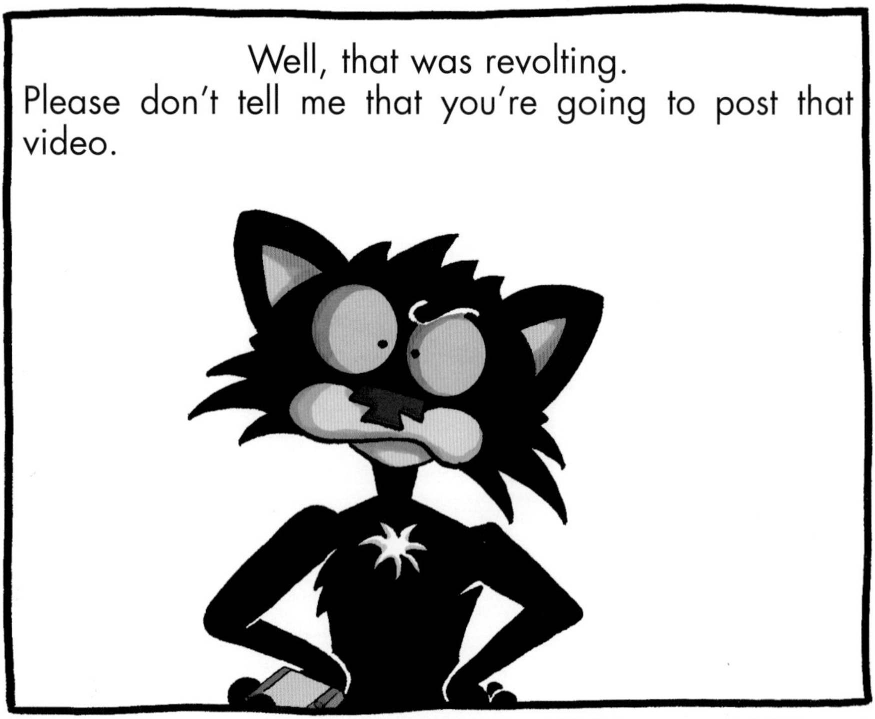
Well, that was revolting.
Please don't tell me that you're going to post that video.

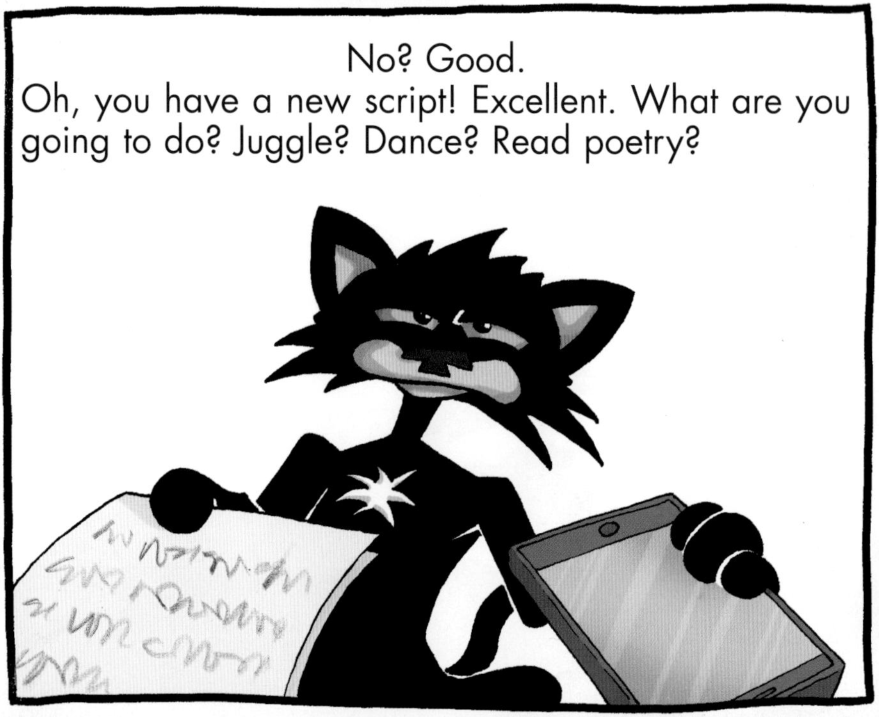
No? Good.
Oh, you have a new script! Excellent. What are you going to do? Juggle? Dance? Read poetry?

What a happy cat!

Oh, no.

My cat is the happiest cat!

I think I'm going to be sick.

My cat likes to watch videos of herself watching other cats watch videos of other cats playing with feathers!
Hap-Hap-Hap-Hap . . .

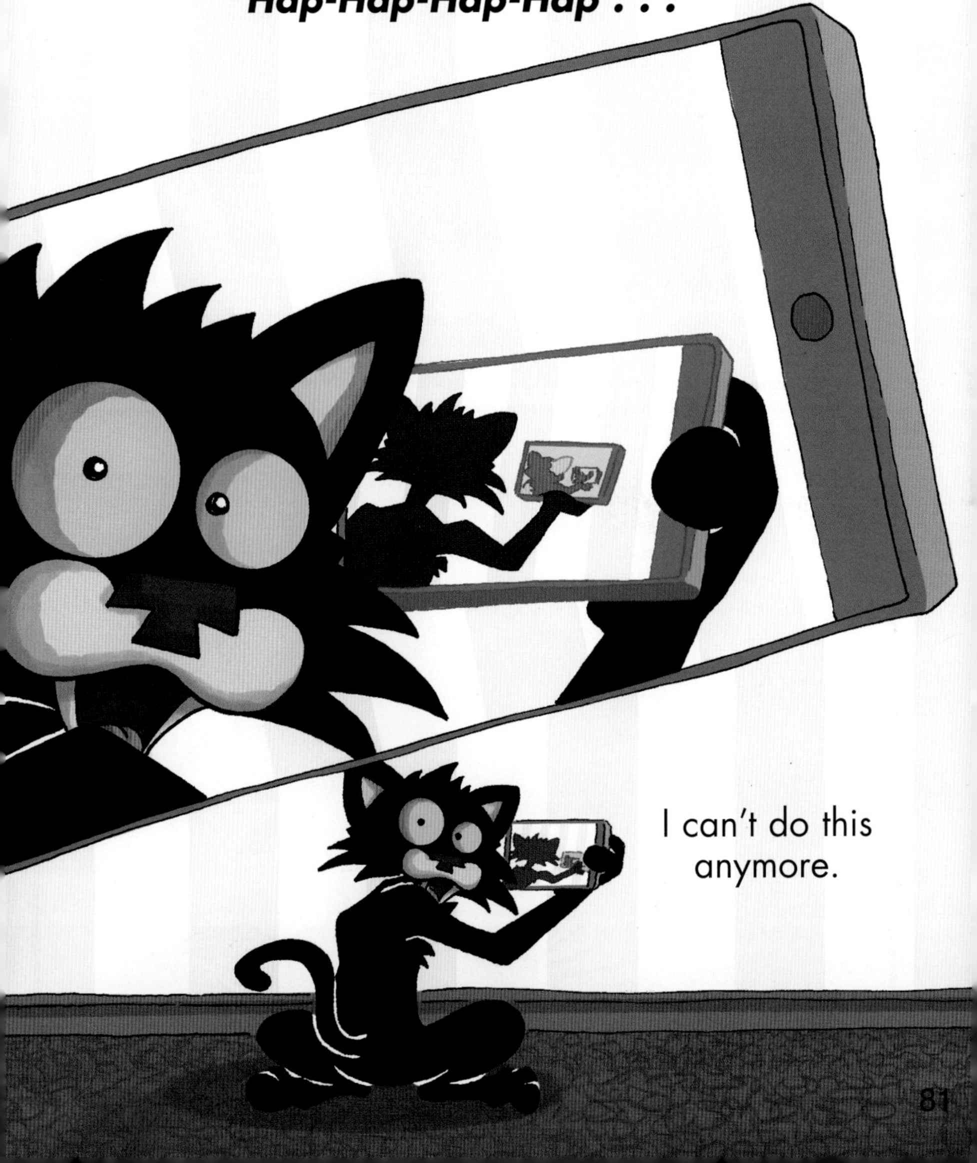
I can't do this anymore.

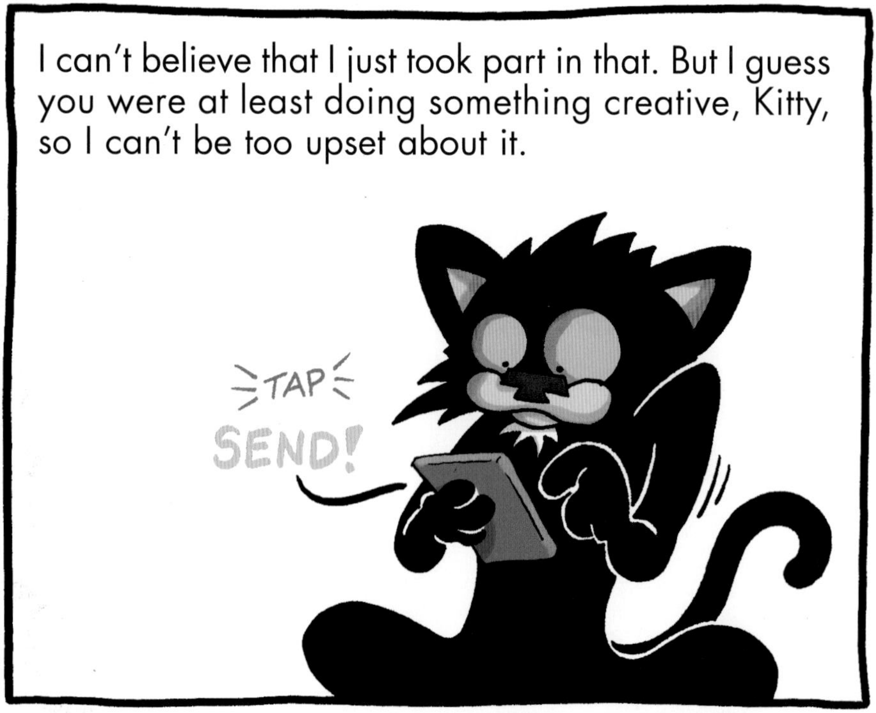
I can't believe that I just took part in that. But I guess you were at least doing something creative, Kitty, so I can't be too upset about it.
TAP
SEND!

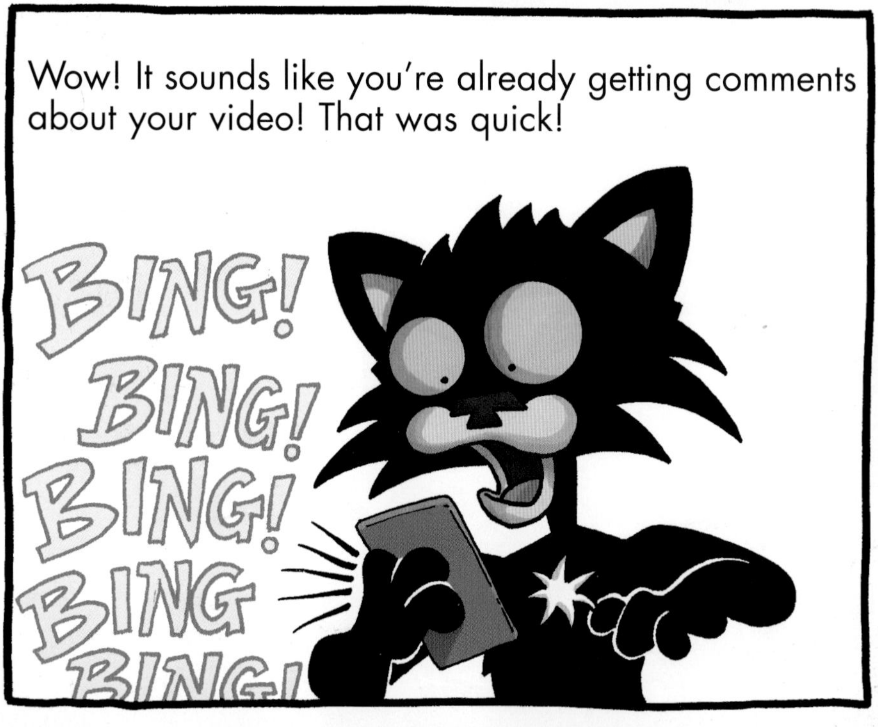
Wow! It sounds like you're already getting comments about your video! That was quick!
BING!
BING!
BING!
BING

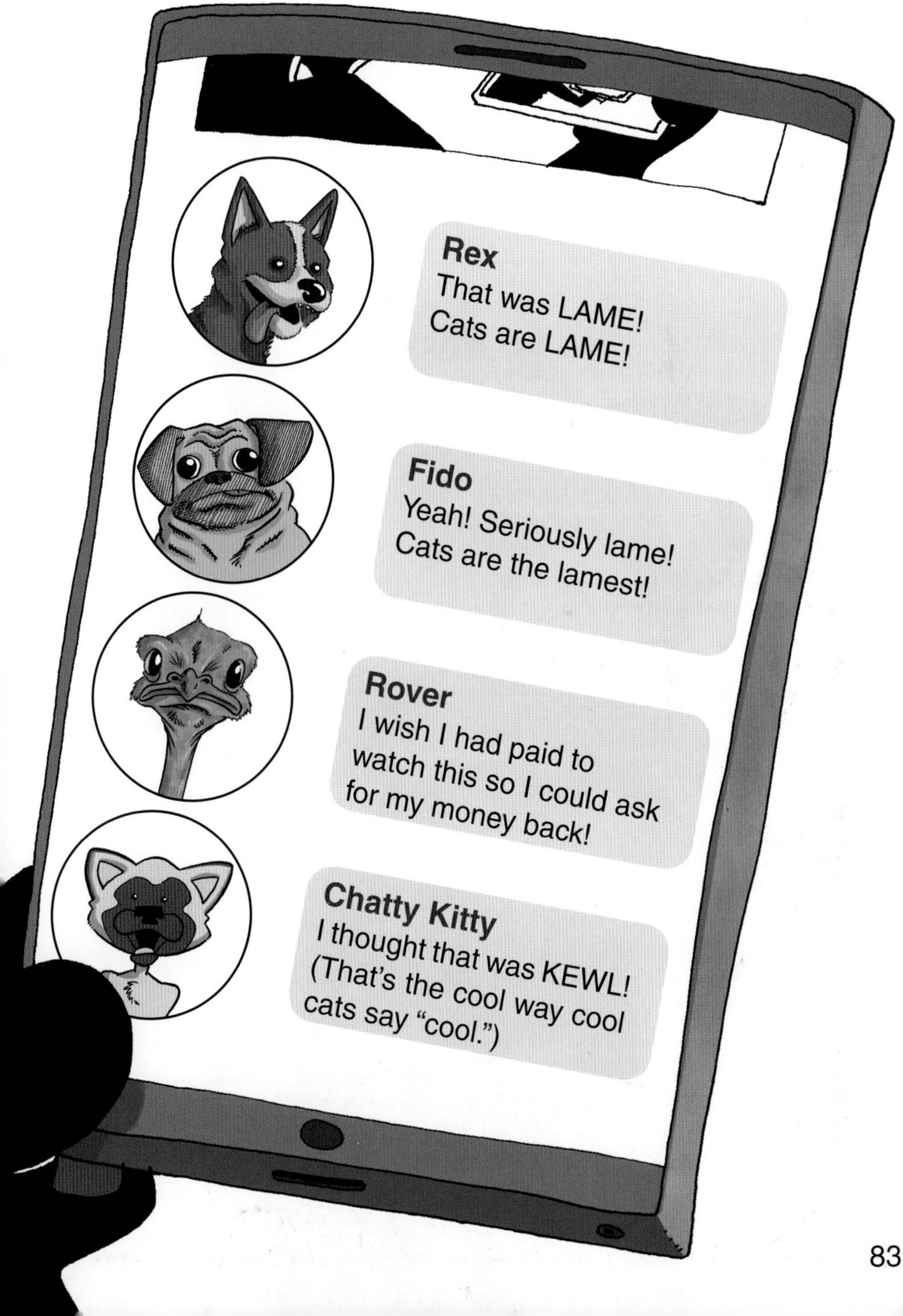
Rex
That was LAME!
Cats are LAME!
Fido
Yeah! Seriously lame!
Cats are the lamest!
Rover
I wish I had paid to watch this so I could ask for my money back!
Chatty Kitty
I thought that was KEWL! (That's the cool way cool cats say "cool.")

Ouch. I'm sorry, Kitty. That was mean.

Cats and dogs and people being mean to each other on the Internet can be a real problem. Often we're mean to each other on the Internet in a way that we would NEVER be if we were standing face-to-face.

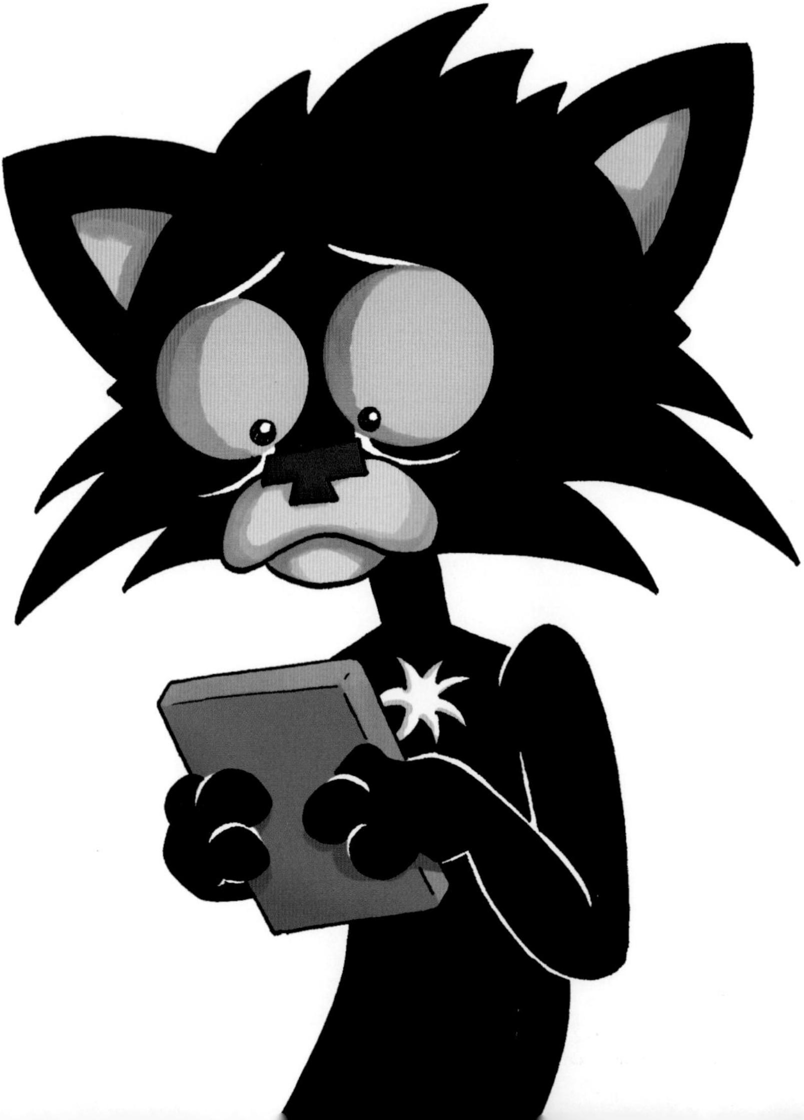

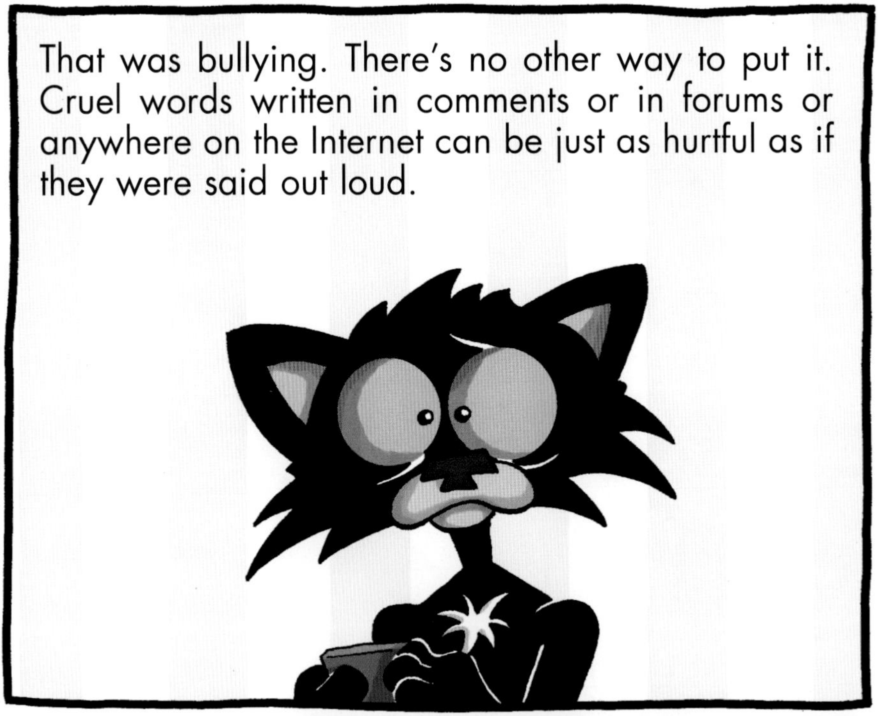
That was bullying. There's no other way to put it. Cruel words written in comments or in forums or anywhere on the Internet can be just as hurtful as if they were said out loud.

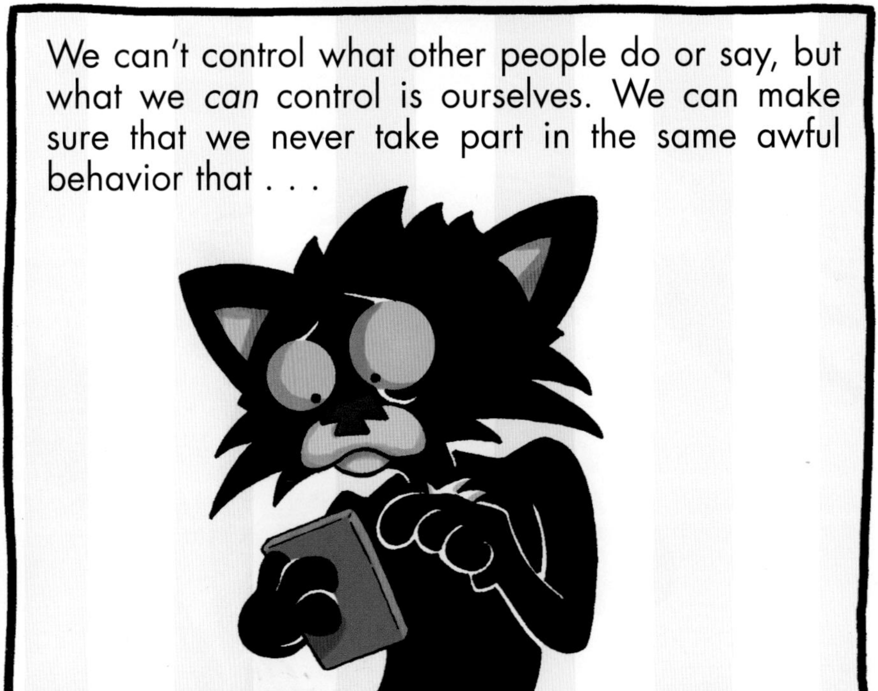
We can't control what other people do or say, but what we *can* control is ourselves. We can make sure that we never take part in the same awful behavior that . . .

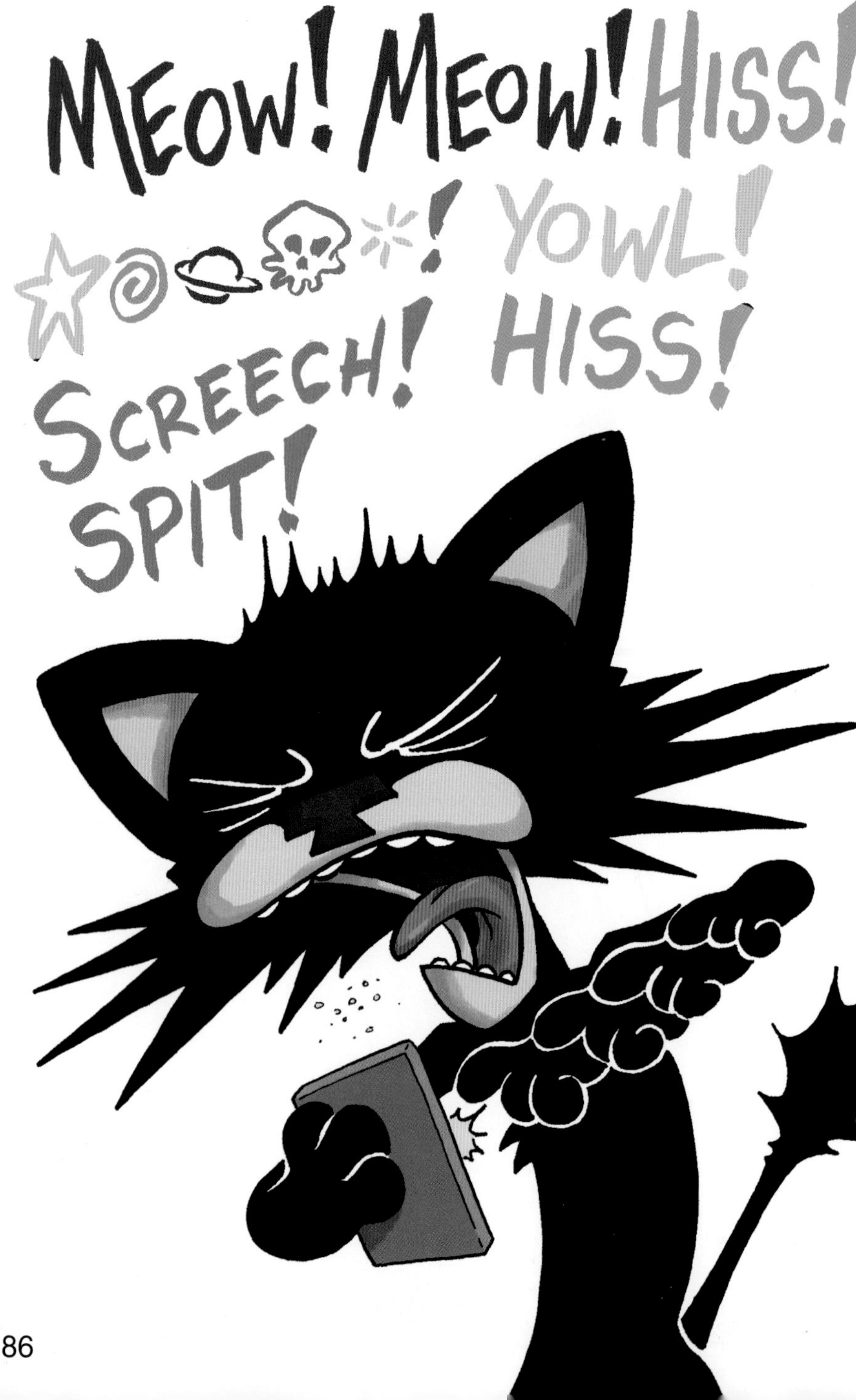
MEOW! MEOW! HISS!
YOWL!
SCREECH! HISS!
SPIT!

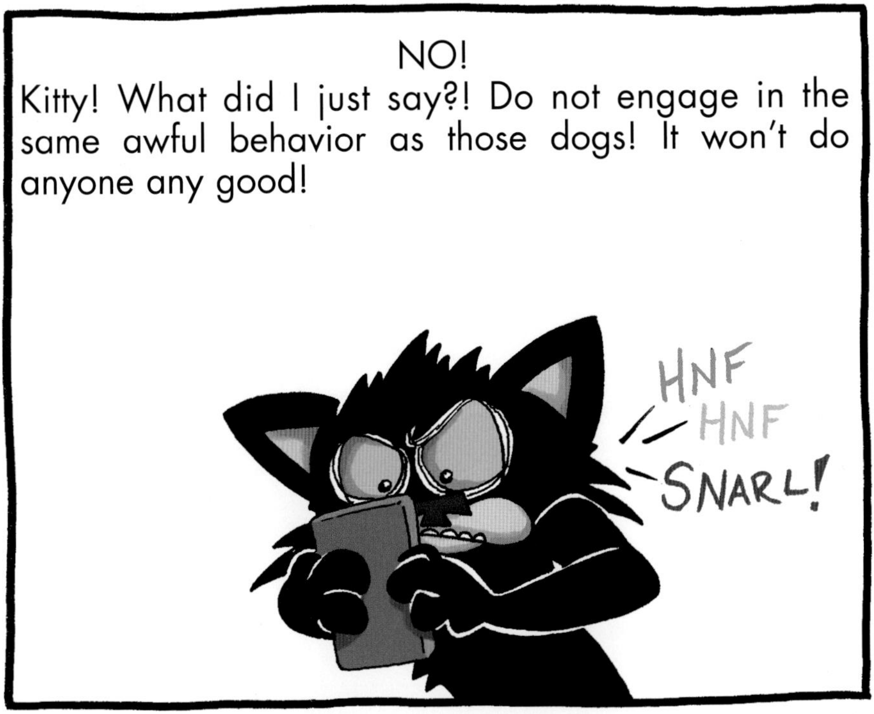
NO!
Kitty! What did I just say?! Do not engage in the same awful behavior as those dogs! It won't do anyone any good!
HNF
HNF
SNARL!

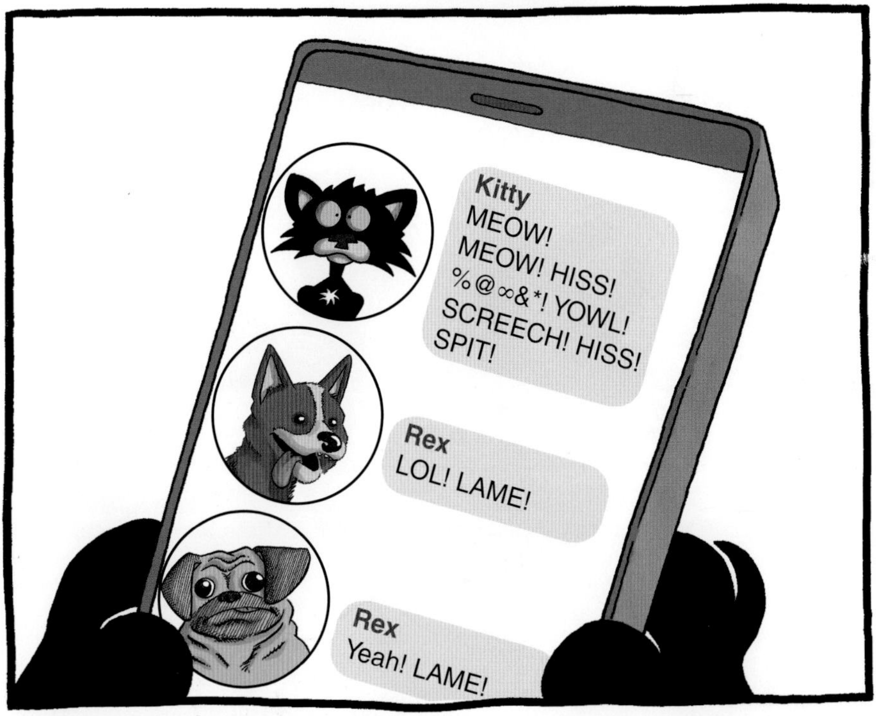
Kitty
MEOW! MEOW! HISS! %@∞&*! YOWL! SCREECH! HISS! SPIT!
Rex
LOL! LAME!
Rex
Yeah! LAME!

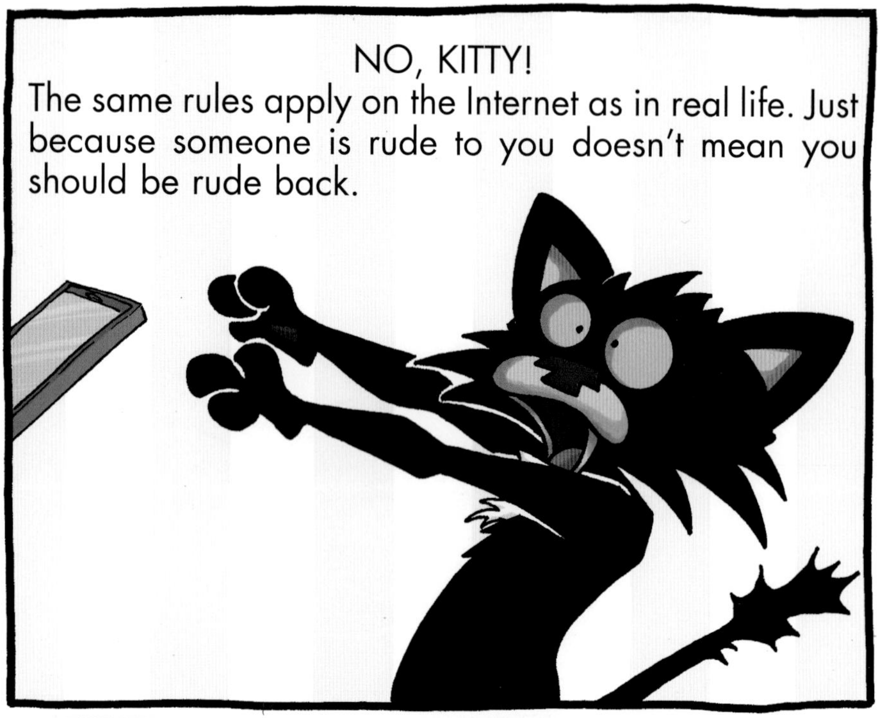
NO, KITTY!
The same rules apply on the Internet as in real life. Just because someone is rude to you doesn't mean you should be rude back.

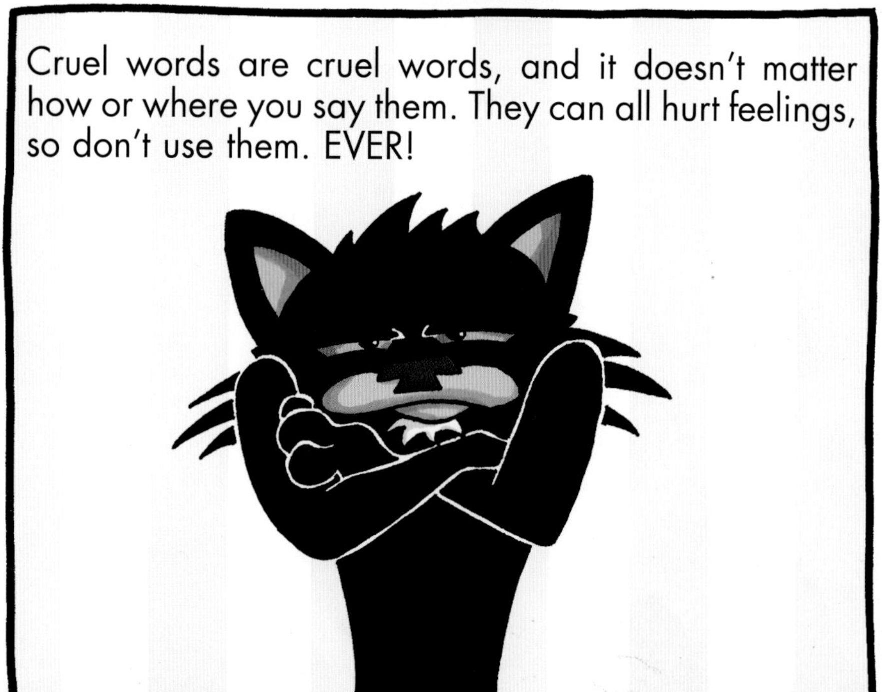
Cruel words are cruel words, and it doesn't matter how or where you say them. They can all hurt feelings, so don't use them. EVER!

Sorry, Kitty, but ViewTube is not appropriate for cats. I can't trust that you won't engage in mean-spirited chats with strangers. And to be completely honest, I didn't care for how dull and listless you were becoming from lying around and doing nothing but watching videos all day. I'm blocking you from accessing this site.

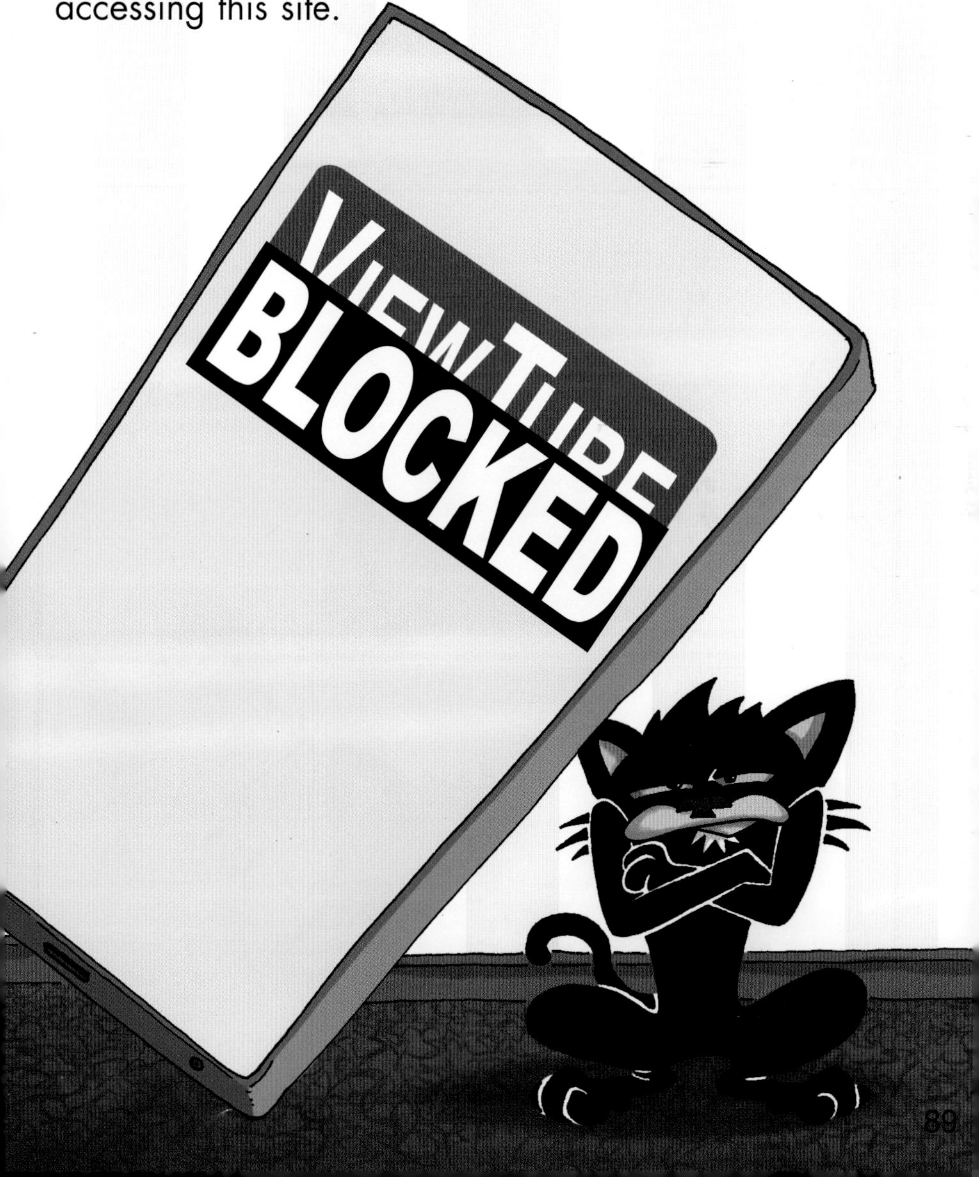
BLOCKED

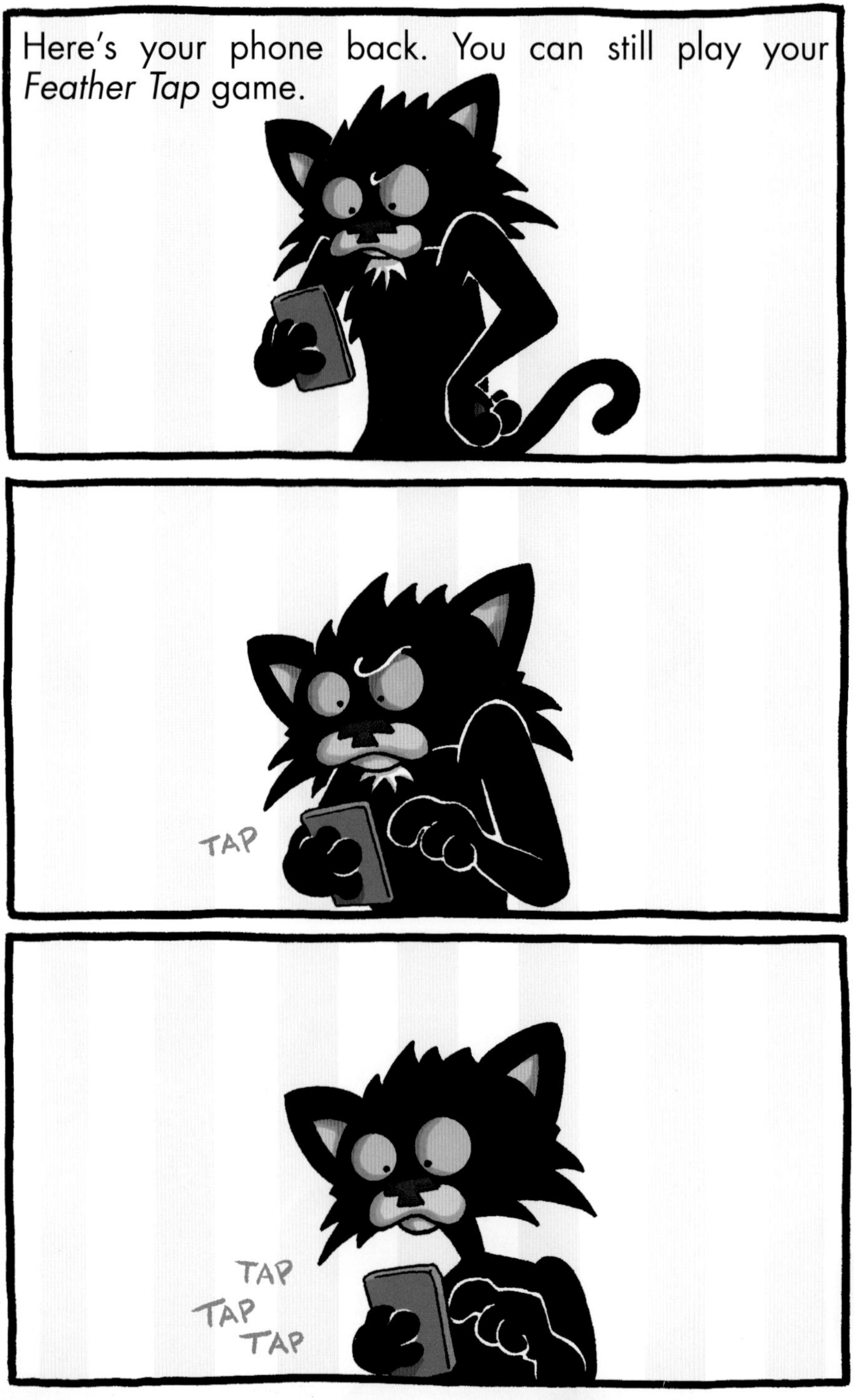
Here's your phone back. You can still play your *Feather Tap* game.
TAP
TAP
TAP
TAP

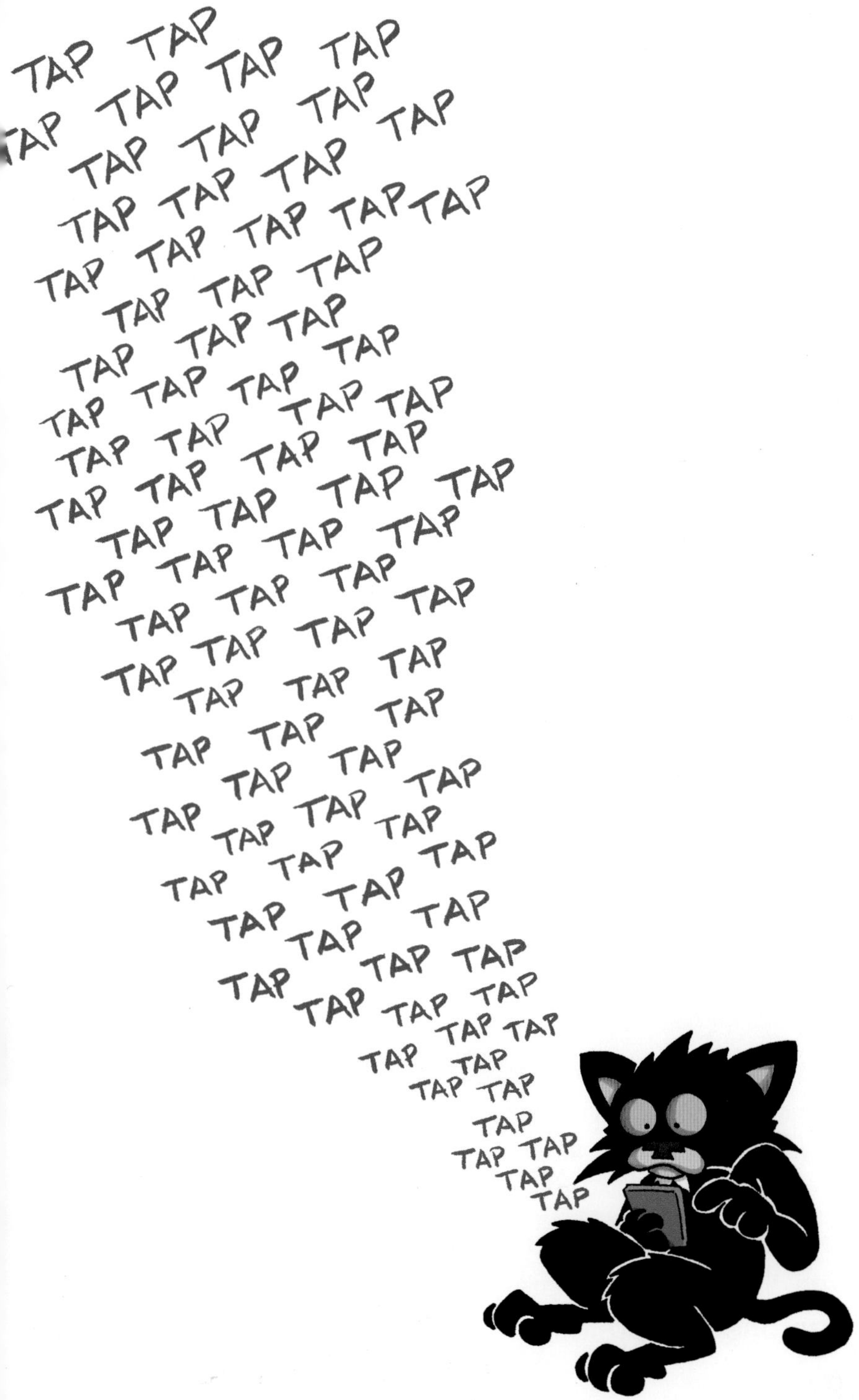
TAP TAP
TAP TAP TAP TAP
TAP TAP TAP TAP
TAP TAP TAP TAP
TAP TAP TAP TAP
TAP TAP TAP TAP TAP
TAP TAP TAP
TAP TAP TAP
TAP TAP TAP TAP
TAP TAP TAP TAP
TAP TAP TAP TAP
TAP TAP TAP TAP
TAP TAP TAP TAP
TAP TAP TAP
TAP TAP TAP TAP
TAP TAP TAP
TAP TAP TAP
TAP TAP TAP
TAP TAP TAP TAP
TAP TAP TAP
TAP TAP TAP
TAP TAP TAP
TAP TAP TAP TAP
TAP TAP TAP
TAP TAP TAP
TAP TAP
TAP TAP
TAP
TAP TAP
TAP
TAP

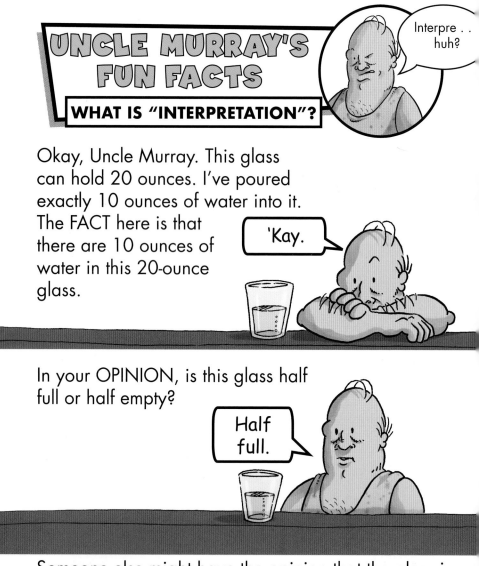

UNCLE MURRAY'S FUN FACTS

WHAT IS "INTERPRETATION"?

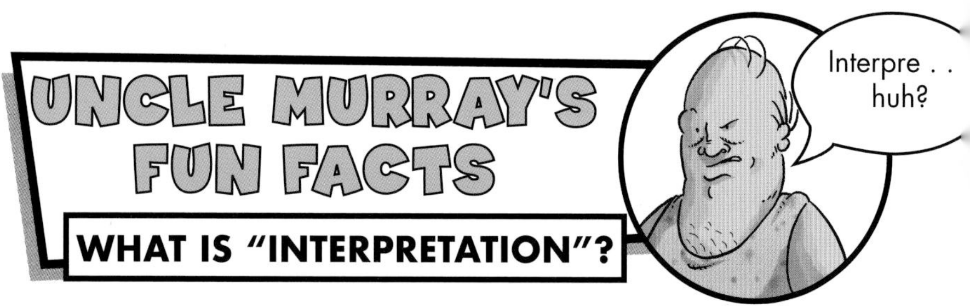
Interpre . . .
huh?

Okay, Uncle Murray. This glass can hold 20 ounces. I've poured exactly 10 ounces of water into it. The FACT here is that there are 10 ounces of water in this 20-ounce glass.

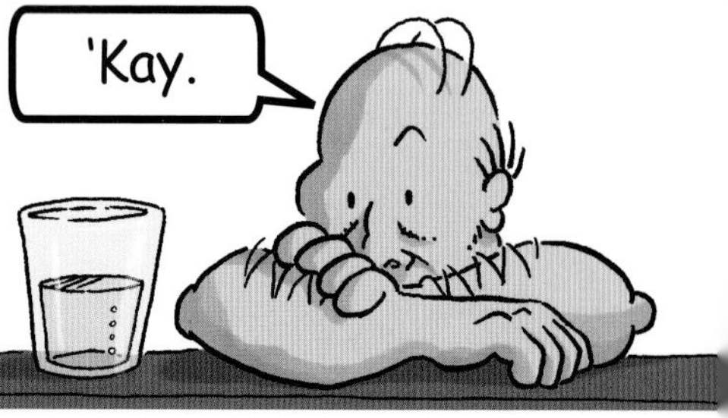
'Kay.

In your OPINION, is this glass half full or half empty?

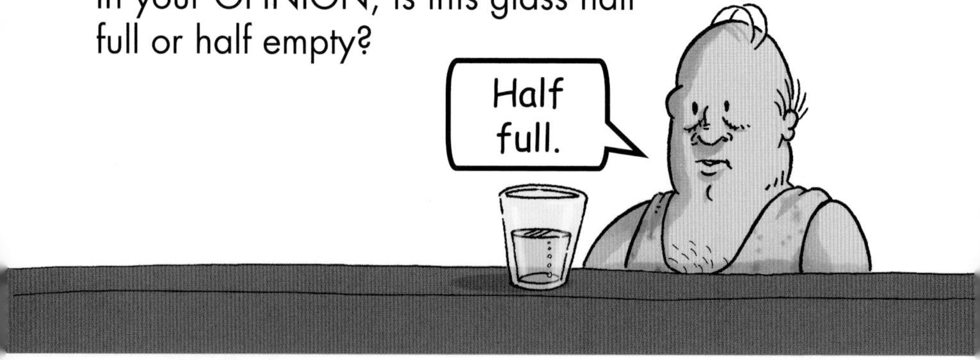
Half full.

Someone else might have the opinion that the glass is half empty!

An interpretation is a way to explain a fact. But as with this glass of water, a single fact can have more than one interpretation.

One interpretation is that the glass is half full. Another interpretation is that the glass is half empty. In this case, BOTH interpretations are true, even though they lead to opposite opinions.

Waitaminnit! What does any of this have to do with cats and phones?!

Phones are a very popular way to access the Internet. And the Internet can be an amazing source of information. Buried in that information are lots of facts and lots of opinions. Cats of all ages need to understand the difference between the two.

Cats also need to realize that people may take their opinions very seriously. But facts can have more than one interpretation, which leads to different opinions that can all be true.

This is all very confusing.

That's your opinion.

Stop it.

•CHAPTER SEVEN•

THIS IS *FEATHER TAP*

Kitty, it's 4:00 in the morning. Why aren't you asleep? It's time to stop playing that game.

Kitty?

Kitty?

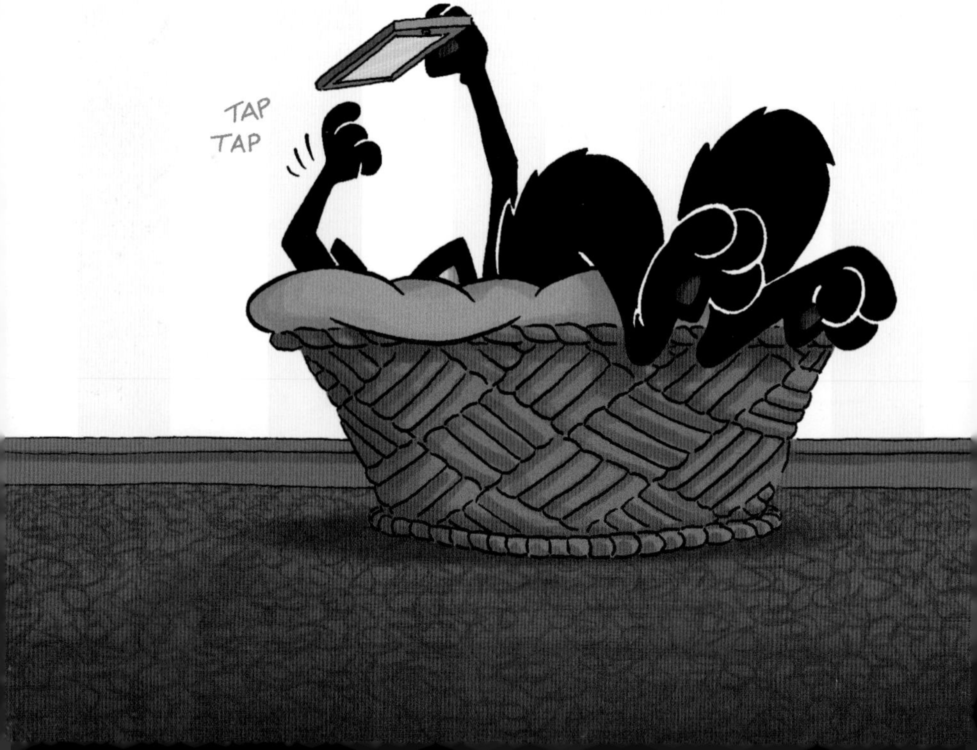
TAP
TAP

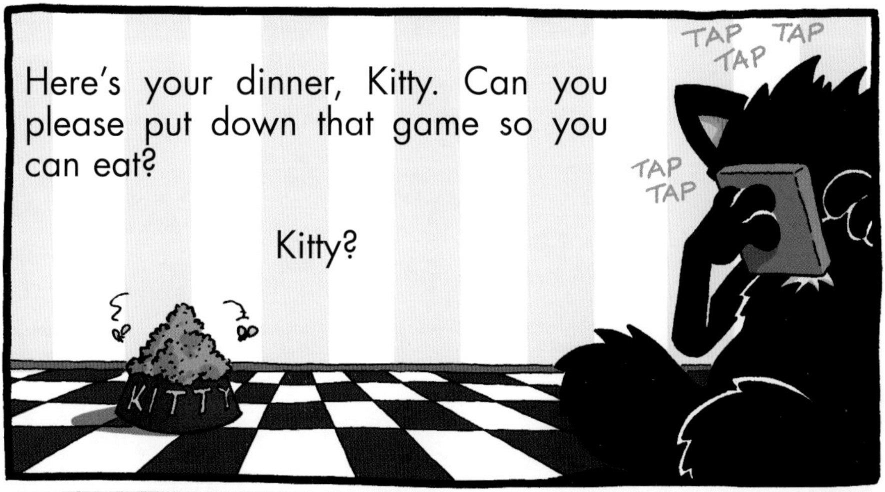
Here's your dinner, Kitty. Can you please put down that game so you can eat?
Kitty?
TAP TAP TAP
TAP TAP
KITTY

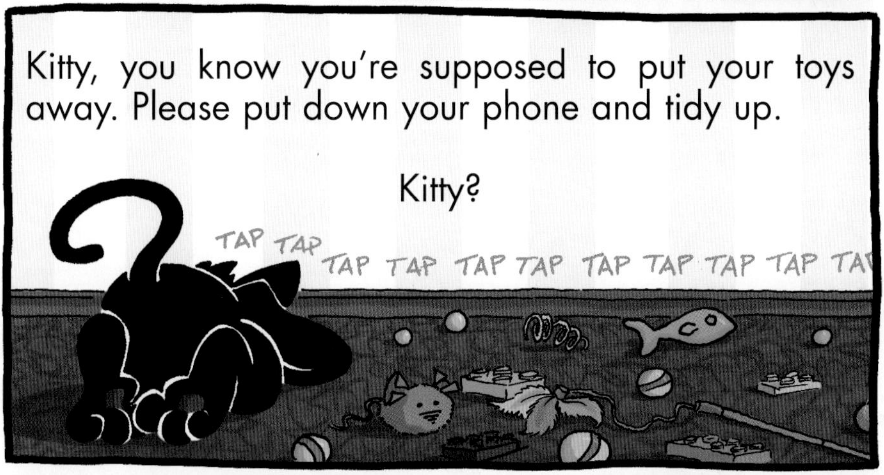
Kitty, you know you're supposed to put your toys away. Please put down your phone and tidy up.
Kitty?
TAP TAP TAP TAP TAP TAP TAP TAP TAP TAP

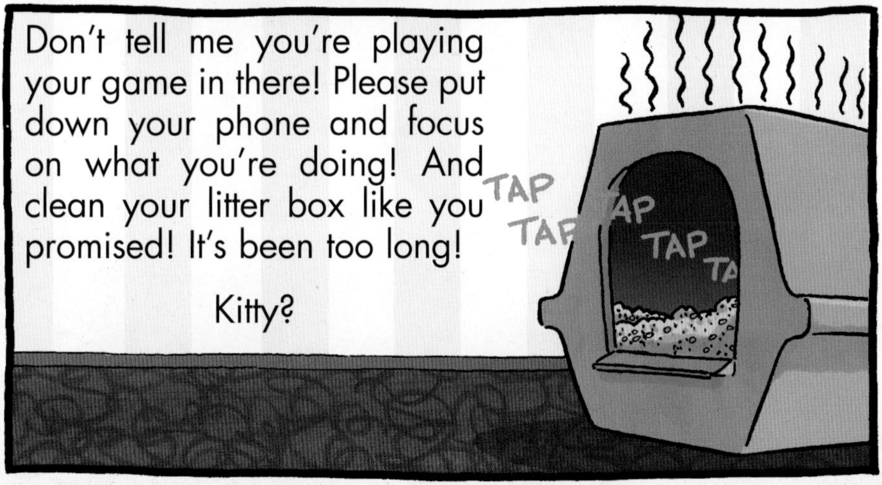
Don't tell me you're playing your game in there! Please put down your phone and focus on what you're doing! And clean your litter box like you promised! It's been too long!
Kitty?
TAP
TAP
TAP

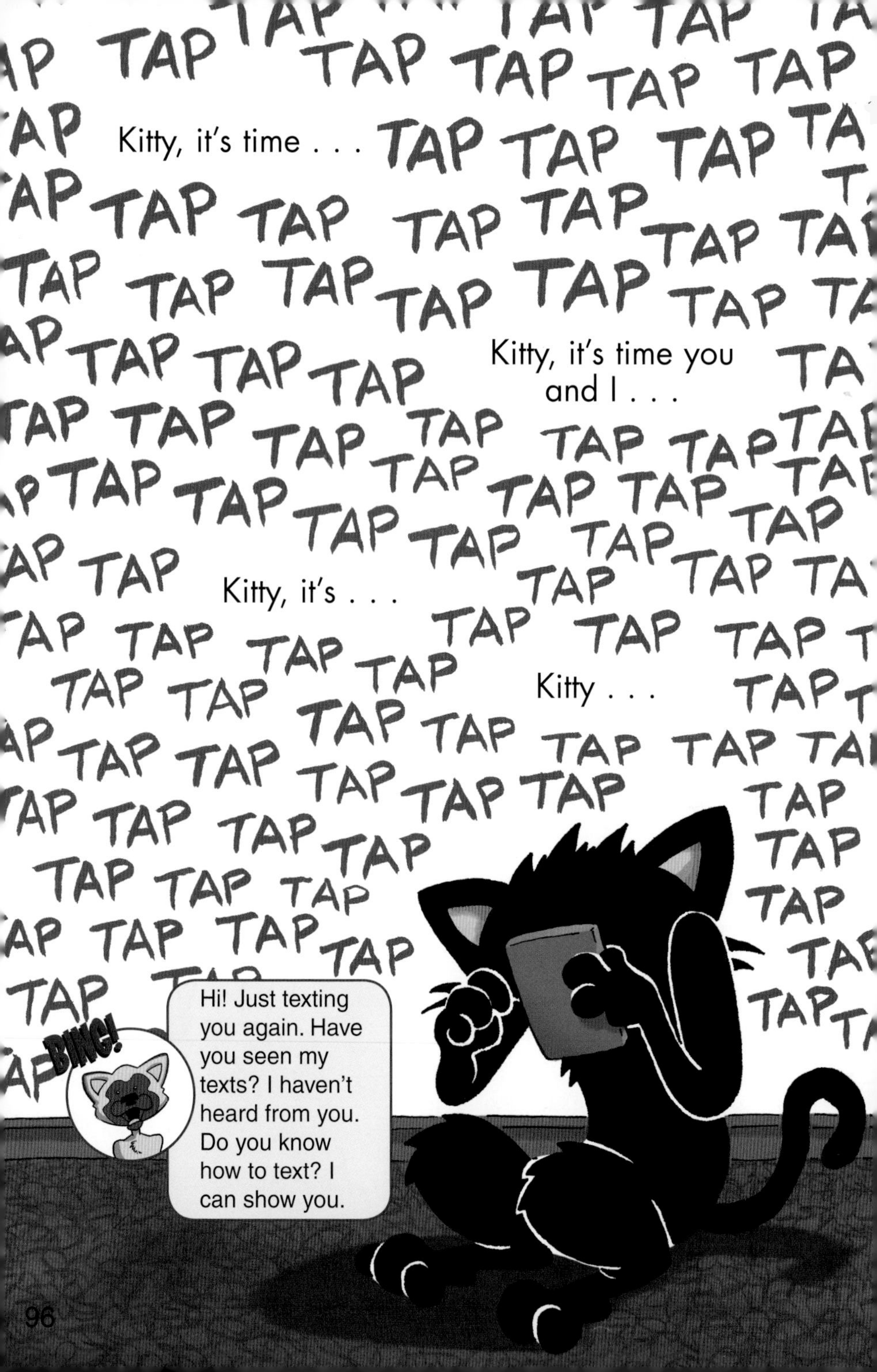
TAP TAP TAP TAP TAP
Kitty, it's time . . .
Kitty, it's time you and I . . .
Kitty, it's . . .
Kitty . . .
BING!
Hi! Just texting you again. Have you seen my texts? I haven't heard from you. Do you know how to text? I can show you.

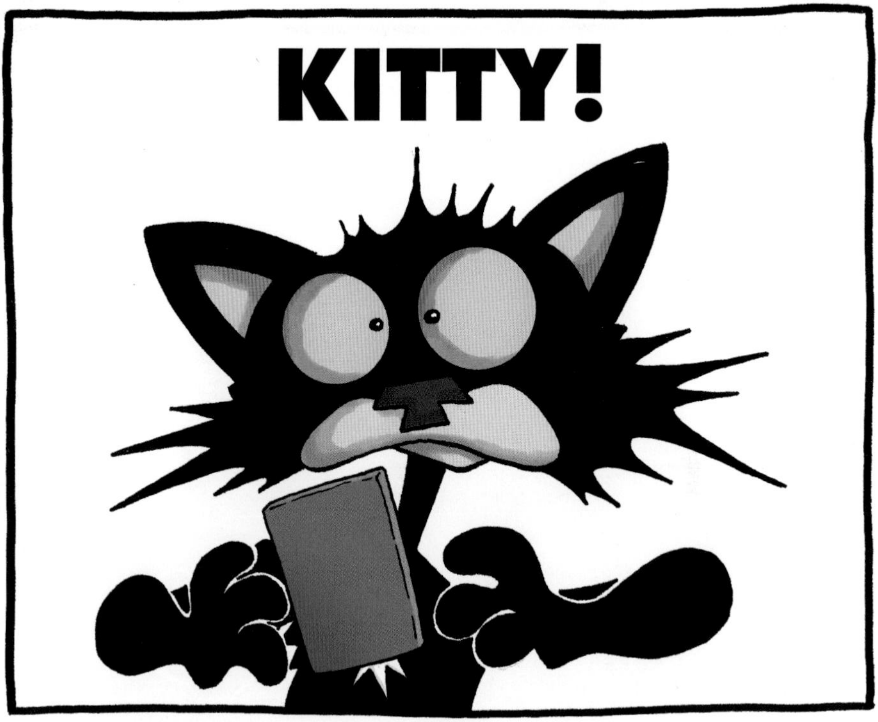
KITTY!

Kitty, it's time you and I had a conversation. You need to take a little break from your phone and from playing that game. You're not eating enough. You're not sleeping enough. Your toys are all over the place, and your litter box is disgusting.

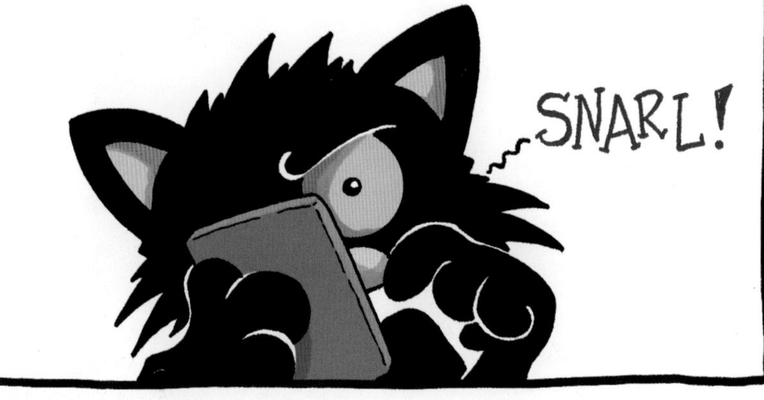
SNARL!

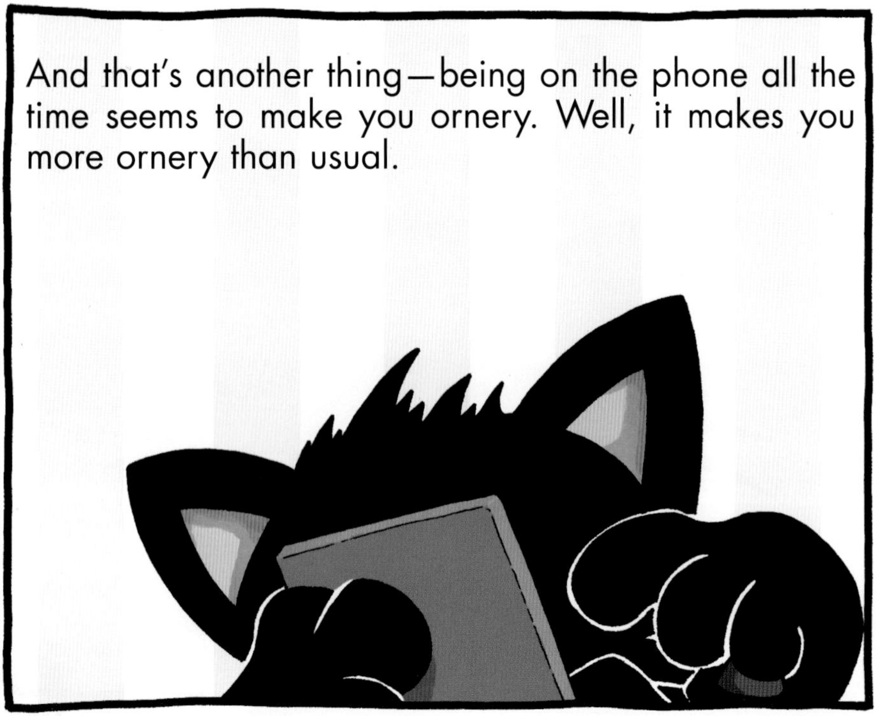
And that's another thing—being on the phone all the time seems to make you ornery. Well, it makes you more ornery than usual.

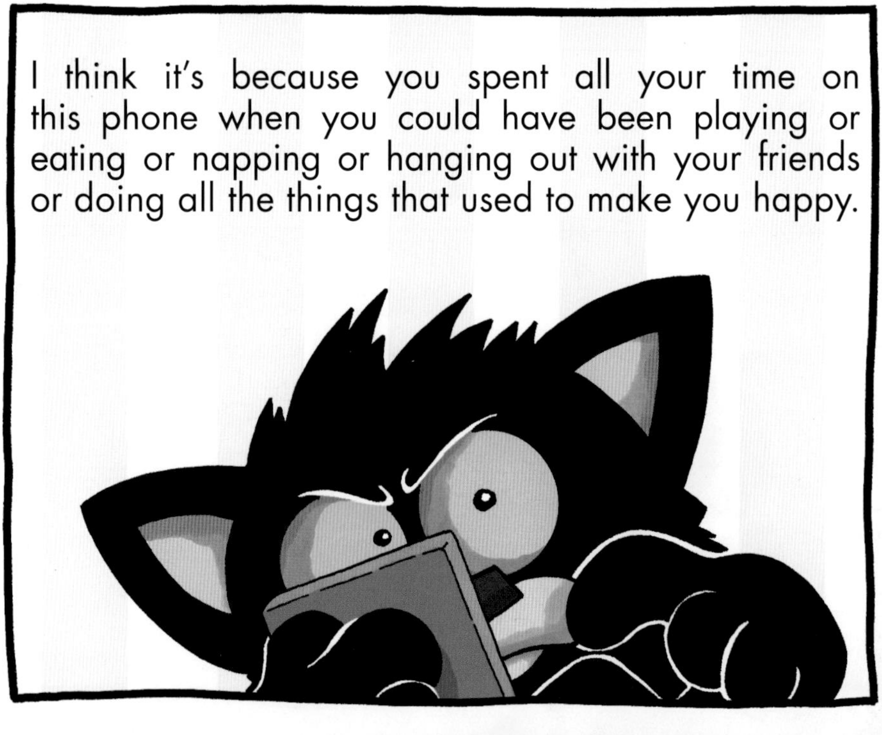
I think it's because you spent all your time on this phone when you could have been playing or eating or napping or hanging out with your friends or doing all the things that used to make you happy.

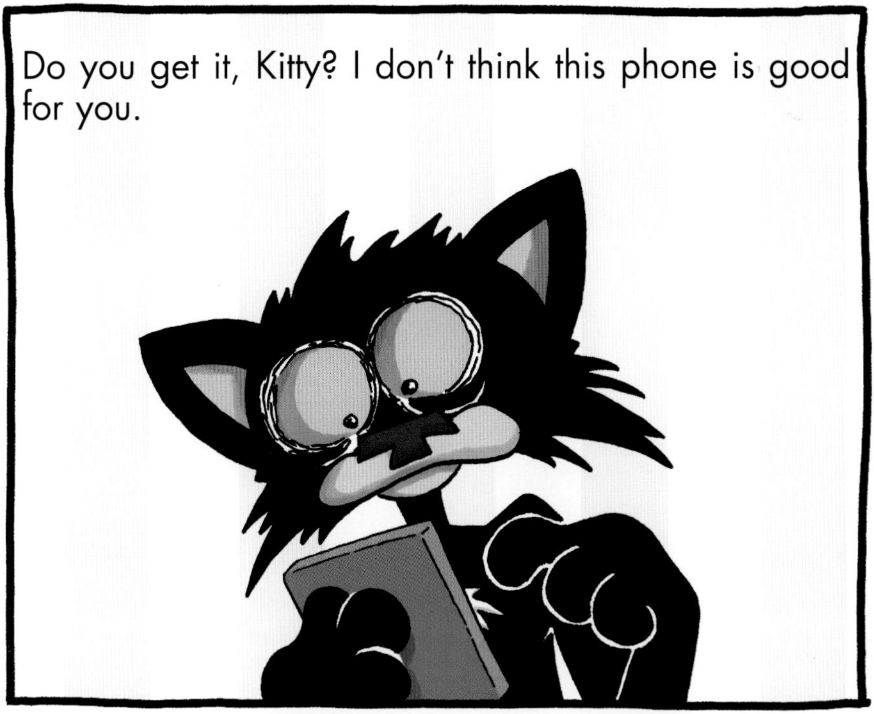
Do you get it, Kitty? I don't think this phone is good for you.

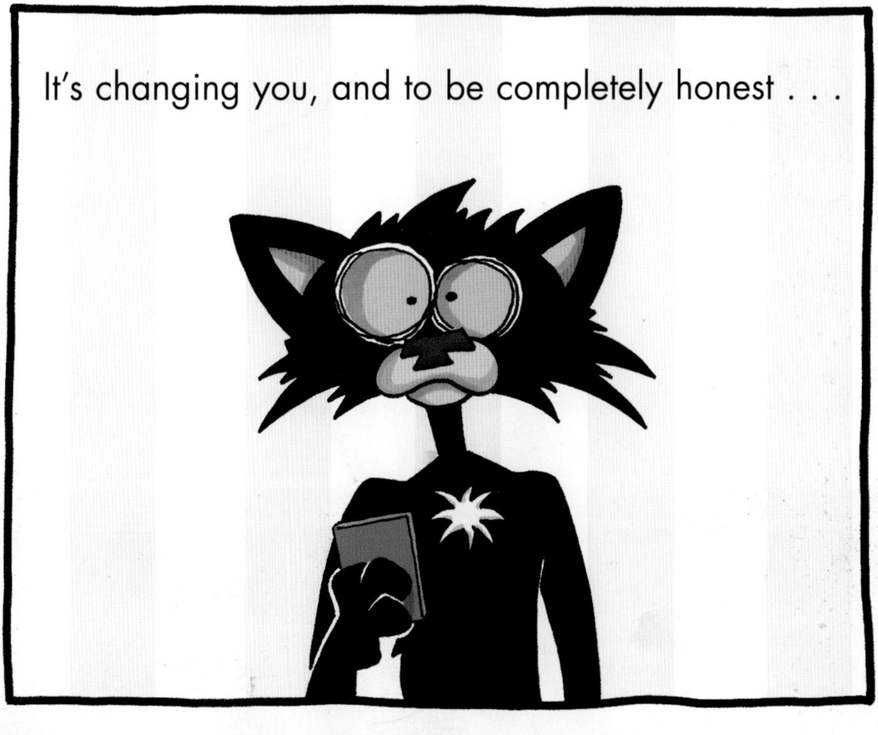
It's changing you, and to be completely honest . . .

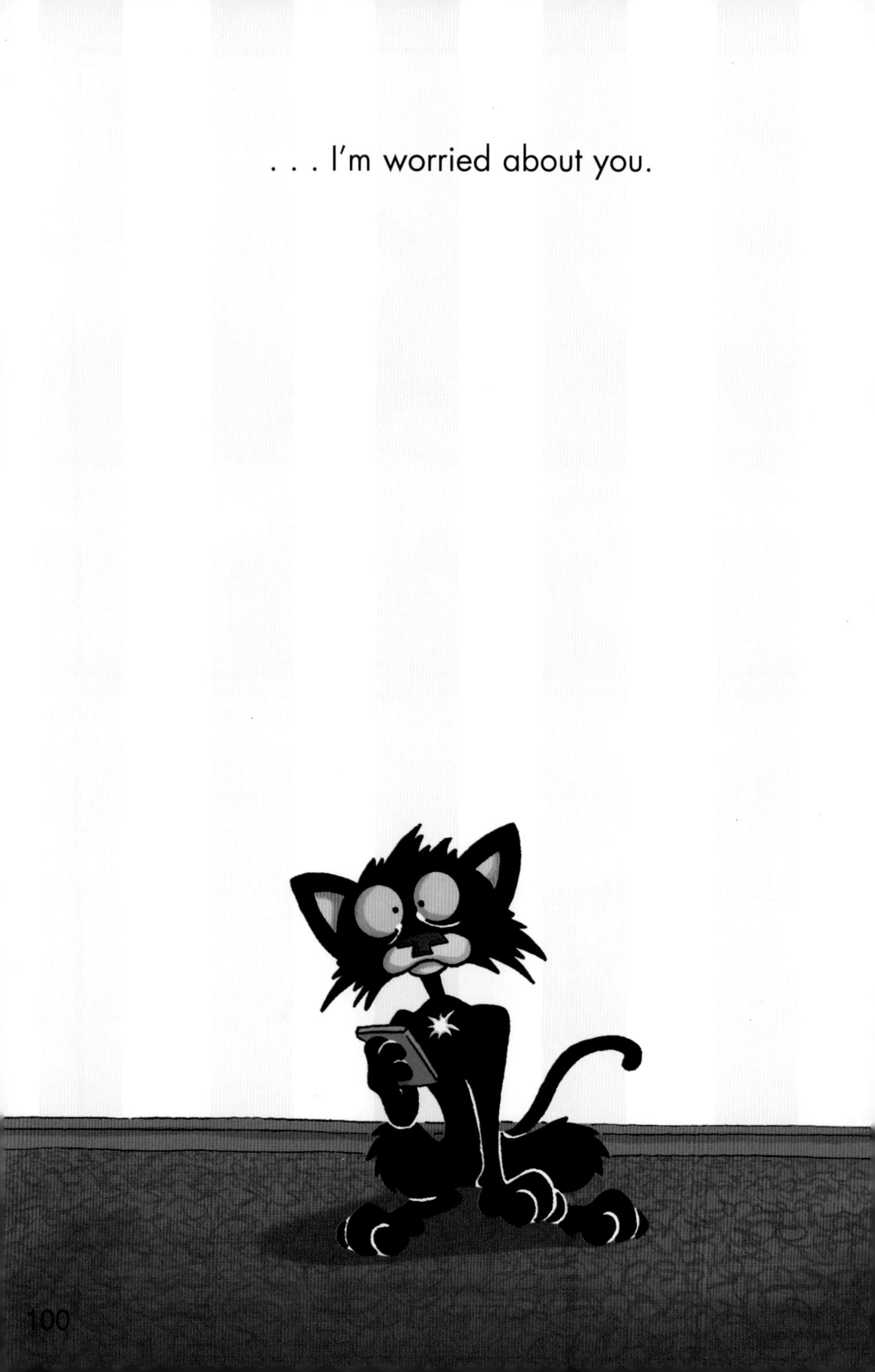
. . . I'm worried about you.

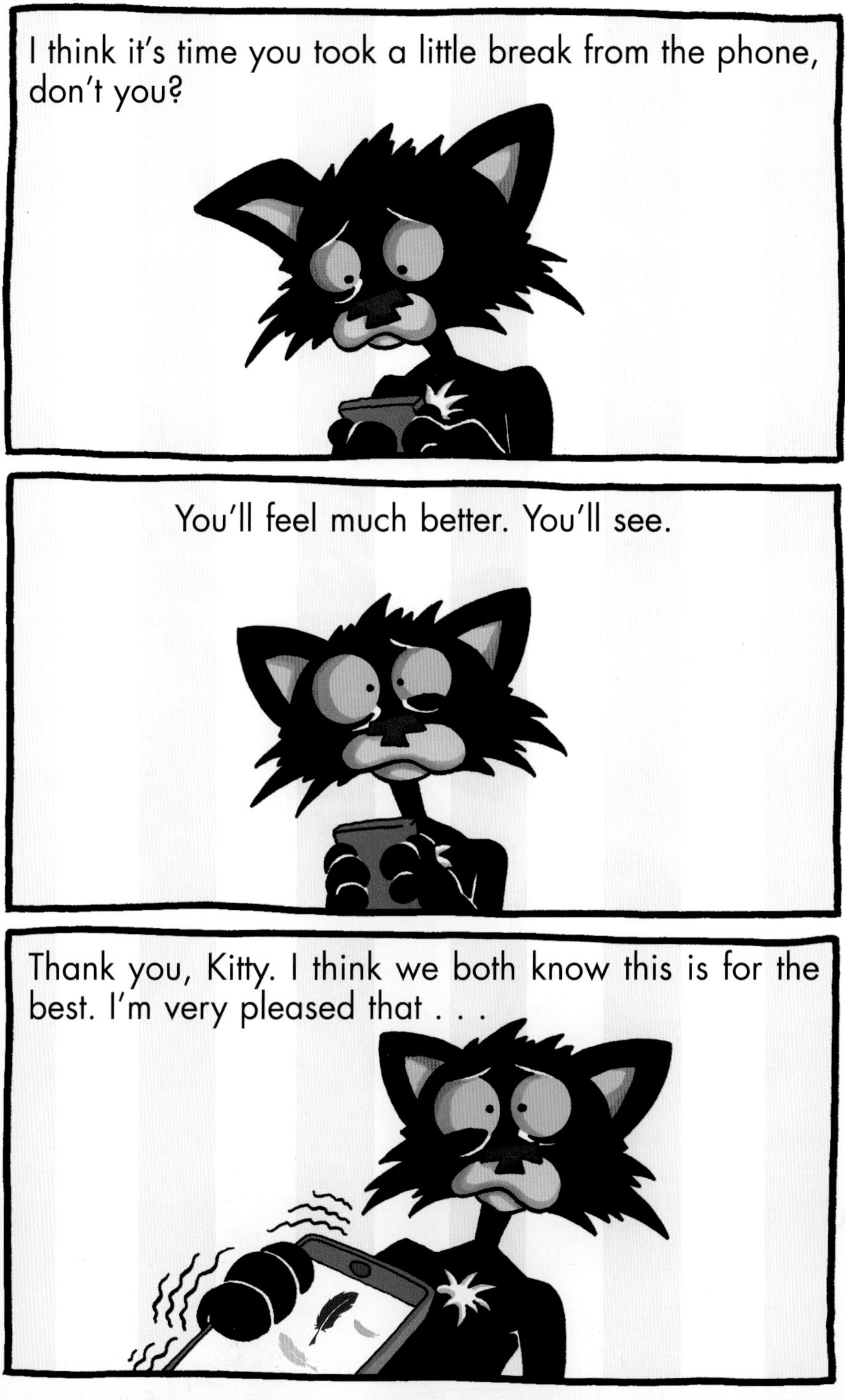
I think it's time you took a little break from the phone, don't you?
You'll feel much better. You'll see.
Thank you, Kitty. I think we both know this is for the best. I'm very pleased that . . .

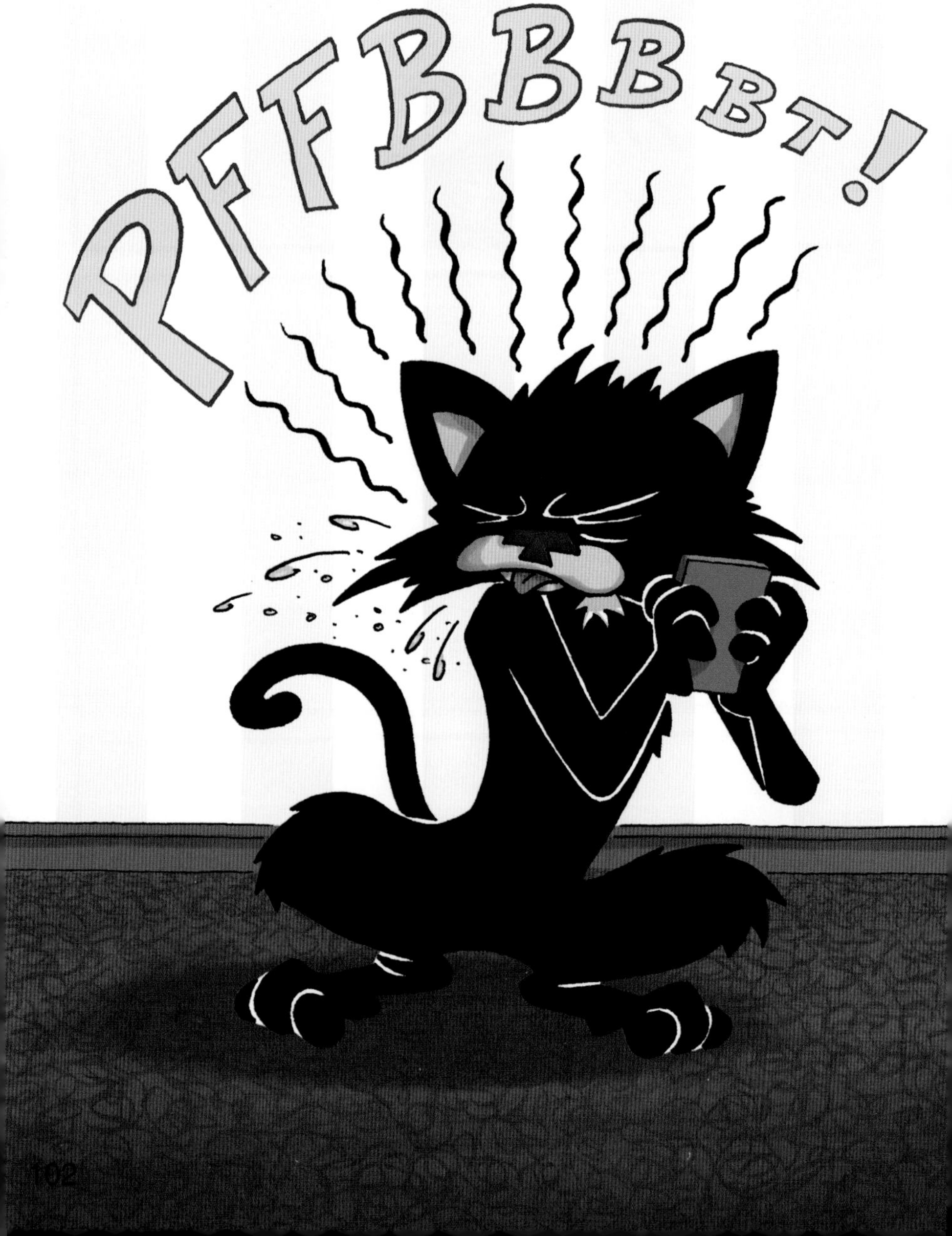
PFFBBBBT!

Sigh.

I should have known it
wouldn't be this easy.

•CHAPTER EIGHT•

HOW TO TAKE A PHONE AWAY FROM A CAT

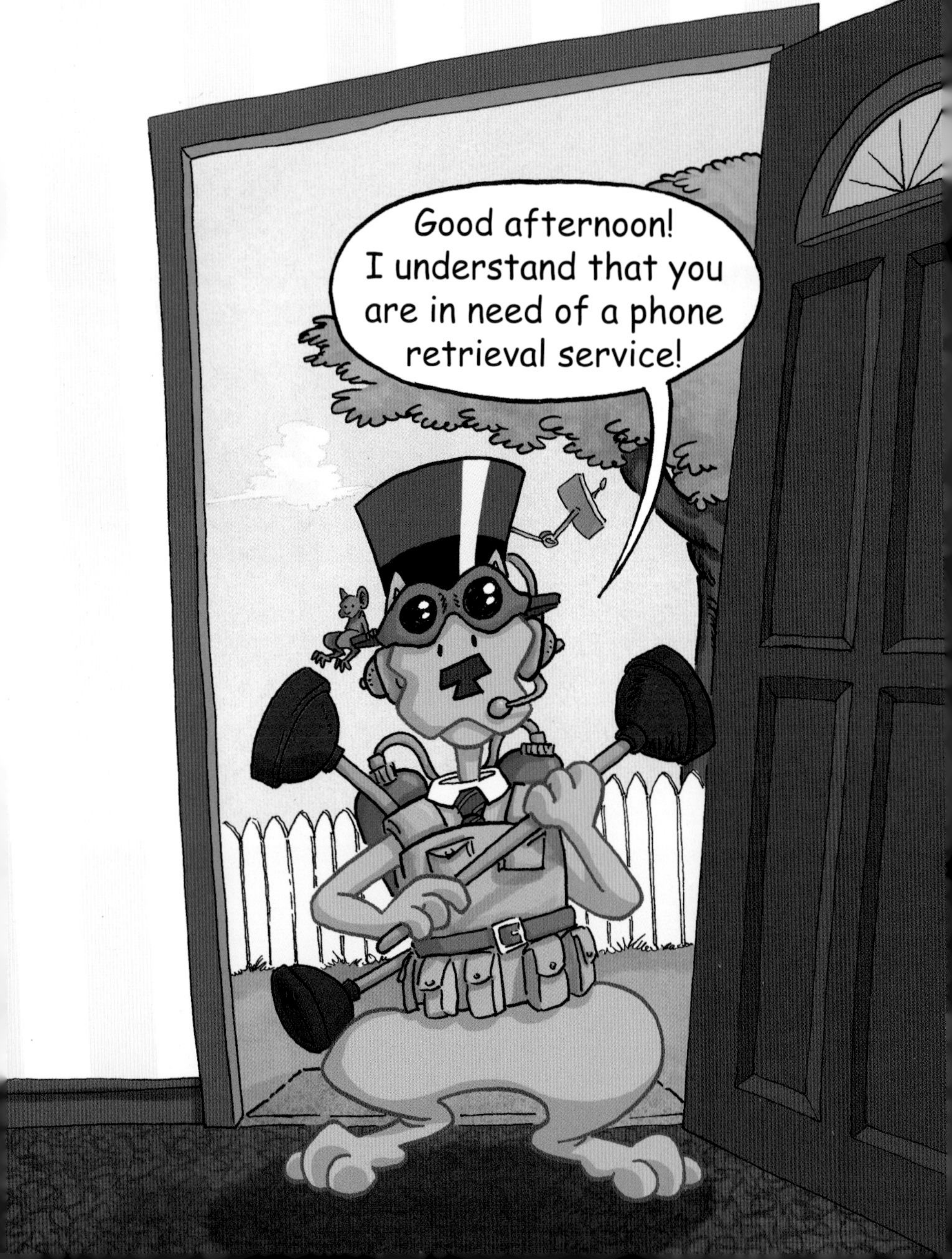
Good afternoon! I understand that you are in need of a phone retrieval service!

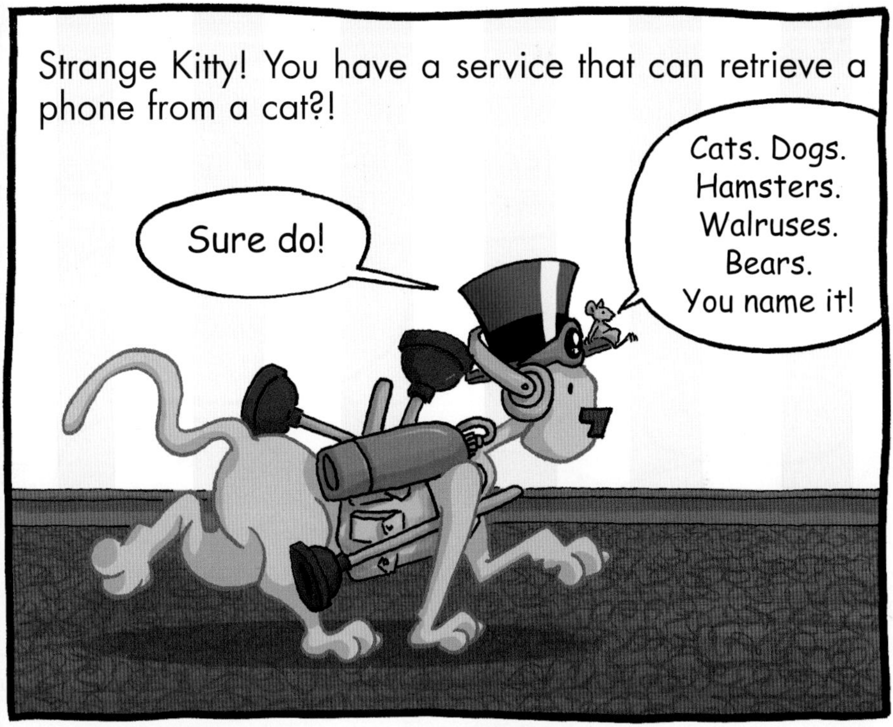
Strange Kitty! You have a service that can retrieve a phone from a cat?!
Sure do!
Cats. Dogs. Hamsters. Walruses. Bears. You name it!

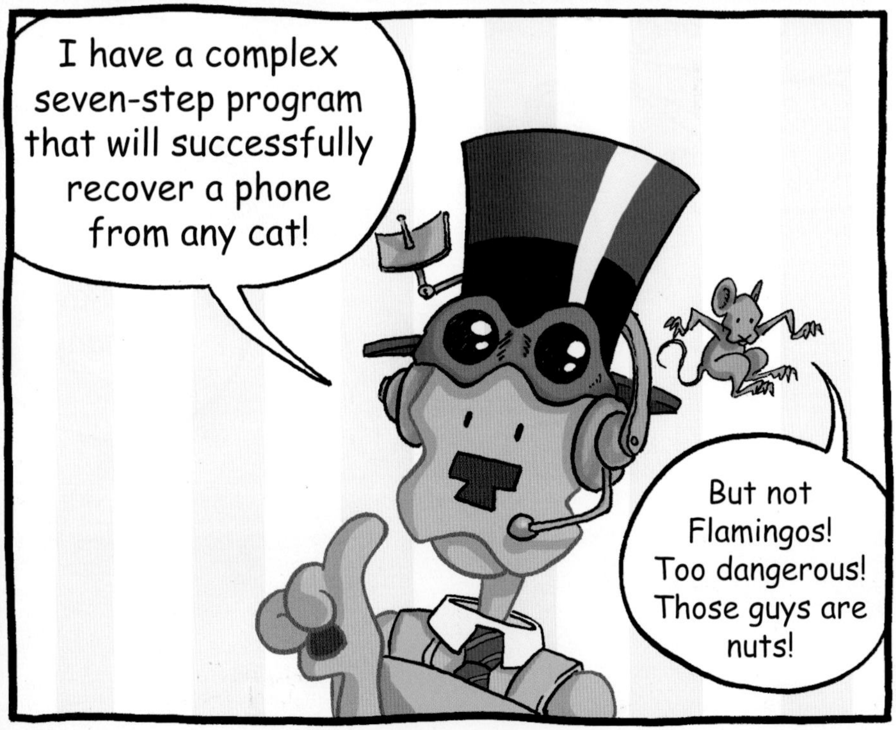
I have a complex seven-step program that will successfully recover a phone from any cat!
But not Flamingos! Too dangerous! Those guys are nuts!

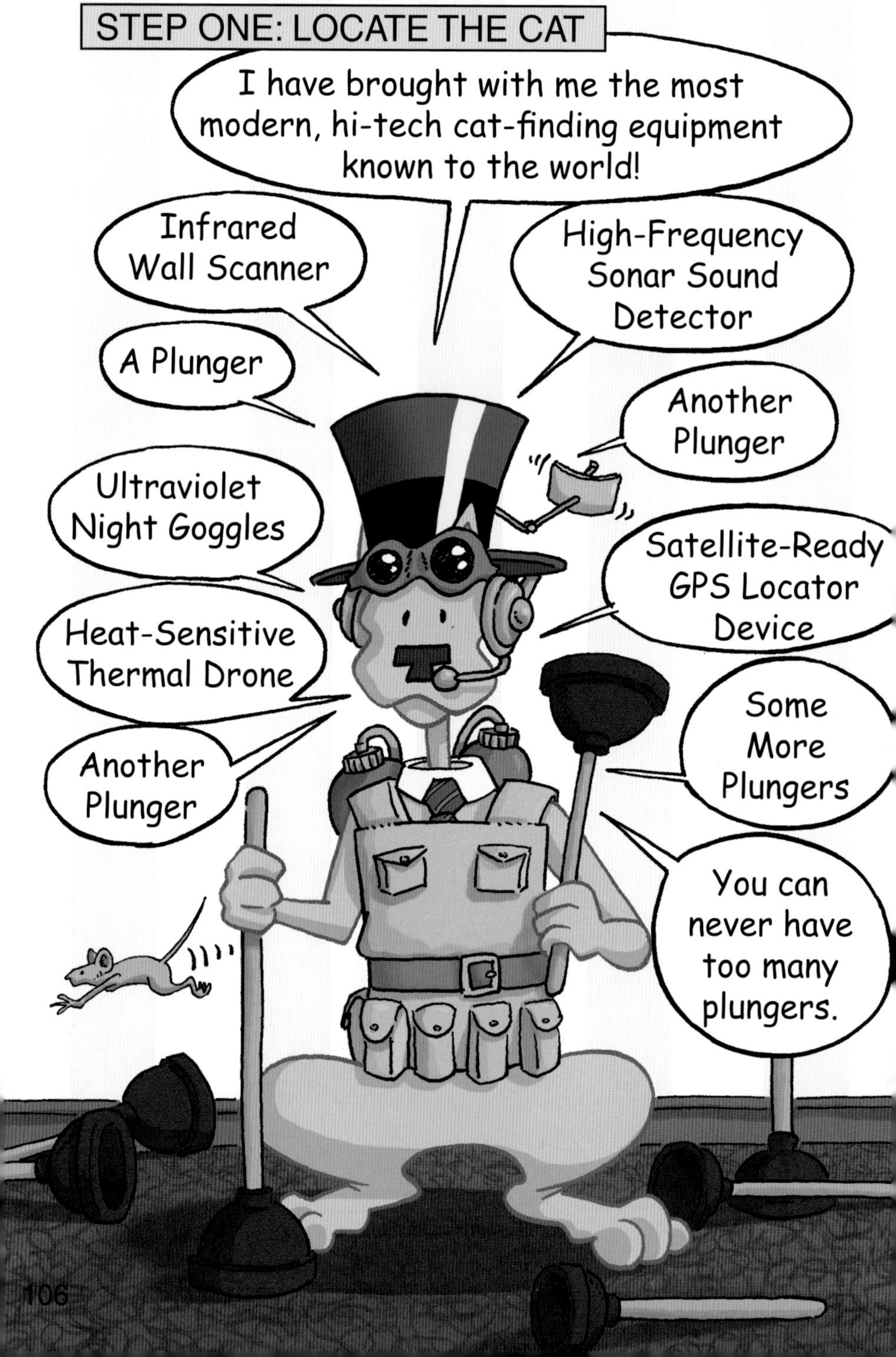
STEP ONE: LOCATE THE CAT
I have brought with me the most modern, hi-tech cat-finding equipment known to the world!
Infrared Wall Scanner
High-Frequency Sonar Sound Detector
A Plunger
Another Plunger
Ultraviolet Night Goggles
Satellite-Ready GPS Locator Device
Heat-Sensitive Thermal Drone
Some More Plungers
Another Plunger
You can never have too many plungers.

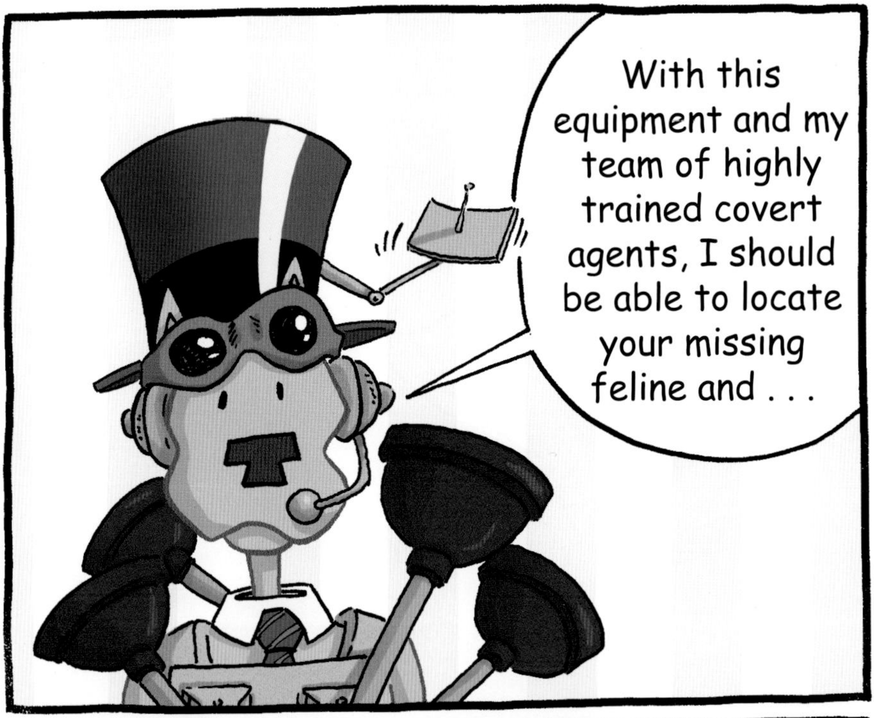
With this equipment and my team of highly trained covert agents, I should be able to locate your missing feline and . . .

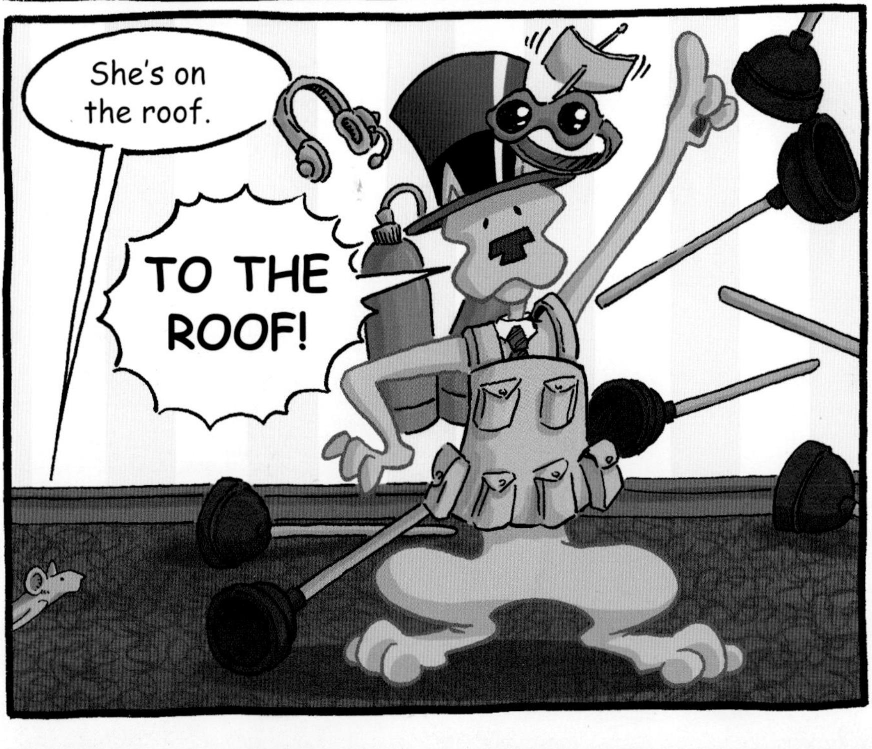
She's on the roof.
TO THE ROOF!

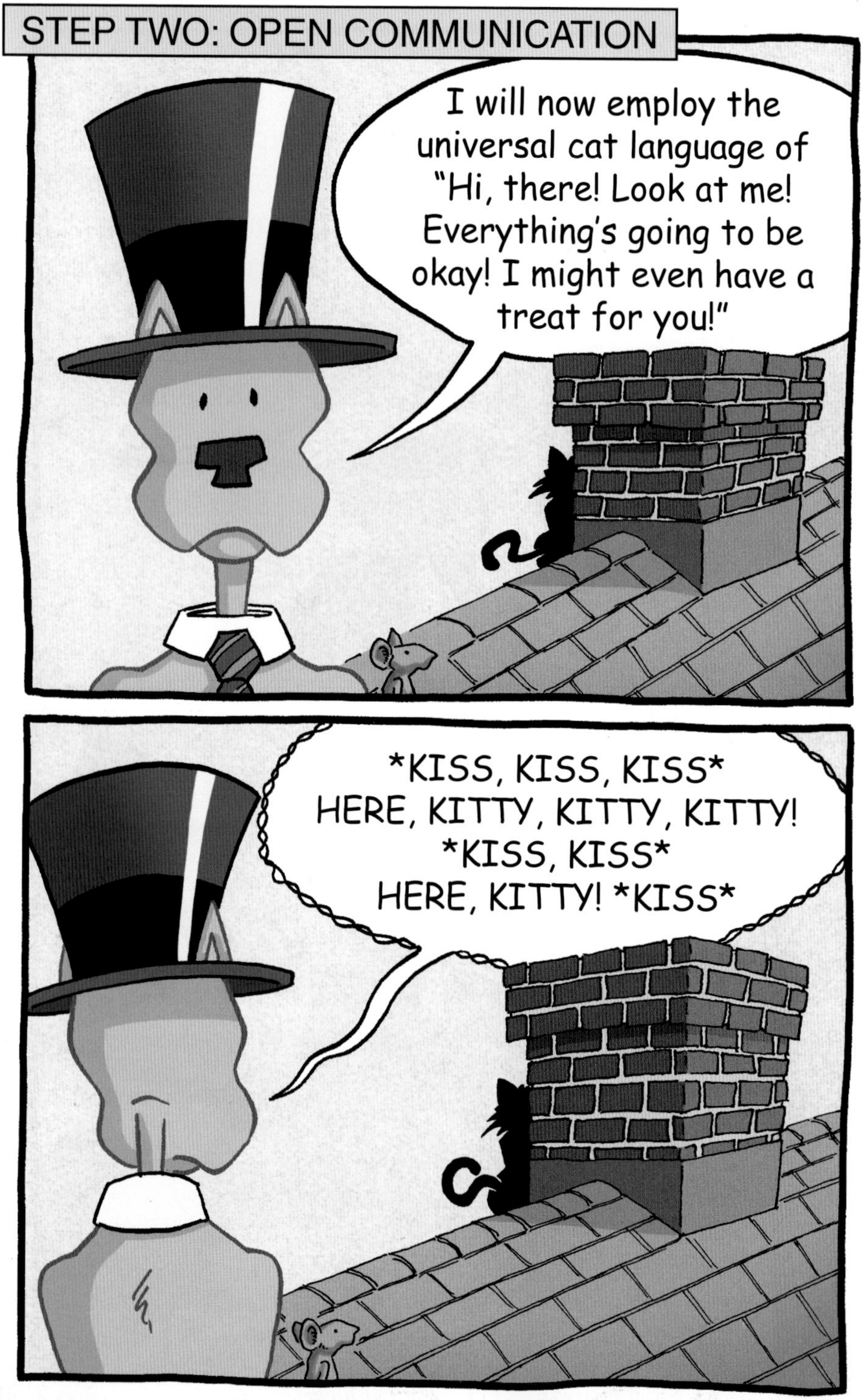
STEP TWO: OPEN COMMUNICATION
I will now employ the universal cat language of "Hi, there! Look at me! Everything's going to be okay! I might even have a treat for you!"
KISS, KISS, KISS HERE, KITTY, KITTY, KITTY! *KISS, KISS* HERE, KITTY! *KISS*

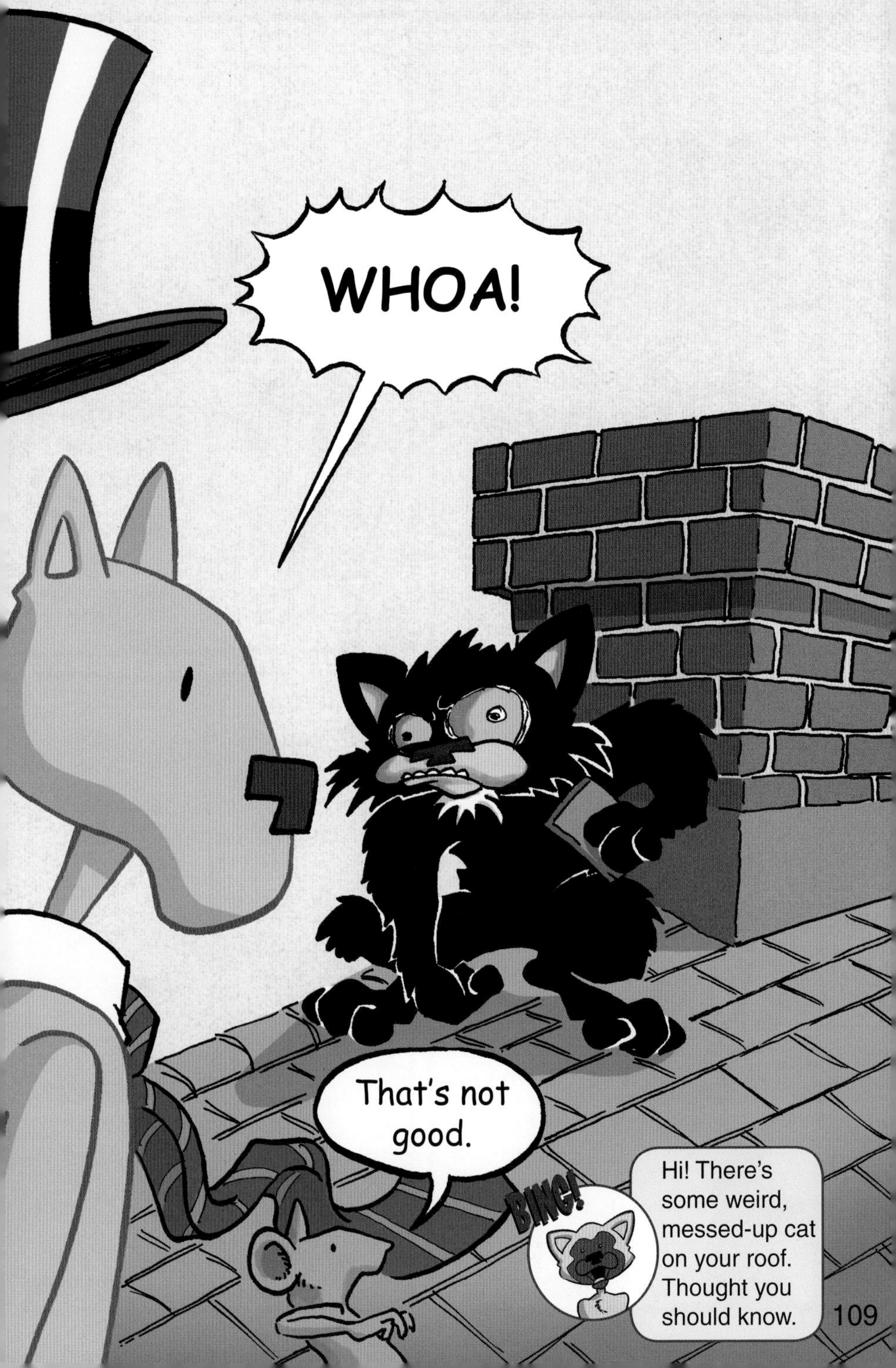
WHOA!
That's not good.
BING!
Hi! There's some weird, messed-up cat on your roof. Thought you should know.

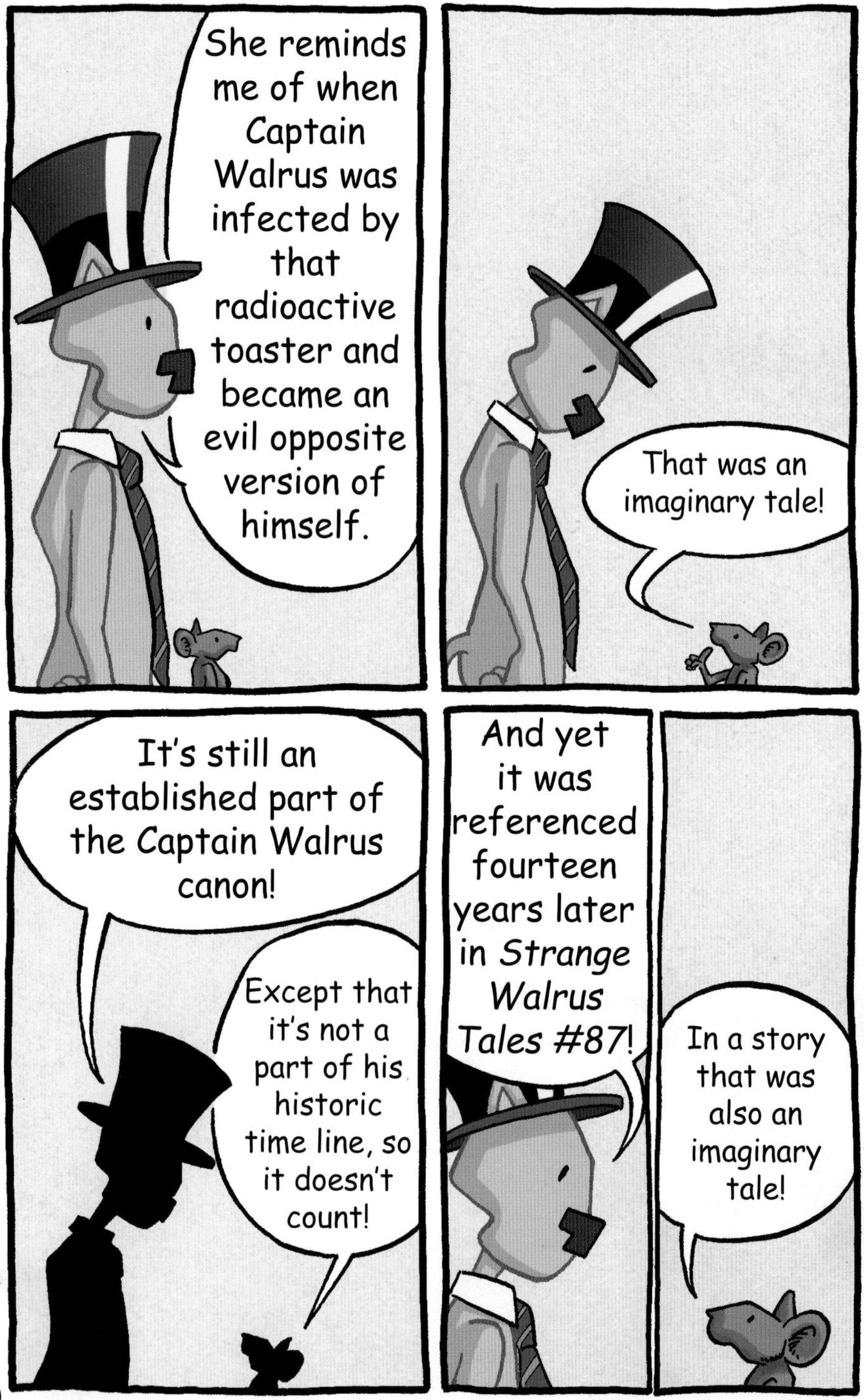
She reminds me of when Captain Walrus was infected by that radioactive toaster and became an evil opposite version of himself.
That was an imaginary tale!
It's still an established part of the Captain Walrus canon!
Except that it's not a part of his historic time line, so it doesn't count!
And yet it was referenced fourteen years later in *Strange Walrus Tales #87*!
In a story that was also an imaginary tale!

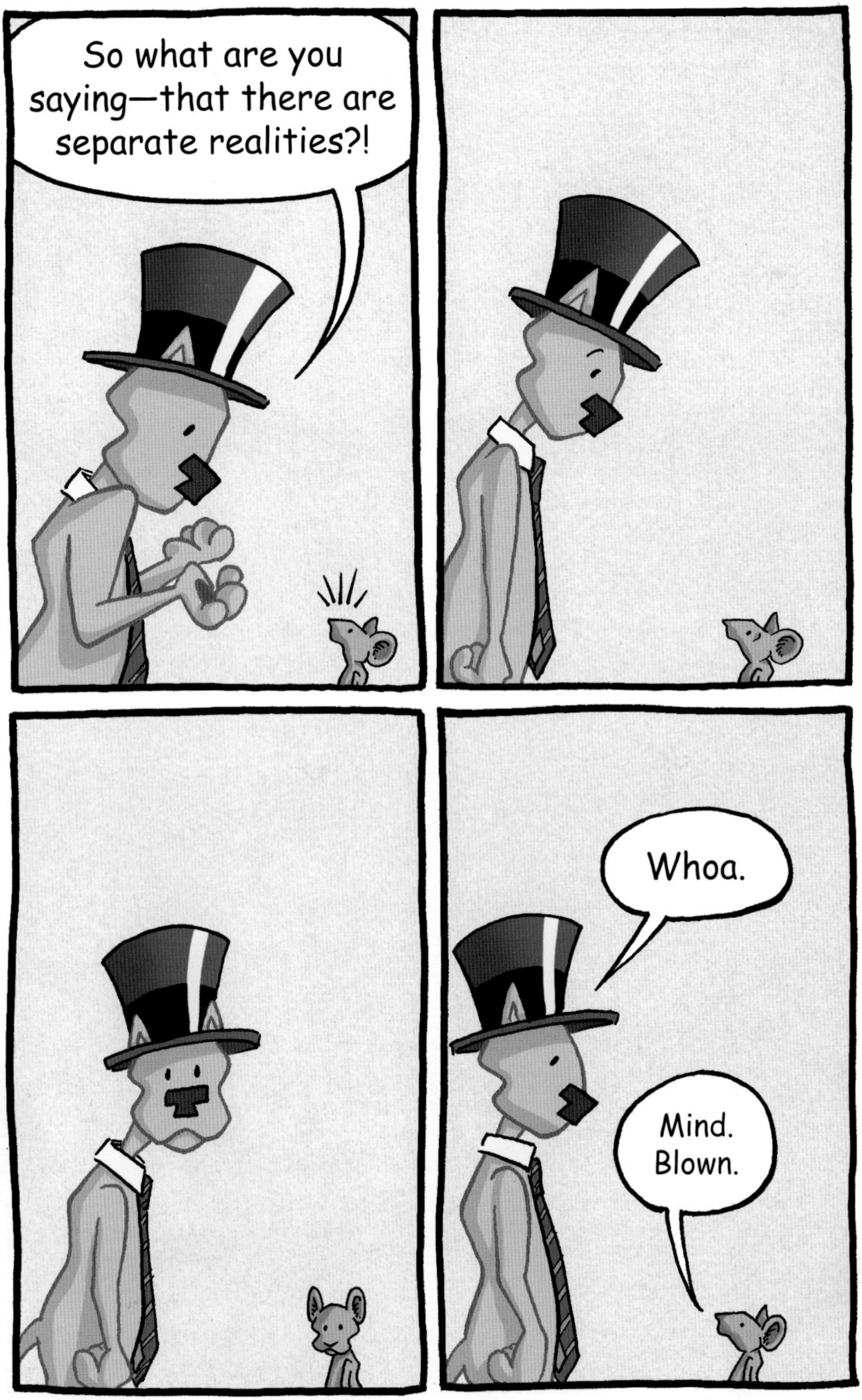
So what are you saying—that there are separate realities?!
Whoa.
Mind. Blown.

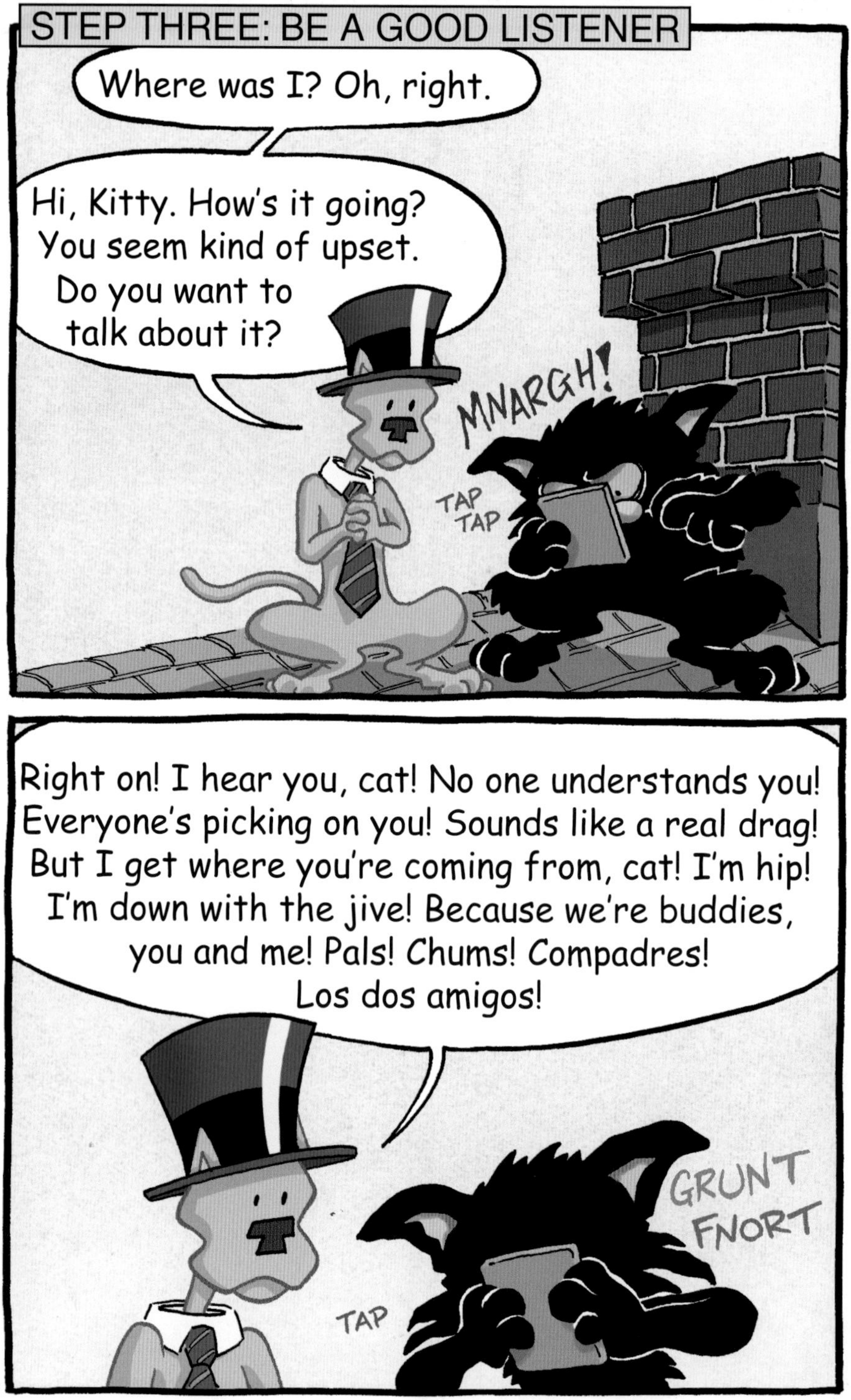
STEP THREE: BE A GOOD LISTENER
Where was I? Oh, right.
Hi, Kitty. How's it going? You seem kind of upset. Do you want to talk about it?
MNARGH!
TAP TAP
Right on! I hear you, cat! No one understands you! Everyone's picking on you! Sounds like a real drag! But I get where you're coming from, cat! I'm hip! I'm down with the jive! Because we're buddies, you and me! Pals! Chums! Compadres! Los dos amigos!
GRUNT FNORT
TAP

STEP FOUR: FIND COMMON GROUND

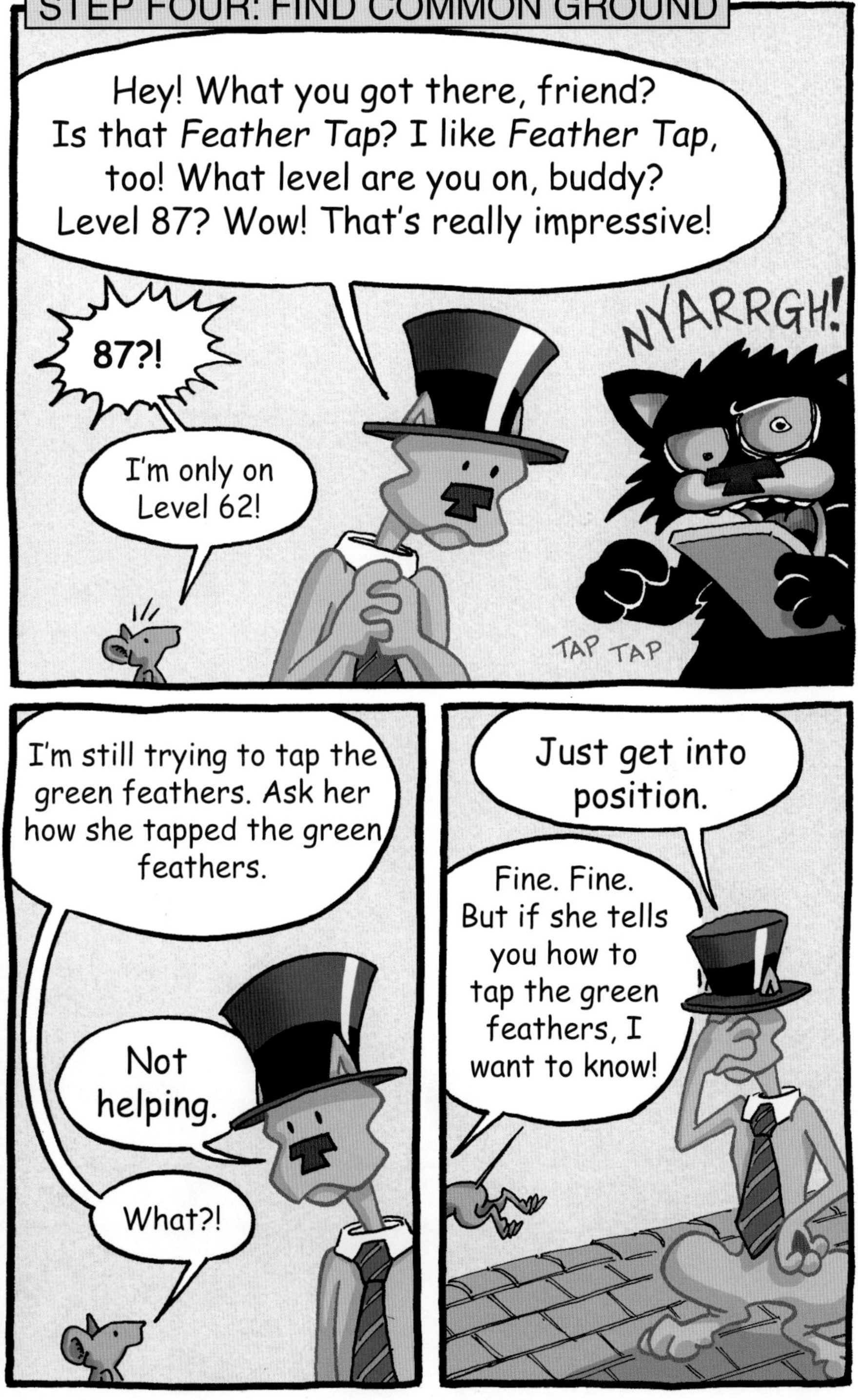
Hey! What you got there, friend? Is that *Feather Tap*? I like *Feather Tap*, too! What level are you on, buddy? Level 87? Wow! That's really impressive!
87?!
I'm only on Level 62!
NYARRGH!
TAP TAP
I'm still trying to tap the green feathers. Ask her how she tapped the green feathers.
Not helping.
What?!
Just get into position.
Fine. Fine. But if she tells you how to tap the green feathers, I want to know!

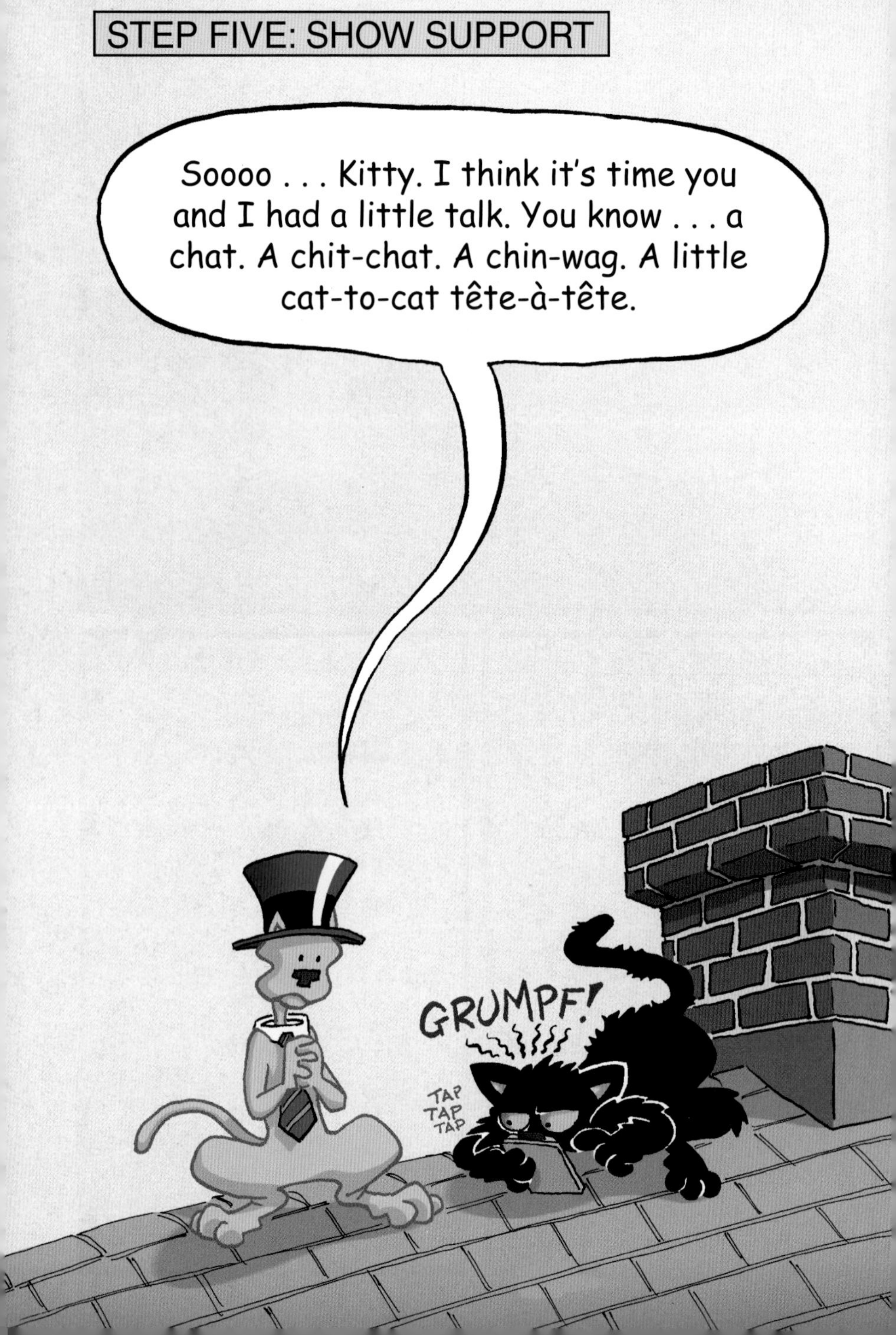
STEP FIVE: SHOW SUPPORT
Soooo . . . Kitty. I think it's time you and I had a little talk. You know . . . a chat. A chit-chat. A chin-wag. A little cat-to-cat tête-à-tête.
GRUMPF!
TAP TAP TAP

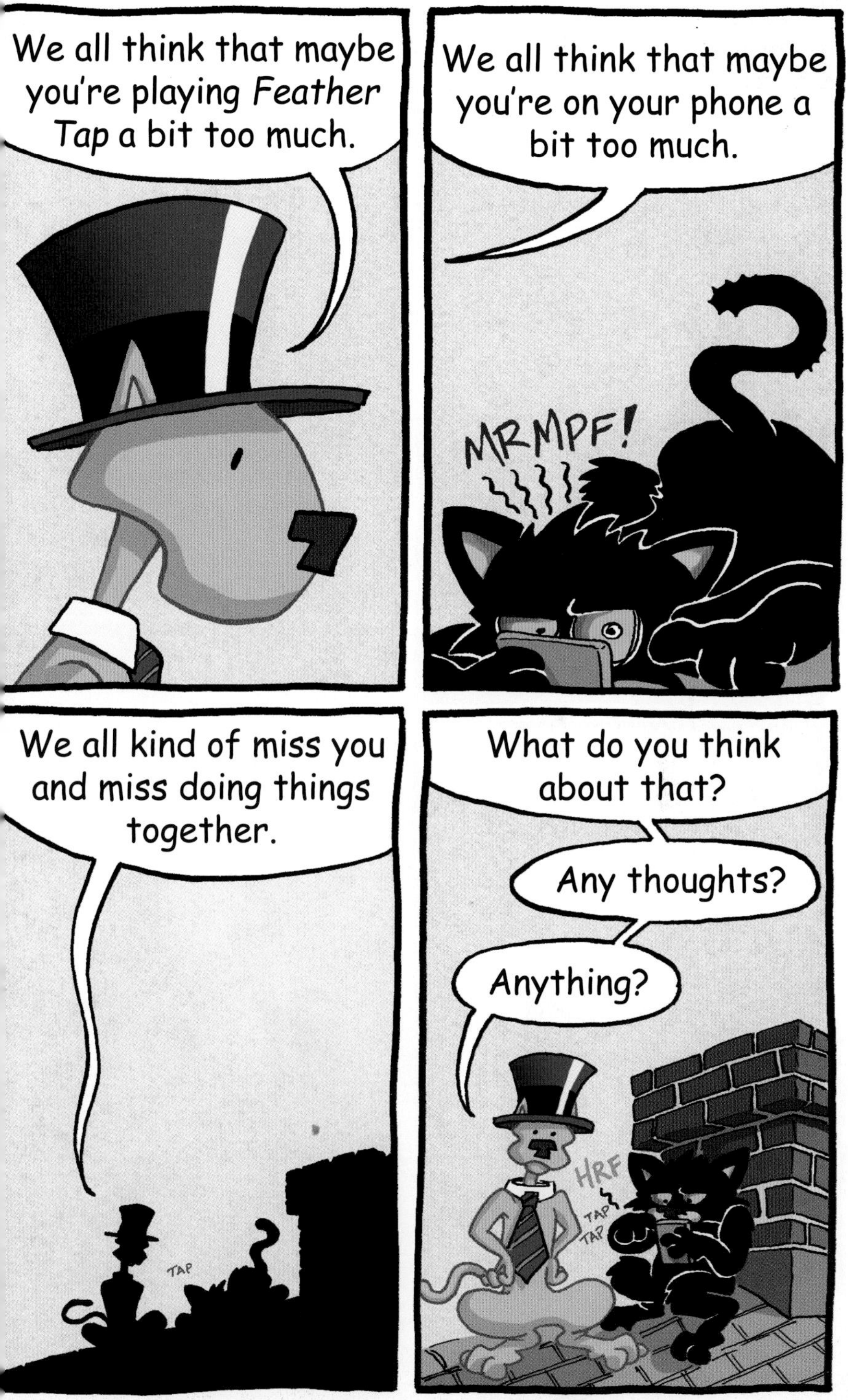
We all think that maybe you're playing *Feather Tap* a bit too much.
We all think that maybe you're on your phone a bit too much.
MRMPF!
We all kind of miss you and miss doing things together.
TAP
What do you think about that?
Any thoughts?
Anything?
HRF
TAP
TAP

STEP SIX: SHOW THAT YOU'RE SERIOUS

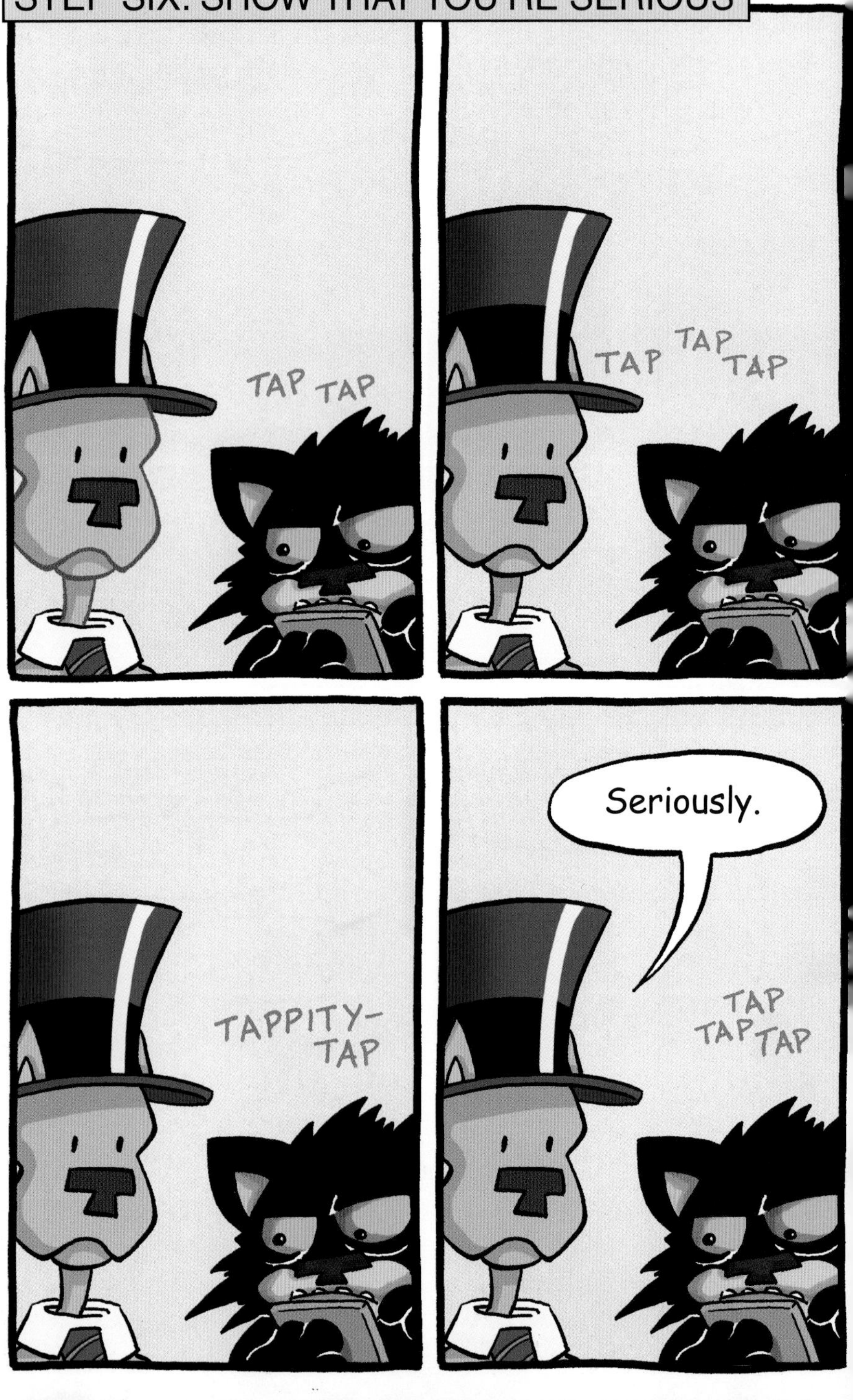

TAP TAP
TAP TAP TAP
TAPPITY-TAP
Seriously.
TAP TAP TAP

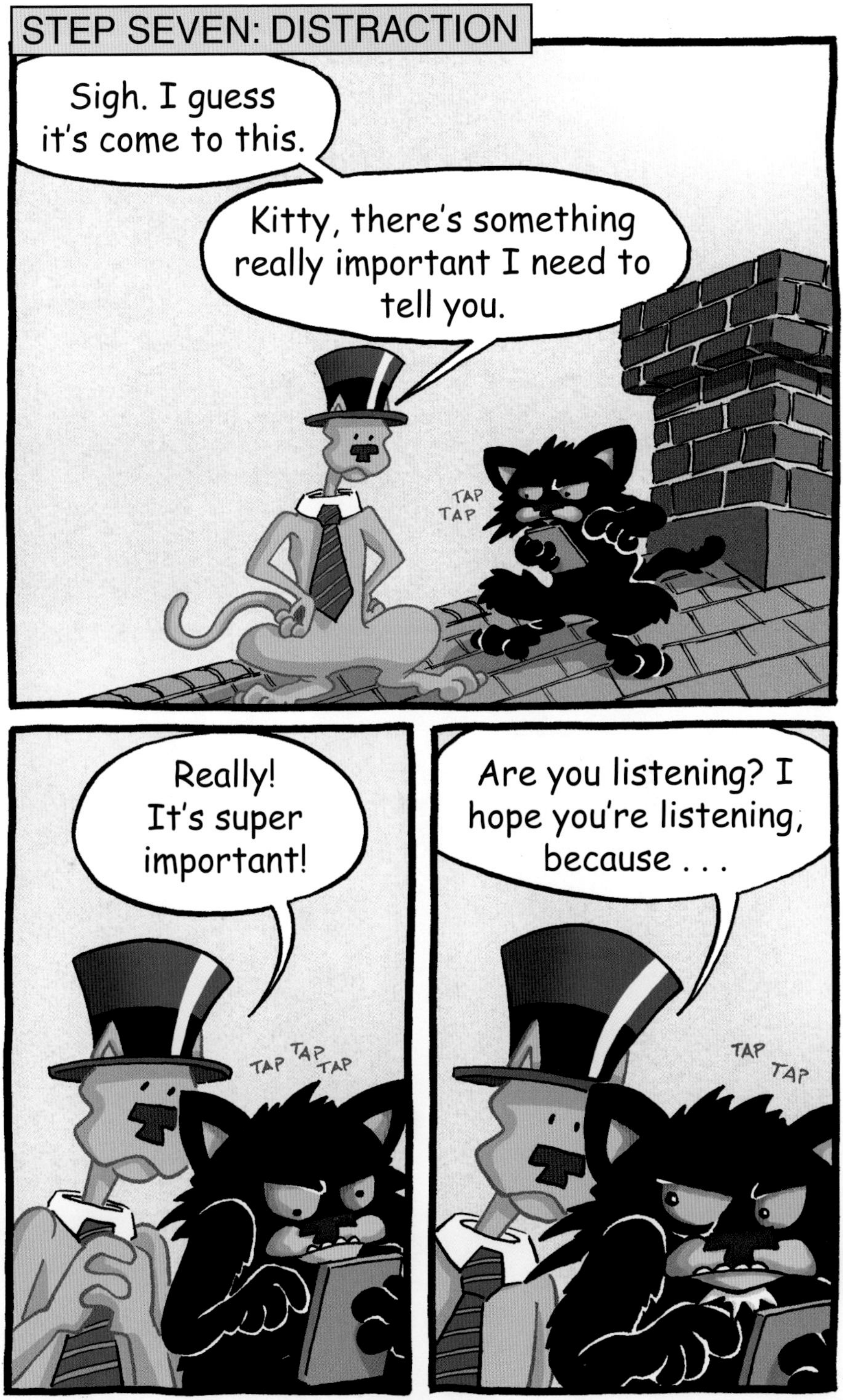
STEP SEVEN: DISTRACTION
Sigh. I guess it's come to this.
Kitty, there's something really important I need to tell you.
TAP TAP
Really! It's super important!
TAP TAP TAP
Are you listening? I hope you're listening, because . . .
TAP TAP

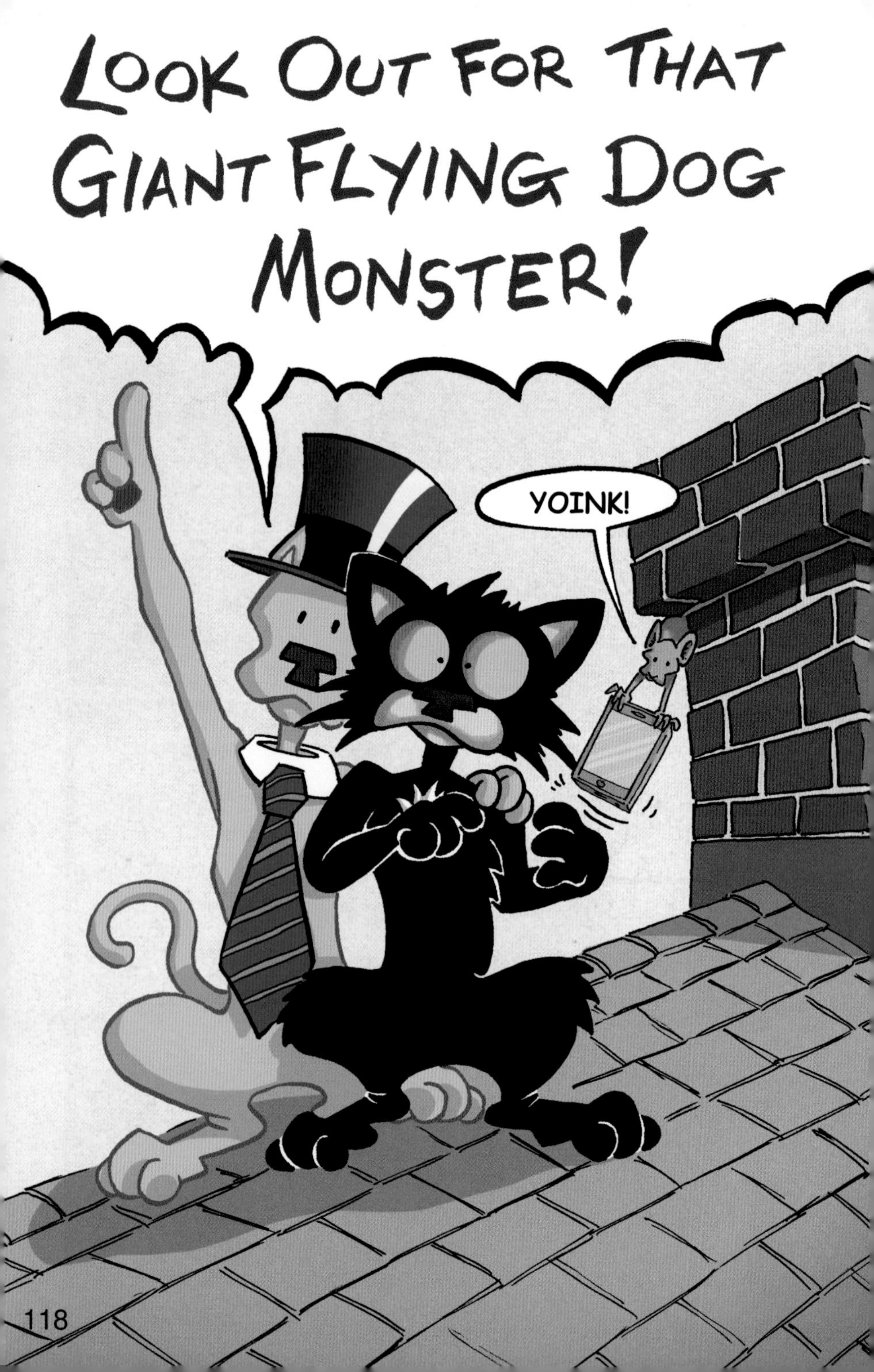
LOOK OUT FOR THAT GIANT FLYING DOG MONSTER!
YOINK!

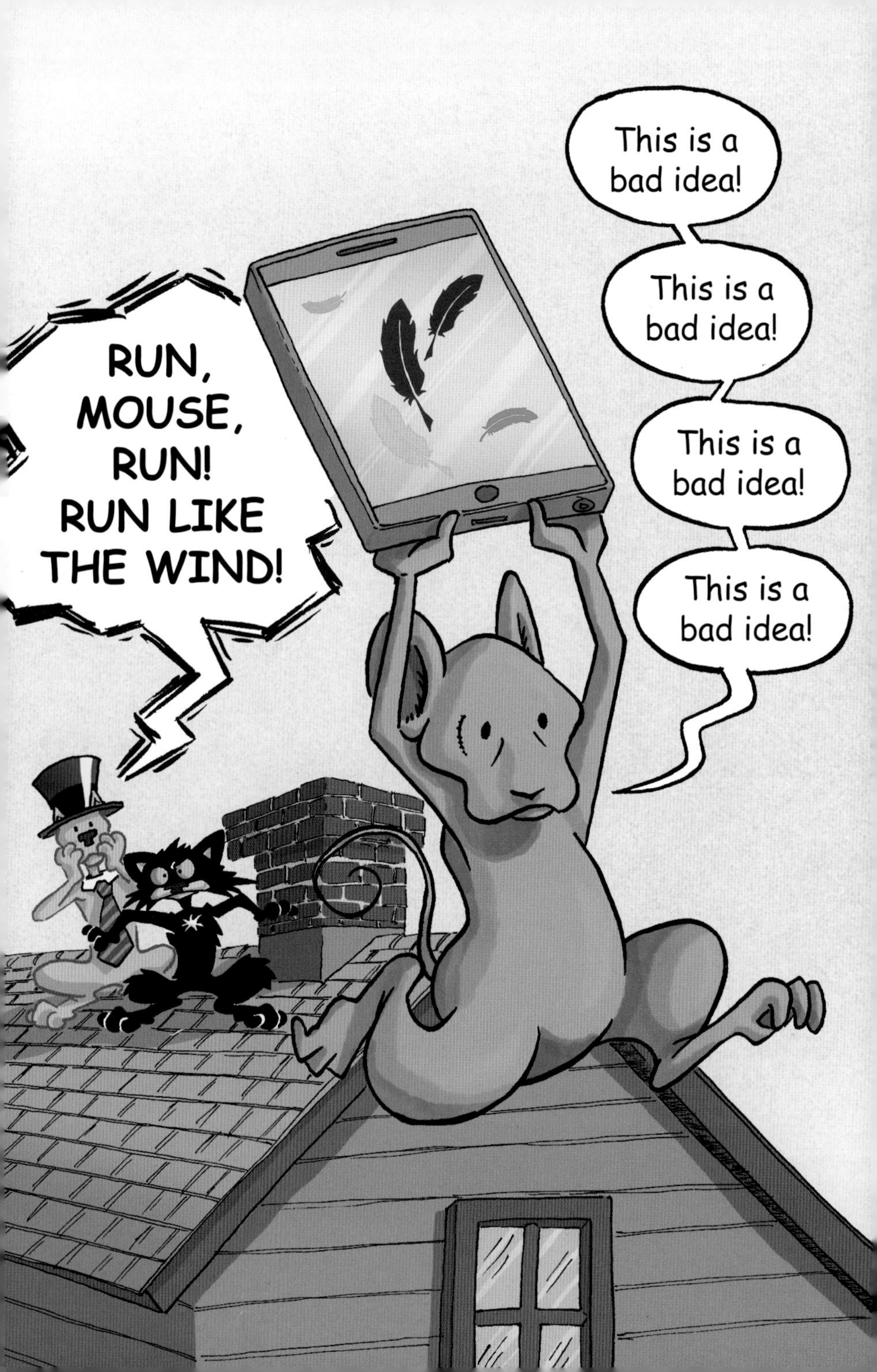
RUN, MOUSE, RUN! RUN LIKE THE WIND!
This is a bad idea!
This is a bad idea!
This is a bad idea!
This is a bad idea!

121

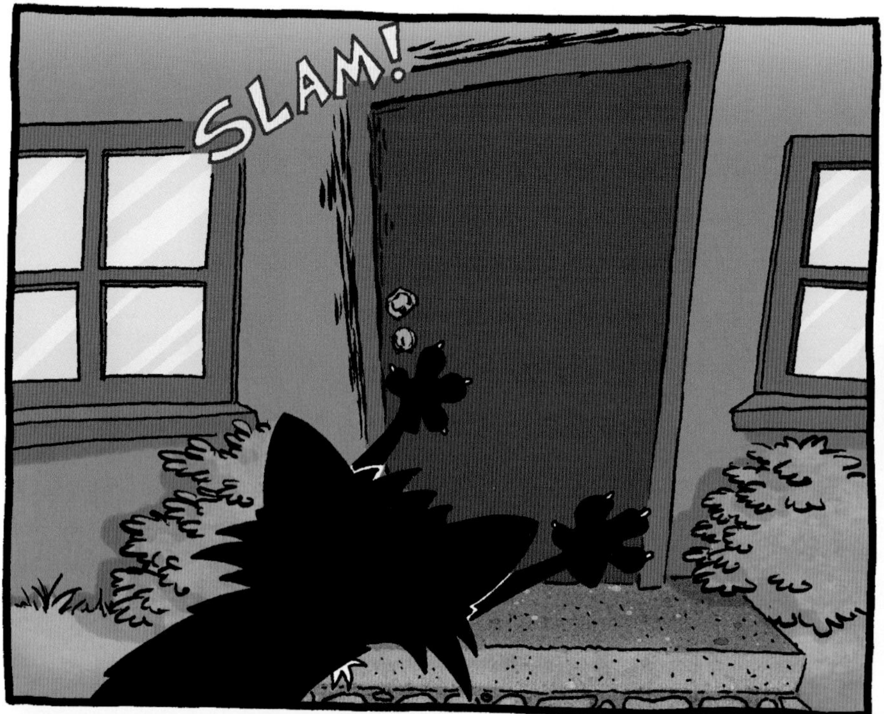
SLAM!

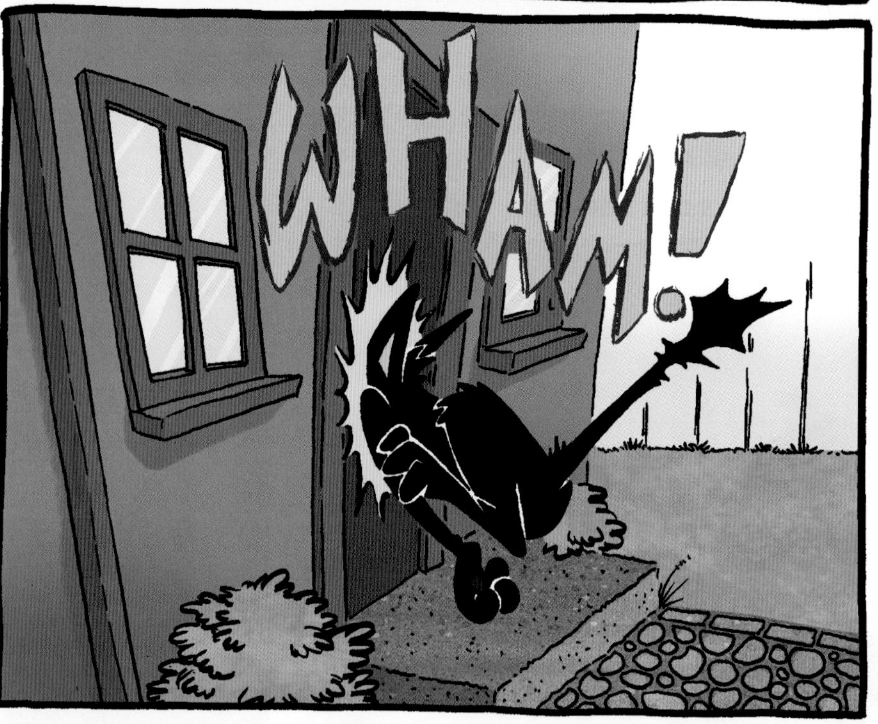
WHAM!

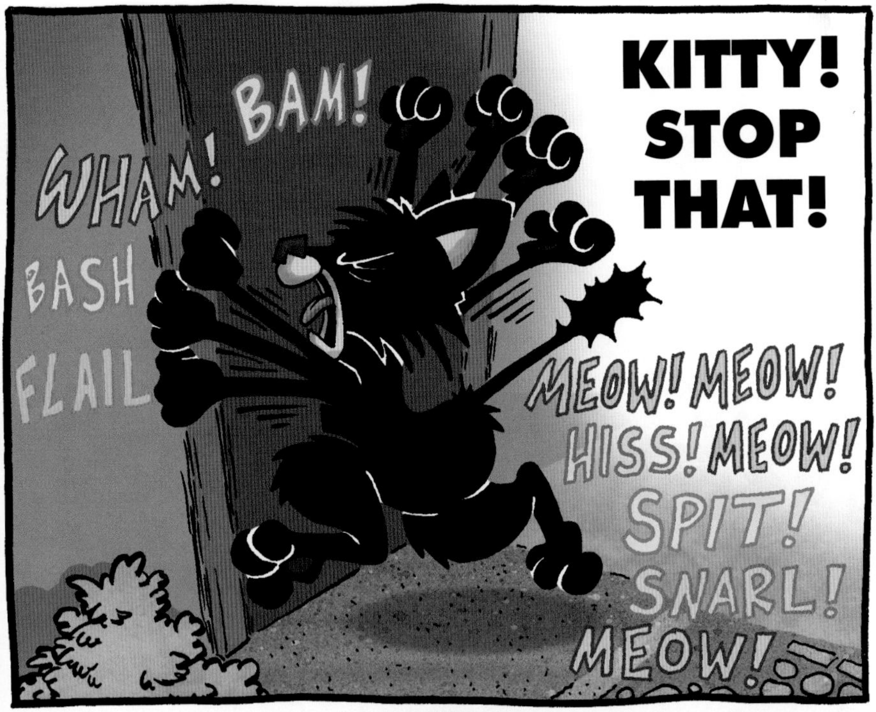
KITTY! STOP THAT!
BAM!
WHAM!
BASH
FLAIL
MEOW! MEOW!
HISS! MEOW!
SPIT!
SNARL!
MEOW!

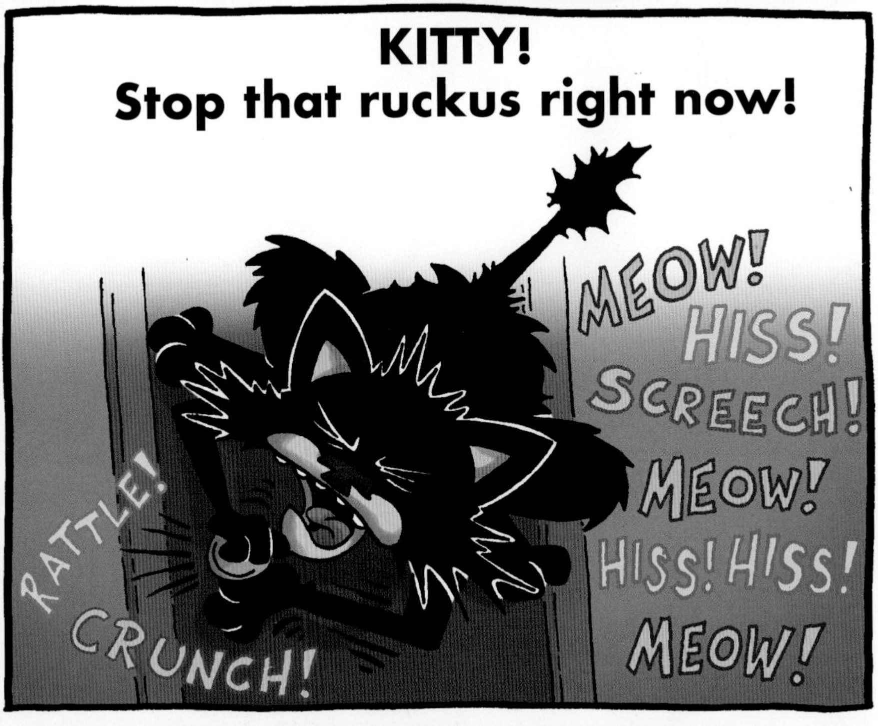
KITTY!
Stop that ruckus right now!
MEOW!
HISS!
SCREECH!
MEOW!
HISS! HISS!
MEOW!
RATTLE!
CRUNCH!

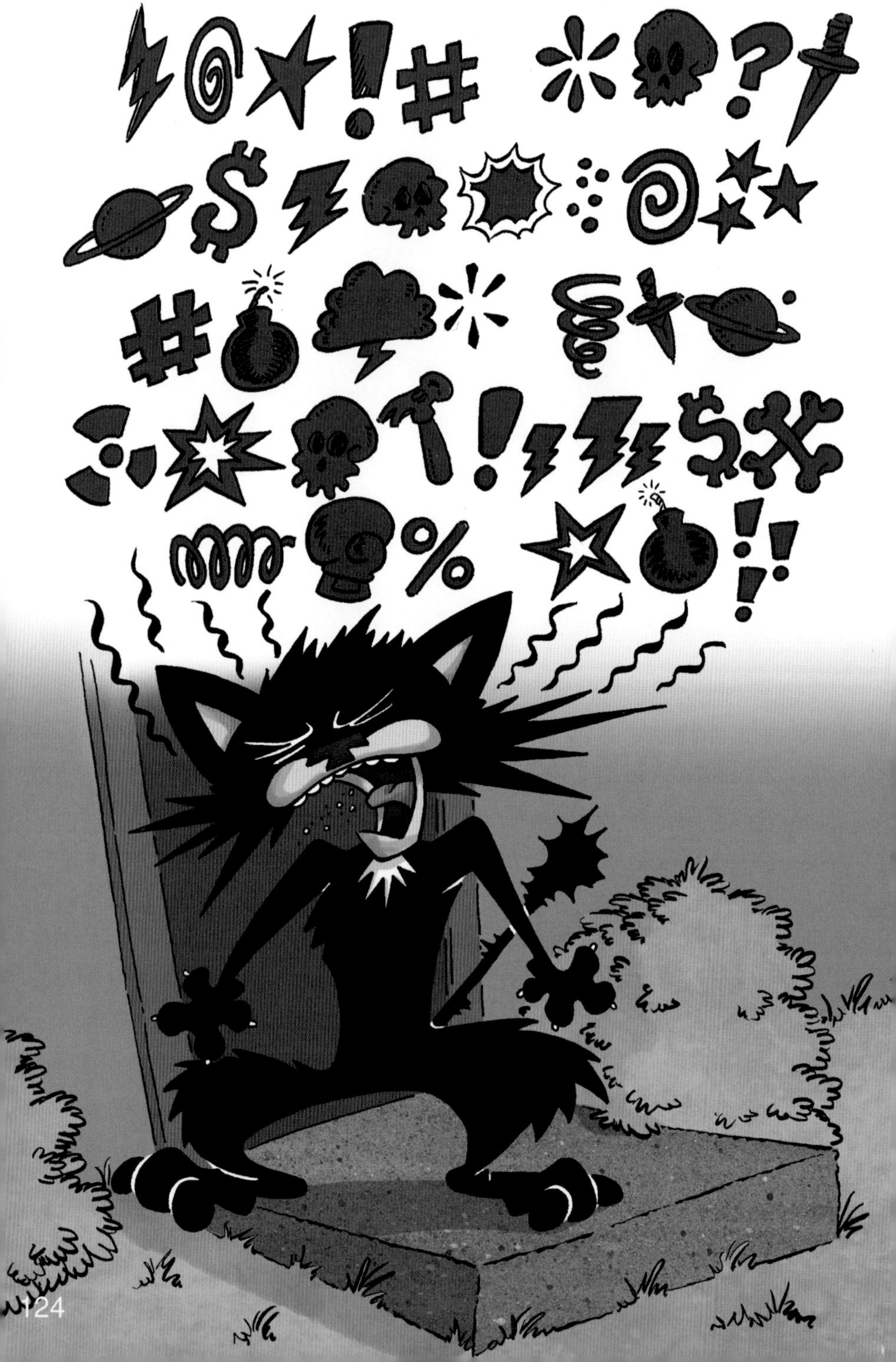

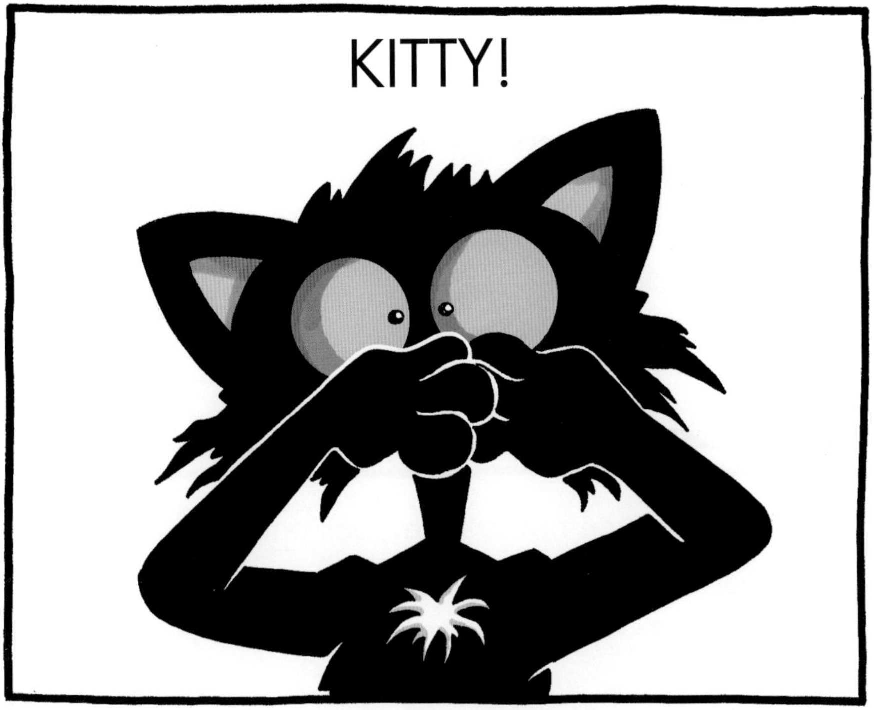
KITTY!

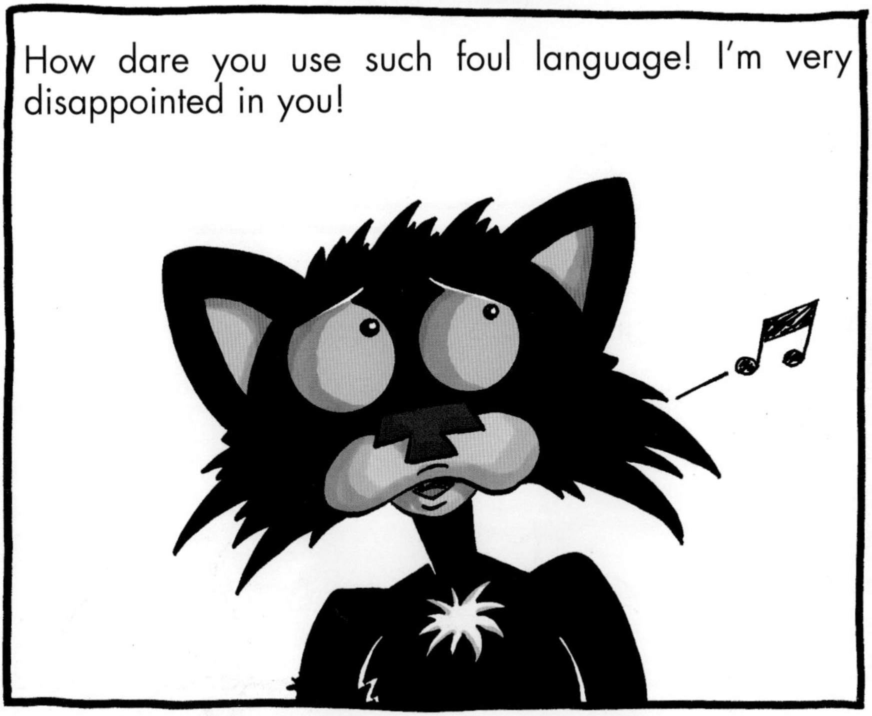
How dare you use such foul language! I'm very disappointed in you!

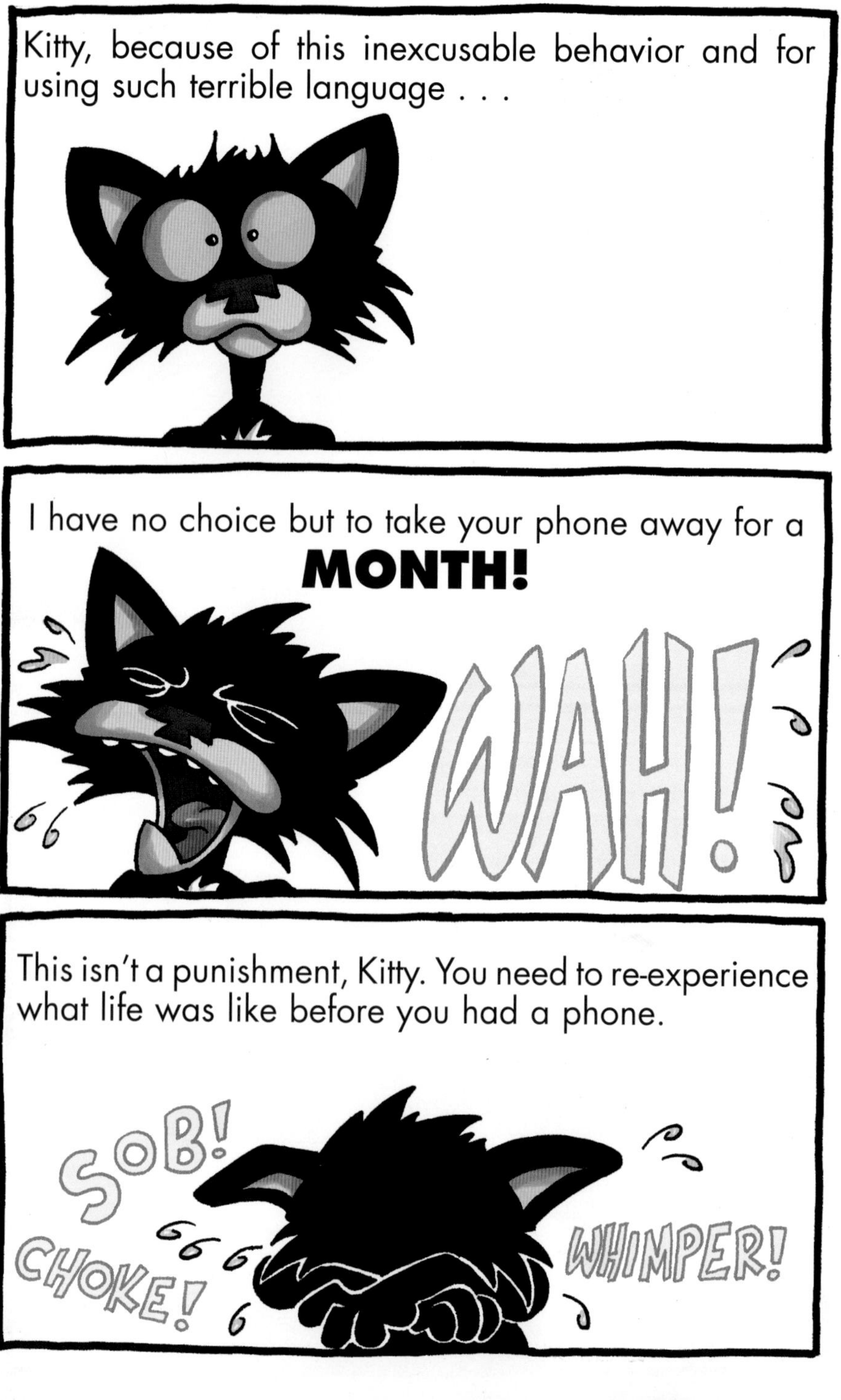
Kitty, because of this inexcusable behavior and for using such terrible language . . .
I have no choice but to take your phone away for a **MONTH!**
WAH!
This isn't a punishment, Kitty. You need to re-experience what life was like before you had a phone.
SOB!
CHOKE!
WHIMPER!

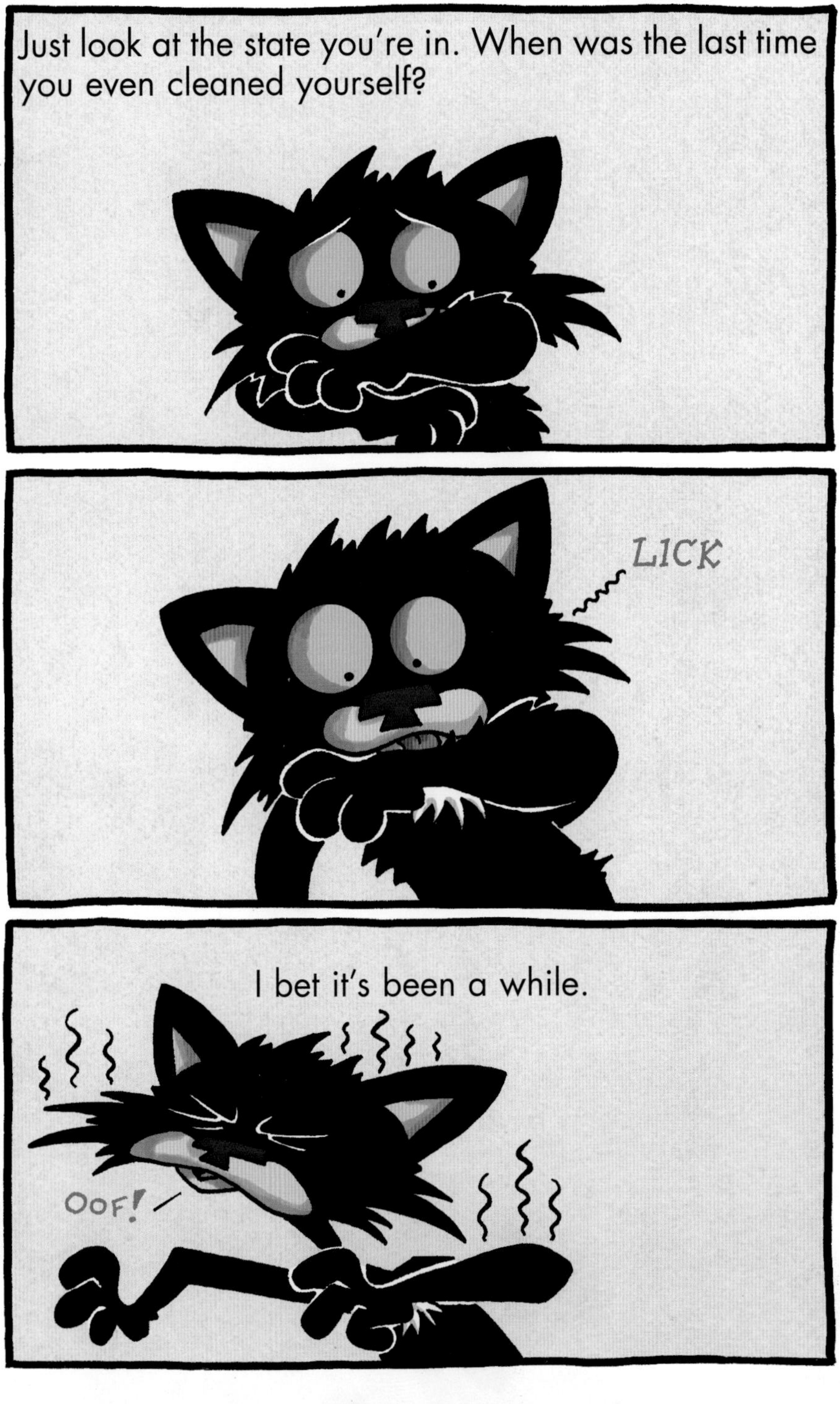

Just look at the state you're in. When was the last time you even cleaned yourself?
LICK
I bet it's been a while.
OOF!

Kitty, a cell phone can be an amazing thing. It can open the world up to you in an instant. But as you've discovered, it can also take you to places that are . . .

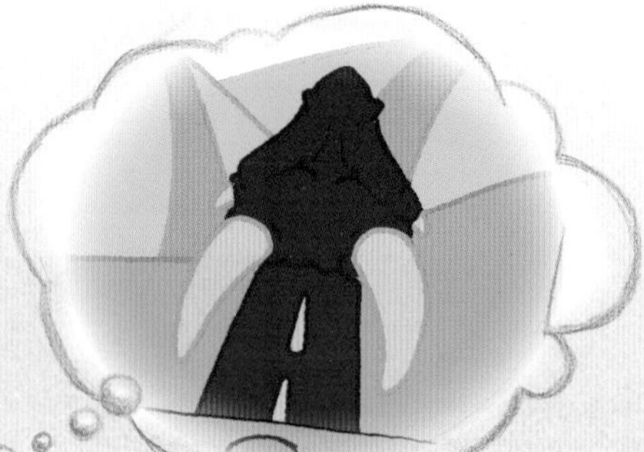

too violent . . .

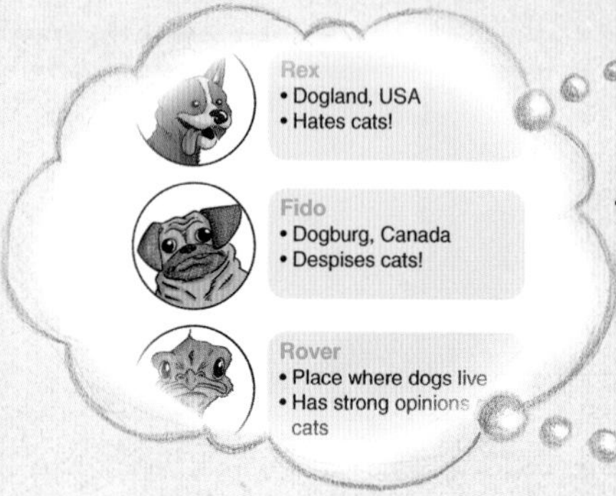
Rex
• Dogland, USA
• Hates cats!
Fido
• Dogburg, Canada
• Despises cats!
Rover
• Place where dogs live
• Has strong opinions
cats

too suspicious . . .

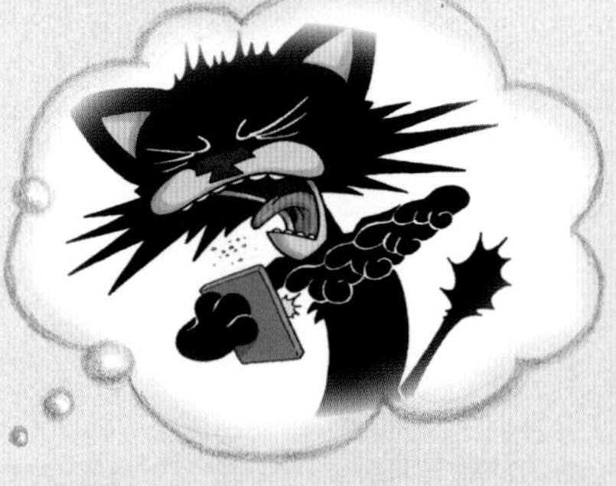

too angry . . .

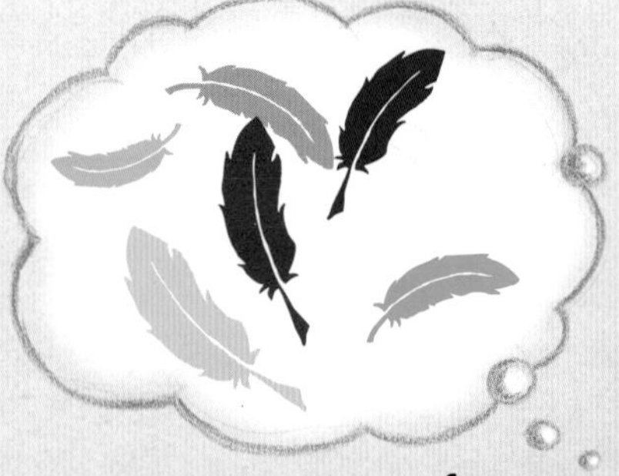

or too tempting for a young cat like yourself.

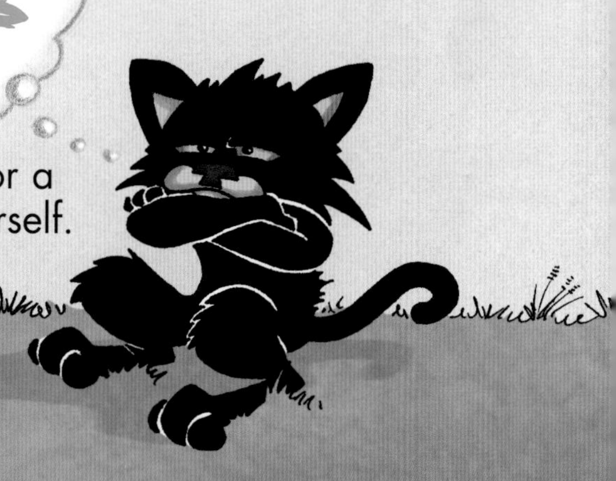

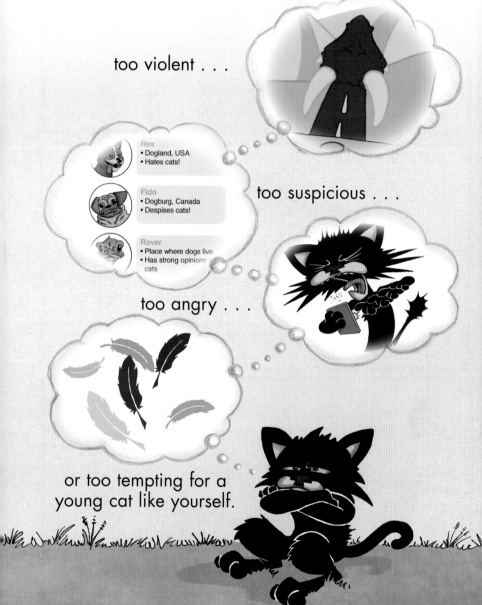

I'm sorry you won't have your phone for a month, Kitty, but I think it's for the best.

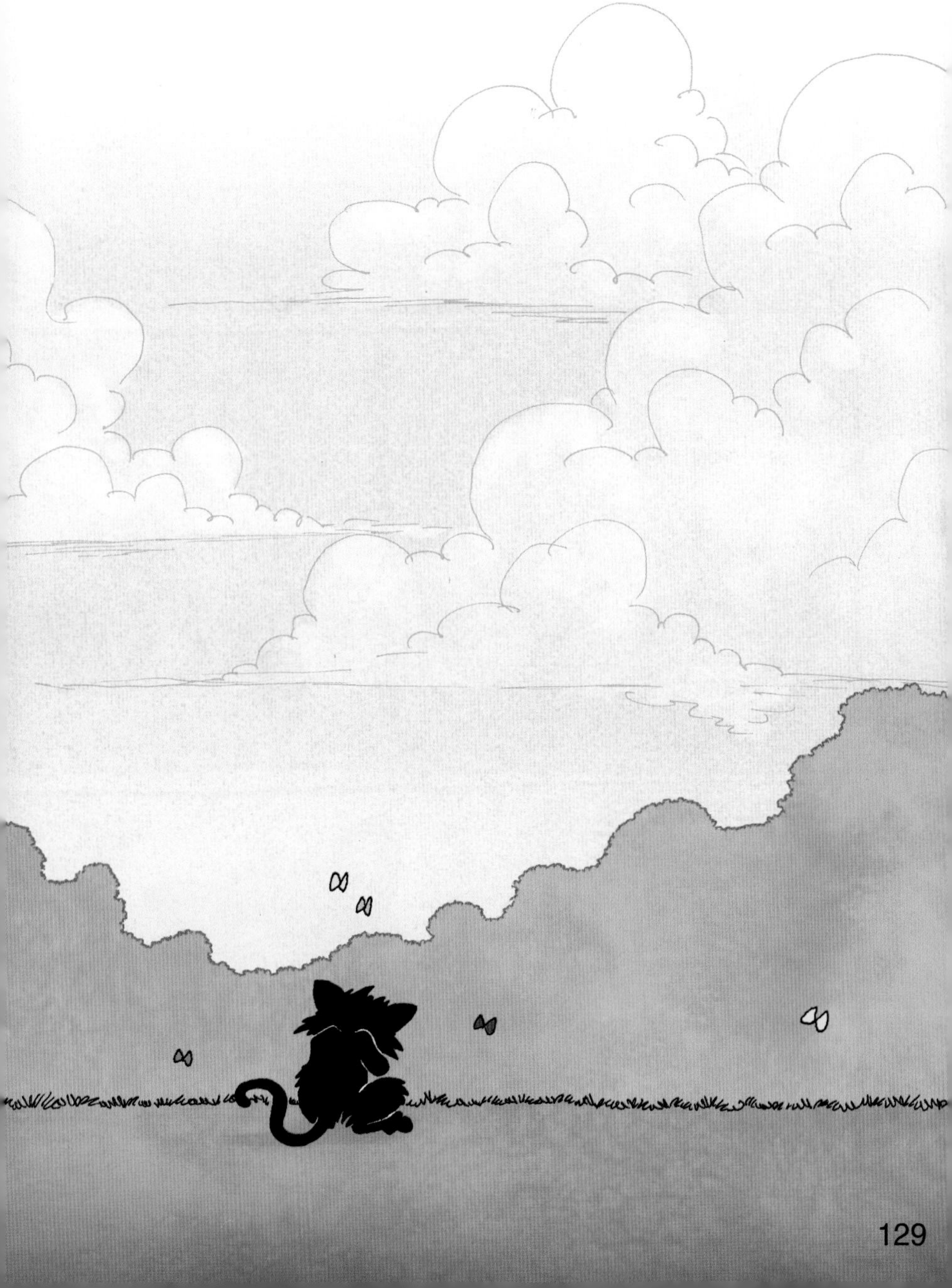

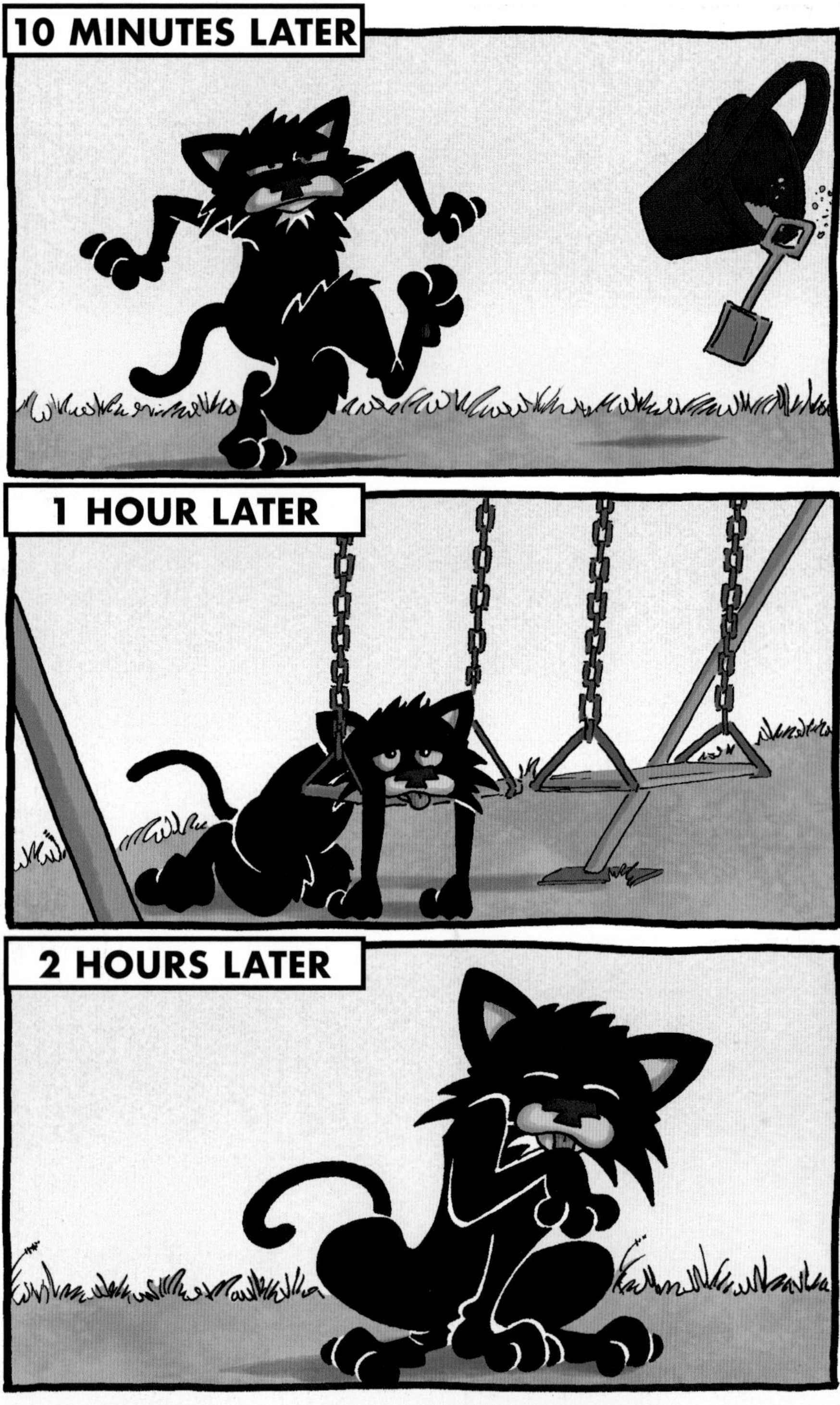
10 MINUTES LATER
1 HOUR LATER
2 HOURS LATER

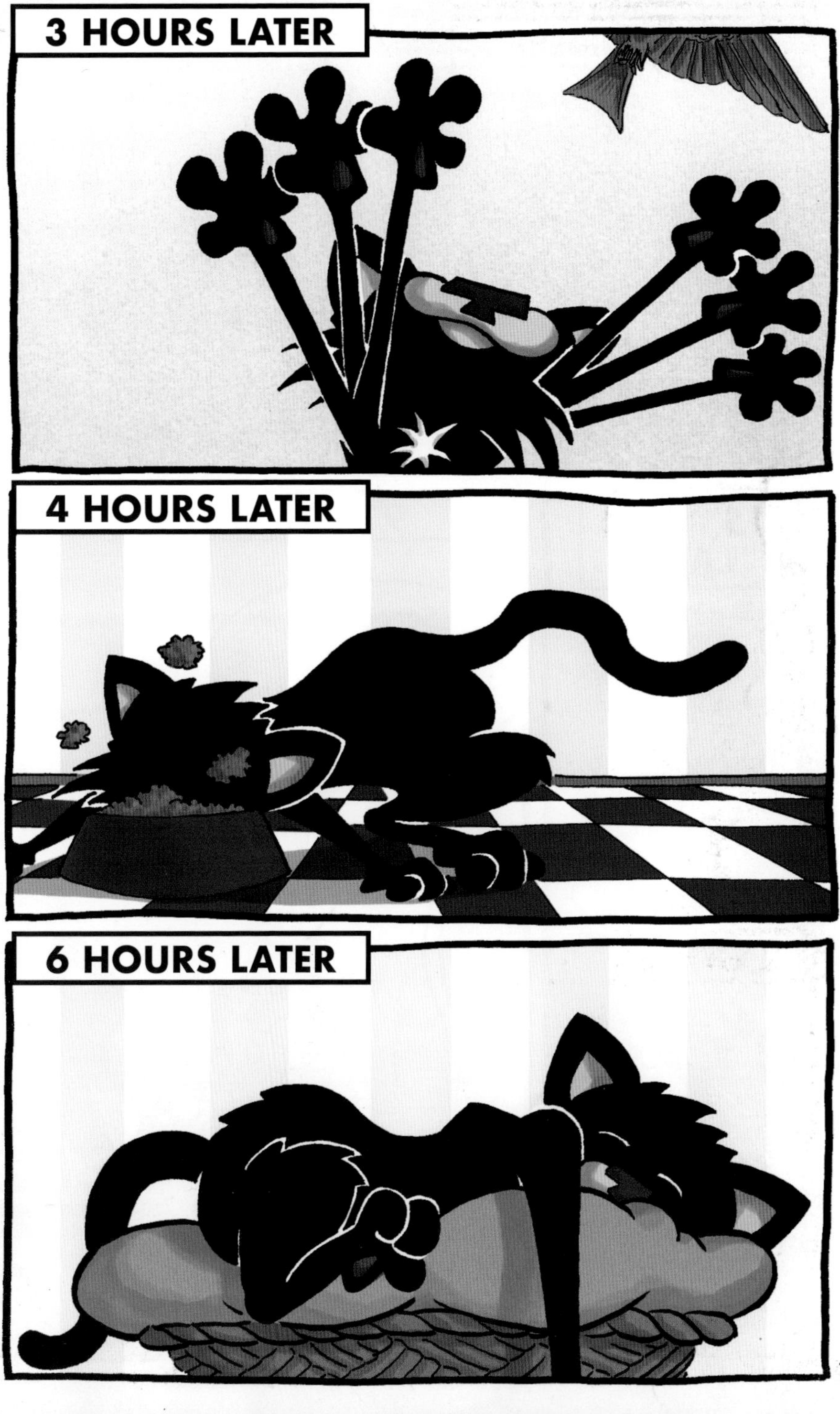
3 HOURS LATER
4 HOURS LATER
6 HOURS LATER

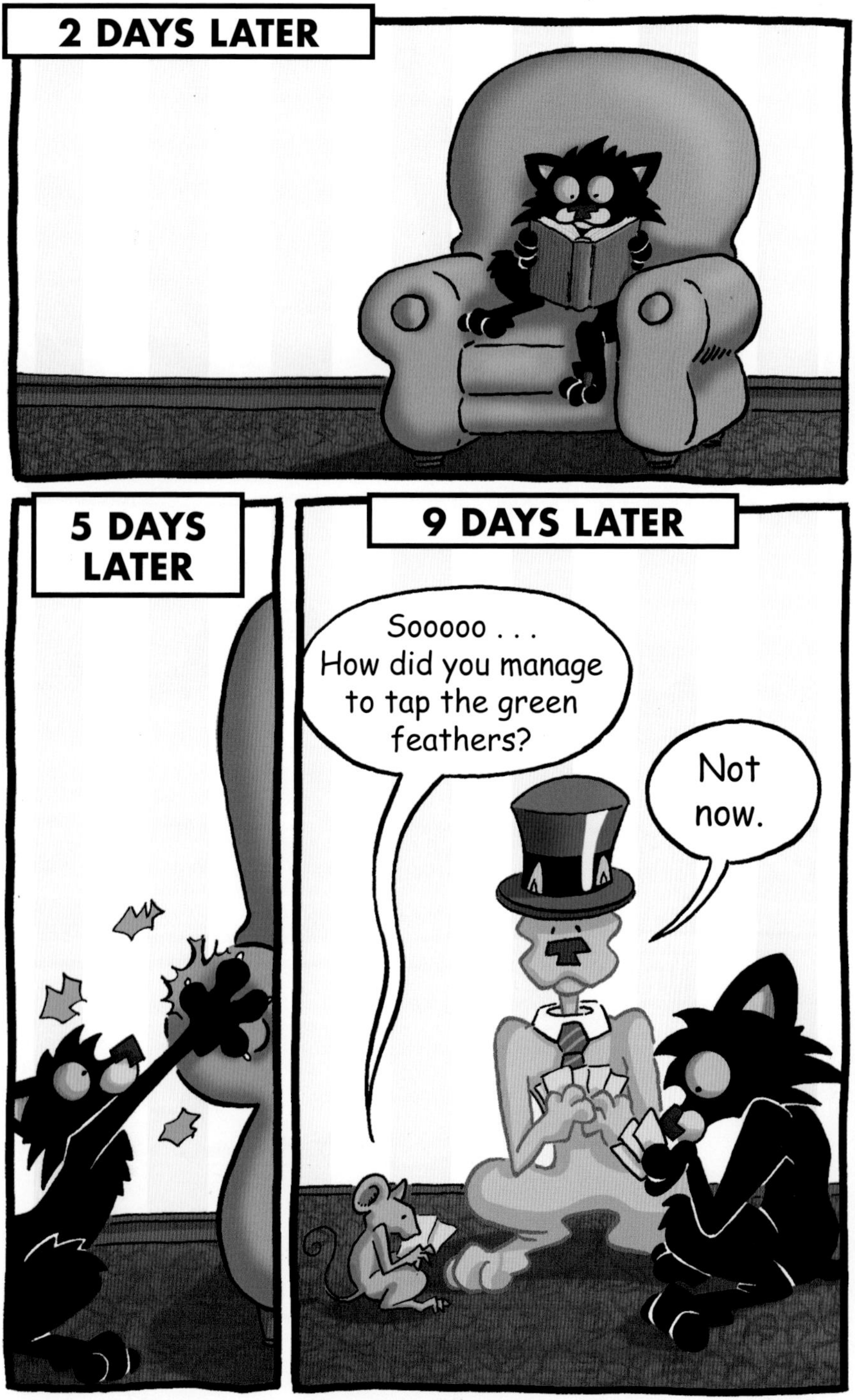
2 DAYS LATER
5 DAYS LATER
9 DAYS LATER
Sooooo . . . How did you manage to tap the green feathers?
Not now.

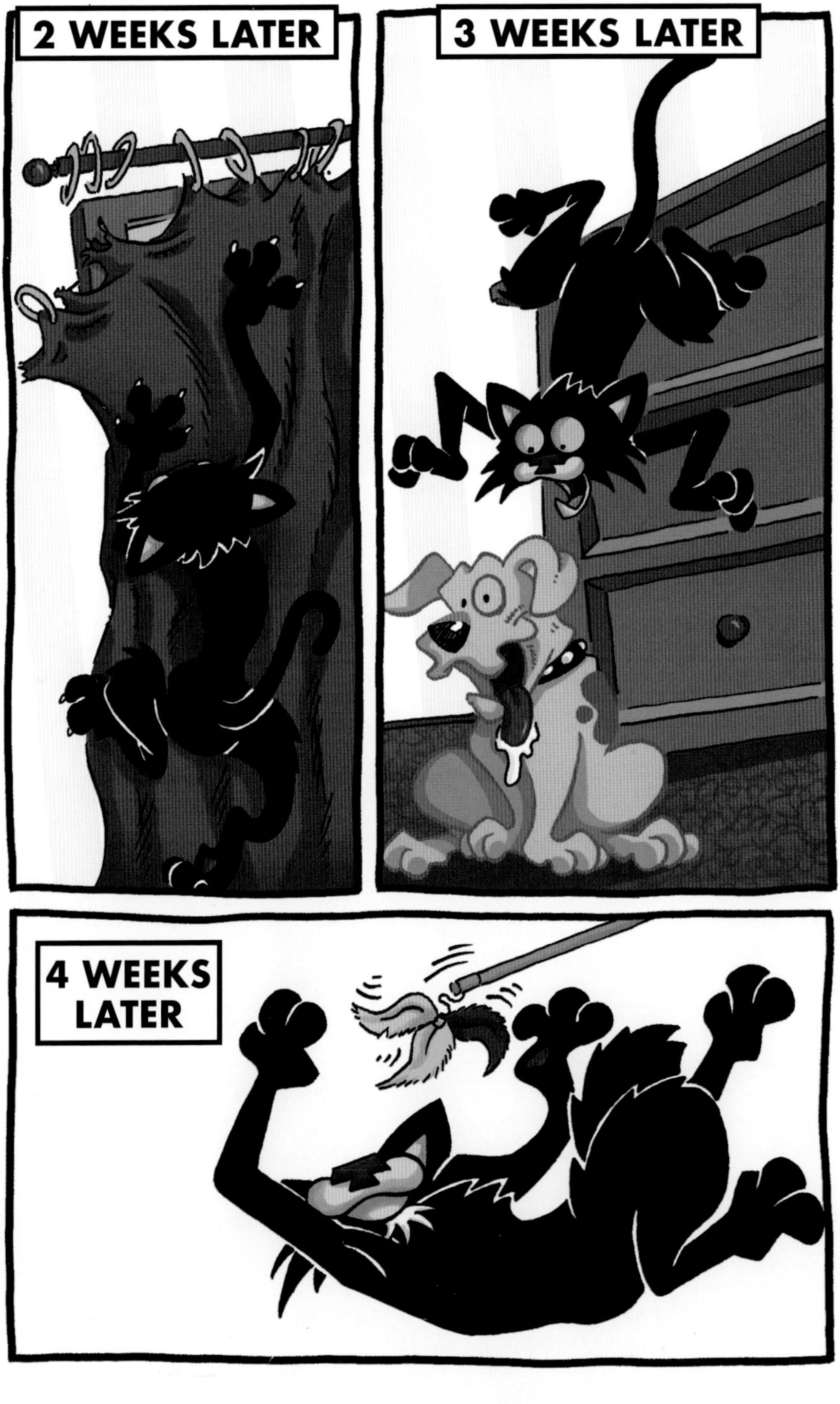
2 WEEKS LATER
3 WEEKS LATER
4 WEEKS LATER

•CHAPTER NINE•

ONE MONTH LATER

Well, Kitty, it's been a whole month. You can have your phone back.

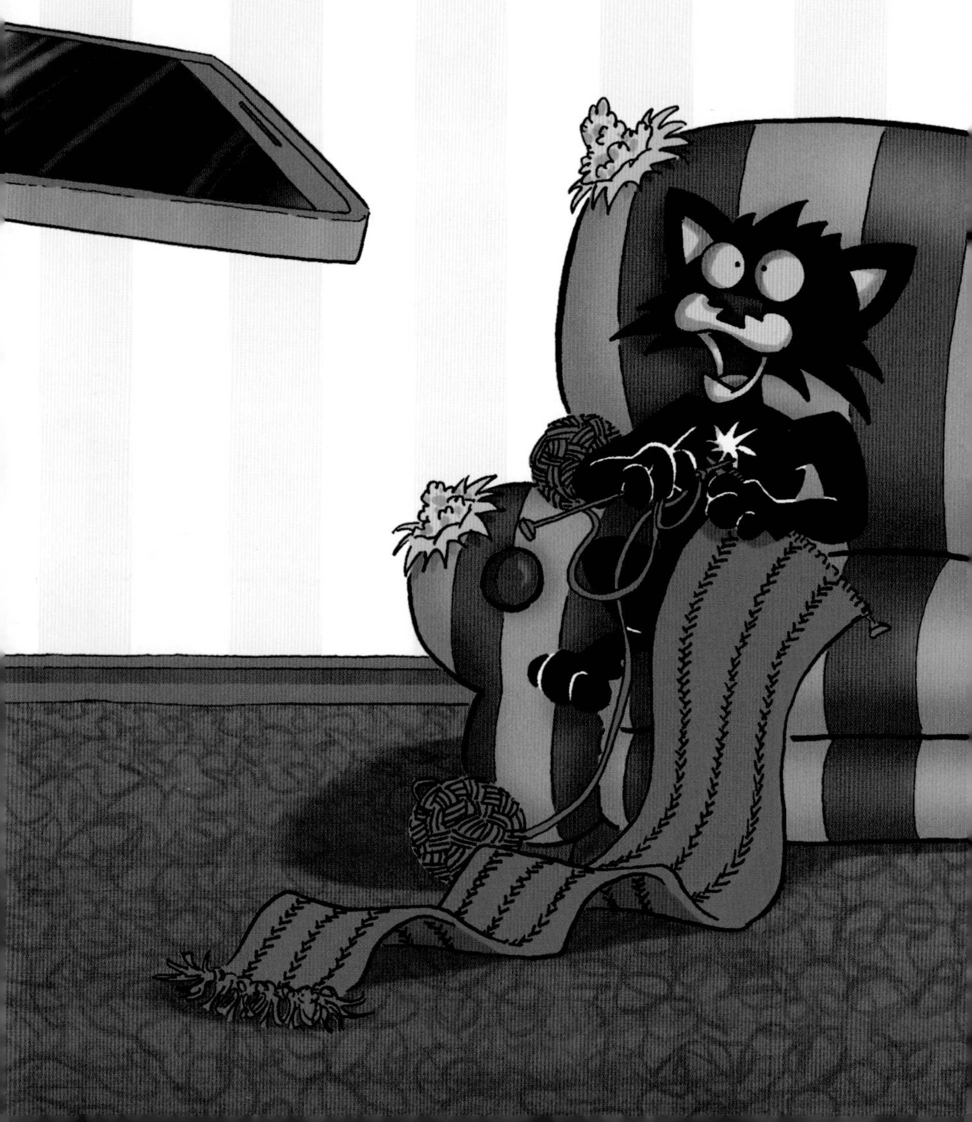

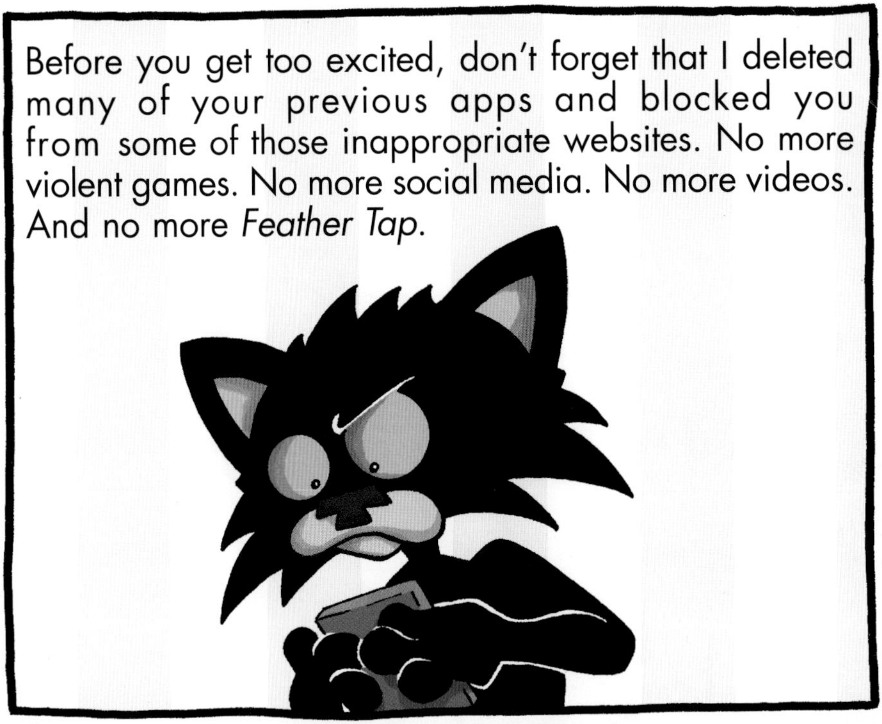
Before you get too excited, don't forget that I deleted many of your previous apps and blocked you from some of those inappropriate websites. No more violent games. No more social media. No more videos. And no more *Feather Tap*.

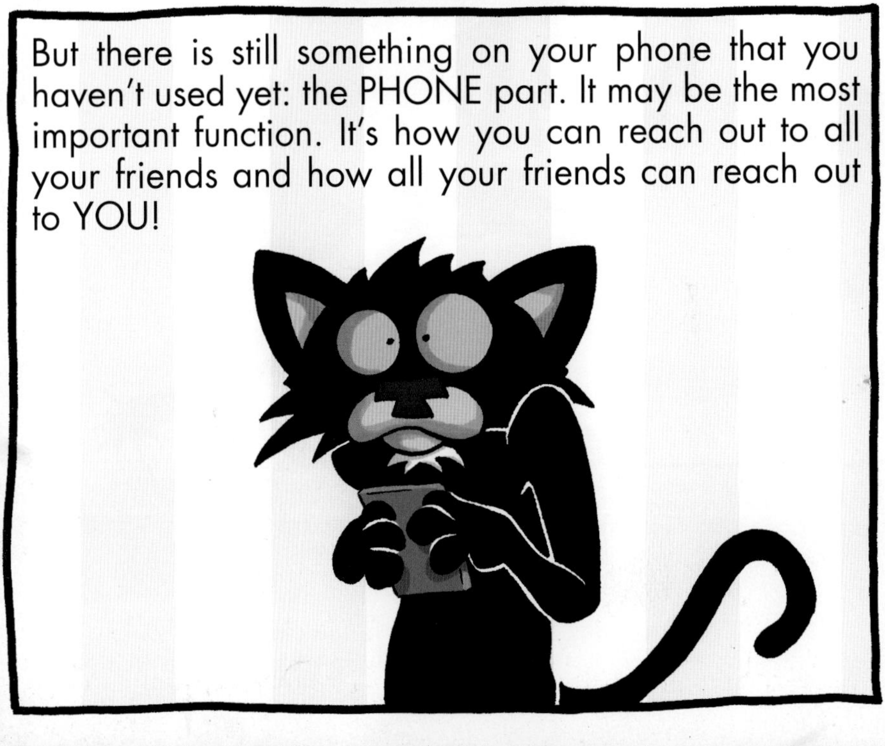
But there is still something on your phone that you haven't used yet: the PHONE part. It may be the most important function. It's how you can reach out to all your friends and how all your friends can reach out to YOU!

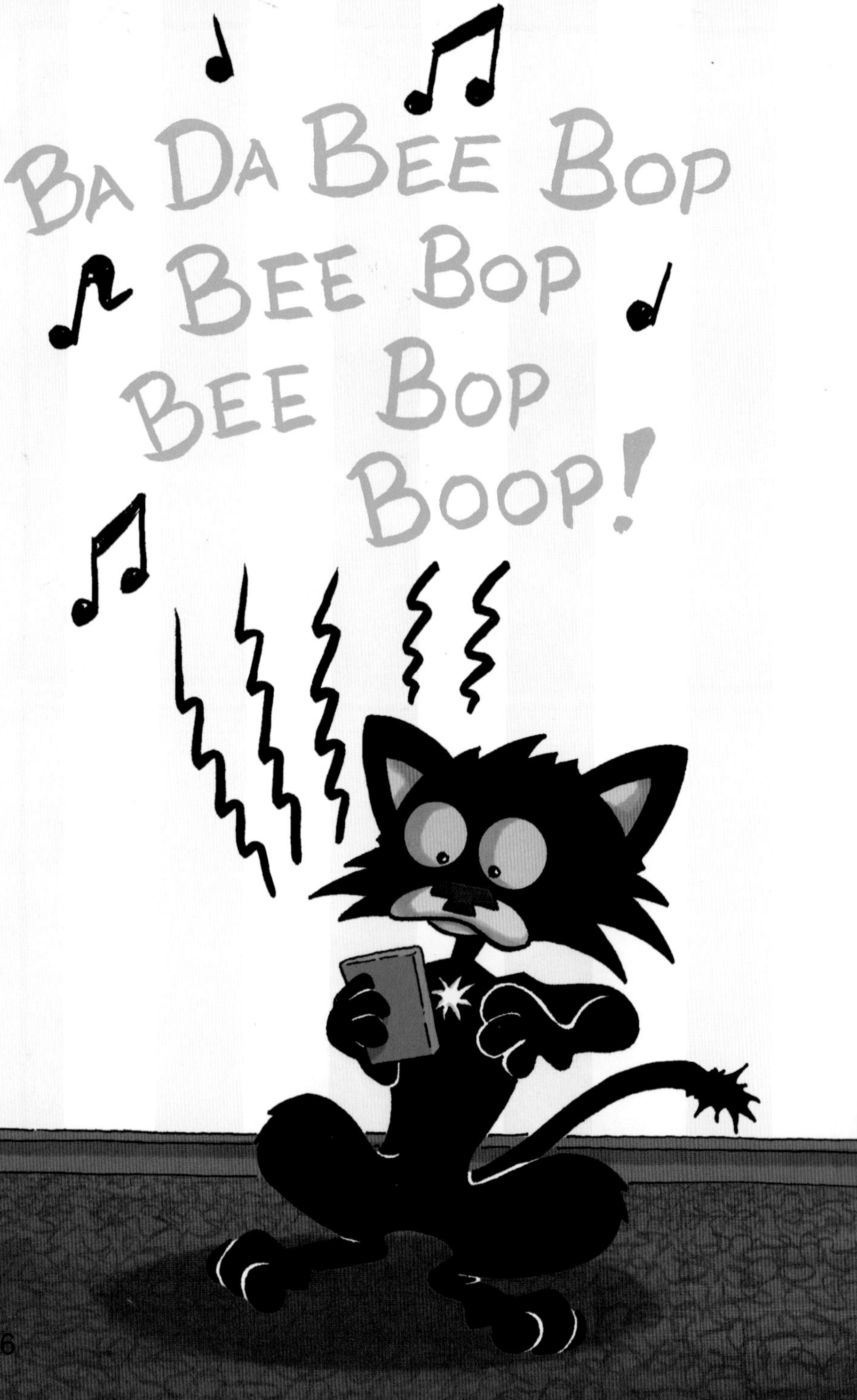
BA DA BEE BOP
BEE BOP
BEE BOP
BOOP!

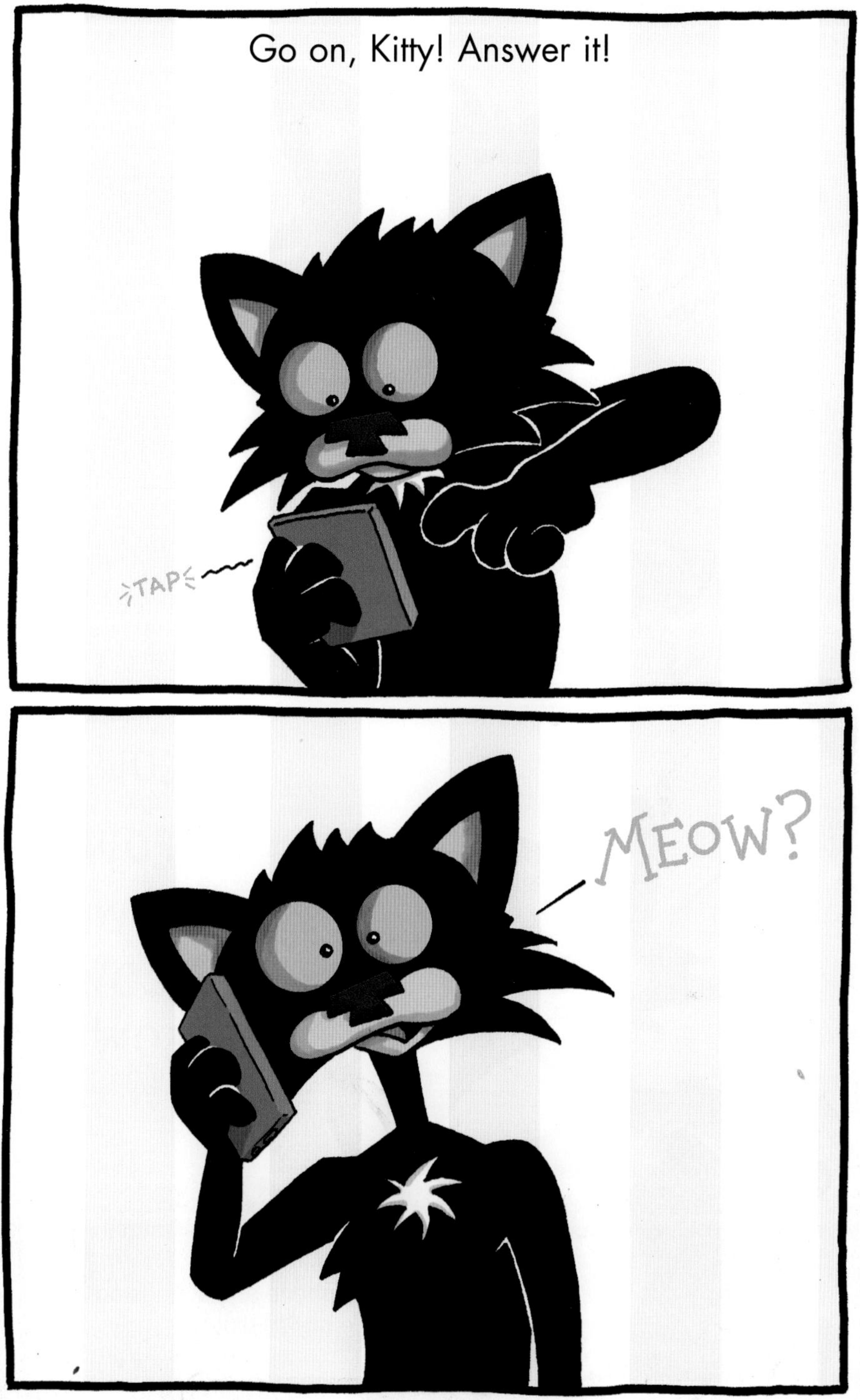
Go on, Kitty! Answer it!
TAP
MEOW?

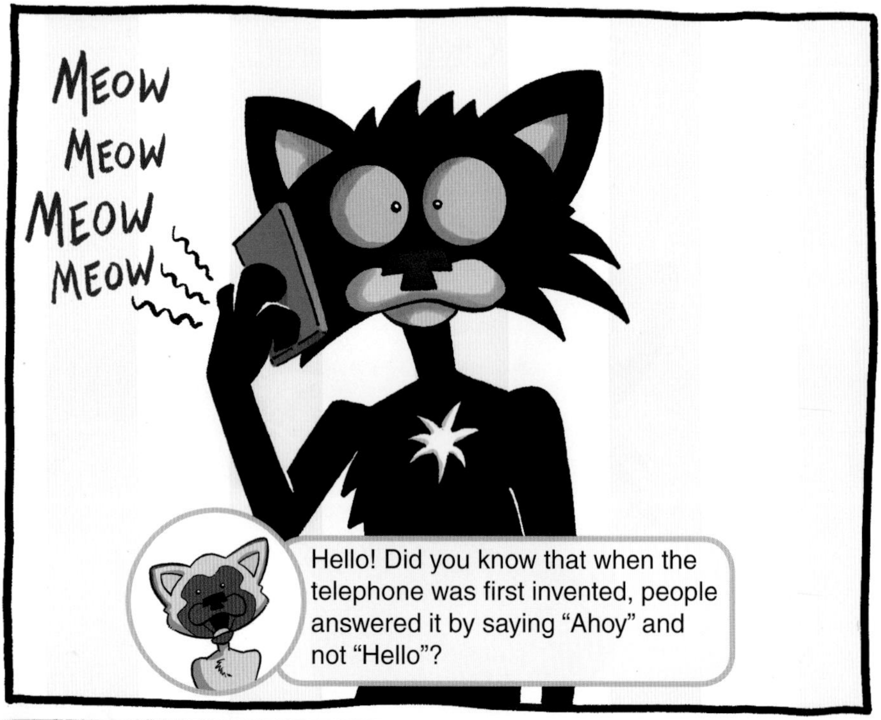
MEOW
MEOW
MEOW
MEOW
Hello! Did you know that when the telephone was first invented, people answered it by saying "Ahoy" and not "Hello"?

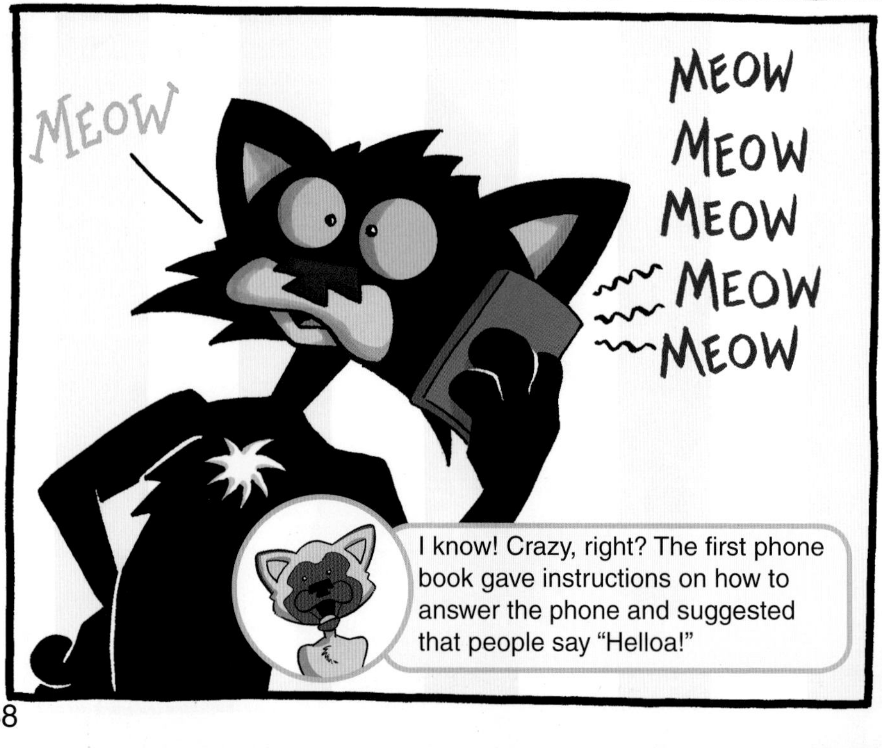
MEOW
MEOW
MEOW
MEOW
MEOW
MEOW
I know! Crazy, right? The first phone book gave instructions on how to answer the phone and suggested that people say "Helloa!"

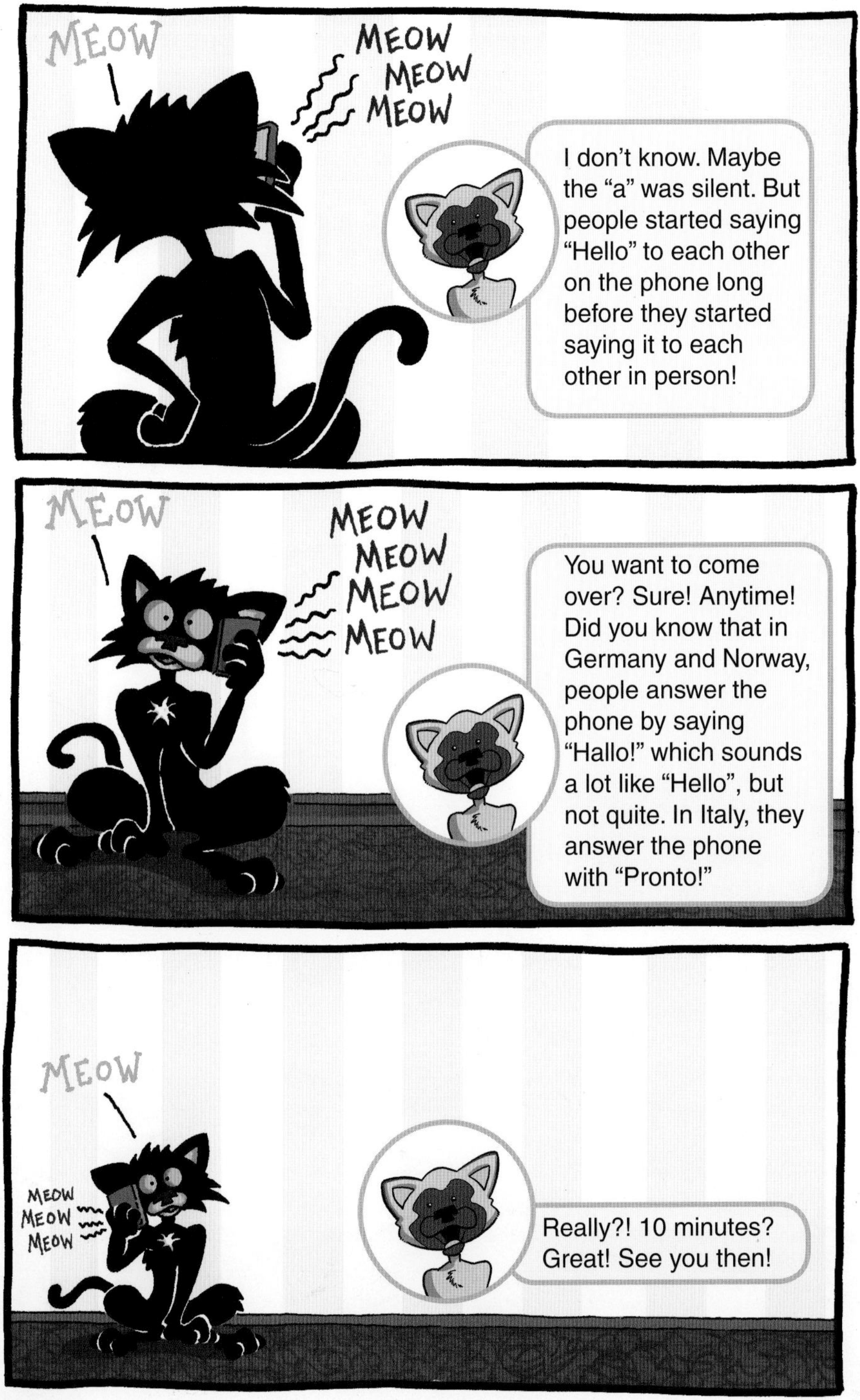
MEOW
MEOW
MEOW
MEOW
I don't know. Maybe the "a" was silent. But people started saying "Hello" to each other on the phone long before they started saying it to each other in person!
MEOW
MEOW
MEOW
MEOW
MEOW
You want to come over? Sure! Anytime! Did you know that in Germany and Norway, people answer the phone by saying "Hallo!" which sounds a lot like "Hello", but not quite. In Italy, they answer the phone with "Pronto!"
MEOW
MEOW
MEOW
MEOW
Really?! 10 minutes? Great! See you then!

THE END

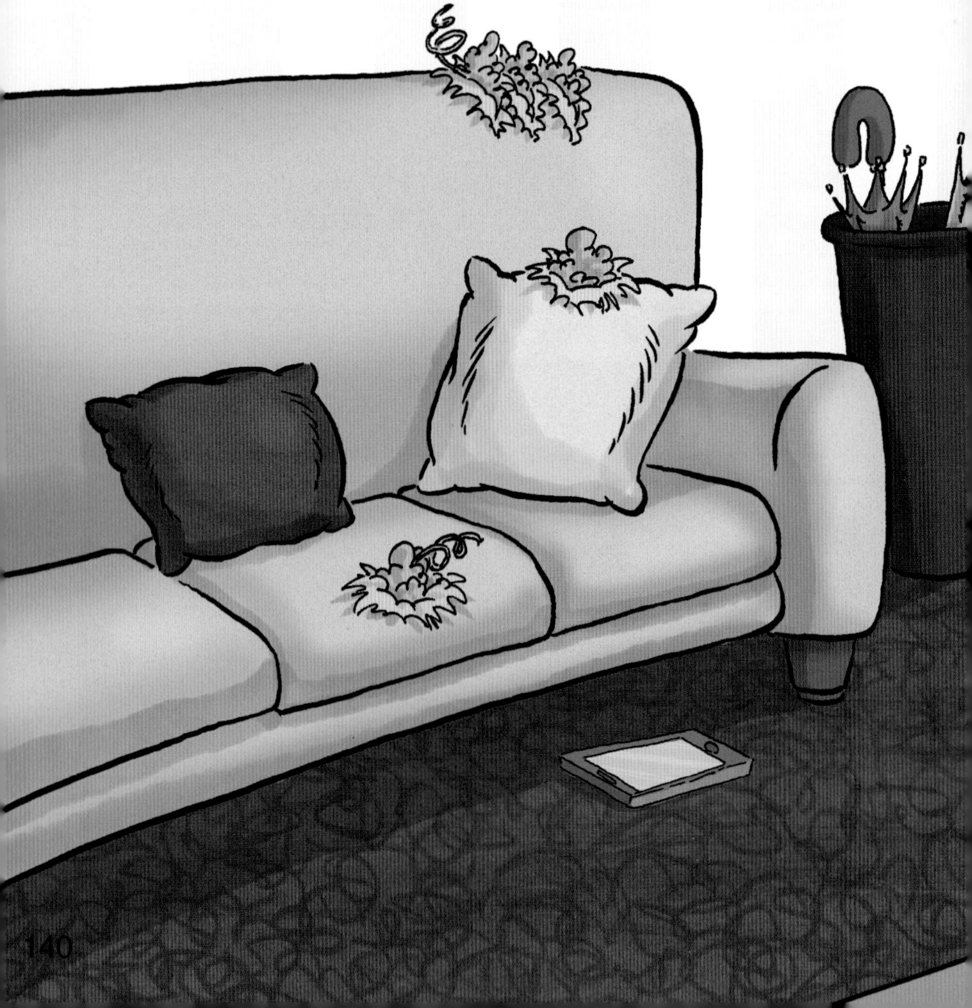

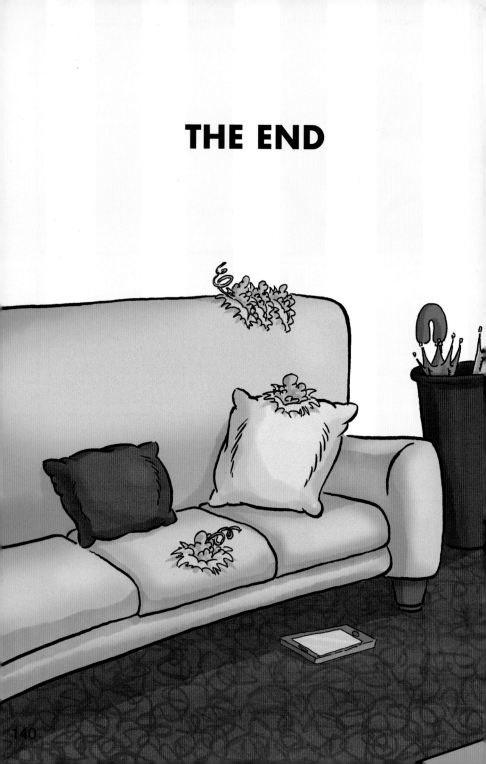

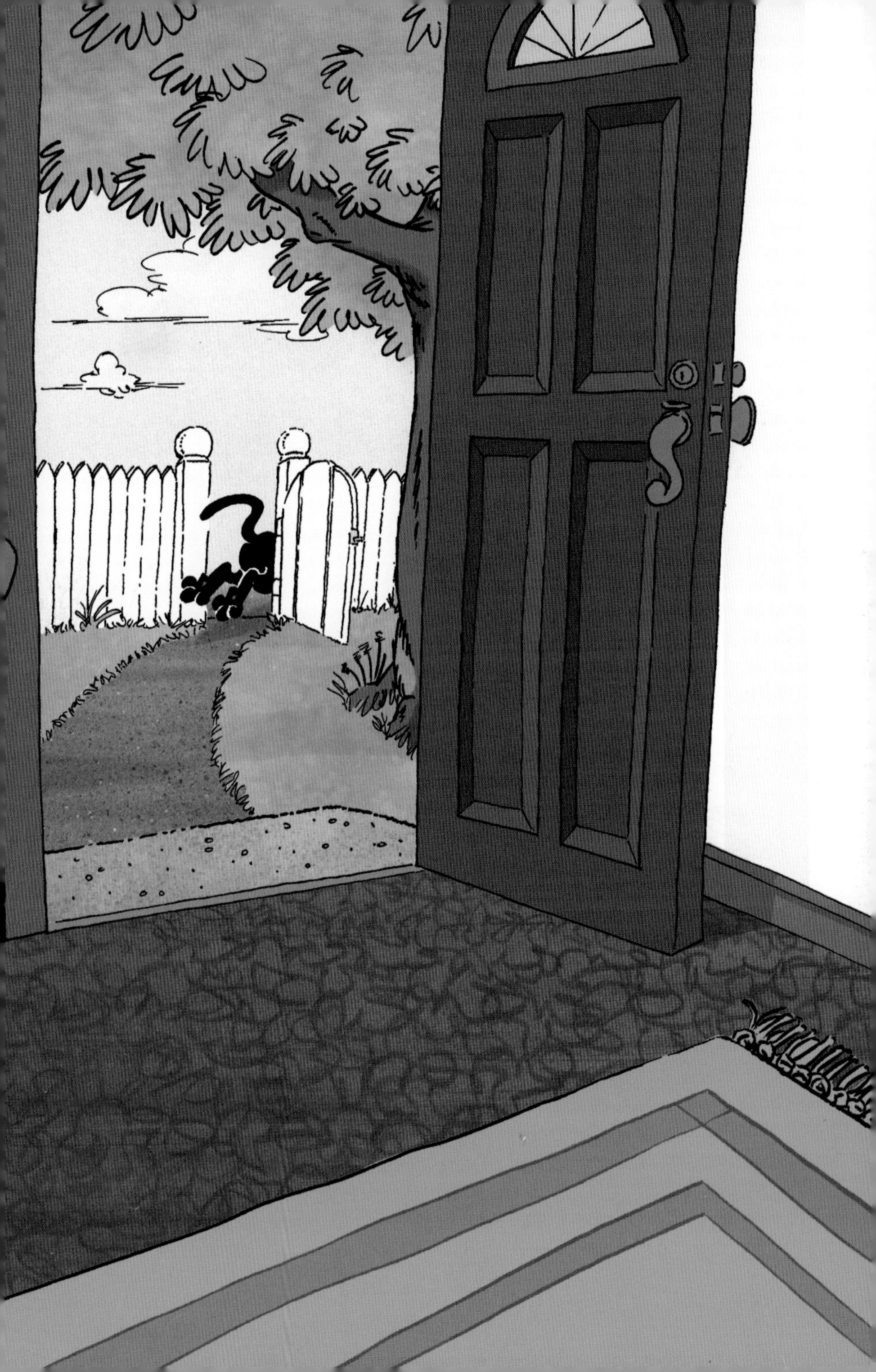